RYAN
GRAUDIN

Orion

ORION CHILDREN'S BOOKS

First published in Great Britain in 2017 by
Hodder and Stoughton

1 3 5 7 9 10 8 6 4 2

Text © Ryan Graudin, 2017

A CIP catalogue record for this book
is available from the British Library.

ISBN 978 1 5101 0286 6

Printed and bound by CPI Group (UK) Ltd, Croydon, CR0 4YY

The paper and board used in this book are from
well-managed forests and other responsible sources.

Orion Children's Books
An imprint of
Hachette Children's Group
Part of Hodder and Stoughton
Carmelite House
50 Victoria Embankment
London EC4Y 0DZ

An Hachette UK Company

www.hachette.co.uk
www.hachettechildrens.co.uk

PRAISE FOR

INVICTUS

'Graudin depicts the futuristic, high-tech world and the fulsome and frenzied historical settings with equal richness ... A madcap, vivid time-travel tale with a strong ensemble' – *Kirkus Reviews*

'If the crew from *Firefly* somehow wound up as teenagers on the TARDIS and had to solve a *Fringe*-type mystery before time literally disappeared, you'd have something like *Invictus*' – *Beth Revis*, New York Times *bestselling author of the Across the Universe series*

'*Invictus* gripped my heart. Graudin's achingly beautiful prose and thoughtful exploration of time, history, and identity create a stunning story. I couldn't turn the pages fast enough, and yet I wanted to savour each decadent sentence. Readers be warned, you'll want to stop time to live in this tale' – *Roshani Chokshi*, New York Times *bestselling author of* The Star-Touched Queen

Also by Ryan Graudin

The Walled City
Wolf by Wolf
Blood for Blood

To my mother, whose roots go deep enough to stand
even after a fall

O.

AB AETERNO

RECORDER EMPRA MCCARTHY SAT IN THE bleachers of the *Amphitheatrum Flavium*, her pregnant belly round as a globe under her indigo stola. The Colosseum—not that it was called that, not yet—was a frenzy of life around her. Nearly fifty thousand souls had come to watch the day's bloodbath, filling the seats with earth-toned togas, popping salted peas and chunks of bread into their mouths, screaming last-minute bets and Latin slang as the gladiators marched through the *Porta Sanavivaria* into the arena below. Morning air was already salty-ripe with sweat and blood, scents so thick the crowd seemed drunk with it. They retched and roared and called for more. *Blood! Blood! Blood!*

Two gladiators lined up in front of the imperial box, bowing to Emperor Domitian and handing over their weapons for inspection. Both stood as men prepared to die.

And for what?

Blood! Blood! Blood!

Empra tried to take note of everything—it was her job, after all, the reason she was here, in a time not her own. She tried to ignore the constant ache of her lower back, the throb of her ankles, the flaming, wet misery of her heart.

Usually, when Empra sat in the thick of living history, she thought of her great-grandfather: Bertram McCarthy, professor of history at Oxford. A man whose life was a tidy sum of tweed jackets and pipes and paperbound books. He worshipped the past with a strange fervor. *It was*, he liked to tell her, *the weight all mankind was born to bear. The roots we did not choose, but chose us.*

Bertram McCarthy had terrible timing. Born four centuries too late, dying two years too early. Two years before time travel was firmly within humanity's grasp. Empra often thought about what it would be like to travel back to Oxford's mote-strung halls, to show her great-grandfather the CTM *Ab Aeterno* and take him for a ride through time. But there were rules upon rules regarding this sort of thing. Time travelers were to be unobtrusive observers. Interacting with people from the past was dangerous business, best kept at a minimum. Lest the course of history be altered.

Not, her swollen belly reminded her, *that she'd been so diligent in all the rules.*

Thus, Bertram McCarthy was stranded in his own timeline: dusty life and quiet death. But the love of history he'd planted in his great-granddaughter rooted well. Empra hungered for the past: a world unwired. Without personalized adverts constantly streaming through her corneal implants or meal blocks that tasted suspiciously the same no matter what kind of food she ordered.

That was why she'd worked her tail off to become a licensed time traveler by age eighteen, why she'd joined the Corps of Central Time Travelers on a yearlong survey expedition to ancient Rome. Traveling, seeing, recording. Blue skies, green plants, real food. These were the things Empra lived for. Also, love...which she hadn't known she was looking for until it found her. Until *he* found her.

Love. Which brought her back here. To this round belly. To this bloodthirsty arena. To the gladiator who stood at the center of it all. Empra wondered if Gaius searched for her among the crowd that roared for his death. She'd already said good-bye, already told him they could never be together. Every moment of their last encounter had felt like plucking out her own heart, string by sanguine string. Empra knew she'd never forget the shadows hooding his already shadowed features, his promise to *live* for her and the baby, his *Why?* so broken and desperate that for just a sliver of a moment Empra considered telling Gaius the truth.

Star-crossed didn't even begin to describe their romance. She loved him to the core, but there could be no future between them, even if he lived. This was because he'd already died. On a day thousands of years before Empra twinkled in her own parents' eyes.

She had a feeling that day was going to be today, though Empra couldn't know for sure. She'd scoured the Historian databases with keywords like *Gaius* and *gladiatorial games* and *95 AD*, but the results were sparse, informationless wastelands. Gaps of knowledge waiting to be filled with her own datastream.

The facts weren't hard to add up: Gaius was a good fighter. She'd seen him train as a retiarius at the gladiator school, snaring opponents in his net to be trapped at the mercy of his trident. But the gladiator Gaius was pitted against today was one of the empire's best. A secutor with a brutish blade and fifteen victories under his belt.

Empra hated watching the violence, but more than this, she hated not knowing. Did Gaius die today, his blood just one more reason for the crowd to cheer? Or did he survive this fight? Gaius was a man long buried. His ending did not matter in the scheme of things, but Empra knew if she didn't watch this battle, did not see his past future ended or extended, it would haunt her.

This was why, after nine months and one day of pregnancy, Empra sat in Rome's barbaric heart instead of coddled up in some Central hospital, plugged into an entertainment system to distract her from the oncoming woes of childbirth.

"You're pushing it," Burg, her ship's Historian, had warned her the night before. "The Corps isn't going to like that you've stayed so long."

"Just one more day." This could have been a plea except for the way Empra had said it. With the same determined gravitas that had secured her this post in the first place. "That's all we need to finish out the survey year. Besides, tomorrow's fight . . . it's important."

She'd never told anyone about Gaius. Simply speaking to him—sitting down for that first off-the-record interview to learn more about gladiatorial life—had been a massive breach in protocol. What followed was unforgivable, and if word of it slipped out, Empra's Corps license would be revoked forever. She'd be as stuck as her great-grandfather Bertram.

"Watching men hack each other to bits for fun is *not* what I would consider good maternal preparation." Burg frowned. "You can't have the baby here, Empra."

The baby's paternity had been a point of contention among the three male crew members of the CTM *Ab Aeterno*, each of whom regarded the others with raised eyebrows and unvoiced suspicions. As long as they didn't suspect the truth . . .

"It's not like we can't come back," he'd gone on softly. *Too* softly for her liking.

Maybe she'd get a chance to return after all this, but Empra wasn't willing to bet on it.

She could feel the baby kicking, even now, tiny heels thumping against her gut as the gladiators took their positions, weapons gripped with lusty fists. Gaius was the fighter on the right, standing under the box of Vestal Virgins. Had Empra's eyesight been limited by biology, she would've been too far away to see his face. Her Recorder equipment magnified the details. Gaius's proud falcon nose turned into the ring, dark-as-earth eyes calculating his opponent. His calf muscles rippled against his sandal straps, ready to spring.

Empra's heart swelled: sick, sicker, sickest.

And then it burst.

She thought it strange that she felt it leaking, wet and warm against her stola, until Burg's voice buzzed into her comm implant. "McCarthy! Your vitals are spiking! Are you going into labor?"

Below, the fight had started. First blood had already been drawn—not Gaius's, but the secutor's. The crowd went feral at the sight.

"McCarthy! Answer me!" Burg shouted louder this time.

"I think my—my water just broke," she whispered into her hand, and stood on shaky legs.

There was a louder roar. Empra didn't want to look, but she had to. This time it was the secutor's blade that had landed a blow. There was a bright smear on Gaius's left arm, mixing with the fibers of his net.

"Get your hashing tail back here this instant!" Empra could just imagine Burg sitting at the *Ab Aeterno*'s Historian console, rubbing his bristly silver crew cut with an agitated palm. "Don't make me come get you, McCarthy. You don't want to see me in a toga."

"I'm coming, I'm coming." She didn't want to leave, but Burg was right. She couldn't have the baby here. The event would attract too much attention.

Time was not on her side today.

Most of the crowd was too riveted by the fight to pay attention to the pregnant woman stumbling down the bleacher steps. Two more blows had been struck by the time Empra reached the exiting arch. Her back was to the arena, but she could tell by the round after bloody round of cheers.

One last look. She could risk that, couldn't she?

And there was Gaius, her Gaius, still fighting. His trident seemed a part of him. It was a terrible, wretched scene, but somehow he was beautiful in it.

Already dead, she reminded herself. *It doesn't matter if it's a second from now or decades.*

This didn't make it any easier to turn away. Neither did the fact that the red-notched secutor had managed to slice away Gaius's net and was backing him slowly, surely, into a corner.

"McCarthy, Doc says your stats are off the charts. Kid's coming fast. You need me to come get you?" Burg's question was low and steady in her ear.

There was nowhere for Gaius to run. His back was to the wall, dark curls splayed. The point of his enemy's blade drew closer, closer.

Empra changed her mind. She couldn't watch this.

No one should have to watch this.

"No, I—I'm coming." She turned her back and stumbled

away. Blinded by the pain of a white-hot contraction. Deafened by the roar of a gore-glutted crowd.

❖ ❖ ❖

The CTM *Ab Aeterno*'s engine purred as Burgstrom Hammond waited by the hatch. According to the infirmary monitors, Empra's contractions were crowding closer together, and judging by the cries that burst through Burg's comm, they hurt like nothing he'd ever felt before.

"C'mon, McCarthy! Keep going. You're almost here!" Burg wasn't sure if he was telling the truth—the visual on his Historian screen was blurry with Empra's tears and the field where their time machine was parked looked like every field surrounding it. His fist was white on the latch, five seconds from running to the Appian Way in his coveralls.

There was no need. Empra beat him to the punch, crumpling into Burg when he opened the door. Her tears dampened his chest as he carried her to the ship's infirmary. Doc already had his sleeves rolled up, med-patches fanned out in his hand like a card deck. One was enough to fool pain receptors for an average wound, but Burg counted ten. After Empra's next scream—a sound that cleaved everything around it—he wondered if even ten would be enough. They hadn't planned for Empra to have her baby on the *Ab Aeterno*.

"We need to get her back to Central, *stat*!" Doc's yell carried into the console room, where the CTM's Engineer was doing last-minute landing calculations. "Nicholas, get us out of here!"

The ship lurched in response, engines propelling it into the aching winter sky. Again, Empra screamed—new life's pain made all the louder by their comm connection. Burg pressed a hand to his ear, surprised not to find blood trickling out.

"Deep breaths! Hold tight. Just a few more minutes and we'll get you to a proper hospital." Doc applied med-patches to Empra's arms as fast as he could, adhesive peels flurrying across the floor. They didn't seem to help. Burg's eardrum threatened to rupture as he made for the console room—an uphill incline to the ship's bow—where Nicholas was hunched over the controls.

"Hades's clangers!" Sky glared at Burg through the vistaport, its blue too bright for the future. "What are we still doing here?"

"Gotta get the right elevation or things could get a mite toasty." The Engineer wasn't wrong. Central—the crew's home city, seat of the Central World Republic—sat on this exact spot some twenty-two and a half centuries in the future. If the *Ab Aeterno* didn't climb high enough, its jump through time could send them careening into hovercraft traffic. "Trust me, I'm as ready to say good-bye to this year as the rest of you."

Nicholas's voice cracked with a strain they all felt—364 days spent inside a 65-square-meter CTM, watching Empra come and go and grow from the belly out. Back issues of holo-paper zines and two hours a day on the walkabout machine could only do so much to ward off cabin fever. In fact, the sight of Rome spread below was one of the best Burg had seen the whole hashing year. From this elevation, the capital was a model maker's dream—hills crowned with temples, Colosseum the size of a coin. The *Ab Aeterno* leveled above it, letting only a second pass before the city—and the time that held it—vanished. They'd peeled out of 95 AD, into the Grid. Darkness pressed against the vistaport, endless and eager.

The screams from the infirmary grew louder. Burg wanted to tell the Engineer to *hurry up*, but there was no point. The Grid was a timeless place. Clocks stopped and what you thought was a second could be an hour, a week, a year, a decade. He stared through the vistaport instead, willing the world's capital to reappear in its twenty-fourth-century iteration. Rome had changed a good deal in the last two millennia: from dusty republic city to *Caput Mundi* to selfie-stick-wielding tourist destination to *Novum Caput Mundi*. The heart of the ancient world had risen to new, all-powerful heights. Its cityscape even resembled a crown. Zone 1—the Colosseum, the Vatican, countless basilicas and fountains and piazzas—sat at the center, the buildings of Old Rome protected by the Global Historic Preservation Act of 2237 AD. Modernity hemmed it in on all sides. Zone 2's jutting skyline was bejeweled with neon adverts, hovercraft traffic dotting the slices of intervening sky. The centerpiece of Central was—without question—the tiered New Forum skyscraper designed by the famed architect Biruk Tekle. All 168 floors of the building were sheathed in gold glass. Six hundred senators worked inside these gilded walls, representing half as many global districts, headed by a dual consulate.

Earth's capital was the seed of a million migraines, with its smog and tangled lights, but there was a pause every day when it transformed. Locals like Burg knew this as the "Flaming Hour," when the setting sun caught pollution particles at just the right angle to spread orange bright into every corner of the evening. The city became fire itself, unmatched by anything in history. One world, one light. It was Rome ascended, forged from peace instead of war.

None of this materialized from the black. Nicholas stayed hunched over his screens, taking strings of numbers and crunching them into the precise result that would land the *Ab Aeterno* when they wanted: April 18, 2354 AD, 12:01 PM. One minute after their departure one year ago.

Burg sat down at his own station to disconnect Empra's feed from his comm, but there was no need. Her shrieks had gone silent, a rougher, wordless cry taking their place.

Nicholas looked up at the sound, cheeks ashen. "Is that—"

It was. Newborn lungs drunk on their first swig of air. The cries kept on and the Engineer made the eight-pointed sign of a cross over his chest. Burg felt his own color draining while he looked toward the infirmary, then back to the dizzying dark of the Grid. As a time traveler, he was used to bending the laws of nature, sometimes all the way backward.

But this...a child born outside of time...

Such an event didn't just distort the laws of nature.

It broke them.

Burg switched off the datastream and ran to the infirmary. It was a sight: Doc tending to Empra on the floor. Her stola had gone purple with bloodstains, and she could not stop crying as she rocked her child with med-patch-covered arms. The infant was already squirming, as if he was ready to fight something. His head bloomed full of dark curls.

Though Burg was a large tree trunk of a man—built for bar brawls and bouncer jobs—he was also very intuitive. He'd noted that Empra's datastream lingered a bit too long on the gladiator with those same dark curls. He'd noticed how, at night, always hours before she returned to the *Ab Aeterno*, she would switch off the recording devices and mute her mic. He'd watched love like stars shine through her eyes—the kind of love she never shared with him. Or Doc. Or Nicholas. Or her ex-fiancé, Marin.

The Historian was watchful enough to pick out these things, smart enough to piece them together. Like all registered members of the Corps, Burg had memorized the Corps of Central Time Travelers' Code of Conduct to the extent that he could recite it in reverse. When it came to this child's father, Empra had gone well outside her jurisdiction, and if the Central authorities caught wind of her actions, there would be consequences. Ruthless ones, applied to mother and son alike.

Burg looked down at the baby—so breakably small in Empra's arms—and swore he'd never tell. When the infant's clear eyes latched onto his, the Historian went a step further, doing some calculations in his head. In order for Empra's secret to stay a secret, there had to be bribery involved. Burg knew if he could get the right amount of credits to the right lab techs, then the child's DNA tests could be fudged. Senators did this all the time to cover up unwanted paternity claims.

But the senators' pockets were far deeper than Burg's. He didn't time travel for the money. No one did. Most of the Corps' cash flow went to the mechanical side of things: fuel rods, CTM maintenance, server space to host the datastreams Recorders were collecting from all across time.

How many credits would it take to bribe the lab techs? A thousand? Five thousand? Maybe even more, to hide a misstep as large as this...

"Would you like to hold him?" Empra asked.

Burg nodded. How could he say no? The baby squirmed as he was transferred, curls tickling the inside of the Historian's elbow. It was then that the bearish man decided to hash it all. What were numbers to a life? Whatever price it would take to keep this child alive... he'd pay it. There wasn't much that could be done to cover up the birth outside of time. He just had to have faith that that anomaly would sort itself out.

Burg cradled the boy who should not have been—close as a heart—waiting through the timeless time-between-times for them to land.

PART I

Out of the night that covers me,
Black as the pit from pole to pole,
I thank whatever gods may be
For my unconquerable soul.

— WILLIAM ERNEST HENLEY
"INVICTUS"

1.

THE BOY WHO SHOULD
NOT HAVE BEEN

"STATE YOUR NAME." THE MED-DROID'S AUTOMATED voice was cut clean, every syllable filed down to replicate a Central accent. Why machines needed accents, Far didn't know. Maybe the programmers added this touch of humanity to put the med-droid's patients at ease. The tactic had failed, though the robot couldn't be faulted for Far's discomfort. Sitting tail-naked on an examination tabletop wasn't exactly Relaxation 101. The stainless steel surface was a few degrees shy of frosty, nipping places on his body where cold had no business going.

"Farway Gaius McCarthy," he answered.

The med-droid recorded the reply, shifted into the next query. "State your date of birth."

Far sighed. They asked this question. Every. Single. Time. And every single time he answered, the med-droid's computers would whir through the census databases, find nothing, and state in its elegant accent: "Answer invalid. Restate your date of birth."

This routine was old hat. He'd done it scores, if not hundreds, of times, for all the scores, if not hundreds, of Simulator exams he'd taken at the Academy. The anticheating measures—a full stripping and thorough identity scan before every Sim session—seemed extreme, but as Far's instructors had taught him, time travel demanded flawless precision. Cheating now could lead to world-ending catastrophes later. Maybe. Time's immutability was something much debated by the Corps, who were too afraid to test their theories in case they ended up changing the future they lived in—butterfly wingbeats and whatnot. Thus, perfection was their MO.

Traveling the Grid—exploring the past in real time—was all Far dreamed of. He'd been raised on a steady diet of serialized datastreams and Burg's expedition stories: outrunning velociraptors, witnessing Vesuvius's rage against the night sky, surveying the great Dust Bowl of the 1930s. But watching pixels flicker through screens and listening to an old man's recounted adventures wasn't enough to sate Far's hunger. Even the Sims' state-of-the-art sensory replications, with their sounds and smells and hologram people imbued with enough artificial intelligence to mimic an interactive scene from history, weren't enough.

He wanted to meet history face-to-face. He wanted to be

the blood in its veins, as it was in his. Far was a McCarthy—son of one of the most beloved Recorders of her generation. Everywhere he went, Empra's name followed. Older Academy instructors always did a double take when they came across Far in their class rosters. *You're Empra's boy*, they'd say, along with some version of: *She was a bright girl, one of my best students. It's such a shame about what happened to the* Ab Aeterno....

His mother's legacy and loss were always there, pushing Far to be the best, always the best. And he was. Today he'd pass his final exam with flying colors, like he always did, and receive his license. Today his Sim score would earn him a coveted space on the crew of a Central Time Machine. Tomorrow he'd be exploring many yesterdays ago, documenting momentous events for scholars, scientists, and entertainment moguls alike.

But first—first!—he had to get past this pragmatic med-droid. "State your date of birth."

"Can we just skip this part?" Far shifted on the table, a vain attempt to keep his unmentionables from going numb.

"Answer invalid. Restate your date of birth."

"April eighteenth, 2354 AD." Far tried the date that made him seventeen and a smidge. It wasn't his true birthday, but that didn't stop his cousin Imogen from buying him gelato and sticking sparklers in it every year. He'd tried to make 4/18/54 official, but no clerical worker could be persuaded to fill the blank gap on his birth certificate. Far's birth outside of time had to stay on the public record, for historical purposes. Med-droid malfunctions be hashed.

Speaking of: "Answer invalid. Restate your date of birth."

Far attempted the date he used whenever he was trying to impress a girl. The date that made him 2,276, minus a smidge. "December thirty-first, 95 AD."

"Answer in—"

"I know, for Crux sake! I don't have a hashing birthday!" Far knew it was useless to get mad—*he* was the glitch, not the med-droid's programming—but sometimes it just felt good to yell. "I was born on the *Ab Aeterno*!"

The examination room door slid open. A living Medic stuck her head around the corner. Her features were as edged and elegant as the Hindi on her ID card. A stethoscope dangled from her neck, competing for space with gold-tinted headphones. "Is something wrong—oh!" Her face brightened. "Hello, Far!"

"Hey, Priya." He grinned at the Medic and tried oh-so-subtly to tense his abdominal muscles. "Like the headphones. Where'd you find them?"

"Some hawker in Zone Four was trying to pass them off as genuine BeatBix, asking three thousand credits for them. Can you believe it? With the BB logo facing the wrong way and everything."

"I'd expect nothing less from a Zone Four hawker," Far told her. "One of them tried to convince my cousin that a kitten with an awful dye job was a red panda cub."

"Aren't red pandas extinct?"

"Exactly. So what'd you haggle him down to?"

"Two hundred and fifty credits." Priya's rip-off headphones gleamed as she shrugged. "Could've gone lower, but some prices aren't worth the fight. Hawker gets to pay his bills and I get to listen to Acidic Sisters through something other than my comm."

"Answer invalid," the med-droid informed them in its tireless cadence. "Restate your date of birth."

"Ah. Birth date question again?"

"Never not," Far said.

Being a Medic in an age where droids made up fifteen percent of the population required training beyond human biology, so like most of her peers, Priya doubled as a mechanic. She pried open the med-droid's chest plate and rearranged some wires—a routine Far had seen her perform scores of time—to bypass the question manually. "You'd think they'd have this bug fixed by now."

Far laughed as he offered his arm for the inevitable blood sample. Of all the Medics who came to intervene with his examination hitches, Priya was his favorite. She always pretended the problem lay on the med-droid's end and not his. And where her coworkers were quick to scurry off—their silence like fear— she lingered, often close enough for him to hear the notes beating through her headphones. Today it was a punk-tech ballad. Catchy to the max.

"So...your final exam Sim. I'd ask if you were nervous, but who am I kidding?"

He laughed again. Nerves were for people who didn't know what the future held, and his was pretty clear: valedictorian of his Academy class, acer of Sims. Sure, final exam Sims were the toughest of the bunch. You could get anything from Neolithic bonfires to a twentieth-century high school keg party to watching King John sign the Magna Carta. The goal was simple— record the event and study the people without being noticed. One misstep and you could be thrown out of the Academy tail-first, banned from time travel forever.

Far didn't make mistakes, however, just calculated risks. "Got any song suggestions for my impending victory dance?"

"Classic or current?"

"Classic. I'll need to get used to some historic beats once I'm licensed."

"Let's see." Priya tapped her chin. "There's Queen's 'We Are the Champions' and DJ Khaled's 'All I Do Is Win.' Oh— and you can't go wrong with Punched Up Panda's 'Top of the Rise.' M.I.A. has some good ones, too."

Far made a note of the band names on his interface so he could look them up later. "Queen, Khaled, Panda, M.I.A. Got it."

"You should breathe." The Medic's smoky eyes flickered from Far's exaggerated, oxygen-starved abs to the vitals graph on the med-droid's chest. "You're skewing the readings."

Ah! She'd noticed! Perhaps not in the way he'd intended, but still...

"When will you go once you pass?" Priya asked.

That was the question, wasn't it? Far had spent his entire life watching other times. A whole quilt of cultures and humanity... prehistory, ancient Greece, ancient Rome, medieval Europe, the Renaissance, the Age of Enlightenment, the Industrial Revolution, the Age of Progress, all the way to Central time. And that was just the Western Civilization track. So much was still unexplored—for while there were hundreds of licensed time travelers, there were only so many CTMs to go around. The finite life spans of the explorers they carried covered just a fraction of history.

The possibilities were endless. Almost.

"I could go back and kill Hitler," Far joked. "Isn't that every time traveler's dream?"

Priya shot him a *you shouldn't kid about that* look from under her bangs.

"Whenever the Corps wants to send me, I guess," he recanted.

"You don't have any preferences? You aren't scared you're going to get stuck trying to collect bubonic plague cultures from corpses in the name of science?"

When Far was fourteen, he watched a datastream of the Black Death. Even at that age he could tell it was highly edited: choppy shots, faded audio. The Recorder taking the footage had gagged at a blurred-out cart piled high with bodies. "Not my first choice."

When the med-droid finished its ritual pricking and prodding, it rolled toward the door, calling Far along. "Proceed to the next chamber to acquire your final exam Sim wardrobe."

"I want to see it all," he told the Medic.

"Speaking of seeing it all..." Priya bit her lip, but her smile was too strong to hide. Every other corner of her face lit with it as she nodded to the door where the med-droid had vanished. "You should go get dressed."

Far found his final exam Sim suit in the next room, pressed to perfection and composed of too many pieces. Wool stockings went on first, followed by knee-length breeches and a dress shirt with rabid lace frothing from its ends. These ruffles peeked out of a blue waistcoat embroidered with vines and some long-extinct flower Far couldn't remember the name of. A green-and-gold-striped coat weighted all this into place. The outfit was bookended with leather shoes and a powdered wig.

"Not the plague, then," Far muttered as he reached for the stockings.

He'd experienced a few Sims from the eighteenth century—witnessing the signing of the United States' Declaration of Independence, sailing the Pacific as part of James Cook's crew, watching the streets of revolution-era Paris crumble into parades and chaos—but it wasn't a time he'd studied thoroughly.

It made sense. The point of the exam was to demonstrate how well you could improvise. Time travelers had to use costumes, knowledge, and technology to blend into their surrounding environments. On board a traditional CTM, the responsibility for providing flawless covers fell to the Historian. They assembled the Recorder's wardrobe: clothes, hairstyle, and translation technology...the works. They were responsible for briefing the Recorder on the time period they were walking into. They ID'd key historical figures and sent instructions about how to behave over the comms.

During examination Sims, the Historian's role was played by a computer linked directly to Far's comm. It greeted him with the same accent as the med-droid: "Welcome to your final examination Sim, Farway Gaius McCarthy. Your mission is to observe and record an hour-long datastream. You will be graded on the quality and content of your datastream as well as your recording methods."

The usual, then. Far snapped his breeches into place. For Crux sake, they were tight. It was a miracle the human race managed to keep procreating after years in pants like these.... "When exactly will we be going?"

"May fifteenth, 1776 AD. Seven o'clock in the evening."

The shirt was snug, too, and the waistcoat pushed the ruffles up so they feathered Far's neck, making him feel ostrichlike. "Who wears this many layers in May?"

"The residents at the Palace of Versailles," the computer informed him.

Versailles. A glamorous den of royals, where the air was prickly with wig powder and the golden halls swished with gowns so voluminous they could second for circus tents. There were girls in Far's Academy class who would kill—or at least significantly maim—to be placed in such a Sim.

Far shouldered the overcoat, secured his wig, and ran through his pre-Sim mantra: *I am Farway Gaius McCarthy, son of Empra McCarthy. Birth date unavailable. With timelessness in my blood and nowhere calling to my heart. Born on the* Ab Aeterno, *for* Ab Aeterno. *I am a single Sim away from all of time.*

The Palace of Versailles, France, 1776 AD would be a cinch.

He switched on his recording devices and stepped into the Sim.

2.

LET HIM EAT CAKE

PLUNGING INTO ANOTHER TIME WAS ALWAYS a dizzying affair. Vertigo and culture shock and déjà vu all crushed together. Far found the reeling sensation passed sooner if he focused on a single point. The first sight he caught in Versailles's Hall of Mirrors was, well, a mirror. Far hardly recognized himself—white-wigged and poufy. Only his sharp cliff of a nose helped anchor his own reflection.

The rest of the room settled into place. Far knew he was surrounded by hologram plates—how else would you train would-be time travelers without screwing up the world?—but they did a hashing fine job of convincing his senses otherwise. Cavernous ceilings arched above him: chandeliers dripping like a goddess's tears, gold pouring from every surface. There were gueridons in the form of sumptuous women, seats embroidered with squirrels and flowers, courtiers buzzing high on gossip and champagne. And courtiers, and courtiers...

He'd walked into the middle of a party.

Dozens, if not scores, of people milled through the room. How many eyes that might see Far? How many ears that might hear him? Yes, the partygoers were products of the hologram plates beneath his feet, but their programming was meant to mirror flesh and blood. If Far did anything to attract their attention, his score would suffer.

At least his getup blended in. Their outfits were as outlandish as Far's. Frill and color mixed through the mirror's mercury gloss like a bad med-patch trip. The women's beehive hair climbed impossibly high. Makeup caked their faces to cover the smallpox scars of sickly youth.

One woman was brighter than the rest. She didn't stand in the center of the party yet she *was* its center. Her dress billowed seafoam green—light as air, with a spring-day glow. Real ostrich feathers sprouted from the whorls of her hair. Her makeup was as heavy as the others: gossamer powder, eyebrows perfectly arched as if they'd been drawn on. The woman wore these things like magic, trapping an entire ring of courtiers in her spell.

"ID?" Far asked into his cupped palm.

"Maria Antonia Josepha Johanna. Better known as Marie Antoinette. She is currently twenty years of age and the queen of France. She registers as a Tier Three mark on the important-persons scale."

"Tier Three?" Far, half afraid that the computer was lying, turned to get a better, mirrorless view. It was indeed Marie Antoinette. One of the most hated women of her age. One of the most beloved queens of history.

"Hades's clangers in a hashing bluebox," he whispered to the back of a gueridon's gilded head. The Academy had really tossed him into the deep end this time. Being a Tier Three mark meant any interactions with Marie Antoinette beyond a *bonjour* were forbidden. It also meant that datastreams of the flamboyant queen of France were rare. Valuable. Such footage could send Far's exam marks through the roof, maybe even land him a score high enough to enter the Corps as a ranked official. He'd be that much closer to becoming a captain of operations on a CTM, calling the shots....

The safe thing to do would be to play the wallflower for fifty-nine minutes. Stick to the mirrors' edge, drink in every detail of the party from the outside. Note the food being served, the brand of champagne being poured (Veuve Clicquot), every stitch of the courtiers' frocks.

But being so conservative held its own danger. Too much Central money was poured into the Corps to commission travelers who skulked on the sidelines. If Far didn't score high enough, he risked being licensed but never selected for an actual CTM mission. Just the thought of being grounded to a single time, when his mother and Burg no longer existed, made Far's insides go dark.

That couldn't be his future. It *wouldn't*.

His choices were the following:

1. Fade into the background. Be lost.
2. Step out into the thick of the crowd. Be seen.
3. Walk the line between.

Far had pulled off anonymous observations of Tier Three marks before. Keeping beneath a gossipy royal's radar would be nothing compared with stowing away on the HMS *Endeavour* for two days. He was as good as this. Better than. Number three was all his.

Scores of people wasn't quite a large enough number to get lost in. Far kept to the crowd's outer layer, drifting quickly enough to avoid getting caught in conversation. He circled the party once, twice, soaking Versailles's nightlife into his datastream. Always Far's gaze went back to the queen: her dreamlike dress, her smile—so buoyant beneath all that makeup.

He itched to get closer. His path coiled inward like a nautilus shell, making smaller and smaller circles. With every new step, Far felt the points racking up in his favor: *Captain here I come!*

"Proximity to Tier Three mark has breached recommended distance," the computer cautioned at ten meters out. "Risk of detection imminent."

Far could hear the queen detailing her latest Parisian adventures to a rapt audience. "One *must* go to a masquerade at least once in one's life. It gives one such a sense of power, to be faceless. To be free of who you are, if only for a moment."

Marie Antoinette's admirers nodded. The women's hair feathers bobbed and the tips of the men's wigs fluttered: *yes, yes* in fervent agreement. Far pushed closer, taking care not to jostle any hemlines. So far no one in the crowd had tossed him a second glance, and he aimed to keep it that way.

The warning in his ear blared louder: "Risk of detection imminent."

He wasn't in any danger. Marie Antoinette's back was to him, and the listeners around her had formed a wall—three bodies thick—to be first in the queen's line of sight. The taller courtiers' shoulders provided more than enough cover.

"To walk unknown in the midst of a hundred strangers is simply exhilarating." Marie Antoinette began spinning. "Don't you think?"

There was another chorus of *yes*es, but the queen waved these off as she turned. Far stayed on the crowd's outer edge, his datastream capturing every detail as Marie Antoinette came into view. The lace edges of her Rose Bertin gown. The beauty mark that dotted her right cheek. The diamonds lassoed around her swan-pale neck.

Oh, this was *good* footage! Possibly some of his best to date. If it were real, Far was positive it would've become a published datastream: *An Evening with Marie Antoinette.* Much more entertaining than medieval, rat-gnawed corpses. Cheerier, too—if you disregarded how it all ended.

This would get him assigned to a CTM right away. Far was already dreaming of the sergeant bar that would be pinned to his jacket when the queen spoke again.

"Don't you think?"

Two men in front of Far nodded, but Marie Antoinette paid them no mind. She stepped between the pair. The queen's pale skin, the dark flash of her eyes, her regal stride all reminded Far of a white reindeer he'd once seen in a snow-laden nineteenth-century Swedish Sim. This was all he could manage to think as the queen of France stood in front of him. Anything else was too terrible.

The computer wailed useless warnings. "DETECTED BY TIER THREE MARK! ABORT MISSION IMMEDIATELY!"

"I know an outlier when I see one." Marie Antoinette leaned in. Her cheek brushed Far's, accented with scents of rosebushes and bergamots. "You don't belong here."

This couldn't be happening. This *shouldn't* be happening. None of the normal triggers were there—Far had stayed out of the line of sight, lips sealed, wardrobe well worn. His proximity was closer than the computer preferred, but that had never mattered before. An average Marie Antoinette in an average Sim would still be addressing her courtiers, not holding Far's stare like this, dark eyes into dark. They were, he noted distantly, similar to his own in color. A brown so deep it tangoed with black.

"ABORT MISSION IMMEDIATELY!" the computer screamed.

The exam was over. EVERYTHING was over. Marie Antoinette stepped back with a wink. The motion was smooth and deliberate, just mocking enough to let Far *know* this wasn't some curveball failure.

This Sim was corrupted.

He'd been set up.

Versailles vanished, reduced to a warehouse of hologram plates that glimmered mother-of-pearl in their resting state. Far stood alone in the sudden silence, breathing heavily. Patches of cold sweat spread under all those hashing layers of clothes. His body shook—not out of fear, but with anger.

"Bring it *back*! That wasn't my fault! It wasn't—"

"Farway Gaius McCarthy." The computer in his comm gave way to Instructor Marin's voice. Oh Hades, Marin would be *loving* this. "Please proceed to the exit for your debriefing."

SUBJECT SEVEN HAS BEEN SUCCESSFULLY
REDIRECTED.

3.

LOOPS WITH THE BIRD

THERE WAS A TWO-WAY MIRROR IN the debriefing room, capturing Far's reflection with unforgiving detail when he entered. His wig was still on, flowered waistcoat in place, and the ruffles were threatening to grow. He felt shell-ish as he stared, as if his *self* were elsewhere, tethered to this courtesan gentleman like some child's balloon.

The chamber, with its table and two chairs, was a long leap from Versailles's gilded halls. It gave the appearance of solitude, but Far knew he wasn't alone. An entire jury of instructors sat on the other side of the glass, stripping his datastream to centimeters and syllables. Surely they'd deduce that the mistake wasn't his. It *couldn't* be his. He'd logged thousands upon thousands of successful Sim hours. *Hades*, there was a plaque sporting his name in the Academy's main hall: FARWAY MCCARTHY, BEST CUMULATIVE SIM SCORE OF 2370. Being engraved in solid 24-karat gold had to count for something.

Seconds stretched into minutes, and the initial anger at the Sim reduced to a simmer, tunneling beneath Far's skin like fire ants. The debriefing instructor was usually here by now, congratulating him on this or that evasive maneuver. Delay meant conversation, conversation meant doubt. Who wouldn't be reexamining the Sim's technological integrity after a wink like that?

He wanted to say his piece, sans shouting, so he walked over to the mirror and spoke past himself. "Look, we all know this was a programming problem. I can come back and retake the exam once it's fixed."

"Have a seat, Cadet McCarthy." Instructor Marin's voice slid through the comm—sterling, austere.

Neither of the room's chairs had been designed with ergonomics in mind: steel surface as flat as Homer's view of the earth. Sitting would not only be a sentence to a numb backside, but also any other terms Edwin Marin set forth. The Academy instructor was armored with spite when it came to Far, chips sheathing both shoulders. The grudge weighting them was over twenty years old, born the moment Empra McCarthy had tossed an engagement ring at the man's face. Rumor had it that the princess-cut diamond had left a scar on Marin's upper lip, but this could neither be confirmed nor denied because of the handlebar mustache that had taken up permanent residence there.

Water was not under the bridge that had been burned, and Far was too proud to let Marin jerk him around. As long as the instructor didn't order him verbatim, he'd stay on his own two feet, a fog's breath away from the mirror. His exhales clouded the glass, peeling back and replacing themselves, thick enough to trace shapes in. Far drew an infinity symbol with his forefinger—loop, loop, never-ending loop—until Instructor Marin spoke again.

"Sit down, Cadet McCarthy. *That's an order.*"

Far huffed out the remaining hot air in his lungs and traced one last round with his middle finger. Marin wouldn't miss the switch, but there was no standing rule against doodling with "the bird."

Loopholes were a wonderful thing.

He took a seat and began downloading Punched Up Panda's victory anthem. "Top of the Rise" had a beat that demanded movement, thumb drums to steel tabletop. Who'd have the gall to sabotage his final exam Sim? Far was no tech-head, but he knew hacking into a time-travel Simulation required smarts, not to mention a willingness to break digital trespassing laws. That ruled out Instructor Marin, who'd follow Corps' protocol off a cliff if said command was written in the Corps of Central Time Travelers' Code of Conduct. Far's best friend, Gram Wright, had the brainpower for such a hack, IQ on the right side of 160, but never in a million years would he use his keyboard wizardry against Far.

Who, then?

And why?

By the time Marin entered the room, Far's nerves were amped up to eleven. The instructor smiled in an off sort of way as he took a seat in the opposite chair, lips cozying to the ends of his waxed mustache. "Cadet McCarthy, the licensing board and I have just finished reviewing your datastream—"

"The Sim was compromised, sir." Words were sparks on Far's tongue, too hot to contain. "Marie Antoinette was expecting me. Someone must have hacked the systems—"

"Do not interrupt me while I'm speaking, Cadet. I'd take marks for it, but we both know there'd be no point in my doing so."

No...no point? Far's confidence sputtered, his insides left singed. If he opened his mouth now, ashes might spill out, so he kept his molars locked.

Marin continued, "Nineteen years I've taught here, trying to mold wide-eyed datastream addicts into effective time travelers. This isn't the first time I've heard the programming excuse. Hades—it's not even the tenth time I've heard it."

"It's not an excuse, sir. It's true." Far's gaze darted back to the mirror. He hoped the licensing board had remained to hear him out. "I'm wearing a poodle wig and purse-pinching pants. I was standing two men deep and the queen's back was turned. There's no way Marie Antoinette could have seen me."

"You were two meters away from a Tier Three mark. That's inexcusable in any scenario!" There was a reason Instructor Marin hadn't been assigned to a CTM in multiple sun orbits. The man was all structure, no stretch. Perfect fit for a desk.

"Only because I got caught."

"Exactly, Cadet. You got caught. If what I just witnessed on that datastream occurred during an actual mission, you would have disturbed the past with unforeseeable consequences!"

"It wouldn't have happened on an actual mission. Someone—I don't know who—hacked the Sim and programmed it against me. They wanted me to fail." Once more Far stared past Marin's shoulder, into the infinity-smudged glass. Why couldn't they see what was in front of them? "Go over the datastream again. You'll see how she winked at me."

"Marie Antoinette was a notorious flirt," Instructor Marin pointed out. "For her to wink is hardly an indication of program corruption."

"I know a flirty wink when I see one. This wink was a message—"

"Cadet, please. You're embarrassing yourself. Diagnostics showed all systems are untampered with. You *failed*." Marin's last word curled along the edge of his mustache, pushing out at a merciless volume. It crawled through Far's eardrums, working its way past the final notes of "Top of the Rise," spiraling down a throat full of cinders into a stomach that was trying to digest an impossible possibility and was collapsing as a result.

He'd failed.

Ashes ashes we all fall dead end black hole no no no no . . .

NO.

"Someone screwed up the hashing diagnostics!" Far's yell sounded tinny to his own ears. It was a very *Alice in Wonderland* feeling—shrinking inside oneself, until you had to stand on tiptoes to stare out of your own eyes. "This isn't my fault! I've been framed!"

"Lower your voice," Instructor Marin said.

"Or what? You'll take marks?"

Far knew he'd gone too far when the instructor's smile flatlined. The man cleared his throat. "I don't care who your mother was. I don't care that you were born on a CTM. I don't care that you're first in your class. You hashed up, McCarthy. You hashed up royally.

"You want to know why? Hubris. You think no one can touch you. I've watched you bend the rules again and again without consequence, because you think you're the exception. But I'm going to let you in on a little secret, McCarthy.... You're not special. You aren't important. You are arrogant and disrespectful, and I have no doubt you'd obliterate history if given the chance. Crux help this world if you ever set foot on a CTM. I'll be hashed to the moon and back before I let that happen. Cadet McCarthy, I'm sorry, but you are not a good fit for the Corps. You're hereby expelled from the Academy and banned from ever applying for a license."

"You can't expel me," Far croaked. "I'm the valedictorian."

"Not anymore," Marin told him. "Final exams are *final*, Mr. McCarthy."

Mr. McCarthy, not *Cadet*. Far hadn't missed this change in Instructor Marin's address, the double-syllable shift that stranded him in life as he knew it. There would be no sergeant bar. There wouldn't even be a CTM.

"I'd advise you to hand over your practice Sim pass and campus credentials before security has to get involved," the instructor said.

Security? No, if Far had to leave, it'd be on his own terms. He stood slowly for the sake of his pillaged soul, peeled the lanyard of badges from his neck, and tossed it across the table. An impertinent motion, perhaps, but what did manners matter when he was a hashing civilian? This time Far wasn't subtle about releasing "the bird," on his left hand or his right. One flew toward the mirror, the other toward Marin. Though he was dragged down by the weight of his own sweat, both gave him wings enough to fly toward the door. It felt like waking from a nightmare, this dread trembling through all corners, but Far knew he wasn't so fortunate. The real nightmare lay through this exit, stretching out into inescapable linear years.

The real nightmare had only just begun.

4.

OLD PAPER, REAL INK

AFTER A LESS-THAN-STELLAR SIM, FAR USUALLY found solace on the pull-up bar in his room. He faced his feelings in ten-rep sets: pumping anger out, muscle mass in. Making himself better, getting ready for next time. This evening when Far stepped inside the Zone 3 flat he shared with his aunt, uncle, and cousin, the exercise equipment seemed to mock him. What was the point of burning muscle pain now? There was nothing more to work toward.

Marie Antoinette and Instructor Marin had seen to that.

Dreams, badges, his will to fight...all that was gone. Far didn't even have the energy to make it past the entertainment room, and so he sprawled across the rug, performing a scrupulous examination of the ceiling. There wasn't much to study: just white interrupted by a light fixture and a single crack that whispered along the room's length. He'd spent the past forty minutes watching a jumping spider begin an epic trek from one end of the room to the other, ignoring the messages Gram kept pinging to his interface: WHAT HAPPENED? WHERE ARE YOU? I THOUGHT WE WERE SUPPOSED TO MEET FOR LIBATIONS???

Priya's question was even worse: HOW'S THE VICTORY DANCE GOING?

There was music, but it wasn't the happy kind. Punched Up Panda's anthem had gone straight in the trash, replaced by the cyber-metal radio station thrashing through Far's comm. He'd turned it up to max volume in a vain attempt to drown out Marin's speech about hubris and history hashing. The rant cycled through Far's thoughts on repeat, angrier than the synthesized song screams. Louder, too. *Diagnostics showed all systems are untampered with. You hashed up royally. YOU FAILED.*

He didn't hear Imogen press her palmdrive to the front door's lockpad. What he did hear was her yell, "Sorry I'm late! I picked up some gelato on the way home. I thought we could celebr—Far?"

There was a thud—she'd dropped something, the gelato probably—followed by panicked steps.

Far was still staring at the ceiling when his cousin's hair spilled into his face: bright pastel color, stabbing ends. The closest he'd ever come to describing Imogen McCarthy's personality was by comparing it to a kaleidoscope. Always changing, always surprising. COLORFUL. She flowed from one thing into the next in a way that was never expected but made perfect sense.

Imogen's hair was the most obvious canvas for this. In the 366 days since her Academy graduation, Far had seen his cousin's hair 366 variations of colors. She chalked them in every morning, washed them out every night. This seemed like an inordinate amount of work to Far, but Imogen would have it no other way. Dye was too permanent. Natural blond was too boring.

Today it was violet and very much in his face. Far couldn't find the strength to wave, so he huffed the offending strands away.

"Crux! I thought you were dead or something!" Imogen leaned back on her heels. The ceiling returned. The spider was still marching, eight legs milling across the plaster wasteland. Where was it going? All Far could see in the arachnid's immediate future was blank space....

His cousin frowned. Her stare lingered on the wool stockings and waistcoat Far had still been wearing when he stormed out of the Academy—*hash you very much!* "What happened?"

"I failed."

Imogen didn't move. She sat on the floor beside him, silent for the length of another cyber-metal song. It hammered through Far's ear. The ceiling melted orange with the light of the Flaming Hour, and the jumping spider reached the other side of the room, disappearing behind a HAPPY 17TH UNBIRTH-DAY, FARWAY! banner. The sign had outlived its usefulness by half a month.

"I failed," Far said again, thinking that maybe the words would make him feel better, or at least give the day some sense. All they did was punch the spiderless ceiling.

Imogen left and returned with a carton and two spoons, settling cross-legged next to him. "I got honeycomb flavor. Your favorite."

If anything, the gelato made Far feel worse. The silky treat—real cream, genuine sugar—was a luxury. Something only senators and high-ranking Corps members and people with connections could afford. When he and Imogen were younger, his mother spoiled them with cartons of the stuff. As if pints of pistachio or key lime or raspberry sweetness could make up for the fact that she was still going on expeditions, aging months in the span of minutes. Chocolate was the flavor she'd bought before she boarded the *Ab Aeterno* ten years ago and never came back. The ship was declared untraceable by the Corps, lost in a way that could never be found again.

At least, that was what the Corps officials told him. There'd been chocolate then, too—a mug of cocoa going cold on the coffee table. Far ignored it, staring hard at the officer's infinity hourglass badge, eyes traveling its loop around and around. *Your mother is lost. . . . Sergeant Hammond, too. I'm sorry, son. We've done everything we can. What happened to them will remain a mystery.*

Even at seven years old, Far refused to believe this. He knew, he just *knew*, that when he wore a badge like that, he'd go back in time and find the *Ab Aeterno*.

"Eat." Imogen held out a spoon, waiting for him to take it. "Sugar and fat heal all wounds."

"You can't afford that," Far said to the ceiling.

She shrugged and dropped the utensil. It landed with a thud

on his chest. "I've been saving up some credits, working OT in the shop."

Imogen had attended the Academy on the Historian track, which was popular and thus overpopulated, producing more licensed Historians than expeditions could take on. Imogen applied for every single CTM mission she could, only to watch the position fall to another, more experienced Historian. Once she'd been put on standby (she'd bought gelato in celebration of that occasion as well—lemon lavender), but nothing came of it.

In the meantime Imogen worked as a style consultant in a boutique, dressing the rich and fabulous according to their favorite datastream era. The work at Before & Beyond was menial and underpaying, but Imogen always came home with stories. She liked to reenact incidents featuring her more dramatic customers. There was Eleanor Chun, a senator's wife who was so addicted to Roaring Twenties datastreams that it was rumored she'd tried to bribe her way onto a 1920s New York City CTM expedition. There was Lucille Marché, who only ever wore white stolas with embroidered edges and was on a strict diet of soy-flavored meal blocks. There was Patrick Lucas, who always custom-ordered top hats and other elaborate millinery but never paid the credits when they arrived.

Far had never met these people, but he felt like he knew them. Imogen's impersonations were almost better than datastreams, which was good, because Far didn't plan on watching a datastream ever again.

"What happened today?" He needed a story now. Anything to derail his mind from the dark track it was going down.

"I got chewed out for bringing Mrs. Chun a flapper dress a size too large." The silver bangles Imogen wore chimed as she stabbed her spoon into the gelato. "Another costuming order came in. The CTM *Churchill* is preparing to explore fourteen hundreds Florence. So I'm going to be drowning in Renaissance gowns for the next week. Checking the Recorder's entire wardrobe for accu—"

She stopped midsyllable, a sudden jerk in conversation that startled Far. Why had she—Oh. Right. CTMs. Time travel. Wardrobes.

So much for derailing.

Imogen stayed quiet for another moment. The spoonful of gelato in her hand was starting to drip all over the rug. "I'm sure you can file a formal appeal."

That was Imogen. Eternal optimist. *The grass is still green on this side* and *never ever ever give up* type of girl. Usually Far found her view refreshing. A dose of color and sugar to counter the cynic inside him.

She meant well. She always did. But today Far found no comfort in her encouragements. Hashing up in an Academy Sim was the end of your career. Hashing up in actual history could be the end of the world. When it came to time travel, there was no such thing as redos, and as Instructor Marin had so bluntly reminded Far, he was not an exception.

"I'd rather not talk about it," he said.

"Right." Imogen's mouth twisted. "Well, I didn't spend fifteen hundred credits on gelato to watch it melt. So you better get your tail off the floor and eat it with me."

Far didn't want to move, but fifteen hundred credits was over twenty hours clocked at the boutique. The thought of Imogen's hard work melting into nothing forced him to grab the spoon and sit up.

Enough had been lost today.

They took alternate jabs at the golden cream. Imogen filled the spaces between bites with New Forum gossip and dress dramas, trying her best to edit any mentions of time travel. But the gaps were too obvious. Time travel was discovered only thirty-one years ago, but its cultural presence was inextricable. *Everything* revolved around it: entertainment, fashion, science, architecture, agriculture. You couldn't walk outside without seeing a twenty-second-century flash-leather suit or triggering an implant advert for ZOMBEES© HONEY—THE SWEETNESS IS BACK (APPROVED BY THE CENTRAL BOARD OF AGRICULTURAL REHABILITATION). No matter how carefully Imogen censored her tales, stinging details still slipped through.

BUZZ.

Far was almost relieved when the flat's doorbell jerked Imogen to her feet. She bounded to the door—purple hair flouncing—and opened it to find nothing but hallway.

"That's weird. Oh—" Imogen bent down, staring at something Far couldn't see.

"What is it?" he asked.

"It's...a letter." His cousin nudged the door shut. "For you."

A letter. Far felt the hair on the base of his neck bristling, though he wasn't quite sure why.

"This is old paper. Real ink," Imogen noted as she handed the envelope over. Elegant penmanship marked Far's name on the front. "I've only seen stuff like this in museums and Sims."

The prickly feeling spilled down Far's shoulders and back as he tore open the envelope. The card inside was covered in the same loopy writing—

Second chances are rare. Don't waste yours.

Eleven o'clock tonight.

The Forum, Zone 1

Far stared and stared at the letters, waiting for them to rearrange or vanish in front of him. The card was wrong. Second chances weren't rare. They just... *weren't.*

"What is it?" Imogen asked.

Old paper, real ink, second chances, a night-cloaked meeting in Old Rome... It reeked of danger and black market schemes, calling to Far in a way he could not ignore: *DON'T WASTE THIS.*

He didn't want to lie to his cousin, but he wasn't ready to tell her the truth, either.

"An invitation." Far folded the card into quarters and tucked it into the pocket of that ridiculous waistcoat. His chest one gram of paper heavier, one whole future lighter.

5.

YESTERDAY YET

ZONE 1 WAS MORE OF A museum than a neighborhood. Rent in the Old Rome district reached astronomical heights, despite its leaky roofs and primitive plumbing. The only people who could afford the luxury of nonluxury were the very same people who frequented Imogen's shop. They shelled out credits by the zeros for flats they used once or twice a month. If that.

As ridiculous as it seemed, Far understood the draw. The buildings might be crumbling, but they were also mesmerizing, covered in wistful vines, their stucco as colored and cracked as Easter eggs. When you walked the streets cobbled with fountains and gelaterias, grooved with the tracks of automobiles and horse-drawn carts, it was almost like stepping back in time.

Almost.

But the present circled the ancient capital in the form of skyscrapers and satellite towers. Even if you didn't look to the horizon, it came to you—hovercrafts weaving a constant blanket of noise overhead.

Walking through Zone 1 never failed to stir the hunger in Far's heart. It tumbled and yawned, reminding him that he wanted so much *more* than this world of Sims and datastreams and *everything*-all-of-the-time. He wouldn't have been able to stand passing the Colosseum without the card tucked inside his waistcoat: Second-chance hope, you'll walk these stones yesterday yet. Every few steps, he patted his pocket to make sure the invitation hadn't vanished.

The old Forum felt anything but welcoming when Far arrived. Two minutes early. He scanned the ruins—broken stones flickering under hovercraft lights—but they were empty. Tourists often visited this place in the daylight hours, shuffling from one site to the next while conjunctive datastreams flowed through their corneal implants. With one eye they took in the present; with the other they gazed at the past. Digital ghosts enacted history right in front of them: triumphal processions, temple ceremonies, gladiatorial fights...

Right now, with the deep gaps of darkness between the Temple of Saturn's freestanding columns, it was easy for Far to imagine ghosts in their truer form. Shadows kept crowding his vision. He found himself getting fidgety.

"Switch off your comm." The voice came from behind Far, but when he turned, there was nothing but night and stone.

"If you wish to proceed with this meeting you'll switch off your comm."

No—not behind him. Inside him. Someone had linked to his comm without a contact request. Second hack of the day? Far's stomach cinched as he ordered his comm offline.

A man stepped out from behind a column. He sported a black cape, complete with a hood that made him look like some sort of Renaissance assassin. With a wordless wave, he beckoned Far to follow him through the old Forum's scattered stones and weeds, all the way to the ruins' southern perimeter, where he stepped behind a second column. When Far followed suit, he found a row of arid shrubs hugging an old-as-dirt wall. His guide stood between the shrubs, face to the huge stones. Waiting.

Far was starting to wonder if he'd made a terrible mistake. Had he been lured out here by some psychopath to get gutted for the credits on his palmdrive? If so, the caped criminal wouldn't get much. Far lived on a student's budget. Ten measly credits were all he had to his name....

This dissuading banking information was on the tip of Far's tongue when the figure placed his own palm against one of the rocks.

It opened.

What looked like first-century Roman stonework was in fact a door. After reading the caped figure's prints, it rolled back, expelling air heavy with must and darkness. The guide waved again: *You first.*

None of this helped Far's apprehension. He breathed deep, felt the real-paper crinkle of the card against his chest.

DON'T WASTE THIS.

It took a few minutes to get used to the dark and the cobwebby smell. The tunnel seemed to be going down, along a course that threatened to collide with the Tiber. The electric light in the caped figure's hands glistened across wet walls, carved out Far's path in the shape of his silhouette. He kept moving at the cloaked figure's wordless urging, until he was positive he'd walked a few kilometers. Maybe more.

The tunnel ahead opened into a great cavern. How great, Far couldn't tell. The only light was the figure's, and it touched no walls, just globed against the dark. As soon as Far walked into the open space, this, too, clicked off....

It was a darkness he'd never experienced before—complete absence of light. Far wondered if this was what it felt like in the Grid. As if everything in the universe was spread in front of him, or possibly nothing at all.

He shivered.

"What's going on?" His question's echo was faint. This cavern was extensive....

"I'm pleased you could join us, Mr. McCarthy." The voice came from in front of him, and he'd heard no footsteps. It couldn't belong to the cloaked figure. No, it had to be someone who was already here. Someone who'd been waiting for him.

"Who exactly is *us*?" Far asked the darkness.

"We'll get to that," the voice drawled, confident. The more it spoke, the more Far felt he should recognize it. "But I have a few questions for you first."

"Go on."

"Who do you love the most?" It seemed like a dangerous query, the way it was asked: razored syllables, hungry breath beating, beating against the black.

"Myself." This was not the full truth, nor was it a complete lie, but Far's answer filled the dark well enough.

"Who do you hate the most?"

At the moment?

"Marie Antoinette." And the person who hacked the Sim, but Far kept that addendum to himself in case said person was standing before him now.

"What is your deepest fear?"

"What is this?" Far deflected. "Twenty questions?"

A sigh. "Just answer me, Mr. McCarthy."

"Dying without living."

There was a moment of silence before the answer. "How poetic."

"My favorite color is beige and I have a purple narwhal tattooed on my tail cheek. His name is Sherbet." Not knowing what the hash was going on was starting to fray Far's calm. "Anything else you want to know?"

"I can see why you get under Marin's skin," the voice said. "But I'm not so easily rattled."

Marin. The name set Far's jaw on edge. He was about to ask the voice *how* he knew about the irate Academy instructor when the world reappeared. Rows and rows of industrial-sized bulbs burst light into what Far now understood was a massive underground warehouse for honest-to-goodness CTMs. Four time machines reared in front of him: sleek as cats, big as houses.

The *Galileo*, the *Ad Infinitum*, the *Armstrong*... None of these were names Far recognized—nor were the actual CTM initials stamped onto the vessels' bows.

The closest one had no name at all. Its holo-shield invisibility plates were unscratched. Far would've bet his tight, tight breeches that the ship's maiden voyage had yet to be taken.

"Like them?"

The man standing to Far's side was colorless. The white linen loungewear he had on did nothing for his leached gray hair and pallid skin. His eyes were dark but flat. Lacking some essential *-ness* Far couldn't quite place. He was the type of person you wouldn't look at twice if you passed him on the street. But he was also the type of person who wanted you to forget, who watched you, drinking in your every move, filing facts away for later.

As Far watched the man watching him, he got the very distinct impression that he himself was a file already written. Highlighted and starred. "Why am I here?"

"I think you know."

"Right, well, since we're playing guessing games..." Far walked to the nameless time machine and placed a hand on the hull's pearly plates. It was a hulking, elegant thing, with a three-inch-thick lead body and engines powerful enough to bear it. "How long have you been watching me?"

"You've always been a point of interest, given the circumstances of your birth. And then what happened to your mother... a shame."

Far's reflection shimmered back at him: opal shades and

anger. *Shame.* He hated that word, never understood why people used it in the wake of tragedies. To him, it always sounded like surrender.

"Your Sim performances have always been superb. Today's notwithstanding." The man drew closer until his reflection appeared in the hologram plate as well. "You fear nothing that's inconsequent. You aren't overly stiff, nor are you reckless. Your judgment calls are bold but clean. Risk done right. The potential, the talent, the fearlessness, the drive…all of my requirements are there. Now, thanks to a flirtatious Tier Three queen, we can both have what we want. You need a time machine, and I need a captain. You've got the drive and the talent. I've got the ship and the fuel."

"*Captain?*" Far's mouth went dry at the word, cracked with the possibilities of it. His heartbeat oozed through these gaps.

"I need someone of skill to go back in time and—acquire— certain items for me. I'll give you and your crew five percent of the cut, as well as appropriate amounts of fuel and use of the TM."

The black market trade of past-snatched luxuries wasn't so much a secret as a conveniently ignored fact. Central's upper crust was attached to such creature comforts: Vintage wines, artisan cheeses, coffee, and fresh flowers could all be found floating around the mansions of the Palisades. According to Imogen's shop gossip, even senators were in on the indulgence, which was why no formal raid had ever been made by the government. What did history's integrity matter if there was non-synthetic *chocolate* for the tasting?

Never mind a single wink. Hashing hypocrites.

"Were you the one who corrupted my exam Sim?" Because Far was as sure as shazm that *someone* had, and he couldn't imagine that a mogul whose operation was twenty types of illegal would have qualms about cracking the Corps' computer systems.

"When it comes to your Sim, I was a mere observer." It was a cool response, chill over the shoulder. "The queen's attentions were a stroke of luck."

Far turned to face the man. "I don't believe in luck."

"Then I'm doubly fortunate." The black marketer's grin was as wan as the rest of him, crowded with canines. "A man who doesn't believe in luck works twice as hard. If someone did sabotage your Sim, you should be thanking them. Souls like yours were never meant for Corps work. Did you really want to spend your life picking flowers for the Central Board of Agricultural Rehabilitation? Filming parties and battles for perpetually discontented datastream addicts? No, Farway McCarthy. You would have choked to death on the Corps' protocol. Wearing their uniform would have been its own prison."

These words struck a chord. The Corps had only ever been a means to an end. The end itself remained: a time machine at Far's back, centuries for the seizing, the *Ab Aeterno* waiting to be found sometime among them. As tempting as it was to go full-on Pavlovian—drool on the warehouse floor, et cetera—Far knew dreams weren't handed over without a price.

"So making wine runs as your bootlegger errand boy is a life of free-range fun by comparison?"

"I have more than enough couriers." The man nodded at the other three TMs. "What I *need* is a thief. History is brimming with lost treasures. The Fabergé eggs. Art sacked and burned by the Nazis. Blackbeard's hoard of gold. Things that will never be missed or noticed by the Corps. Things you're going to help me obtain."

"You want me to plunder time for you." Far let the thought sit a moment. It was more exciting than loading up crates of cheese wheels. Riskier, too. "Aren't you afraid that I'll slip up and screw over history as we know it?"

"The universe always has a way of righting itself, Mr. McCarthy. Course correction. God's will. Karma. Fate. Call it what you will. Things tend to balance themselves out." The man's eyes never left Far as he said all this. Crux! Did the man *ever* blink? Was it possible he was a droid? Though most droids *had* eyelids...

"Speaking of balance. Seems a bit unfair you know so much about me and I don't even know your name."

"Lux Julio," the man said. "Anything else you'd like to know?"

"Plenty." Far looked around the warehouse. It was a warren of a place, walls riddled with tunnels. Exits, exits, everywhere, and while some of them were large enough to accommodate magcart tracks, none were suited for a time machine's girth. "How do you get the TMs in and out?"

Lux pointed past the lights, where the cavern vaulted with cathedral-esque aerobatics. "This ceiling wasn't always made of earth. My ships leave the anchor date—our present—by jumping to June 2155, a time when the Tiber's riverbed carved through here. From there they fly to their physical destination, and jump to whatever year is necessary. The return trip is the same."

"Four jumps for one load of cargo?" Far whistled. "That's a hash ton of fuel."

"Discretion has its costs," Lux said. "This isn't a job for the faint of heart. Should you agree to my terms, I expect results. Failure to deliver my cargo will lead to...unpleasantness."

Ah. Now they were getting into the nitty-gritty—sell your soul for silver coins, *Doctor Faustus* territory. "Care to elaborate?"

"The items I'm sending you after are one-of-a-kind. Irreplaceable. My buyers are willing to put down millions of credits. It's my opinion that the forfeit should be equivalent to the loss. Say you return with a partially burnt Van Gogh. I'd be inclined to fire you, but not before I wiped your palmdrive and blacklisted your name for every future employer. Cross me and I can end your dreams, your freedom, your life."

"You sure know how to pitch yourself," Far said, making a mental note to never, ever flip off Lux Julio.

"You're still free to walk away, though here's what will happen if you do. Once I dope you up with Nepenthe, you'll wake up with no memory of this meeting, an empty ache inside your chest. Datastreams will torment you. You'll watch your licensed friends grow decades older in the span of days, living the life of adventure you were destined for. The despair will eat you alive until all you can think about is how to end it." The words alone were terrifying, but the way they left Lux's lips made them darker still. Ruthless truth, said with a smile no droid programmer would ever authorize. "Work for me, and time is yours for the taking."

A second chance. And Far's last.

For the taking.

He wasn't quite snatching yet.

"Seven percent," Far countered. The black market mogul cocked his head at the number. The air around him sharpened, and Far found himself wondering what a halo was called when it did not shine gold. "I want seven percent of the cut, plus enough fuel for a free trip every heist we complete. Also, I get to choose my crew."

Getting away with highly illegal, unregulated time travel was enough of a challenge. Doing it without souls Far trusted—and liked—would be impossible. He already had a running roster in his head.

"Why should I be inclined to give you these things?" Lux asked.

"If the forfeit is equivalent to the loss, the reward should be equivalent to the gain," Far reasoned. "I'll be making you millions. Another two percent and a few vacations is an even trade."

"We have ourselves an agreement, Mr. McCarthy." Lux gestured to the figure in the corner. The hooded man moved between them, pulling out a sheet of parchment very much like the one tucked in Far's waistcoat.

I hereby enter into the service of Lux Julio under the agreed-upon terms, it read, followed by a blank dotted line.

"I like sealing deals in writing," Lux explained. "That way if you rat, you burn."

The stationery felt awkward in Far's hands: too heavy and *there*. Though pen to paper was a dead art, he'd learned handwriting during his first year of Academy—just one of the many strange skills they had to learn to fit into other eras. Along with horseback riding, operating an automobile, cooking with a microwave, and loading a rifle.

He held the pen over the document, fingers cramping with muscle memory. There was just one more request.... "I get to christen the ship."

Lux nodded, trying his best to appear benevolent. The look didn't suit him.

Far's pen was too close to the paper. Its ink seeped out, a disturbing red, pooling at the base of what would soon be an $\mathcal{F}$. He scrawled out the rest of his name in an unpracticed hurry. The whole thing looked off-kilter.

Lux accepted the signature, rolling the paper into a scroll. He nodded at the TM. "What will you call her?"

Why were ships always *her*s? Imogen would know. Far would have to ask his cousin when he got back to the flat. "I haven't decided yet."

"Make it good." Lux's fist closed over the document, covering the spot where Far's name had bled through. "You're stuck with it, Captain McCarthy."

Captain. I am the captain....

Far looked back at the ship. Its holo-shield plates swallowed the overhead light, made it mesmerizing. He could still hear the parchment wrinkling against Lux's palm as he stared at the hull: plain bright bursting into pink, green, blue shimmer.

"There are worse things to be stuck with," he said.

PART II

How Time is slipping underneath our Feet:
Unborn TO-MORROW, and dead YESTERDAY,
Why fret about them if TO-DAY be sweet!

—OMAR KHAYYÁM, AS TRANSLATED BY
EDWARD FITZGERALD
"THE RUBAIYAT OF OMAR KHAYYÁM"

6.

PRETTY, PRETTY PLUNDER

INVICTUS SHIP'S LOG—ENTRY 2 (THOUGH TECHNICALLY
IT SHOULD BE ENTRY 345 IF FARWAY WEREN'T
SLACKING ON HIS CAPTAIN DUTIES)

ANCHOR DATE: AUGUST 22, 2371

CURRENT DATE: JUNE 11, 2155 (HOW ELSE WOULD
WE LAUNCH OUT OF OUR TOP SECRET DOCK LIKE
SUPERHEROES?)

CURRENT LOCATION: SOMEWHERE OVER THE ATLANTIC?
PROBABLY?

DESTINATION DATE: APRIL 14, 1912

DESTINATION LOCATION: ATLANTIC OCEAN, RMS *TITANIC*

OBJECT TO ACQUIRE: A PRETTY, PRETTY BOOK

IMOGEN'S HAIR COLOR: AQUAMARINE WITH A HINT OF
BUBBLE-GUM PINK

GRAM'S *TETRIS* SCORE: 354,000

CURRENT SONG ON PRIYA'S SHIPWIDE PLAYLIST:
"EVERYDAY PAST" BY ACIDIC SISTERS

FARWAY'S EGO: AVERAGELY INFLATED)PAL.
NX^&54LLLLLLLLLL

IMOGEN'S VIEW OF THE SCREEN WAS invaded by cuteness in the form of fur, four paws, and BOUNCING. The red panda danced across her digital keyboard, paws lighting up random letters. Decades of domestication hadn't prevented these ginger fluffballs from dying out in the twenty-third century, nor had extinction deterred Imogen from acquiring one. Saffron: cutest pain in the tail there ever was.

"Off!" She clucked at the animal, which proceeded to rest his rump exactly where Imogen did not want it. AW;EOFFF FFFFFFFFFFFFFJNSKMMMMMM She picked Saffron up by the scruff and set him on the floor, surveying the damage. Nothing a good, long session with the Delete key couldn't fix.

Delete. Delete. Delete. Back to AVERAGELY INFLATED.

Imogen nibbled at the end of her aquamarine-with-a-hint-of-bubble-gum-pink hair and stared at the entry, trying to scrounge up adjectives to describe her cousin's most defining trait. Maybe she should create a sliding scale: size-of-a-pinhead-pride to dictator-of-the-month all the way to RED-ALERT-the-wax-of-your-wings-is-melting-and-we're-all-going-down-in-flames.

"What are you doing?"

Speak of the devil! Imogen twisted around her chair— it was her one nonnegotiable request in joining the *Invictus*'s crew, a seat that spun—to face Farway. One look and she could tell her cousin wasn't actually angry. When he was fake-mad his eyebrows trembled. Actually pissed and those suckers would be stock-still.

"I'm writing a ship's log," she told him. "Which, incidentally, is the captain's job. I've told you I don't know how many times that the *Invictus*'s logs need to be kept. Keeping track of birthdays is hard enough with one timeline, but when you start mixing our cover lives with our historical gallivanting it's hashing impossible."

Due to the less-than-legal nature of their activities, the crew kept up with their old jobs in Central time. The result? Three months of life as they knew it—long shop hours and family dinners. Almost thrice that had been spent aboard the *Invictus*, which made a proper mess of their biological calendars. It'd take more than math, however, to keep Imogen from celebrating a birthday.

"I keep records!" Farway waved at the wall beneath the ship's vistaport—as dark as the chalkboards of old, covered in descriptions of their missions. Imogen's hair chalks had been press-ganged into the effort. They weren't meant for writing with, but that hadn't stopped her cousin from spelling out his successes in silver and blush, white and aqua. Farway's highlight reel was bright indeed.

```
1945: RESCUED GUSTAV KLIMT PAINTING FROM
EXPLODING NAZI CASTLE.

1836: BRUSHED ELBOWS WITH DAVY CROCKETT. DUG UP
GOLD AT THE ALAMO. HEAVY AS A THREE-HUMPED CAMEL.

1511: EVADED THE SWISS GUARD TO RETRIEVE
MICHELANGELO'S PAINTBRUSH FROM SISTINE CHAPEL
SCAFFOLDING.
```

There were thirty such descriptions, each a testament to some treasure and the trouble they'd gone through to get it. Imogen appreciated the list's multihued aesthetics, but in terms of record-keeping it was...smudgeable. A brush of Saffron's tail had turned Blackbeard's name into *Bla—rd* and *cutlass* into *cut-ass*. Imogen giggled whenever she saw it.

She choked back the laugh as she addressed her cousin. "We need something more bona fide than your brag wall. Records that capture our comings and goings, the day-to-day spirit of the *Invictus*."

"Oh." Farway leaned in to read the text. "Bubble-gum pink? Looks more coral to me."

"Coral?" Imogen gave a mock gasp. "In what world would

this color be considered *coral*? Are you sure you don't need to have your vision checked?"

"I've got eagle eyes and you know it." Farway pressed the Delete key.

Good-bye, AVERAGELY INFLATED. Nice knowing you.

"Hey!" Imogen dropped her not-coral hair and swatted at her cousin's knuckles. "I spent, like, thirty seconds typing that."

Farway endured her assault, kept typing: FARWAY'S EGO: RIPPED TO SHREDS BY CRUEL, UNFEELING COUSIN. RIP. Imogen was positive her cousin would've droned on with his pride's digital eulogy if Saffron hadn't decided to tackle Farway's calf.

"Crux!" He swore as ten claws needled his shin. "Get the cat off me!"

A snicker came from across the room. Gram, the *Invictus*'s Engineer, cleared his throat and pretended to be wholly engrossed in his *Tetris* game.

"Red panda." Imogen leaned down to remove said creature from Farway's pants. "*Ailurus fulgens* in your mother tongue."

Her cousin's expression soured, not so much with pain as with the word *mother*, made all the more aching by Imogen's use of Latin. Neither McCarthy child needed translation tech for the language because Aunt Empra always spoke it with them. Imogen could still conjugate the shazm out of words in her sleep, though she hadn't used the skill in eleven years. Neither of them had since the *Ab Aeterno* had vanished. Thinking about her aunt's disappearance made Imogen's throat tight. She couldn't imagine how Farway felt about it.

He brushed the subject off like he always did: "So what's the scoop? Or were you too busy doing my job to do yours?"

Right. Imogen should probably add DASH OF CROTCHETINESS INDUCED BY RED PANDA CLAWS to the day's tally. She'd do that later, when Farway wasn't watching. He'd never read the logs anyway.

"Boss-man's got you going after some pretty-pretty." Imogen pulled up the mission specs Lux's assistant Wagner had downloaded into the *Invictus*'s mainframe during their last stint in Central. "The *Rubaiyat*. Also known as the Great Omar. It's a book of Persian poems. This particular edition went down with the *Titanic* in 1912. Bookbinders in Britain spent two years snazzing it up with gold and semiprecious stones and then sold it to an American. Obviously it never actually finished the journey across the pond. The bookbinding firm tried to make a second version, but it was crispified down to the jewels during the Blitz in World War II. Rumor has it the book was cursed."

The image was a drawing based on archival descriptions. Three peacocks flocked across the cover; their proud tail feathers sprayed with amethysts, topazes, and rubies. The book's edges were detailed with golden embroidery. Most of the things they stole were pretty, but this was by far Imogen's favorite. Hence the extra *pretty*.

"Cursed or not, it's got a lot of bling." Farway whistled at the sparklies; Saffron cocked his head at the sound. Imogen scooped the red panda into her lap before he could play pincushion with Farway's calf again.

"Over a thousand jewels," she told her cousin. "It was worth about 405 pounds at the time. But I had Gram run the numbers, and he's guessing with inflation and overall rarity it's well over eighty-five million creds."

"Eighty-five?" Farway straightened and looked over at the Engineer. "Eighty-five mil?"

Gram was doing three things at once: running pre-Grid numbers, flipping a T-shaped *Tetris* piece so it fit between two I-shaped ones, and shrugging a reply. "Easy. Could even inch up to one hundred if Lux fences it to the right buyer."

"A cut from that would buy us a real nice vacation." Imogen nudged Farway. True to the agreement he'd struck with Lux, they got one free trip to any time they wanted for every heist they pulled. This was the *Invictus*'s life between the hair-chalk letters: thirty R&Rs for thirty snatches. India, Walmart, the Maldives, the Giza Plateau, China's Bamboo Sea. Imogen couldn't recall every place they'd been—her memory was going slippery before twenty, bad sign; she needed to remember to ask Priya for fish oil pills, if she could remember to remember to ask—which was why she'd decided to start keeping the ship's logs. These trips were worth documenting, though lately their extra comings and goings had erred on the side of errands. Going back to the 1990s for a vintage replacement part to Gram's busted NES console, picking up specialty food for Saffron, and...looking for Farway's mother.

The last one was never voiced aloud, but Imogen knew it for what it was. They'd been to third-century BC Egypt three times, and it wasn't a coincidence that was the last date and location stamped into the *Ab Aeterno*'s official Corps logs.

"Somewhere nice," she went on. "Somewhere fun."

Gram looked over his shoulder. His dark eyes widened, urging her on. She was hardly the only crew member who wanted a vacation. It was easy to get cabin fever in a ship as small as the *Invictus*.

What looked like some hulking, iridescent snow dragon from the outside was actually…not as big on the inside. Their TM was stuffed to the brim with stuff. The bow held workstations: Imogen's database and the blank-faced dummy she coordinated Farway's mission outfits on; Gram's U-shaped console, where the Engineer ran numbers and systems checks before weaving them through the Grid; Farway's captain's chair—facing his wall of accomplishments, the vistaport above—though he hardly ever used it. Priya's infirmary was port side, attached to the engine room. Her time there was spent patching up Farway's scrapes, keeping the *Invictus*'s fuel rods from turning them all into radiated fritters, and creating playlists for "team morale."

The TM's starboard was a washroom—smeared with the fluorescent remains of Imogen's former hair colors—and a small kitchenette, where rations were stored. Most of the cabinets were filled with recycled nutrient meal blocks, which tasted like plastic foam and lasted just as long. Usually the stock stayed untouched, for EMERGENCY—if you're on your last HANGRY legs and anything within arm's reach is edible—situations. Nicking fresh ingredients from days-past was a much more popular option.

The central common area was where they ate meals, sipped tea, watched datastreams, and plotted their next vacation. The space also doubled as a wardrobe. Clothes from all eras hung from the ceiling pipes, long enough to brush the crew's heads every time they moved from one end of the *Invictus* to the other. It wasn't rare to spot Saffron's tail hanging in the mix. The rest of them bunked at the stern of the ship. Their cabins were stacked in a honeycomb formation, each large enough for a bed and half a crouch. Too tiny to do anything except sleep and snag some alone time.

There wasn't much solitude among four souls, one mannequin, and a red attack panda. Something was always happening. A heist, or dinner, or a clandestine snogging session between Farway and Priya, or Gram hitting *Tetris*'s highest score in record time, or Saffron getting into Imogen's hair chalks thinking they were treats and staining the floors and pipes with pastel-yellow paw prints for days afterward.

The *Invictus* was family, life, home, and despite its cramped quarters Imogen wouldn't trade it for anything. Unless anything happened to be a nice vacation.

"We could go mingle with artists in Belle Époque Paris. Or go diving in the Great Barrier Reef." Imogen realized she was still staring into the Engineer's eyes. Their darkness had a mesmerizing quality—much like a sustained cello note—flowing into his hair, his skin. Too many beats she'd held his gaze, and now her face was aflame. Such snitches, her cheeks! Blushing at every inopportune moment... "Or Las Vegas before the great drought?"

"Vegas?" Priya's voice drifted from the infirmary, along with the syncopated beats of her playlist. "I second Vegas! Poolsides, parties..."

"Motion denied. For now," Farway said, loud enough for the whole crew to hear. "We can start thinking about vacations once this job is out of the way."

Imogen swiveled her chair 180 degrees in the opposite direction, where Bartleby the mannequin stood, fully clad and faceless. At least she could blush in front of him. Being eyeless and unjudgy and all.

"You've got two outfits. The *Invictus* will drop you off on the smokestack closest to the first-class promenade, so you've got to be a bit snazzed up." Imogen pointed to the swallow-tail coat with a top hat, white waistcoat, and cane, before she unbuttoned the dress shirt. "You'll be wearing worker clothes underneath, so you can strip down once you leave the first-class section of the ship. Trousers, suspenders, and a button-down I greased up in the *Invictus*'s engine room. It should get you easy access to the cargo bay."

"That's where the *Rubaiyat* is being held?" Farway asked.

"Probably. Problem is there's no record of where the book was actually stored. All we know is that it's on the ship." Imogen brought up the *Titanic*'s layout on her screen. It reminded her of Gram's everlasting *Tetris* game: stacks and stacks of cabins, forced to fit together in block formation. She pointed at the highlighted areas. "The only thing documented in the specie room is opium, so you shouldn't bother with that. The cargo bay is down here, by the post office. I'll guide you through the comms. We'll drop you off at six PM April fourteenth, 1912. Everyone will be preoccupied with dinner and you'll have hours to look."

"Before it sinks."

"Yep."

Farway sighed. They both knew an earlier landing time wasn't an option. The entire point of collecting history's lost treasures was to let history believe they really had been lost. Not stolen.

"You've survived worse," Imogen reminded him. The wardrobe above the common area was testament to that. Sleeves edged with singe marks, a tricorne sporting a musket-ball-sized hole through one corner, pants pocked with blood from *Blard's cutass*. War, pirates, burning buildings, disgruntled gangsters...Farway had faced all these and more with minimal damage. He was pretty hashing lucky for a person who swore off the concept of luck altogether.

"Any Recorders?" her cousin asked.

"None that we know of." Which meant none sent before or during 2371 AD. Future missions might well have landed there. Imogen wouldn't have been surprised. The sinking of the *Titanic* was tragic in the most magnetic of ways. A serialized datastream of the event would make billions.

But it was also a landmark moment, prone to all sorts of interference. Lots of deaths. Lots of lives saved. Lots of press. It was the kind of event the Corps tended to shy away from for fear of altering the future. Lux hurled them into such scenarios without hesitation. It always came down to the same two things: money or fear. Which one was stronger?

Farway was fearless in a way Imogen simply could not grasp. If she were the one who had to put on that suit and descend into that soon-to-be watery grave, she—she just couldn't. She was comfortable being a Historian, guiding Farway through the comm, dealing with danger sans bullets and adrenaline.

Her cousin watched this screen, which would soon be linked to his corneal implant, showing Imogen history through his eye.

"How close are we to the landing coordinates?" he called out to Gram.

"Autopilot's got us ten minutes out. We'll be ready to jump in fifteen." Sonatas and cedarwood. That was what Gram's voice reminded her of.

Oh hash it all. Her cheeks were going red again. Imogen buried her face into Saffron's fur to hide it. The red panda chirruped and, instead of being a cooperative muff, hooked around her neck like an old woman's stole. Gram hadn't even looked up from the numbers he was running. Imogen didn't know whether to be disappointed or relieved. Maybe both?

SUCCESSES IN IMOGEN'S LOVE LIFE: 0. BLARGH.

"Right, then." Farway grabbed Bartleby by the waist and started dragging the mannequin toward the washroom. "I better get suited up."

7.

WHOOPS

GRAM WRIGHT'S STATION WAS MORE OF a shrine than a console. An homage to blocks and order. There were the usual buttons and screens, the navigation systems vital to any TM worth its stock. And the numbers... there were always the numbers, streaming through his brain at a rate that'd break a lesser genius. Gram's own gray matter had bandwidth to spare. School was so easy he'd done it twice, cycling through the Academy first as an Engineer, then doubling back for Recorder training. Why contain knowledge to a single degree? Why trap yourself in a tiny box?

Maybe that was what made Gram so fond of Rubik's Cubes. Yes, they were boxes—squares within squares within squares— but they held over forty-three quintillion color combinations. He was the proud owner of six of these toys, all vintage 1980, fresh off the assembly line. They lined his console in solid colors—red, orange, yellow, green, blue, white—the promise of a solution always within reach. A few twists + abstract thoughts = disorder reversed.

There was nothing Gram loved more than wrapping his mind around chaos, solving it. This was why he'd joined the *Invictus*. Piloting ships through time was a demanding job, but it was also short-lived. Engineers on a normal CTM often kicked back their feet and watched datastreams during the meat of the mission. Life aboard an illegal time machine was much more free-flowing. Dull moments need not apply. Gram could fire at all cylinders here: helping Priya tweak the engines, running heat scans for Imogen, and, every once in a while, getting off the ship to rescue Far's tail.

But the numbers were Gram's task and Gram's alone. These tangled equations kept the *Invictus* on course through the Grid, providing specific landing points down to the year, month, day, hour, minute, second, millisecond. It was a bit like doing a Rubik's Cube backward—twisting out of the present into a specific pattern of time. The astrophysics was so complicated Gram had to put his *Tetris* game on pause.

His score was frozen at 360,000. The *Invictus* spun through the nothingness that was the Grid. Gram ran through the numbers. Wrenching, twisting, solving, trying to land them on April 14, 1912 AD, 6:00 PM.

Wrenching, twisting, not-quite-solving, not-quite-solving...

Though timelessness was all around them, a tangible lack of passage that felt akin to an astronaut's lack of gravity, Gram had the cutthroat sensation this was taking too long. He stared at the screen, reviewing the equations until their white pixel forms burned into his vision.

Not-quite-solving...

An eternity passed, crammed inside a nanosecond, until Gram knew for certain that something was wrong. He couldn't make the numbers click and fit. Not the way he normally did.

It didn't fit. It didn't fit.

Why didn't it fit?

The equation was unsolvable. Impossibly impossible.

They couldn't land.

Gram tore his eyes from the screen and looked around the *Invictus*'s console room. It was oddly peaceful. Priya was helping Far smooth out the lapels of his new costume. Imogen was engrossed in her Historian screen. Saffron was draped over her shoulders, his striped tail twitching like an old clock pendulum: tick-tock, tick-tock.

Except there was nothing to keep time to. Nothing. Nothing. It didn't fit. They couldn't land. Couldn't—

It was only when Imogen looked up—a burst of green eyes, and then blush—and frowned that Gram tried to silence these thoughts. If he wasn't careful, the panic would stack on top of itself, block after misplaced block, until it choked him.

He looked back at the screen's pale numbers, took a deep breath, and ran through them again. Wrenching, twisting, not-quite-solving...

One of the numbers changed.

If Gram hadn't seen it happen with his own two eyes, he'd

never have believed such a thing could occur. Though the physics of time travel was a twisty, turny business, there were rules to it. Sixes didn't just turn into eights. Numbers in equations couldn't change, according to the laws of the universe.

They couldn't, but they had.

"Everything okay, Gram?" Imogen asked.

"Everything's fine." It was only when Gram ran through the equations again that he realized he wasn't lying. The numbers worked! He could thread them through the *Invictus*'s landing gear, out of the Grid, and straight into April 14, 1912 AD, 6:00 PM. First he had to check that the TM's holo-shield was on, autoset to mimic the surrounding environment. If it did, anyone looking up at the sky would see exactly that: stars, blue, perhaps a cloud. If not—well, there goes history.

The shield was in tip-top shape. Gram typed his solution to the equation into the navigation system and pressed Enter. The landing was so seamless that he started wondering if the panic he'd felt in the Grid was somehow a side effect from traveling through an eternal void. Integers didn't change. They just didn't.

Live footage from the *Invictus*'s hull began streaming through Imogen's screen. Her frown changed every angle of her face. "Um…"

"What is it?" Far gripped his cane.

Imogen looked at Gram instead. "What's the clock say?"

"April fourteenth, 1912…" If he were a real *Tetris* game, he'd be stacked up too high: GAME OVER. As he was, he just sat there, staring at the last few numbers on the clock. The numbers…

"Why's it dark out?" Far's stare bounced from the vistaport to his cousin's screen. "Where is the hashing *Titanic*?"

"Gram," Imogen said softly, "what's the rest of the time stamp?"

The numbers had changed and they'd landed wrong. Off not just by a few seconds or minutes, which would've been bad enough, but by hours. Four whole hours.

"Ten o'clock in the evening," Gram heard himself say.

Priya made a small in-the-throat sound. Far straightened, fists choking his gentleman's cane. Gram couldn't tell if the O of his friend's lips meant shock or anger. Probably both. In nearly a year of flights and heists, Gram hadn't screwed up once. He was convinced he still hadn't.

"I—I'll go check the engines," Priya volunteered. "Something must have fritzed."

Fritzed, yes. Engines? No. The numbers had failed somehow, but Gram knew how crazy that sounded: *Yeah, I'm gonna go ahead and blame the laws of the universe for this glitch. Not machines or human error.*

"We don't have to waste fuel on another jump," Imogen informed them. "There's still time. The *Titanic* has an hour and forty minutes before it hits the iceberg. We just have to fly a few knots west. Should only take ten minutes."

Far shut his mouth.

"You didn't need all that time anyway," Imogen told her cousin. "You always work better under pressure. We can get the mechanics of this sorted later, after you snatch up the pretty-pretty."

"Later." Far nodded. "Let's get hauling."

A Rubik's Cube got caught in Gram's haste to turn back to the nav systems. Fingers to squares to floor. He let it lie between his feet, channeling every ounce of concentration into guiding the *Invictus* where it needed to be.

❖ ❖ ❖

The *Invictus* hovered just meters above the *Titanic*: engines silent, elegant V shape melting into the night. If one looked closely enough, one might see the distortion—patterns of stars where stars had no business being—but the few people smattered on the decks below weren't watching the sky. Their gazes were turned out to sea, or to the windows inside, or to each other. Even the lookouts in the crow's nest were too busy wishing they had a pair of binoculars to notice the dark figure appear out of nowhere onto the second smokestack's top rung, balancing a top hat on his head and a cane in his mouth.

Far wasted no time descending the smokestack's ladder, because there was no time to waste. It had taken fifteen minutes, not Imogen's predicted ten, to catch up to the ocean liner, and now there was only T minus one hour and twenty-five minutes until iceberg, panic, doomsday. He wanted to be far away when that shazm hit the fan.

The rungs were cold enough to burn. Wind from the *Titanic*'s forward motion lashed Far's back as he hurried down. By the time he planted two feet on the deck his teeth were chattering, beaver-fast. It was too hashing cold for just a fancy dinner jacket and a workman's shirt. Imogen should've known better, added in a sweater or something.

She didn't usually make mistakes. Neither did Gram.

"I'm on d-d-deck," he shivered into his comm.

"I see that," Imogen replied. "Kind of. The visual's shaking a lot."

Far sucked in a breath. No point in pointing out her wardrobe oversight now. It'd only distract her from the more important task of giving him directions. "Which way?"

"All the cargo rooms are on the orlop deck, which is the second level from the bottom. You have to go through first class. Find the Grand Staircase....It should be close."

Far looked around. The night was clear and moonless, with stars, stars, stars overhead and glassy water in every direction. The *Titanic*'s boat deck stretched out, its pitch pine planks littered with chaise lounge chairs, edged with too few lifeboats. Imogen was right. The door to the Grand Staircase was close, literally a hop, a skip, and two short ladders away from the smokestack's base.

"Got it." Far ducked under the railing and down the first ladder.

"Good, good. Now, when you reach the Grand Staircase, you're going to go down two floors, to B deck. While looking snazzy and dapper and all that. Don't rush too much. Gentlemen don't rush."

"Why would I rush when I have so much free time?" he muttered.

Imogen's *don't be a jerk, Farway* sigh fuzzed through the

comms. Far ignored it, pushing through the door into the Grand Staircase.

It was a nice place, for a ship. White tile floors bloomed with black geometric patterns. A vast dome of iron and frosted glass stretched over the stairs, netting the night's shadows and pouring them into the halls. There were passengers here, chatting despite the late hour; faint conversations weaving beneath the notes of a pianist in the corner.

Far didn't look directly at any of these people. Avoiding eye contact was the best way to go unnoticed. He kept a healthy pace to the first landing, where the stairs spilled into a grandiose show of oak carvings. At the center of these sat a very fancy clock, which caused Imogen to *ooooooh* through the comms and offer one of her Historian tidbits. "The clock's famous, you know, called Honor and Glory Crowning Time."

Far didn't really care about the angels' names so much as the time they crowned.

10:20.

T minus one hour and twenty minutes. Gotta keep moving.

Past the bronze cherub candelabra, down to A deck and another collection of chatty passengers. He was just curling around to the second flight of stairs, past a young couple seated on a settee, when Imogen spoke again.

"Um, Farway."

That tone—stretched, a little sticky, the one that only meant trouble. If Far never heard it again it would be too soon. There were too many people around to reply to his cousin without drawing attention, but Imogen knew this and kept talking.

"Gram just did a heat scan of the ship. There are 2,225 people on board. The manifest in the databases has 2,223 names. You're 2,224, so...there's someone else on board who isn't supposed to be."

Who? Who was the 2,225th? A Recorder? Or worse, security from the future who'd figured out what they were up to, come to prevent it? If that was the case, they were already hashed. Unless they dumped the mission and returned to Lux empty-handed. That would go over well: lots of screaming, guns pointed at them, the *Invictus* seized and given to another crew. And Far, back to square one...

No no no no. An old fear stirred inside him, whispering that he was on the wrong side of a dream, that this life could get torn away, that everything would crumble to nothing again and Far would never be what he'd hoped: heroic son, unstoppable wanderer.

NO. Fire threaded through his veins, fight hot. Running wasn't an option. Far belonged here, sneaking through a soon-to-be-sunk steam liner like the spectacular thief he was. Besides, if it was Corps Security coming to intervene with this mission, there'd be more than one extra body. It was probably a CTM Recorder. All Far had to do was keep his head down, blend in like he always did, and keep walking.

8.

A ROYAL GREETING

"THERE'S SOMEONE ELSE ON BOARD WHO isn't supposed to be."

Eliot fiddled with her bracelet as she eavesdropped on the *Invictus*'s comms. A few subjects ago this statement would've summoned a smile. As things stood, her pulse pushed between the tendons on her wrist, a scattershot tempo it had kept up since the afternoon, when she strolled up to the first-class promenade and saw everything she feared beyond the ocean.

"I hope I'm not boring you, Ms.—" the gentleman across the settee from Eliot faltered, blushing. "Forgive me, my memory has been wretched today. What did you say your name was?"

She stared at the sandy-haired man. Man? No, even at nineteen Charles was more of a boy. Baby fat clung stubbornly to his cheeks, and there was such a hope in his eyes. The kind that looked like fresh-smelt copper, before the world ate it away in cruel patina chunks. Eliot couldn't remember the last time she felt so bright....

Unfortunately, the shine was about to end for Charles as well. She'd made the mistake of running his profile as soon as he'd sat down to chat. He wasn't one of the 710 souls who survived the night. Throughout their entire conversation together, this knowledge boiled inside her: *He's going to die.*

Eliot wanted to stay and give him a piece of happiness to hold on to when he plunged into the frigid water and his fingers, toes, arms, legs, thoughts, heart withered under the cold. That was the way destruction always crept: outside in. From the edges to the core.

He's going to die.

Aren't we all?

In a perfect world Eliot would linger on this settee and teach Charles some foreign curse words. It was a hobby of hers, learning obscenities in other languages: The French always sounded like poets when they swore, while Latin often felt dusty off the tongue. Her favorite insult was in Japanese: *Hit your head on the corner of tofu and die!* Charles would laugh when she translated it for him. Eliot would smile back. The *Titanic* would push on into the dawn, all the way to New York City.

The entire scenario was a paradox, though. 'Twere this world perfect, Eliot wouldn't be here at all. She couldn't spend the evening with Charles any more than she could warn the boy of his fate. If she didn't go do her job, there were going to be even more deaths. A whole haze of a lot more than a shipful.

"I'm sorry," she told Charles. And she really was. "I've got to go."

With that, Eliot left the boy, beet-faced and stuttering. She walked fast so she didn't have to hear him. It helped to have other voices buzzing through her comm.

"Once you get to B deck, you'll round back to where the elevators are and go through the baize-covered doors. Walk to the end of the hall and take the door out to the deck." The Historian was getting ahead of herself, Eliot noted, rushing despite her own instructions *not* to do so.

They could hurry all they wanted. It wouldn't help. Subject Seven—aka Farway Gaius McCarthy—had failed before he'd even stepped foot on this boat, because Eliot had boarded first. She'd already combed through the cargo bay's FRAGILE THIS SIDE UP crates, collecting splinters in her fingertips during her search for the *Rubaiyat*. To some, the book was a fount of wisdom: poetry that dissected birth and death and the life between. To others, the Great Omar was art bound in fortune, a collector's dream.

Yes, it was beautiful. Yes, it was wise. But to Eliot, it was so much more.

She paused by the Grand Staircase, watching Subject Seven as he descended to B deck. Her heart rattled over the steps. What a wonder it kept beating so fiercely when her weariness went so deep: down to the level of atoms and quarks, to fraying threads of fear and an always dreamless black sleep.

Disaster was exhausting. She'd lived so much of it.

And now, through Subject Seven, she was about to live it again.

❖ ❖ ❖

Far was only too glad to ditch the first-class getup. He didn't even wait around to watch them hit the water as he tossed the clothes overboard: Good-bye, bird-tail jacket! Peace out, top hat! *Vale*, gentlemanly cane!

The second outfit, with its trousers and rough shirt, was much more flexible. No one looked twice at a scuffed-up workman windmilling down five flights of stairs to the orlop deck. He was deep in the ship now, beneath the waterline, where engines hummed like warring whales and the dim lights served only to silhouette the mountains of crates and luggage. There were ranges of wooden boxes, leather wardrobes, even cars.

"Now what?" Far asked his cousin.

"You're looking for a small oak case. Probably near the top of one of these piles."

"Probably?" Far walked toward the nearest pile. Boxes on boxes on boxes, all netted together like a bunch of king mackerel to keep from tumbling with the ship. No small oak case here. Unless it was buried deep.

T minus one hour and ten minutes.

"It's the best I can do, Farway." Imogen sounded as stretched as Far felt. "You'll find it."

He moved to the second pile, using a Louis Vuitton trunk as a launch point for his climb to the top. Once there, Far pulled aside some crates, peering into the maze of leather and wood. Nothing of note. It was on to the next stack. And the next. He scaled mound after mound of expensive luggage, his stomach shrinking a size with every overturned crate, every passing minute.

T minus one hour and five minutes. T minus fifty-five minutes. T minus forty minutes...

Though Far kept searching, his mind was starting to wander—picturing his own empty hands outstretched, and Lux before them. Even in imagination the man was cold—no sneer on his face, no rageful tone: *I gave you a 1.2-billion-credit TM and three million credits' worth of fuel and you've brought me nothing. What am I supposed to do about that, Mr. McCarthy? What forfeit is equivalent to this loss?*

The answer that was sure to follow made Far search harder, but this mission had turned into a handful of dust and the tighter he gripped, the faster everything slipped. The *Rubaiyat* wasn't in this stack or the next or the last, and what else could he do except swear?

"We are so hashed."

"There's another cargo room with a lot of first-class luggage one deck up," Imogen told him. "The *Rubaiyat*'s probably in there."

True or not, this didn't make up for the thirty-minute countdown. Twenty if you counted the time it'd take for him to return to the *Invictus*—

Far halted, trying to understand what he was seeing.

An entire ship away, Imogen processed the same image. "What's a first-class lass doing in the cargo bay?"

The girl in the door *was* decked out in first-class frippery—floor-length daffodil-colored gown; chestnut hair coiled and pinned—but just from her stance Far could tell she was out of her era. She stood with her shoulder to the doorframe, elegantly slumped, an oak case propped on her hip. Far was a universe and a half certain this box contained the *Rubaiyat*, but it was what he saw on the girl's face that rendered him speechless. Or rather, *who* he recognized there.

Marie Antoinette.

The queen of France was on the hashing *Titanic*.

It was her, and yet…it wasn't. There was no beauty mark. No beehive wig. Her eyebrows still appeared scripted, the product of a pen nib. The gaze beneath was unmistakable: dark as glistening.

"You," he croaked.

Marie Antoinette—Far was certain that wasn't actually her name, but what else could he call her?—smiled and opened the case. Peacock jewels gleamed under the cargo bay's flimsy light. "Looking for this?"

"Um." Imogen's bewilderment was palpable. "Who is that? And why does she have the Great Omar?"

Far wanted these answers, too, but with T minus twenty-seven minutes to disaster and the *Rubaiyat* in the hands of another, there was only one question that mattered: "What do you want?"

The girl shut the box and tucked it under her arm. "To get your attention."

"Consider it obtained." Far took a step forward. "Now can I have the book?"

Marie Antoinette didn't move. Her smile was as unnerving as it had been in Versailles, just a twitch away from becoming a snarl. "You didn't say the magic word."

"Now can I *please* have the book?" he tried.

"You're going to have to work a little harder than that."

"Pretty please?" Far raised both eyebrows. "With a cherry on top?"

She winked.

And then she ran.

9.

RACE AGAINST TIME

YOU'D THINK A FLOOR-LENGTH DRESS, BUTTON-UP boots, and a hefty oak box combined with five flights of stairs would put a damper on someone's running skills. This didn't seem to be the case. *Hash it all*, this girl was fast! She leaped up the stairs with a springbok's grace, two flights to Far's one. He was still huffing up the third level when she slipped out of the stairwell.

"I told you we need to get a walkabout machine. Cardio is important. Your exercise routine can't be all pull-ups and push-ups and up-ups." Imogen's nervous chatter filled Far's ear. He wanted to tell her to stop, but he couldn't gather the breath for it. Every gram of oxygen in his lungs was dedicated to reaching Marie Antoinette before she disappeared altogether.

Where was she going? Far supposed she'd gotten here by means of a different TM. But TMs were crewed by many bodies, and the heat scans Gram ran only detected the two of them as anomalies. This girl was here alone. But to what end? If it was the *Rubaiyat* she was after, why dangle it in front of him like bait? If it was his attention she wanted, as she claimed, why run? And why run *so fast*?

Far panted through these questions, step by step. Nothing made sense, but it didn't have to. This girl wasn't going to ruin his life again! Come Hades or high water or stupid cardio staircases, he was going to get the *Rubaiyat*!

When Far blasted out into the cold night, he found C deck deserted. Two cranes bent like a giant's skeleton fingers, propped on glossy lengths of pitch pine. Marie Antoinette was nowhere in sight.

"Rat farts! Where'd she go?" Imogen's shout burst firework red across Far's eardrum, making him wince. "Sorry. But who is she, Farway? She acted like she knew you."

"It's a long story. I'm pretty sure I don't know the half of it." Far stepped into the middle of the deck and did a 360-degree sweep of the ship. There were plenty of places the girl could've gone, but based on her dress, Far figured his previous route was the best bet: up the iron staircase by the second crane, through the swing gate, into first-class territory.

He started running.

"Your clothes!" Imogen warned.

Clothes be hashed! These trousers were better for running in anyway. Far vaulted over stairs and gate alike, blasting past a steward on his way to the door. Through it, he caught sight of the yellow gown: Marie Antoinette was a whole quarter of a *Titanic* away, clutching the case to her chest. The corridor between them was ill lit, but Far could've sworn the queen of France was smiling as she slipped through the door. A silken ghost—there and gone.

"Oi! You!" It was the steward. "You can't be here! First-class passengers only!"

"Farway, you're being noticed," Imogen's voice jittered through the comm, shaken double by Far's sprint. "This is bad. This is bad, bad. The Corps is going to figure out we're here and haul us off to jail for the rest of our lives. Who's going to feed Saffron? *I can't go to jail, Farway!*"

So much for her *grass is green on any side* attitude.

Far tore down the red carpet corridor, past B deck's berths and lavatories, barreling through the door back into the Grand Staircase, making eye contact with at least four very startled late-night socialites as he did. All of them gasped. None of them wore yellow gowns.

Which way had she gone? Up? Down? Forward? There were too many choices and no time to choose. The steward was shazm hot on Far's heels. He'd be swinging through the door any second now—

Canary fabric flashed through the gaps in A deck's banister. Far looked up to see Marie Antoinette leaning over the railing. She wasn't even breathing hard....

"There she is! Go up, Farway!" His cousin hyperventilated useless instructions as Far ran for the staircase. "Go up! Go up!"

The girl was gone by the time he reached A deck. All Far found were settees full of wide-eyed passengers and the glory-honor-angel clock, its hands ticking closer and closer to T time.

"There!" Imogen caught the yellow this time, with Far spotting the color a second later. Again, it was a flight of stairs away, quick to vanish. "She's going out to the promenade!"

It struck Far as eerie, that this girl knew exactly how he'd arrived on the ship, knew exactly what item he was looking for, not to mention the fact that she was A HISTORICAL HOLOGRAM FROM HIS FINAL EXAM SIM.

She acted like she knew you.

Did she? If so...how?

Far ran outside, cheeks burning, arctic air knifing his lungs. Wind, water, sky, everything around him was moving. Their vastness accented the fact that the promenade deck was empty. He climbed to the base of the smokestack, where a full view of the *Titanic*'s top decks pooled out under starlight.

Marie Antoinette and the *Rubaiyat* were nowhere to be found.

"What the Hades?" he hissed at the night.

"Um...maybe she went back inside?" Imogen suggested. "Or maybe she's getting a head start and hiding in one of the lifeboats?"

Maybe. Far didn't have time to play detective. The doors to the Grand Staircase opened to reveal the steward, flushed and fuming. He'd collected a wake of curious passengers, who trailed him onto the deck.

So much for going unnoticed.

Far scanned the promenade again, but of all the gowns

belonging to the scandalized ladies who fluttered after the steward, none were yellow. And beyond them? No one. Nothing but the void of surrounding ocean and...an iceberg.

The iceberg.

It was a small thing at the moment. If Far hadn't already known it was there, he would've passed over the faint silhouette, just as the lookouts in the crow's nest were doing now. Just as they'd keep doing until the chunk of ice was undeniably *there*, scraping back the steel hull with curtain-like ease.

Imogen saw it, too. Her breath cut against the comm: "You have to come back."

Even though Far's hands clutched the ladder rungs, they felt so empty. He couldn't leave without the *Rubaiyat*. He just couldn't. He hadn't failed a mission yet....

Then again, he hadn't failed a Sim exam, either, until this girl showed up.

The iceberg rose higher, higher. How couldn't the watchmen see it? Even the tip was a minor mountain, close to one hundred feet high, according to Imogen's study of eyewitness accounts. Far suspected, as he watched the ice draw closer, that it was really more in the range of one hundred and twenty or so. All of that doom and death, sitting on waveless waters, and the *Titanic* plunging full speed toward it.

"You don't have time to chase that girl!" Imogen warned. "All Hades is about to break loose on that ship, and I am *not* sending Gram down there to rescue your tail from drowning."

A sharp cry left the crow's nest, but it had come too late.

The path was set; the *Titanic*'s fate was sealed. The unsinkable ship under Far's feet would soon be dragged down to its grave of darkness, swallowing all these people with it. Maelstrom swirling vortex black cold drown gently down no need to fight...

The end had begun. The ice of the headwind slid under Far's skin, crackled through his joints. He hunched his shoulders, but the chill stuck, following him as he turned his back on the tragic past-future and hauled tail up the smokestack.

10.

THE GIRL IN THE
YELLOW DRESS

IMOGEN WAS ALREADY DRAFTING HER NEXT ship's log when the *Invictus*'s rear hatch opened, spitting in a wind-licked, royally peeved version of her cousin. His curls were everywhere, hands clenched into fists.

```
RMS FARWAY HAS TAKEN AN ICEBERG BLOW. ABANDON
SHIP! WOMEN AND RED PANDAS FIRST!
```

No...*delete* that. It was too lighthearted.

None of this was funny: The look in Farway's eyes as he stomped into the console room sans the *Rubaiyat*. All of those faces of all of those passengers Imogen saw through the datastream. The tooth-raking sound of ice on steel as the collision took place just meters below. It was an awful noise. Imogen covered her ears, and she wasn't the only one. Both Gram and Priya paused from their tasks—booting up the nav systems, latching the *Invictus*'s door shut—to block it out.

Farway alone listened. He stood in the console room—eyes scalped, hands bare. She'd seen this look on her cousin only once before: the evening she force-fed him honeycomb gelato and found that exquisite real-paper message.

It meant the loss of everything.

When the iceberg and the *Titanic* parted, all was quiet. None of the *Invictus*'s crew wanted to be the first to test the wounded-animal look on their captain's face. Even Priya, who always gave Farway a once-over for injuries, hovered to the side, scanning him with eyes alone.

This was uncharted territory. They'd never not pulled off a heist.

They'd never returned to Lux empty-handed.

The thought turned Imogen's stomach. She'd only met Lux once, but that one time was more than enough. There was something *off* about the man they called boss. She got the distinct impression that he was a devil without the *d*. Not the sort of person who'd forgive the loss of eighty-five mil. Imogen wasn't sure *what* the black market mogul would do in mercy's stead, and she really, really didn't want to find out.

Similar thoughts layered Farway's face—denial, anger, desperation—sketching his emotions into new dimensions as he strode to Gram's station. "We have to go back. I have to try again."

The Engineer was staring at the numbers in front of him and whispering to himself, traces of gibberish syllables. He held one of his prized Rubik's Cubes in his hands, twisting without thought. Imogen had never seen Gram so imprecise, in word or motion. Muttering into unhearing screens was usually *her* forte....

"Gram! I need you to focus! I need you to skip us to earlier in the timeline, so I can get that hashing book before the girl does! Go back to the time we were supposed to land in before this whole mission went to shazm!" Farway's voice was sharp enough to make Imogen look at his eyebrows.

No trembling. This time he was truly pissed.

Gram looked up. There was sweat on his face; it caught the display's glow, shimmering from his cheekbones and brow. "Can't."

"What do you mean, you can't?"

"I don't know why or how, but we can't jump to that time. I tried plugging the numbers in—"

"So fix it!" *Smack.* Farway hit the frozen *Tetris* screen. Its glass held, but the rest of the *Invictus* flinched. "Isn't that what I pay you to do?"

"I tried," Gram said again. "I tried, and I'm telling you, I can't. It's impossible."

His sweat had collected into beads, rolling down his face so profusely that Imogen knew the Engineer—though he made no sense—was telling the truth. Farway must have come to the same conclusion, because he started back for the hatch.

"Imogen, get the feed back online!" he barked.

"*No!*" Imogen swiveled her chair too hard in her franticness. "You can't go back down there! The ship is sinking. There are too many variables now—"

"Do I look like I give a hashing bluebox about variables?" Her cousin halted. "That's two hundred mil I just lost down there! Lux isn't going to let that go easy, and I sure as Hades won't, either! Bring back the feed!"

Lux's wrath loomed, true, but Farway's descent into the gathering deep wouldn't change that. "The girl's gone," Imogen reasoned. "She's not gonna stick around with loot like that when the ocean's knocking!"

Yet stubborn is as stubborn does, especially where McCarthys were concerned. Farway made for the console room door, only to find Priya blocking its threshold. She stood there with her arms crossed, eyes relentless. "Imogen's right. You can't go."

"Move," Farway said. "Please."

"Sometimes," Priya spoke in a whisper, "it's okay to fail."

Imogen watched her cousin's face turn a shade darker and found herself wondering if there was any gelato left in her freezer stash. She could use some right about now, but she had a feeling the last carton of raspberry had fallen victim to nighttime cravings over a week ago.

NOTE TO SELF: SAVE AT LEAST ONE PINT OF GELATO
FOR EMERGENCIES.

"I didn't fail." Farway's words seared. "I never fail. I was robbed."

"Can you really be robbed of something you never had in the first place?"

The whisper had come from Imogen's corner, just over her

shoulder. Gram, Priya, and Farway all turned to look. When Imogen followed suit, all she saw was Bartleby, but once her sight started to adjust, she realized there was another human shape cookie-cuttered into the darkness behind the mannequin.

The shadow stepped forward.

It was the girl in the yellow dress.

11.

SCANNING WILL NOW COMMENCE

Eliot had seen her fair share of time machines and TM crews. They all had their quirks—you couldn't expect to survey the whole of time without a few personalities—but this took the cake. Clothes hanging from the ceiling. A girl with hair the color of a nebula. The Medic in grease-stained scrubs. And—oh haze—was that a raccoon?

The *Invictus*'s crew stared at her with the same scrutiny, trying to process her out-of-thin-air appearance. It wasn't as sudden as they thought. Eliot had been lurking behind the mannequin for several minutes, observing. She'd already gathered quite a lot about how this particular engine of teenagers ran. The Engineer, he was the steady *click, click* of gears. The dark-haired girl in the doorway was something of a radiator, monitoring temperatures, keeping things cool. The Historian—colorful like motor oil, running everything through the chaos.

But Eliot wasn't here to pick apart the interpersonal web of the ship. That was extra credit. The real assignment was Subject Seven, whose gaze was fuel-rod hot, aimed straight at Eliot. Had she been anyone else, she might have melted.

"You!"

Eliot was beginning to wonder if that exclamation was all he was capable of saying when the others chimed in.

"How'd she get in here?"

"Where's the book?"

"Who the hash is she?"

The ginger raccoon hissed at her, darting under Nebula Girl's chair.

"The *Rubaiyat* is in a safe place." Eliot gathered her skirts and stepped into the center of the console room. Nebula Girl scooted her chair back, accidentally rolling over the whatever-kind-of-animal-that-was's tail. The creature bounced away, yowling.

Subject Seven didn't seem to notice the mayhem. "What do you want?"

That question again...It was almost as if Seven were reading from a script, just like all the others. Same scene, different setting. Eliot brushed this thought aside. The other subjects, those other scenes, were done. Closing acts and curtains drawn. Her focus needed to be here and now. Subject Seven had to be the center of her universe...in case that was what he was.

"I want a job." Eliot moved to the empty captain's chair, sank into its tangerine-colored leather—haze, it felt good to be off her feet—and twisted to face her audience. "I want to join the *Invictus* as part of your crew."

The Medic's eyebrows tilted: one up, one down. Gingerbread Rodent kept hissing from the safety of the mannequin's shoulders. The rest of the crew continued to be dumbfounded, staring at Eliot as if they couldn't quite grasp her dimensions. Real? Hologram? Bad med-patch trip?

If only they knew the half of it.

Nebula Girl was the first to respond. "But...why?"

This was the hard part—knowing how much to say. The truth was off the table, but Eliot knew her time with the *Invictus*'s crew would be smoother if the conversation felt two-sided. "The black market is more crowded than Lux has led you to believe. I've been working the scene as a freelancer for a while, but that gets lonesome. Not to mention exhausting."

"Yes." Seven's voice brought new meaning to the word *scathing*. "Hashing up other people's lives must be very tiring."

"Freelancer?" The Engineer frowned. "But—how do you jump through the Grid without a TM crew?"

A rabbit-hole question, best skipped. "With great difficulty. As I said, I'm looking to ease things up, so I thought I'd give the whole teamwork thing a try."

"Teamwork?" Subject Seven spat. "You just sabotaged our mission!"

"No," she corrected. "I gave you incentive to hire me. Consider this past hour my test run, a demonstration of my top-notch thieving skills."

"I'm all the thief this ship needs!" Nothing had caught fire yet—a miracle considering how Seven's stare burned. "I can handle heists just fine, when you're not there tossing everything to shazm! What the Hades were you doing in my final exam Sim anyway?"

"Your—what?"

"My final exam Sim. You were dressed up as Marie Antoinette. You rigged the whole hashing thing! You *winked* at me!"

"I have no idea what you're talking about." Eliot did, of course. "If we work jobs together, we can maximize our thieving capacity. Twice the loot, twice the payout."

"You were inside Versailles's programming," Subject Seven pressed. "I'm not crazy and I'm certainly not delusional enough to invite you to join my crew—"

"No invitation needed." She shrugged. "I'm already here, and if you try to kick me off, you'll never see the *Rubaiyat* again."

The four exchanged glances—a web of silent conversations. Seven's eyes linked most with the Medic. There was such a familiarity in the pair's body language. Nod, shrug, eyebrow twitch; everything meant something. How long had it been since someone had looked at Eliot that way?

"This ship," Seven began, "it's built on trust. I trust Imogen knows where she's sending me. I trust Priya to clean my cuts and keep the engines going. I trust Gram to guide us through the Grid...."

The Engineer fidgeted with the cube he held, brow furrowed. When his gaze landed back on his console screen, it wavered, as if stumbling through a foreign language without translation tech, all meaning lost.

Eliot took a deep breath, shook the shake from her pulse.

Seven went on, "I've got no idea what I'm going to get when I toss you into the mix."

"You'll just have to sit back and see." Had there been a table in front of Eliot, she would've propped up the ridiculous button-up boots she was wearing, just like the men in old Western movies did when they had the upper hand. But the captain's console was behind her, and the *Invictus*'s crew all had a grasp on her superior position without the body language.

"You're in my seat," Seven said.

"It's all yours as soon as you show me to my bunk," Eliot told him. "I'd like one close to the floor. Heights aren't really my thing."

The moment sat and sat. Seven was sizing her up, running through his options, and realizing it was a very short sprint. "So you produce the *Rubaiyat* when we reach Lux?"

"That's right." Eliot smirked.

He crossed his arms and stepped close, only a few centimeters short of crushing the hem of her dress. "What's to stop us from throwing you out on your tail once we deliver the goods?"

"The same thing that will stop me from giving Lux a matinee datastream of our chase and lobbying for your job. Mutual trust." Eliot's smirk-smile remained steady. It was her default expression as of late, because she couldn't sustain any other emotion. Not after what she'd seen. Not with everything that was at stake.

Subject Seven's eyes narrowed. "We don't even know your name."

"Eliot."

"That's it? Just Eliot?"

"Only Eliot." What use were surnames when there was no family attached to them? "A girl used to reciprocal introductions. I realize bursting in on you like this was rude, but let's not make that our standard."

The crew wasn't quite sure what to do. The Medic moved to Subject Seven's side—a closeness that melded her scrubs with his workman's shirt. Nebula Girl blinked, while the Engineer looked up from his screen. His stare hadn't changed, gentle dark mixed with doubt. It reminded Eliot of an overcast dawn. "You want to know our names?"

"I want—" Here she paused, struck by the word's danger. The taste of it on her tongue—*What? What do you want, Eliot? Can you even recall?*—made her swallow. "A fresh start. Look, I'm not asking for friendship tattoos or a forever home, just a chance to try a new life on for size. If it doesn't fit, no harm done. If it does, your palmdrives will get so loaded you won't even be able to wave. Knowing your names would be a nice bonus."

The *Invictus* was so quiet, with its stealth engines and haunted crew. Noises from the outside were leaking in, the calls of officers who started to uncover the lifeboats. Theirs were calm, routine voices, unaware that things were about to get much, much worse. *Ignorance is bliss*, it was said, and maybe it *was* better that they could stare into the star-strangled sky and breathe deep, before the dark crashed down in fathoms....

"I'm Imogen McCarthy." Nebula Girl continued the

introductions when no one else offered. "Gram's our resident genius. Priya keeps busy keeping us alive. Farway—"

"That's a family name," Subject Seven interrupted. "Everyone else knows me as Far."

"That's it?" Eliot prodded. "Just Far?"

"Call me what you will, but don't mistake this impasse as an excuse to get chummy." Each word of his was a pulled tooth. Subject Seven should've been bleeding from the mouth. "Bunk on the bottom right corner is all yours, Eliot. I'd like my chair back now, if it's all the same to you."

"It's never not the same." With the help of Eliot's boots, they were equal silhouettes when she stood. "Now if *you* don't mind, I'll be turning in. I've had a trying day and these shoes are as painful as they are pretty."

Imogen gave an appreciative grunt. The rest of the *Invictus*'s crew watched, shell-shocked, as Eliot swept past their captain to her new quarters. She stole glances into the others' bunks as she did. One was strung with twinkle lights, with a holo-paper issue of *Style Yesteryear* faceup on a brightly woven Kilim rug. Another had a pair of antique wireless BeatBix headphones on top of the pillow. The adjacent pod was cluttered with kettlebell weights and dirty socks, and had the distinct scent of *boy*. The bunk above was meticulous in comparison—its bed made up with hospital corners. A poster of the periodic table brought blocks of color to its far wall.

Even after just a few minutes of study, Eliot could pin which crew member each room belonged to. Fitting then, that hers was so bare. The walls had the sterile feel of a science lab—all white in an effort to disguise the bunk's tininess. Paint could only do so much. Her dress took up half the hexagon, making it nearly impossible to turn.

Good thing my luggage is so compact, she thought, after the acrobatics of sliding her door shut. When the lock lit, Eliot flopped onto the bed, unbuttoned her boots, and rested her head against the wall.

Too much running, too much death. Couldn't she shut her eyes for just a moment?

When Eliot did, she could hear the crew just past her sliding door, bursting with questions: "Who is that girl, Farway?" "What's she doing here?" "Where is the book bling?" None of which Subject Seven would be able to answer. Beyond and below, she heard the *Titanic*'s orchestra launch into the beginning notes of their lives' final songs. She tried not to think of Charles, with his peach-fuzz face, and failed.

It was good that she remembered him, though it was exhausting to do so.

No rest for the weary. Or the dying. Or the dead.

Eliot's eyes remained closed when she brought up her interface. A family snapshot was the first thing to appear: Mom, Strom, and Solara on a boat ride through the drowned city of Venice. Towers rose from the water behind them—half elegant, all eerie. Strom wrestled into scuba gear while Solara knotted her hair in a bun. Eliot's mother was midconversation, words forever suspended. Eliot used to study these pixels for hours, trying to conjure the sights, sounds, scents of that day. Now it was a placeholder as the menu loaded.

Figures and charts and forecasts and six separate files of datastreams spackled the darkness. Eliot flicked past these to the newest file: SUBJECT SEVEN. It contained a comprehensive profile of Farway Gaius McCarthy...fudged DNA tests, school scores, palmdrive accounts, past residences, current address: Via Ventura Zone 3. It also held a spectacular datastream of the May 5, 2371 AD, Sim hack and the resulting expulsion.

The rest of the file's space was waiting to be filled. Eliot transferred her past few hours into it. Her life had become a constant datastream—recorded, stored, labeled, rinse, repeat. This episode went down as *Subject Seven Second Encounter. April 14, 1912 AD.*

"Evening, Vera." Eliot kept her voice soft when she addressed her interface, in case Subject Seven's crew had taken to pressing ears to her door. "What's the weather like on your end?"

I AM A COMPUTER, INCAPABLE OF EXPERIENCING PHYSICAL CLIMATES. Vera replied the way she always did—a dry voice-text combination. Programmers had given her a British accent from the olden years. Often Eliot took comfort in the sound, but this evening it reminded her of all the passengers she'd mingled with.

History could be such a betch.

"The climate here is terrible," she whispered.

ACCORDING TO MY DATA, THE TEMPERATURES AT THIS DATE AND LOCATION ARE BELOW FREEZING. Vera wasn't much of a shoulder to cry on. The interface's range of support was strictly technical. WHAT CAN I DO FOR YOU, ELIOT?

"Subject Seven should be within range." The *Invictus* fit in a one-hundred-meter radius, which was all Eliot needed. "Lock on and start the countersignature scan."

TARGET ACQUIRED. SCAN OF SUBJECT SEVEN FOR COUNTER-SIGNATURE EMISSIONS WILL NOW COMMENCE. READINGS ARE 0% COMPLETE. WHAT ELSE CAN I DO FOR YOU, ELIOT?

That was all. The scan's climb to 100 percent could take days, and there wasn't much Eliot could do before the results accumulated. Positive or negative. Catalyst or casualty. Here was a chance to keep her eyes shut, to lure sleep to her like some wild beast for the trapping. It did not come gently. How could it, when the cold night cried out below, awash with violins no pillow could mute?

Eliot piled blankets over her gown. Her bones sagged into the mattress; her heart would not stop shivering.

12.

CHORUS OF THE DAMNED

WHEN IN DOUBT, MAKE TEA. IT was a rule Priya Parekh lived by, upheld by her mother and her mother's mother before that. How many all-nighters spent studying for her Medic examinations had been made bearable by the constant supply of masala chai her mother brewed?

They were in for a long night. Or day. Or whatever time it was. Time traveling never failed to screw up the internal body clock, one of the reasons Priya kept her infirmary cabinets stocked with melatonin med-patches. She doubted even those would help Far now. He was wound up tighter than Saffron on a sugar high. Priya's own movements were methodical as she put a pot of black tea leaves on to boil and gathered the spices—ginger, cardamom, star anise, cloves, cinnamon, nutmeg—all stronger than the ones from her childhood, and fresher, too. The manufactured ingredients her mother was forced to use couldn't hold a candle to past-procured karha mix.

The water came to a boil as Far paced. Priya added the spices, poured in fresh milk, and fought the urge to embrace her boyfriend every time he passed the kitchenette. After almost a year together, she'd learned that what calmed *her* only made Far antsier.

"What. Just. Happened?" Imogen flopped onto one of the common area couches. Only her bluish hair was visible over the armrest. Saffron was batting at it. "Who is that girl, Farway? What's she doing here?"

All apt questions, though the mystery that piqued Priya's interest the most was: "Marie Antoinette?"

"Freelancer, my tail! Liar's trying to gaslight me," Far said. "She showed up in my final exam Sim in the Hall of Mirrors dressed as Marie Antoinette. She was the one who made me fail. I *knew* I'd been framed!"

Imogen sat up, frowning. "Marie Antoinette had *blue* eyes, Farway. Not brown. Everyone knows that."

"Your assessment of global knowledge is generous," he told his cousin. "The computer said she was the queen of France and I had no reason to doubt it. Neither did the licensing board, apparently."

Priya poured tea into four mugs and passed them along. Gram first—he looked like he needed a caffeine jolt the most, face lost inside his console screens. She set his drink by the green Rubik's Cube, where it'd be least likely to spill. "That's one Hades of a hacking job, though, fooling the Corps like that."

Imogen's eyes wavered behind steam as she accepted her

mug. "*Was* she fooling the Corps? Maybe this Eliot character is with the Corps. Think about it. She's got access to TM tech. She not only knew we were going to be here, but she also knew what Farway was looking for."

Far stopped under a heinously bright three-piece flash-leather suit—the one he'd donned to snatch the Cat's Eye Emerald from the Caponian Collective minutes before their headquarters were destroyed in the millennium's biggest organized crime raid—and shook his head. "The Corps would've arrested us as soon as we landed. They wouldn't remove the *Rubaiyat* out of its original time."

"Speaking of," Imogen interrupted, "where *is* the book bling? How do we know Eliot is going to produce it when we arrive on Lux's doorstep?"

"We don't. Thanks, P." Far nodded when Priya handed him the chai, polishing it off in a single swig. He claimed he hated hot drinks losing their heat, but Priya had no idea how his throat could stand the scalding. Even *he* grimaced a little at the end of the swallow. "What about the second *Rubaiyat*? The remade one? Imogen, you said it burned in World War II....Any way we could get to it before the bombs do?"

"It's not salvageable." The Historian shook her head. "That copy wasn't incinerated—its jewels were reused in a third iteration. And before you ask, no, we can't steal that Great Omar, either, because it still exists in Central time. Eliot's our only hope, which means if she *is* Corps, we're royally hashed."

"None of this fits the Corps' MO." Far set his mug on the common area table. Priya's eyes drifted to the real-paper copy of the Corps of Central Time Travelers' Code of Conduct beside it. After every mission, she and Imogen went through the guidebook, marking every rule they managed to break. Over half of its three hundred pages were covered in checkmarks and Xs and swirly hearts. Cat ears bedecked every *C* on the front cover. When had those been added? Imogen must've broken tradition by doodling solo.

"Not the current Corps, no," Priya said. "But MOs change over time."

Far frowned.

"You think Eliot's from the future?" Imogen asked.

The future. It was one of the few Code of Conduct rules they hadn't broken: *No CTMs are authorized to travel more than one day in the future from their anchor date.* The crew of the *Invictus* never had a reason to travel ahead of their native time. Lux's missions were bound to historical events studied well enough to sidestep. The future wasn't just unknown but also full of potential complications: learning their own fates, crossing timelines, getting caught by future authorities. It was a sticky business—best avoided.

But that didn't mean the future couldn't come to them.

"It's the most likely explanation," Priya said. "That or some sort of Corps black-ops program."

"Black-ops, future, whatever." Far started pacing again. "What are we going to *do* with her?"

Imogen looked pointedly at the door to Eliot's bunk—not 100 percent soundproof—then back at Priya. "You should turn that music up."

"I'm afraid I can't." There *was* a song playing in the background, but Priya hadn't started any of her playlists during the mission. This music—strings-based, classical—was far more poignant than the beats she usually listened to.

They fell silent as the notes crept on. Imogen's face drained whiter with each bar. "Crux, it's—it's the *Titanic*'s orchestra. Farway, why are we still here?"

Here: hovering above the song of the dying. Most time travelers Priya knew preferred to say *already dead*, as if the inevitability of the tragedies they encountered made them less tragic. Her Medic training couldn't write off a life so easily. How many people were about to freeze to death down there? How many *children*? It hurt even more to think of these numbers, these *lives*, when the *Invictus* hovered a mere thirty meters away.

Bitter, bitter symphony; every new note haunted Priya more than the last, until she couldn't bear listening any longer. It was possible to switch on a playlist remotely, but she took the chance to duck into the infirmary. Sometimes she hated how secluded it was from the console room, but then there were moments like these, when the wall was a relief. She didn't like to cry where others could see.

Tears clogged Priya's lashes as she scrolled through the playlist. Pick a song, any song—it didn't matter, as long as it drowned out the dirge below. *Thrash & Hash: Live from the Pantheon [uncensored]* began beating through the speakers. Priya slumped down to the infirmary floor, staring at cabinets full of med-patches and scanners. Tools of the trade she'd wanted to practice ever since she was a gap-toothed girl welcoming her father home from hospital shifts. Long work's grit often lurked beneath his eyes, but Dev Parekh never failed to play scan-the-patient with his only daughter. He crafted splints for dolls' arms out of tongue depressors and taught Priya various suture techniques as he helped her sew stuffing back into Madam Wink.

"All better now," he'd say when the thread was cut. No hero in the world could be bigger, and Priya knew that when she grew up she'd save not just polyester unicorns but people, too. Who wouldn't?

It wasn't until later that she registered something else in the crescent shadows of her father's face: the grief that came with truth.

Some people were past saving.

It didn't help that Priya couldn't hear the lifeboats being lowered, the deckhands crying out, the chorus of the damned playing on and on. She knew these things were happening, had happened. The already dead were dying and nothing was better now....

"Hey, P. Can I come in?" Priya recognized the shape of Far's shadow against the med-cabinets, as familiar as her own.

She nodded. Her face was a mess—trying to blot out the tears with her sleeve only succeeded in smearing snot everywhere. She'd only ever seen Far weep twice: teardrops small enough to blot with a single finger. Priya didn't understand how you could keep such a strong emotion so *clean*. Every crying session of hers ended up with her resembling a drowning walrus....

Far sat down next to her, full mug in his hands. "I brought you your tea."

There was still warmth in the ceramic, in the fingers that brushed hers as they passed off the chai. When Priya took a sip, the heat spread through her chest.

"You okay?" Far asked.

"Yes. No. I—I know the *Titanic* sank before we—before *I* was born," she corrected herself. "I know it's in the past."

Far rested his head against the wall. His curls had unraveled to frizz during his chase for the *Rubaiyat*. "The past isn't as distant as it used to be. When Burg told me bedtime stories about traveling on the *Ab Aeterno*, it was all about adventures and new sights, never the bodies they had to leave behind."

Or the family. Time travel cost more than billions of credits. Corps workers often caught up with their parents in age, while their own children grew at a snail's pace. Priya had sworn never to date Academy cadets for this reason. Love should be all or it should be nothing. She had no interest in playing a Central anchor-girlfriend, absent for most of her boyfriend's life until it looked like he'd robbed her from the cradle. If she was going to be with someone, she'd be *with* them: step for step, year for year, growing old in tandem.

The rule wasn't too hard to keep, since the med-droids completed the bulk of face time during the cadets' routine checkups. Then came the boy who crashed the system. Skewed DNA, blank-space birth date. One glance at Farway McCarthy's chart and Priya assumed he was a senator's bastard, the type the Academy halls crawled with: rich with hush money, bored out of his brains. Oh, how wrong she'd been. Far crackled with life, or life crackled with him. (It was difficult to tell which force was stronger.) His ever-movement—legs shifting, fingers drumming—was contagious. Jokes, too. The way he talked about history made Priya miss times she'd never known. On the hoverbus home that evening she found herself scrolling through her music for a song that captured the boy's longing zest.

It was the beginning of many playlists.

Her choice to join the *Invictus*'s crew was easier than it should've been. Far needed a Medic, and though it wasn't quite love—not yet, not then—Priya didn't want nothing. The year since had been a juggling act, two lives crammed into one. She kept up her Medic shifts, as well as Saturday dinner with her parents, though every trip home Priya found it harder to pick up where she'd left off. *What's new in your world,* beti? took on a different angle when your mother's week operating an antique shop was your month spent illegally hopping from World War II Europe to Gold Rush America to *Queen Anne's Revenge*, all while kissing a boy your parents knew nothing about.

Imogen and Gram performed the same verbal gymnastics with their parents, though ultimately conversational lag was a small price to pay. Priya was reminded of this every time Far talked about the *Ab Aeterno*, with a gap in his words no larger-than-legend energy could fill. Though he tried.

He tried.

"Would you save those people down there, if you could?" she asked.

Far frowned. "Imagined heroics make the helplessness worse, don't you think?"

"Better than feeling like a vulture."

121

"We *are* vultures, P."

Like it or not, that was the truth of them. "I prefer the term *relic relocaters*."

"It'd be great if we had a relic to relocate." Far's lip twitched. "What do you think of our new guest?"

"I haven't seen someone get under your skin so badly since Instructor Marin. Not even the pirate who gave you that scar." Priya touched his right biceps—where, just under the workman's shirt, she felt a hard welt of skin, one that curved into brachial artery territory. It was the most of Far's blood she'd ever seen outside of his body, brought forth by a rusty cutlass, closed shut by thirty stitches. *A mere flesh wound*, he'd joked with blue lips as Gram dragged him back onto the ship. If Imogen hadn't been there to offer her vein for a transfusion, the story wouldn't have had such a happy ending.

"Swords, I can handle—whack and hit! But this?" Far massaged his face. Most of the anger had rubbed off, giving way to starker things. "After I got thrown out of the Academy, I swore I'd do anything I could never to feel so...so *defeated* again. Here we are nearly a year later—after all these successful heists—and the exact same girl is dangling our futures on a string, and I don't know what to do. If I don't deliver the *Rubaiyat* to Lux...we could lose everything, P."

A shudder passed from him to her. It wasn't like Far to be afraid, and it wasn't like Priya to squeeze his arm so tight, but here they were. Each other's only.

She drew strength from her next sip of chai. "Let's not lose our heads, though. The fact that Eliot diverted your timeline makes me think there's some sort of long game at play here.... We need to learn more about her. If we can get our hands on a DNA sample, I can run it through the diagnostics machine. Could give us something to go on."

"The washroom floor looks like it's covered in spaghetti confetti from Imogen's shedding," Far said, nose wrinkling. "Scrounging up an Eliot hair shouldn't be hard. We have the time—I've asked Gram to take us to Las Vegas."

"Vegas? As in an actual proper-vacation destination?"

"The only other option is limping back to Lux, and I'd prefer to delay that demise for as long as possible. We'll use the trip to get a handle on things. Figure out who Eliot is, find the *Rubaiyat*. All of this assuming we can make the jump to the next century—"

"We should. I checked the engines and the fuel rods." As evidenced by the spots on her scrubs. Grease this time, not blood. Fixing things tended to get messy. "Everything's smooth on the mechanical end."

"You sure?" The question stayed in Far's stare even after she nodded. "It's not like Gram to hash things up."

"Gram spoils us with that brain of his, but he's not a droid. Mistakes are what make us human. I hope you've apologized for assaulting his *Tetris* screen."

"Gram knows I was frustrated."

"But he won't know you're sorry until you tell him." The tea's extra dash of ginger burned gold on Priya's tongue, adding fire to her grandmother's favorite saying: "'The world misses bees for their honey, not their sting.'"

It would've been easy for Far to bring up the fact that the proverb was outdated—bees were back thanks to time travelers. He rubbed his knuckles instead, as if wiping away the memory of the punch. Determination settled in the darker edges of his profile.

"I'll make it right." He leaned forward to plant a kiss on her forehead. Priya shut her eyes and soaked in every warmth: the mug of tea in her hand, the press of his lips to her skin, the radiance from the *Invictus*'s engines as it tore west, through the night.

13.

THE HILLS REMAIN

GRAM STARED AT THE NUMBERS.

They were changing, but it was a slow, expected shift. Seconds ticking along. Time's natural passage as morning caught up with them—April 15, 1912 AD, 5:32 AM. In just a few minutes, Las Vegas would appear on the horizon, looking like little more than an old Western movie set, with signs advertising BILLIARDS and horse shazm scattered along the dirt roads. Nothing to see, and even less to do. The great state of Nevada had outlawed gambling in 1909, never mind that it would be at least twenty years before the first official casino opened. The flashier stuff came much later.

Could they make the jump? Gram hoped so. He more than hoped. The 1900s wasn't an era he wanted to be stranded in. Skin color wasn't a barrier in Central time, but when it came to the past, prejudice was inescapable. Every time Gram stepped into a new era, he had to brace himself for the hatred of the age.

Sometimes it was just under the surface, lurking in shopkeepers' gazes as they watched him walk down every store aisle. Other times men called Gram words unfit for a dictionary, insulting his intelligence to his face. This stretch of history was downright dangerous. He'd seen photos of lynchings. Even in black-and-white they were graphic enough to make him retch.

They *had* to make the jump.

Gram ran their next landing date over and over again in his head. April 18, 2020, was no golden age, either: slavery's chains exchanged for jumpsuits, *keep your hands where I can see them* a guarantee for nothing. But a successful jump to the twenty-first century meant a future jump home. There was no reason these landing numbers shouldn't work. The *Invictus*'s nav systems were running as smoothly as they had before the hashed landing, but this only made the Engineer more anxious. It'd be better to know *what* was wrong than to just keep floundering like this....

"Is your tail glued to that chair? You haven't moved for hours." Imogen walked in and took a seat at her console. It was a new day, and sure as the sun, her hair was a fresh color. The blue and pink chalks had been washed out, replaced with even brighter shades.

"Green." Gram realized, as soon as he said it, that the word didn't make sense on its own. His brain needed a few extra beats to shift from numbers to language after staring at equations all night. "Your hair, I mean."

But it wasn't *just* green. Imogen's head was phosphorescent. It looked as if she'd snapped a glow stick in half and used the insides as conditioner. The predawn shadows through the *Invictus*'s vistaport made her shine all the brighter.

"'Nuclear Green' is the colloquial term," she told him. "It's a 2020 throwback color. Do you like it?"

"It's…" Of all the times for Gram's vocabulary to abandon him! "Shiny."

"It'd be rubbish for a stealth mission," the Historian admitted. "But Las Vegas isn't really known for its subtlety. When in Las Vegas, glow as the Las Vegans do. Vegans…that can't be right."

"It is," Gram said.

"History's ironies abound much." She swiveled her chair back to the screen, radiant hair aflutter.

Radiant. Resplendent. Pulchritudinous. These were the words Gram should have used, queuing up ten seconds too late. He couldn't voice them now, not when Far appeared in the doorway, scanning the console room with bleary eyes.

It wasn't hard to guess who he was looking for. Gram glanced at the bunk door, still sealed. Eliot: a piece that didn't fit. The girl's sudden appearance was as much of an outlier as the hashed landing, both of which had happened in the span of an hour. Correlation didn't imply causation, but he was willing to bet that the events were linked. Was Eliot the cause of the disturbance?

Or was she here *because* of it?

Twisty, turny, not-quite-solving puzzles. Gram wasn't used to problems that lasted so long. He looked up at his Rubik's Cubes—each solved and back in place, their rainbow row complete. There was an answer out there. There had to be.

Far sidled up to the console. "Think we can land when we want to this time? Ship's guts look good according to Priya."

"Priya checked the engines?"

"Well, yeah." There was a seedling frown on Far's face, threatening to grow. "You asked her to, didn't you?"

"Did I?" It'd slipped Gram's mind, like much of the moment after the landing. Strange...Adrenaline often *heightened* his senses, whetting his memories until their edges were razor sharp. Too much cortisol must've flooded his system. "Mechanics wouldn't make a jump go sideways like that. Last time we were in the Grid, I was running the numbers, but I couldn't solve for the landing time we wanted. That's when..." Both cousins stared at Gram, expectant. He wasn't sure if his words would work—they didn't add up. He said them anyway. "That's when the equation changed."

"Huh." Far took the news far better than expected, though this could be because he didn't quite grasp what the statement meant. Even Gram wasn't sure. What happened when the laws of the universe became suggestions?

Far cleared his throat. "Well, I'm sorry for hitting your *Tetris* screen. And yelling. You were under pressure and I was making a proper tail of myself."

Imogen's mouth opened wide enough to catch flies. Gram didn't need the visual cue to know the behavior was aberrational. Far apologizing was almost as strange as math not being math. Things really were in flux....

"All's forgiven," Gram told his friend. "Just aim for something less antiquey next time."

"Hopefully there won't be a next time." Far took a seat in his captain's chair and stared out the vistaport, where Las Vegas was taking shape in the darkness. One could count the sleepy town's lights on both hands. The horizon was beginning to lighten—black to blooming indigo—revealing hills. These were the bones of the place. For millions of years the earth had been carving out the sky, as it would keep doing four centuries from now, long after the casinos had crumbled, their swimming pools sucked as dry as Lake Mead, their flash and glitz and neon lights fading to nothing. . . .

Through all this, the hills would remain.

Gram guided the *Invictus* into this steady distance. The outskirts of the outskirts. It would be the best place to jump—out of range of future flight paths, close to stretches of empty desert that would be perfect for parking an invisible time machine.

"All of us are stressed and yell-y." Imogen sighed. "That's why it's imperative we stay on track with this vacation. We all need some fun. Dining! Drinks! Dallying the days away!"

"This is a mission, too," Far reminded them. "Eliot's got the drop on us right now, and I need that to change before we return to Central. Vegas affords us some wiggle room to dig up information. Priya has a plan, and I need you two to keep our guest distracted so she won't catch on."

"Consider it done. As long as we *can* wiggle," Imogen added. "There's supposed to be a dance party of epic proportions at Caesars Palace on Saturday night. DJ Rory is hosting."

Far looked less than enthused. "Eliot doesn't strike me as the dancing type."

"Don't be so quick to judge books by their covers, Far. I contain multitudes."

All three of them jumped. Eliot. There was no telling how much the girl had heard, for she was but a shadow in the doorway, and just as soundless. It was as if she'd teleported. Twenty-four hours ago Gram would've deemed that impossible. But the word meant nothing now. . . .

Their captain scowled. "Sometimes the covers *are* all that matter. Particularly when they're loaded up with one hundred mil in jewels."

With a dancer's grace and a smuggler's smugness, Eliot whirled into the console room. " 'One thing is certain, that Life flies; / One thing is certain, and the Rest is Lies; / The Flower that once has blown for ever dies.' Words of wisdom from the very book you deem matterless."

Again, Far was less than enthused. "My life's flight will be a hash of a lot shorter if you keep the *Rubaiyat* stashed away."

"O ye of little faith . . ." A smile twisted Eliot's face as she stared out the vistaport. Not even dawn light could soften her features. In fact, it only brought out the shadows under her eyes, the tendons stringing her neck—things that made Gram weary by proxy. Though both of her feet stood firm on the *Invictus*'s floor panels, it seemed to him that she was standing on some sort of edge, close to tumbling.

None of this helped the anxiety piling in Gram's chest. He tried his best to swallow it back as he shifted the *Invictus* into hover mode.

"We're ready to attempt a jump," he told Far. "Cross your fingers."

Their captain, not one for lucky charms, nodded. Imogen made up for it by crossing both sets of fingers and her arms to boot, as if luck were something you could simply pluck out of thin air, cling to for dear life. Gram knew wishes weren't quantifiable, but he found himself hoping she'd collected enough fortune for their journey.

"Three, two, one…"

14.

THE GRID

BLAST OFF without noise
without anything.
Gone—the hills, the skies, the light
Darkness returns, even deeper than night
unfolding forever and ever, refolding into nothing, nothing.

Here is a place of contradictions.
Here is not here. It is there. And there. And there.
It is everywhere.
Or nowhere.
Time spins around. It stands perfectly still.
Moments within moments between moments
Each contains multitudes larger and smaller…

Find the numbers. Make them fit.
Shift and…
…click!

15.

FOLLICLE FALLACIES

From dawn glow, to searing darkness, to blistering midday light. *Ow.* Far should've known better than to stare out the vistaport during a jump—the shift in views paired with the Grid's timelessness created a special kind of queasy—but it was better than being forced to face Eliot's smirk. He'd thought, after some alone time with Priya and a nap, that the girl might be less infuriating. Not so. Her cockiness was salt in the wound, stinging for how easily she'd sent Far's future spinning. A single wink, a shiny book. Years of work down the drain...

Phosphene stars marred Far's vision, crept through the writing on the wall before him. He stared hard at what chalky fragments he could—*Rembrandt, sapphire, fire, Hindenburg*—and dug his fingers into the armrest. Priya was right: no sense in losing his head. This was far from over. He'd pin his life back into place piece by piece, starting with this chair. He'd never liked the captain's seat—it was uncomfortable and such a **violent** shade of orange—but now it felt like his, because he'd had to fight for it.

"Time?" he asked Gram.

"We hit our target," the Engineer said. He himself had the look of a man who'd dodged ten bullets. "April eighteenth, 2020. Noon."

At least *something* was going Far's way today. "Let the vacation commence."

He really did want a vacation. Ideally, it'd involve him and Priya by a pool, a pale lager with two lime wedges, and a world without cares. Las Vegas had most of these things—true—but Far couldn't rest until he knew what Eliot was up to.

The girl stood close to him, barefoot. Without her boots, she was quite short, small enough to blow away. Her hair was still coiffed in a first-class style, but its fanciness had frayed. Single strands quirked out from the pins, flew around her shoulders. All it would take was a quick pluck....

"I'll gather our wardrobes!" Imogen headed toward the common area closet. "What are your measurements, Eliot? I can lend you one of my outfits, if it fits. Your waist is so tiny!"

"It's this haze of a corset." Eliot turned her back to Far.

There, just there! A lone hair ripe for the taking. He was certain he could snag it without Eliot noticing—working for Lux, he'd developed quite a set of thief fingers—but when he tugged the strand, it didn't break the way it should have. To his horror, Far realized that he'd not only gathered a single hair from Eliot's head but an entire wig. He dropped the hairpiece.

Eliot turned to face him. Where Far expected to see anger,

there was only a hoity twist of lips. Where he expected to find her natural hair, there was none. Eliot's scalp was as smooth as the rest of her. Those eyebrows, the ones that reminded him of penwork—they really *were* drawn on. Even her eyelashes were missing. Far's brain must have autofilled them in before now.

"Well, shazm." He glanced at the wig, now a glossy brown pile by his feet. "This is awkward."

It became even more so when Saffron emerged to attack what he mistook for a fellow fur-thing. The red panda snatched the wig in his jaws and took off for the common area, striped tail waving.

"Saffron! *No!*" Imogen wasn't fast enough to catch him. The animal leaped from couch to shelf to pipes, beyond their reach.

"Your hair..." Far trailed off, at a loss.

"Has been purloined by a ginger raccoon, from the looks of things." Eliot squinted at the wardrobe: army uniforms, a pair of riding chaps, a prison jumpsuit. The original flowered waistcoat he'd worn in the Versailles Sim hung among them. Far wondered if she recognized the outfit. "Or were you referring to my lack of it?"

"Um..."

Imogen climbed on top of the couch, swatting clothing aside to find her furry ward. "Get back here, you scallywag! You can't just steal people's hair."

One of Eliot's inked eyebrows rose as she looked back at Far. Clearly she harbored the same sentiment. He needed to think of an excuse, anything other than the obvious—

"I thought I saw a feather," he said lamely. "I was trying to pull it out."

"How considerate," Eliot grunted. Far doubted she believed him. *He* wouldn't believe him, and so far this girl had outwitted him at every turn.

Imogen continued uttering swears as colorful as her hair, standing on tiptoes in an attempt to reach the red panda's roost. Gram joined her. His reach was longer, but Saffron had scooted so far back into the pipes that they'd have to dismantle the *Invictus* to get to the creature.

"Best surrender." It was all Far could do to keep from laughing, not because this was funny, but because the whole wignapping scene had surpassed absurd. "It's in the lair of the beast now."

"Saffron isn't a beast," Imogen huffed. "He's a *beastie*."

Gram balanced on the couch's highest point, swiping as far as he could. No use. He fell back onto Imogen's cushion. His weight created a seesaw effect—and Imogen, having nowhere else to steady herself, grasped Gram's biceps.

"What on earth is going on?" Priya's bunk door slid open. The gold BeatBix headphones slung around her neck were genuine, BB logo righted, snatched and gifted by Far for their six-month anniversary. She'd worn them to sleep ever since. Indeed, she looked like she did most mornings: hair mussed, eyes misty with dreams as they peered into the common area. "Oh—"

Imogen snatched her hands back. Far had never seen his cousin so pink: hotter than bubble gum, deeper than coral. He wished they'd sort things out and kiss already. The *Invictus* was small enough as it was. There simply wasn't room for so many unaddressed pheromones.

"Saffron ran off with Eliot's hair." Gram stepped off the couch, clearing his throat. "I mean, wig."

Far could pinpoint the moment his girlfriend went into Medic mode. Her stare went sharp, then soft as she examined Eliot's baldness. "*Alopecia universalis*. Right?"

"Ladies and gentlemen, we have a Medic worth her salt!" Eliot's voice held a showmanship boom—all the ship's a stage. "You'd be amazed how many don't know the proper name without a med-droid beeping it in their ear."

"*Alopecia universalis.*" Imogen considered the Latin, face aflame. "Universal foxsickness?"

"A fancy way of saying my immune system isn't such a fan of my hair follicles. Every single hair on my body fell out when I was six years old and never returned."

"It's rare," Priya remarked. "Rarer than rare in Central time. I've only ever read up on cases."

This was yet another sign that Eliot was out of her era. But if her condition was rare in Central time, wouldn't it be almost nonexistent in the future? Was it possible she was from the past? More questions, endless questions. The spinning feeling from looking out the *Invictus*'s vistaport hadn't faded the way it usually did. Instead, Far felt himself winding tighter. This girl. This smirking, roundabout riddle of a girl. She was impossible to get a handle on, and it vexed him....

"I'm so sorry about your wig, Eliot." Though none of this was Imogen's fault, she apologized. "I'll go out and buy you another one before we hit the town. What color do you prefer? Blond? Brunette? Fire-engine red? You'd sport peacock green excellently."

"No need," Eliot told her. "I only use wigs when I need to blend in. No one in Vegas is going to bat an eyelash at the lack of mine."

"You'll turn heads with that dress, though," the Historian pointed out. "The year 2020 wasn't really known for floor-length frills."

The *Invictus* fell back into its pre-expedition ritual. Priya disappeared to change out the fuel rods. Gram returned to his console to find a parking spot, while Imogen weeded out any dollars printed post–landing year from their US cash stash. Afterward, she printed age-appropriate false IDs for the five of them, then reprinted them when Gram pointed out that her math had made them all twenty instead of twenty-one, and what was the use of that? Eliot helped sort bills and clothes alike, making piles of swimsuits and clubwear under the Historian's sporadic direction. Above it all, Saffron nibbled the wig with happy squeaking noises.

The scene felt so...normal. Eliot had Recorder training, no doubt. How else would she sync with the rhythm of the ship so fast? Far settled back into his captain's chair, eyes never leaving the thief. She watched him, too. Her glances weren't subtle or sly or pointed. They just *were*. Straight on, unabashed. Nothing like the *don't blink* duels he held with Lux. He had no idea what game Eliot was playing, much less how to win it. He needed *answers*. There was more than one way to collect DNA. Skin, blood, spit. All were a good means harder to procure than hair, especially now that Eliot was onto them, but Far was up for the challenge.

He'd figure out who this girl was.

He'd take his future back.

16.

WHAT HAPPENS IN VEGAS . . .

INVICTUS SHIP'S LOG—ENTRY 3

CURRENT DATE: APRIL 18, 2020

CURRENT LOCATION: VEGAS, BABY!

OBJECT TO ACQUIRE: FUN TIMES. PEACE OF MIND.
PRETTY, PRETTY BOOK STILL AT LARGE.

IMOGEN'S HAIR COLOR: NUCLEAR-GLOW GREEN WITH
NEON-YELLOW TIPS

GRAM'S *TETRIS* SCORE: 354,000 (ON PAUSE)

CURRENT SONG ON PRIYA'S SHIPWIDE PLAYLIST:
"LIGHT UP THE BRIGHT" BY AURORA WINTERS

FARWAY'S EGO: DO NOT FEED. MAY BITE. HAS BEEN
SEVERELY WOUNDED BY APPEARANCE OF JUST-ELIOT
ANTOINETTE, AKA BLACK OPS FUTURE MAGICIAN.

ELIOT: ????????

IT WASN'T THE MOST VACATIONY OF vacations, with a black-mailing stowaway in tow, but Imogen was determined to enjoy Las Vegas until she dropped. Or flopped. Or got lost in a sea of sparkles. That seemed the most likely outcome. Vegas was so *bright*. Even at midafternoon the place was blinding. LED billboards blazed with adverts: OVER HERE BLING BLING. Women walked by in sequined cocktail dresses that could've seconded as mermaid tails. Tourists toted drinks even taller than themselves, neon straws flitting into a different color every two seconds. It was too bad, Imogen mused as she sauntered down the Strip with the rest of the *Invictus*'s crew, that flash leather hadn't been invented for another century. Her iridescent moto jacket would have fit right in.... Though, to be honest, almost anything would. Las Vegas was one of the few sites in history where the entire crew of the *Invictus* could be unabashedly themselves. Glow hair, no hair, dark skin, light—all of it melted into anonymity here.

Anonymous or not, they walked with swagger. Imogen

congratulated herself on a crew well dressed. The boys she'd fitted into button-ups and charcoal jeans. Gram had consented to sporting a leather vest and a fedora, though Farway would only accept aviator sunglasses as an accessory. It wasn't often Priya traded in her scrubs, but the emerald-green wrap dress was stunning on her. Eliot wore a long jumpsuit, so white it almost disappeared against her skin. Anyone else so pale would've been swallowed, but Eliot looked regal. Little wonder she'd convinced Farway she was the queen of France.

For herself Imogen had selected silver palazzo pants—the ones that made her feel as if she were riding a sleigh through fresh snow—and a white top. She'd started off the day with cat-eye sunglasses but had removed them in favor of a better view. And what a view it was! There was a Ferris wheel! Over there, the Eiffel Tower! To her left, the Bellagio fountains had started their infamous show. Oh, this city was delightful....Never mind the drunk emptying his guts at the base of a palm tree, despite the fact that it was 3:00 PM. Historical accounts were right—this city never really stopped partying.

"What should we do first?" Farway paused to wipe fountain mist from his sunglasses.

"The Bellagio is a logical start," Eliot pointed out. "We could work our way down the Strip."

Farway didn't flinch. It was as if the suggestion had bounced off. "Imogen, Vegas was your idea. What do you think?"

"I think Eliot's right." *Here* her cousin scowled, but Imogen paid no heed. The casino's proximity made it an easy choice.

Easier still, given the hotel held the shop she wanted to visit most. "To the Bellagio! Let's go gape!"

The place certainly was gape-worthy. Air-conditioning sucked the group in through the revolving doors, into a lobby with one of the most stunning works of art Imogen had ever seen—the *Fiori di Como*, two thousand pieces of glass blown into floral shapes and suspended from the ceiling. They were every color imaginable, lit from behind to create a sight both alien and spellbinding. All five crew members paused beneath the installation, necks craned.

Gram halted close to Imogen. *Very* close. Ever since that accidental touch on the *Invictus*, she'd been hyperaware of the Engineer's presence. He seemed to carry his own current, one that leaped from his skin to hers. Any second now the charge would reach Imogen's cheeks, light up her true feelings for all to see. She really should look into finding some blush-neutralizing concealer....

She looked to her other side instead, where Eliot stood. The girl's skin was even more translucent indoors; the colors above seemed to permeate it. Blue, purple, green landing at the top of her head and dripping down, down, beautiful, fragile glass, other-worldly. No one else from the crew noticed—they'd adopted Farway's cold-shoulder approach. Imogen didn't see how this strategy would help their information excavation. How would they discover anything about the newcomer if they ignored her?

"This is a Chihuly sculpture," Imogen told the group. "Every single one of those flowers is handspun glass."

"Imagine how much time that took," Priya said, awed.

"Imagine how many credits it's worth." Of course Farway would put a price tag on the pretty-pretty-pretty. "Whatever happened to it?"

"We wouldn't be able to steal it, if that's what you're thinking," Imogen told her cousin. "The Bellagio sold the *Fiori di Como* to a private collector once the drought got really bad. Ten years later, the buyer sold it off in pieces to avoid bankruptcy."

"A hashing shame," Gram said. "Something so flawless falling to pieces."

"Everything does in the end." Eliot's whisper was quiet. Only Imogen stood close enough to hear. Only she felt a shiver creep through her vertebrae.

The *Fiori di Como* looked just as stunning as it had when they'd walked through the door, but now all Imogen could see when she stared at the clash and swirl of colors was how they would break. *Blurgh.* Farway's pessimism was manageable. She'd been balancing that out her whole life. Now that there was double the dose, Imogen found herself in need of reinforcements.

VACATION. ENJOYMENT. ONWARD.

"Should we see what else the Bellagio has to offer?" She led the way into a corridor flashing with the promises of slot machines—WIN $$$$$ WIN $$$$$ WIN $$$$$ WIN. The casino felt timeless in a way that wasn't like the Grid at all. The establishment pumped extra oxygen through the vents to keep gamblers alert. Night could fall, the outside world could catch fire, and the occupants of the windowless casino floor would be none the wiser. They'd roll their craps dice and place their bets for as long as their wallets would allow. Poker chips clattered and the roulette ball rolled, landing on chance, creating fortunes, breaking them.

When they passed some blackjack tables, Gram gave the dealers and their six-deck arsenal a wistful glance. Did he ever look at her like that? Imogen wondered. Maybe he did. Maybe he didn't. She was so bad at guessing these things. It had been confusing enough when he called her hair *shiny*. Had he meant *I like you* shiny? *We're only friends* shiny? Or was it just an adjective that made her synonymous with the Great Omar's cover and Vegas's lights? Imogen's mind would go through a hundred different iterations and then land on one, rethinking it another hundred times, before deciding she had absolutely no idea what Gram had meant.

Priya would know. She was so very good at peeling back the surface of things. Skin, feelings, souls. Imogen often sought Priya's opinion on her lack of love life. Her friend's diagnosis was always the same: *Just talk to him.*

About what? Shiny hair? She'd tried that already. . . .

Priya's solution: *Tell him how you feel.*

There were times when Imogen wanted to, when *I'm madly in crush with you* lingered at the back of her tongue. It never quite tasted right, though. What if Gram didn't say it back? What if he just stared at Imogen while her heart shriveled to the size of a pinto bean? What if their friendship was spoiled and things turned awkward between them forever after?

Imogen would rather take her chances with the slot machines. She might have, if gambling in a time not theirs wasn't such a bad idea. Trying their luck would alter the odds of someone else's: shuffled decks and spun slots. It wouldn't do to go redistributing future jackpots. Who knew *how* many lives that could change?

There really wasn't much to do in the casino section except walk, dodging cocktail waitresses and grandmothers sporting matching sets of visors and fanny packs—a fashion trend that would never make it to Before & Beyond's racks. Imogen's *real* destination—the one that had kept her mouth watering since Gram first set course for Vegas—was in the next hall. Her treadless Greek leather sandals, purchased in a BC year, slipped and slid along the floor's marble edge. Undaunted, she pushed forward to the promised sign: CAFÉ GELATO ICE CREAM & SWEETS.

Aka reinforcements. Thank the Lady Luck their "look but don't partake" policy stopped short of food.

"We should've known." Priya smiled at the destination. "The sugar, it calls to her. Are we sure she's not part honeybee?"

"There are worse vices!" Imogen said over her shoulder and shuffle-skated into the shop. The place was inherently cute, splashed with color: yellow walls, bright pink chandeliers. Its display case overflowed with gelato. So much gelato. Mint. Mango. Tiramisu. Pistachio. Blackberry cheesecake. Hazelnut. How was she supposed to *choose*?

Priya opted for a banana split. Gram got a scoop of pistachio with chocolate shavings. Farway and Eliot each ordered a scoop of blood orange. All of them were settled around one of the marble-topped café tables by the time Imogen made up her mind. Why choose one flavor when you could get five? Rose, mint, amarena, stracciatella, salted caramel. It was almost a whole carton's worth of cream—she had to use two hands to balance it as she made her way toward the table.

"Wait! Wait!" Imogen set her dessert down and began rummaging through her clutch. "Before I forget!"

It was clear, from the look on Farway's face when she pulled out the sparkler, that he was the one who'd forgotten. *Serves him right for not keeping a ship's log.* Not only had they landed on April 18, but by Imogen's count, it had been 365 days since Farway's seventeenth-year celebration.

She lit the sparkler and stuck it into her cousin's gelato. "Happy eighteenth unbirthday, Farway!"

"Wait." Light hissed around Farway's curls like rabid fairy dust. "Already?"

"Time flies when you're plundering history," Imogen told him. "And in case you were wondering, the gelato is just the beginning of the festivities. We have lots to celebrate! Eighteen is a big year!"

"Or 2,277," Gram added. "We know you're not picky about the age."

"You don't know how old you are?" Eliot stared at Farway through the flare, looking for answers even though *she* was the question. "How's that?"

"He was born in the Grid." It wasn't until the information slipped out that Imogen second-guessed volunteering the fact. Not that Farway's unbirthday was a secret. He was something of a celebrity in Central time for it, which made Eliot's not-knowing that much stranger.

An odd duck, this girl.

"A boy without a birthday?" The sparkler was nearing the end of its run, but the newcomer's expression lit and fizzed. "What a strange wonder."

It was testament to how much Eliot disgruntled Farway that these words didn't serve as instant ego fuel: *Why, yes, I am a strange wonder. The most special of snowflakes! Born out of time, forever running to catch up to it!* He resorted to mumbling instead, "All it's ever done is fritz out med-droids. The bragging rights wear off real quick."

"We should sing," Priya broke in. "Before the sparkler dies!"

"Agreed." Imogen's five-flavor spread was melting, and she preferred to start eating before it turned into a gloppy rose-mint-sour-cherry-salted-caramel-chocolate-eggy soup.

The tune to "Happy Birthday" hadn't changed much in four centuries. Imogen belted it with great gusto—off-key probably; she'd never had the ear for music that Priya did. Priya, who embellished and harmonized and, along with Gram's steady bass, salvaged the song from becoming plastered-karaoke *bad*. Even Eliot joined for a line or two: ♫ *"Happy birthday, dear [Farway/Far]! Happy birthday to you!"* ♫ By the song's end, the sparkler only had a centimeter of flash left. Already it was starting to fade.

Imogen turned to her cousin and recited the phrase Aunt Empra once used every year. A McCarthy family tradition. Words spoken just before the fire died. "Make a wish. Make it count."

17.

STILL POINT

So MUCH DEPENDED ON a plastic spoon.

All throughout the celebratory dessert-before-dinner, Priya kept tabs on Eliot's utensil, noting how the girl ran her thumb over the stem when she wasn't using it. Between that and the dozen or so bites of blood orange gelato she took, there'd be plenty of DNA to analyze. It was just a matter of snatching the spoon and getting it back to the *Invictus* without Eliot noticing.

The task wasn't that risky, or even very thrilling, but Priya's heart thrummed inside her chest—a wild thing—as she watched Eliot toss her waste into the rubbish bin. Priya lingered in the back of the line, waiting until Eliot's stare drifted elsewhere to retrieve the evidence and wrap it inside a clean napkin before stowing it in her purse. Far sometimes teased her for lugging such a large tote everywhere, and even Priya had to admit it could get cumbersome, but she needed its pockets for gauze, Heal-All spray, med-patches, and everything Imogen wanted to bring off ship but didn't have room for in her clutch. Priya slipped the used spoon under Far's swim trunks, pulse thumping all the while.

The group gathered in the hall, looking more tight-knit for the Bellagio's grandeur: sweeping marble and columns. Priya joined them with a smile—one she hoped conveyed *there's nothing at all in my purse, certainly not Eliot's DNA*. It wasn't easy to hold. She didn't have Far's poker face or Gram's ability to drift out of a chaotic room even when he sat in the middle of it. Best to do the analysis as soon as possible.

Imogen's eyes were glazed over in a way that meant she was reading her interface screen. "There's not too much more here in the Bellagio.... We could go down the Strip and try the pool at Caesars Palace, or eat at one of Gordon Ramsay's restaurants. Most of the shows and dance parties don't kick off until later."

"I'm going to have to steal Far away for an hour or two." Priya slipped her elbow neatly through Far's, bag wedged between them. Her smile was starting to feel too tight. "Girl-friend's prerogative."

"You do?" Far asked. Her arm tensed in his—not Morse code, but signal enough. "Oh. Yes. She does. We're off to do, er, couple-y things."

Eliot's eyes narrowed, shifting from Far to Priya. Was that jealousy she sensed, playing tug-of-war between them? Or something else? Priya couldn't get a good read on the girl. She also had trouble gauging Far's reaction—yes, there was anger, yes, there was fear, but a different charge crackled amidst the pair. An absolute sort of energy, felt even on the periphery. Its pang crept into Priya's chest, tendriled around her heart, pried open cracks she hadn't even known were there.

Jealousy...maybe.

"How long will you be?" Gram asked.

"Three hours." This was Priya's best guess, between the journey back to the ship and running the tests. "Or so."

"Hand over the swimsuits and we'll find something to *distract* ourselves." Imogen's voice had a *wink-wink, nudge-nudge* quality. Not subtle at all, if one knew her well. "You two go have some fun."

❖ ❖ ❖

Fun wasn't the word Priya would've used for the hike back to the *Invictus*. The heels Imogen advised her to wear had a six-kilometer-walk span. Maximum. She shucked them off before her toes became totally raw, but walking barefoot on the roadside wasn't much better. Far offered to carry her the rest of the way, but Priya refused. The *Invictus* was within hobbling distance. She could see the parking spot but not the ship—its holoshield was doing its job too well, mimicking the surrounding landscape. Blue sky, bland dirt. Out here, away from the Strip's fountains and well-groomed palms, you could actually remember that Las Vegas sat in the middle of a desert. The air was so thin it felt lonely. There was no humidity, no sweat to smother the skin, just a solitude that stretched for kilometers—up to the hawk wheeling overhead, out to the highway's cracked edge. There were no cars passing and no one to see them, though

Priya was sure she and Far looked odd. Two teenagers clad in party-wear wandering through an empty field, vanishing from sight.

The ship's internal air system blasted Priya's bangs across her face as she tossed her purse onto the couch, narrowly missing Saffron. The red panda was curled among the pillows, clutching his newfound treasure. Eliot's wig was markedly more frayed after hours of gnawing.

"Alone. At last." Far latched the door shut and removed his aviators. The sun remained behind his eyes—desert bright and glaring. "I need a vacation from this vacation. It's bad enough that she's holding the *Rubaiyat* over our heads, but does she have to be so, so…"

"Smug? Smirky?" She tossed out adjectives to fill his pause. "Sinister?"

"Unsettling. You know she hasn't said one word about this detour to Vegas? *Nil.* All that fuss to get on our TM and Eliot doesn't even care where we take her, which raises the question, what *does* she care about?"

"You." The word felt thorny, the way it sprouted. Green, too. Wraparound tendrils climbed all the way up Priya's throat. "Or was that not obvious after two intersecting missions? Her eyes are on you, Far."

"She does stare an awful lot, doesn't she?"

"You stare back."

Far chewed his lip. His cheeks were flushed from their walk, but Priya suspected some of the color had stayed for emotion's sake. She felt hot, too: near a sweat, a shout, a kiss. It was as if someone had come along and twisted off every safety mechanism to her emotions. *Someone had*, she reminded herself. Eliot. Unsettling everything.

"P..."

"I know it's not romantic. But—it's almost as if she's draining you, as if you're letting her. I don't want to be dating a shadow-person."

"This is new ground for us," he said softly. "Like you said, Eliot's running a long game, and I'm still figuring out how to play. Staring, swearing, wig-snatching... The only thing it takes from me is pride, which, according to Imogen, I can spare."

Far stepped closer so the warmth of his sunbaked skin rolled onto hers, fingertips to arms, nose to cheek. Such a different static from before; instead of finding cracks, it filled them, until Priya felt that her skin was no longer an apt container for everything inside. She was breathless and breathed: a song before the first note, after the last.

"Have no doubt, P," he whispered. "I'm yours, at the end of everything."

Their kiss was all tension at first—tight lips, teeth on edge—but it didn't take long to soften. It never did. Far was this at his core: feathery breath, heat of a wandering heart. Priya roamed with him, letting their kiss fall deeper out of their now. Out of time and space, out of the *Invictus*'s common area and the Nevada desert, into a perfect suspension of *them*. Just them, just them, floating and falling all at once, hands in hair tumbling toward the couch, just them—

And Saffron. The red panda's *YOU'RE IN MY SPACE!!!*

squawk yanked their surroundings into focus, and Priya realized she was in danger of crushing her purse, along with its cargo. "Wait, wait! The spoon! I need to take a sample before something ruins it."

Far fell gently to the side, curls amok. "Work first, play later, huh?"

"Isn't that always the case?" Her insides blazed still, would for a while. But, "The answers in this DNA are our next move. The sooner we have them, the better. It'll just take a few minutes to run the test. Why don't you search the ship? There are only so many places Eliot could've stashed the *Rubaiyat*."

"Good thinking!" Far slid from the couch. Destination? The honeycomb bunks.

Priya risked no contamination, donning latex gloves before retrieving the spoon from her purse, unwrapping the napkin with an archaeologist's care. She cupped it in both hands—artifact and offering—all the way into the infirmary. It would only take one swab to get what she needed, but Priya did two for good measure, pausing to fold her hands and whisper a prayer to Ganesh—remover of obstacles, miniature statue at her workstation. The god's elephant head watched, serene, as she placed the sample in the reader. It was an older diagnostics machine, nothing like the fancy scanners in some of the newer CTMs. This had never posed a problem before, but the crew's injuries were often minor: scrapes and burns, food poisoning, a common cold every once in a while. Running DNA aboard the *Invictus* was a first.

When Priya inserted the sample, the diagnostics machine

wheezed so loud that Saffron perked his tented ears and trundled into the infirmary. He sat on the floor, eyes latched to the screen, entranced by the hourglass cursor that never seemed to run out of sand.

"Keep an eye on that for me," she instructed the red panda and went to check Eliot's bunk. The place was wrecked: sheets everywhere, the mattress upended. Far was on his hands and knees, prying up floor panels that had no business being bothered, elbow deep in wires he knew nothing about. Priya, who *did* know about the wires and how they connected to the ship's power grid, was quick to warn him. "Careful. One wrong move and we'll have a fritzed *Invictus* with fried Far on the side."

"The *Rubaiyat* isn't here! Nothing's *here*!" Far scowled. "Eliot was wearing a yellow dress when she showed up, right?"

"Yes."

"Then where is it?"

"Not in the floor." It wasn't in the hanging wardrobe, either, though Priya spent several seconds scanning for the frill. "That's odd."

Unsettling, actually.

Far dropped the floor panel back into place, frowning. "She must have a hidey-hole somewhere. Will you help me check the console room?"

She did, if only to keep him from tugging at even bigger, badder wires. Both of them made a thorough search of it. More floor panels were lifted, drawers were opened, overhead pipes were checked. They even tipped Bartleby over to see if something had been hidden in his hollow torso.

Nothing, except for several tumbleweeds of Saffron's fur.

There was a chime from the infirmary just as Priya set the mannequin back on its stand. *Answers. Finally!* She made her way to the workstation. Gone was the hourglass, a full DNA profile in its place. The report was a mess of *G*s and *T*s and *A*s and *C*s, mapped with graph lines. Data too raw for Priya to read—geneticist she was *not*. The machine had managed the hardest part, turning markers into more familiar language: female, age range fifteen to twenty, *Alopecia universalis*.

Two eyes and a Medic degree had already told her as much. There had to be more juicy secrets hiding in this saliva....She scrolled down the sequence. Reports automatically cited census data—linking chromosomes to ID numbers. Every single person in Central time was stored in the system. Even Far, whose genetic profile was as censored as an ancient war letter, was matched with one of his old Academy pictures: skull-cropped hair, grin thrice as cocky.

Priya kept scrolling.

No picture. No name. No ID number.

NO MATCH FOUND.

She read the results—again and again—until the words disintegrated into letters, the letters into meaningless light. Eliot wasn't just a hologram, but a ghost. She did not exist. Well, obviously she existed; her spit was on a spoon. The phantom status was digital and, according to previous suspicions, logical. Eliot was either black ops or a citizen of the future. Erased or unwritten.

"What's the verdict?" Far had rooted through couch cushions, finding nothing but a *Beats on Blast* holo-paper zine Priya hadn't realized was lost. Its battery was almost drained, review of a 1969 Woodstock datastream in the throes of death. A clip of Jimi Hendrix's legendary "Star-Spangled Banner" performance flickered between his fingers. In and out, in and...gone. Far's expression was the same when he read the screen. "Dead end?"

"Detour," she said, determined. "Just because Eliot is MIA in the system doesn't mean we can't dig up some leads. Ever heard of the Ancestral Archives?"

"The program where you shell out credits to get a pedigree?"

"That's one application." Certainly the most popular. The program was established for learning more about hereditary diseases, but like everything else in the world, it evolved at the eve of time travel. With history forever blasting through people's ears and eyes and hearts, it was natural they'd want to know their place in it. Discovering your many-times-great-grandfather was Albert Einstein did wonders for the ego—never mind that thousands of others could make the same claim. "It cross-references DNA databases for all sorts of things. Estate settlements, medical research, lineage mapping. This program could help us. People don't appear out of nowhere—even future ones. Depending on the types of genetic matches we get, we might be able to figure out what year Eliot's from."

"Great! Let's run it!"

"We don't have the software or the hardware. This two-bit piece of shazm is at its limit." Priya gave the diagnostics machine a healthy *thwack* with her fist. It snarled back. "We have to jump back to Central for answers."

Central, where Lux was waiting for a book they didn't have. A prospect Far summed up with a single syllable: "Ugh."

"*Ugh* is right." Priya moved to the common area, surveying the mess they'd made. Uneven floor panels, dislodged cushions, Eliot's bunk in shambles—so much to clean up and nothing to show for it. She flopped onto the couch. "Seems this trip was a waste. I'm sorry, Far."

"Sorry?" He settled beside her, curl-to-cheek close. "What've you got to be sorry for? I mean, except for getting a banana split when you clearly should've ordered gelato. That's tantamount to a criminal act in Imogen's eyes."

It wasn't quite a laugh-aloud joke, but it did make Priya smile. She rested her hand on Far's, taking a moment to marvel at their physicality. Knuckles, knicks, calluses. Veins, tendons, pores. All touching, not a shadow to be found.

"I know what I want." This, the resonance, a connection past flesh. "How about you—what did you wish for?"

"Wishes have the same weight as luck in my palmdrive. You want something, you make it happen. No need to go spitting on a perfectly nice dessert."

"Play the cynic all you want with the rest of the crew, but I know you made that wish." She'd seen it in his eyes, the way they caught the sparkler, drinking its brilliance spark by spark. It was the look Far got when he honed in on something—intense, fixed, as if nothing in all of time or space could stop him. But what did a boy like Farway McCarthy wish for? There were so many possibilities: amassing a fortune, trumping Eliot, making his mark, finding the *Ab Aeterno*...

Priya could only guess, and that was why she wanted to know. For as many touches and glances and whispers as they'd exchanged, there was still a part of her boyfriend that felt distant. A side of himself he either didn't share...or couldn't. Sometimes it seemed to her like an emptiness. Other times, a hunger.

Love should be all, but *all* was always growing.

"You're right." He smiled at her—there was no sparkler glow in his face now but sunlight. A slant of it reached through the *Invictus*'s vistaport, wrapping around their shoulders. "But if I tell you, it won't come true. Isn't that how the old legends go?"

Priya had no idea, though it did sound like the ragged remnant of a fairy tale, something twenty-first-century people might cling to. That or Far was making the whole thing up. She'd have to quiz Imogen on birthday lore when they reunited.

Which should be soon....Three hours had sounded like an age when she'd cited it, but time passed faster when Priya and Far were alone together. There was never enough—every second, every breath felt stolen.

"The others will be waiting for us." Priya hated to say it. How many moments like this had she wanted to press Pause? To rest her head against his shoulder as long as she possibly could? Instead, their lives felt stuck on Fast-Forward. Flying here and there, caught up in capers, rushing, rushing, rushing...

...to what, exactly?

"Someone's always waiting for something. Imogen and Gram are at the biggest grown-up playground in the world. I think they can manage to keep Eliot distracted for a few more hours." Far smiled. "If you wanted to pick up where we left off."

Oh did she.

Plastic spoons, the missing *Rubaiyat*, the unsettled rush—all this faded when Far's fingers trailed up her arm, along the garment's green gauze, over the bare skin of her shoulder. This was the pause, the beat, the shiver....Something worthy of a snapshot. Priya could command her interface to take an actual photograph, but she preferred collecting the details of Far through memory alone. His eyelashes, thick as ink. The sun spiraling off his curls. The many degrees of emotion caught in the angle of his lips. Herself—far away in the center of his eyes—another world of details and memories made.

It was a still point. A perfect moment.

She let it stretch on as long as she could.

18.

IN THE GARDEN OF
THE GODS

———

SO MUCH WASTE.

It was impossible not to think this, sitting in the Garden of the Gods. There were seven different swimming pools in Caesars Palace, most named after the expected gods: Bacchus, Apollo, Venus. It wasn't the imitation of grandeur that bothered Eliot, though it was underwhelming after standing in the shadows of *real* Roman columns. It was the assuredness of excess: fountains gushing in the desert, middle finger to Mother Nature, partygoers reveling while a few miles away Lake Mead shrank to critical levels.

It was ironic. No, that wasn't the right word. Tragic? Smacking of poetic justice? Maybe she was being too critical. Eliot's mother had always teased her for being a glass-half-empty kind of person.

It's the one thing I can count on, she used to say in her lilt of a voice.

The memory was faint—an echo, really—but it caught Eliot like a blade between the ribs. She sat up in her lounge chair, breath sharp, borrowed sunglasses sliding down her nose.

"Everything okay?" Imogen propped herself up in the next chair.

No. It wasn't. And it wouldn't be. Water wasn't the only thing being wasted. Eliot was on the clock. Subject Seven had been out of scanning range for hours now, and her readings were stuck at 23 percent. *Too slow, too slow*; her lungs shuddered the warning.

"Ooooh." Imogen's nose wrinkled. "You're burning."

When Eliot pressed her fingers to her arm, they left white prints. Unsurprising. It was her mother's skin—pale like the north, ready to take on a thousand freckles at the first kiss of sun. She winced. It helped as much as it hurt, remembering these little things....

"Pink's a great shade for hair, not so much for skin...." Imogen pulled out a bottle of the highest SPF money could buy. "Here. Apply liberally to avoid turning into a lobster princess."

There wasn't enough sunscreen in this world that could keep Eliot from getting fried, but Imogen was one of those people you just couldn't say no to. A glass-overflowing kind of soul. In fact, the Historian was so eager to pass along the bottle that she knocked over her own empty piña colada glass. When she set the barware upright, she salvaged the tiny umbrella to wedge into the base of her bun. On anyone else the decor would've looked ridiculous, but Imogen made it fit. In a way, she made Eliot fit, too. The others seemed wary around her—even that hissy panda thing—but Imogen was a fount of conversation, not to mention knowledge. The offhand comment about Subject Seven's birthday meant more than the Historian would probably ever realize. Eliot had assumed the blank spot by the birth date in Seven's files was an oversight. SYSTEM ERROR. It felt too easy, too much to hope for, that he was, indeed, the one she'd been searching for.

Was he? This boy born outside of time?

Eliot still feared to hope. She feared a lot of things: being wrong, what must follow if she *was* right. There was no room for mistakes, and she couldn't afford to act on impulse. Her certainty had to be at 100 percent, and right now the countersignature scanners were stuck at less than a quarter of that.

"Do you know when—" Eliot caught herself. It wouldn't do to call him Subject Seven out loud. "Far and Priya will get back?"

"That's like asking where a hurricane will make landfall." Imogen laughed. "Farway is a force all his own."

"I've gathered as much." Eliot squirted sunscreen into her palm. "Do you enjoy working for your cousin?"

"I'd say *with* as much as *for.* Farway...he's always been strongheaded, but sometimes he gets that strong head up his own tail. That's when he gets into the most trouble. He needs people. We all do, really." Imogen cast a glance at the Fortuna Pool, where Gram hovered in waist-deep waters, watching the blackjack tables. "I can't imagine freelancing."

"Don't. It's not a life to envy." Eliot had forgotten how nice it was—sitting by a pool, applying sunscreen, chatting with someone who wasn't a computer. "Did you know there's a German curse that literally translates as 'heaven thunder weather'? *Himmeldonnerwetter!*"

"Germans have the best words." It said a lot about Imogen, that she followed this segue. It revealed even more that she appreciated cultured profanity.

"There are fantastic obscenities all over the globe. History, too. I've made it my mission to collect as many as possible. Reminds me that everyone's got something to swear about—no matter where or when they live."

"In Latin you can slander someone by calling them a pumpkin," the other girl offered. "*Cucurbita!* Farway and I used to shout it at each other all the time, until Aunt Empra made us stop."

Eliot emptied more sunscreen into her hand—the bottle was down to the dregs, and the stuff splattered everywhere. "I imagine that was quite an insult, back in the day."

"Most people don't like being compared to gourds," Imogen said sagely. "So what about *haze*? When's that curse from?"

Oh fex…She'd noticed. It wasn't like Eliot to slip from the script: careful vocabulary, galvanized backstory. But the wig-snatching had rattled her more than she cared to admit. She didn't mind going without a hairpiece; in fact, she preferred it (less heat and itch), but the suddenness of the loss—hair and gone—summoned a memory that was all knife. Six years old, stares from every side, cafeteria tears—where did she belong now?

So much had changed, and yet so much hadn't.

"Haze…It's an Australian word, I think. Twenty-third century?" Eliot hoped the Historian knew nothing about Down Under slang. These rabbit holes were getting harder to dodge. "I lose track after a while."

The sunscreen bottle was tapped, but Eliot's skin was too saturated to accept more regardless. She was sure that if she looked in the mirror she'd appear more wraithlike than usual. Blanched to the bone, half past disappearing. It would happen one day, she was certain. The Fade would catch her unawares, in a moment she could not escape.

Eliot pressed her arm again. White prints against white. Still solid. Still here. Even with the new layer of SPF she felt her skin slow-roasting. "I'm going to join Gram in the shade. Want to come?"

"Um, no." Imogen's body language was at war with her words. Calves taut, shoulders turned. "Not this time."

"Most things look good on you," Eliot told her. "Pining isn't one of them."

At this, Imogen removed her sunglasses. "Who told you? Farway? Priya?"

"It's not that hard to see. Your eyes go all galactic when you look at him. Stars and stuff."

The Historian made a mouselike sound and slipped the shades back on as if that could retroactively keep Eliot from noticing the lovey-dovey glow. "Do you—do you think *he* knows?"

"Why don't you ask him?"

"Because…then we'd have to talk about it."

"And?"

The other girl swiped up her piña colada glass and began scraping leftover fluff off its edges. "Why does everyone think it's so easy to bare one's heart for possible laceration? Hmm?"

"Not easy, no," Eliot admitted as she stood. "But it just might be worth it."

The Historian stabbed at dried coconut bits with her straw, grumbling.

"Carpe diem." She shouldn't have pushed, shouldn't have cared at all. Getting attached to subjects and their affiliates only meant there'd be *de*taching later. Still, this rainbow of a girl reintroduced pumpkin profanity into Eliot's mindscape, and that was no small thing. "You should try."

Before it's too late…

"Noted." Imogen waved her off. "Now let me pine in peace!"

For all of Eliot's judgment, the water felt blessedly cool when she waded into the Fortuna Pool, heading straight for the covered part, where people could swim up to the blackjack tables. Staff in shimmery blue shirts dealt the cards from a dry inlet. Gram watched one of the games from a nearby column. His stance was made of intense corners: keen jaw, shoulders straight enough to level a portrait. Eliot could almost see the numbers running through his eyes—*+1, 0, +1, –1,* and on, and on.

"What's the count?" she asked.

"Crux!" The Engineer started, his calculations scattering. "How do you keep sneaking up like that?"

"Was I sneaking?" It wasn't intentional. Force of habit, maybe, the side effect of a year spent in and out of shadows.

166

"You don't even slosh. It's not natural." Gram's stare drifted back to the table. "Negative three. Odds are in the house's favor."

So they were, much to the chagrin of the man who watched his chips get swept away after the next *hit me*. Gram let out a sigh—part satisfaction, part…relief? The people at the black-jack tables kept playing, tapping for more more more as the cards were laid down.

"The landing on the *Titanic* gave you trouble, didn't it?" Eliot asked.

"You could say that." A frown. Slight side-eye. "What would you know of it?"

Everything and nothing. The rabbit hole became an abyss, yet Eliot pressed on. "What time were you aiming for?"

"Six o'clock in the evening. We landed around ten instead."

Did the tear span all four hours? Eliot couldn't count on herself to know. There was no plug-in formula for such growth…merely guesswork. What she needed was a point of reference, a coal-mine canary for the Fade's spread. At 10:20 that evening she'd been talking with the boy on the settee. What was his name? *What* was *his name?* Panic spun through Eliot just a moment before the details landed. Charles. Charles with the baby-fat cheeks, nineteen years old. Sandy hair, bright eyes, over a century dead.

"Remember Charles," she muttered, both as a reminder to herself and for Vera to record as a memo.

Gram glanced down at her. "Who?"

Charles. Charles. Baby-fat Charles.

"It's nothing." Which couldn't be further from the truth. Eliot's memories weren't just an arsenal but a barometer. Once she started forgetting Charles...

"I've never seen anything like it before. The numbers..." The Engineer's voice faded, then picked back up along a different line of thought. "I've spent my entire life learning about order, knowing how to keep it. What do you do when the world stops making sense?"

READINGS REMAIN 23% COMPLETE, Vera reminded her. REMEMBER CHARLES.

Water crashed all around Eliot, cascading from the ceiling's edges, enough to drown in. The man at the blackjack table, who'd been counting on luck to toss him a bone, had instead been beaten by the odds. He threw up his hands and wallowed off.

"There's nothing like the nihilist to bring out the hedonist." Eliot gestured to the empty seat.

"We can't. There's too much reshuffling. The redistribution could—"

But she was already wading over to the table, cash produced seemingly out of nowhere, at the ready. *Carpe the hazing diem. Make it count.* Either Vegas's gilded lifestyle was rubbing off on Eliot or she was just too tired to care. What she needed was a distraction, something to do besides worry herself into bits.

Even Nero had fiddled while Rome burned....

The cute blond dealer checked Eliot's doctored holo-ID before exchanging her dollars for chips—a tidy sum. Eliot didn't care if she lost it or not. The money of this era looked like play stuff, all green and papery, and the chips even more so. She placed the highest bet she could. The cards were laid.

Gram appeared beside her. "Far won't like this."

"Well, your captain isn't here, is he? What's the point of coming all the way to Las Vegas if you can't toss around a bit of cash?"

"It's irresponsible."

Eliot shrugged. "We're young. Isn't that our job? If you don't want any part in it, feel free to join Imogen."

Gram didn't move. The dealer was waiting for a decision, and so Eliot tapped the table.

"She's pretty, don't you think?"

"Yeah. I mean, I guess."

Typical boys and their monosyllabic answers. "Why don't you take her out on the town? Maybe to one of those Penn and Teller magic shows?"

"We're crewmates."

"That doesn't seem to stop Priya and Far."

Gram glanced back through the curtain of falling water—most of Imogen was blurred, but her topknot shone bright. He watched the green glow, something other than numbers flashing through his eyes.

"They're the exception to the rule. The probability of such a relationship not ending poorly at our age…" The Engineer shook his head. "It'd make things too complicated."

Everyone kept getting in their own way today. Must be something in the water.

It felt wrong to laugh, but Eliot couldn't help herself. The sound was unhinged and hysterical and made the dealer do a double take once the cards were placed. Hit or stand? She was at a negative count, but odds mattered less than everyone thought, especially when you pushed back. Life was for the living. She wasn't going to worry about wasting water or time slipping or Agent Ackerman or frozen readings or pivot points or redistribution or Charles or all the undoings she could not undo.

Time to take a fexing vacation.

"Hit me," she said.

19.

WIZIZARDS

FAR AND PRIYA TOOK THE LONG way back from the *Invictus*. They strolled hand in hand, stopping by the iconic Las Vegas sign for a picture, hitting up happy hour at the Cosmopolitan, pausing to watch the song-and-spray number in front of the Bellagio. It was the reprieve Far needed. Big-picture problems fell away when he was with Priya, the world strung together with small joys. An extra side of truffle fries. A kiss enveloped by fountain mist. Jokes and stories and laughter with rubies spilling through it—for Priya's was an outside-in, inside-out beauty. He wanted to be enough for her, and he hated—*hated*—that Eliot had brought this into question. Eliot. Ugh. There she was, under the skin again. A vampire-leech-mosquito taking not blood, or simply pride, but control.

Far wrested these thoughts and sent them splashing into fake Venetian canals. Was it too much to ask for a worry-free walk? Couldn't he stay in this spell of normality they'd woven?

The post-sunset city grew frantic around them—the crowds on the Strip's sidewalks quadrupled, adverts flashed with growing desperation. It was the sort of energy Far thrived on, but he kept his pace leisurely, even pausing to toss some coins to a haggard-looking man whose cardboard sign claimed *ALL I NEED IS WEED.*

At least the guy was honest about his motives. Unlike *some* people...

Eliot, again. Far's shoulders cramped up, ten pounds of tension returning with visions of the girl who'd bested him thrice now. No *Rubaiyat*, no lead. How were they going to get back to Central to tap the Ancestral Archives without Lux tracking them down, demanding what could not be given? Ice in the desert, this prospect, seizing every muscle.

"What's wrong?" Priya paused.

"Is it terrible that I'm thinking about running back to the *Invictus* and hightailing it to a remote tropical paradise where no one will ever hear from us again?"

"Yes." Priya arched her eyebrow—all playful—because she knew it was a pipe dream. He did, too. The only place the *Invictus* could go without Gram was Central time, where remote tropical paradises were few and far between.

"How about Woodstock?" Far fished. Celebrating his eighteenth year of existence reminded him that their anniversary was on the horizon. One-upping genuine BeatBix would take effort.

Her expression lit—a definite *yes*. "Who'd have thought this crisis would make you amenable to vacations?"

"I like vacations." Though he probably *should* take the crew on more of them. He would, if this mess ever got straightened out. Parisian streets and New York fields and wherever Gram wanted to go.

"You like going places to accomplish things," Priya told him. "There's a difference. We'll figure this out, Far. We will. But right now there's nothing we can do except take the night off and go to the pool—"

"The pool?" It was well past dark, but Far couldn't spot a single star when he looked up, just a thick haze of light pollution that reminded him of home. "At this hour?"

"Caesars Palace pool. I got an interface message from Imogen telling us to meet them there. Dance party. Epic proportions. Remember?"

How could he forget?

Far felt the bass rumble at least a minute out when they wove through the casino—which looked nothing at all like the actual *Domus Augusti*, in its ruins *or* its prime. The closer they got, the more Priya's steps started to bounce. The DJ would be hard-pressed to play a song she didn't know; most were probably already on her "Golden Oldies" playlist.

The pools were a sight—waters lit, patterned floors shimmering—dancers in and out, splashing, flashing. Far scanned the crowd's rhythmic mill of heads. Imogen should've been easy to spot, but it seemed she was in her natural habitat: GLOW. Several girls sported hair just as phosphorescent as hers—orange, blue, pink, green. Watching them dance was like will-o'-the-wisps gone wild. There were glow sticks, too, bobbing with wrists and necks.

Far felt very underlit. He let Priya take the lead. Together they skirted the crowd, music buzzing so loud it was almost hard to see. It was Eliot he spotted first. They were worlds away from the mirrors and pastels of Versailles. The night glittered neon, and electronica music clashed about them, yet she was every inch Marie Antoinette—girl at the center of the party, a fixture the crowd gathered around. When she caught Far's stare, he felt his old failure afresh, as if a wormhole had opened up under his feet and slipped him right back into his old skin. He smelled the roses mixed with bergamots. He heard her whisper...*I know an outlier when I see one.*

Eliot stilled. The masses kept moving around her, but she was her own point of gravity. Instead of winking, her eyes held him solid, turning Far's heels leaden. All of his fears fell on him at once, taking and taking.

You don't belong here.

"Farway! There you are!" Imogen blazed into view—green hair, both arms sheathed in glow sticks. She had to scream at his ear to be heard. "You missed lotsa sun! And stuff. You 'n Priya good?"

"Never better," he yelled back. "Where's Gram?"

"Being a wallflower over there!" Imogen's arm streaked— yellow, pink, blue—toward some cabanas. "We rented one.... He's watchin' the bottle!"

"Bottle?" That explained his cousin's breath, though it raised a whole other set of questions. "You rented a cabana?"

174

"Me? No. 'Twas Eliot! She got a lil' *too* distracted and won a bunch of cash at swim-up blackjack."

"Eliot gambled?" *Oh shazm.* How many futures had she changed on Far's watch? He should've known better than to leave her out of sight for so long.

The party suddenly felt more ominous than before, darker gaps between bodies and glow. Far looked over both shoulders, as if Corps operatives were about to leap out of the crowd, armed with stunrods and warrants. All he saw was the thorn in his side herself. She'd gone back to dancing—eyes closed, channeling French royalty at a rave.

Multitudes indeed.

"You're *too dim*!" Imogen tore a blue glow stick from her neck and placed it on his head. "There. Now you look like a wizizard!"

"A *what*? Imogen, how much have you had to drink?"

She held up her thumb and forefinger. "Just a lil' liquid courage!"

"You've never been afraid to dance," he pointed out.

"No." Her frown was a borderline pout. "Not for dancing. For ... other things. Like *talking*."

"About wizizards?"

Priya appeared. Somehow she'd already acquired two glow bracelets. "DJ Rory knows his stuff! This beatmatch is butter smooth! And did you hear that last fade?"

He hadn't. He offered two thumbs up anyway. "I'm going to check in with Gram!"

Both girls wheeled off, and Far wound his way to the

cabanas. He found Gram under a tented area, watching the sea of dancing light.

"Hey, Far."

"Guarding the goods, I see?" Far nodded at the ice bucket, which held a bottle of something clear and strong. There was frost on the glass when he tugged it out. *Belvedere*. He recognized the brand from the shipments Lux's other TMs came back with. Top-shelf spirits. In the Central market, it went for two thousand credits a pop. A third of the stuff was already gone. Not as much as he'd suspected. Then again, Imogen was about as lightweight as pigeon down.

The Engineer shrugged. "Figured this was the best place to plant myself. Least likelihood of getting trampled by stilettos."

"I'm more worried about Corps stunrods." Far looked around the cabana. Lounging cushions, fans, a tray full of snacks…Eliot certainly hadn't skimped on expenses. "All this was bought with table money?"

"The girl can count cards," Gram said. "She made the right bets, pulled in a bundle. I told her you wouldn't approve."

"I'm sure that only encouraged her." Far grabbed two glasses from the tray and started pouring vodka straight up. "At least no one's showed up to arrest us yet."

"Any ripples her actions caused must've been minor." Gram frowned. "Though there was one odd thing…."

"What?"

"She was asking about our landing times on the *Titanic*. When she first appeared, I thought she could be the cause of the aberration. Now I'm not so sure. The events are definitely linked, but it's possible she's here as a result of the disturbance as opposed to the disturbance being the result of her."

Far handed a glass to his Engineer before downing his own. So cold, so burning. "You're making my head spin."

"Yours isn't the only one. Trust me." Gram took a healthy swig, coughing as he set the drink down. "It's all conjecture at this point."

"What isn't?" Far poured another round. "Girl's a no-show in the digital sphere. I'm starting to wonder if she's a figment of my imagination."

"A mass hallucination? That's highly unlikely."

"It was a joke, Gram."

"Ah. I didn't think you were in a humor."

"I'm not." Far looked out at the crowd. Their lights were blurring too fast for him to pick apart. Even so, he could see Eliot: lightless and shining. Her white jumpsuit stood out in the whirlwind of color. *She doesn't belong here. You don't belong here.* Anger and fear, back to back and back again.

Far knew he was being drained. He knew he should stop it. But how?

He slammed his second drink.

"What's your next move?" Gram asked.

Priya materialized from the revelers—a welcome relief. When Far looked to her, the rest of the crowd seemed to crystallize, unmoved in their motion. Her grin called him over before her wave did.

"Dancing, apparently." He set the barware back on the tray, next to the Engineer's unfinished drink. "Have you had enough booze to join the grind yet? Imogen is accusing you of being a wallflower."

"Is she?" The look on Gram's face was pained and determined. He donned his fedora like a helmet as he stood. "Right, then. Let's get this over with."

❖ ❖ ❖

Three drinks, four drinks, five. The night melted into itself—moments without seams, becoming one syncopated blur. Like Gram, Far never went out of his way to seek a dance floor, but he found that once he started moving he didn't give a shazm anymore.

Imogen came by with shots of something that tasted like a candy-shop display. Priya shouted the name and artist of every single song DJ Rory played. Gram tried to make a graceful exit at the five-song mark, but Imogen caught him by the vest and whispered something that made his eyes go wide. The Engineer stayed on the edge of the dance floor, feet shuffling in a way that was too tight to really be called dancing. Eliot flitted in and out of the crowd, always on the edge of Far's consciousness. She was a moving marionette. Weightless limbs, delicate with hints of broken. The metaphor fell apart with her expression—unpainted. Yes, the eyebrows were sketched, but Far now saw how staged everything else had been, such curated smirks.

Collected winks. This face was a good deal younger. It actually dared to smile.

Seven drinks. Eight. Far didn't normally imbibe this much, but they were in Vegas and it was his unbirthday. If there was ever a time to let loose...

Party all night, dance into the dawning light.

Tick-tock, wind the clock, we can't stop.

We can't stop.

We can't stop.

Priya brought a round of water, which the group guzzled down. Eliot did everything right: grin, laugh, *thank you*, drink, and was she actually aiming to become part of the crew? Far spent a good five seconds staring at his cup, marveling at the way the plastic crumpled against his palms. No no no. The *Rubaiyat* should be on the *Invictus*, in his hands. How could she make a whole book go *poof*? Maybe Eliot was a magician? Or an honest-to-goodness wizizard...

Hades, I'm drunk. The realization washed over him, accompanied by dizziness. Everything turned blue—the glow stick, in his eyes. The plastic link snapped off when Far tugged it, the circle becoming a line. He dropped the cup and the shine, watching both get stomped to bits by dancers' frantic feet.

Once the beat fades, we fall apart.

We can't stop.

Tick-tock.

Far stood still, watching everyone else spin around him. Imogen. Gram. Priya. Stranger after stranger. Everyone was covered in sweat, despite the dry air. How long could the night go on? It felt like forever already.

A hand on his arm. Far wasn't surprised to find that the firm grip belonged to Eliot. Her countenance had gone stark... something to match the clench of her fingers on his sleeve.

"What's the first thing you remember about the *Titanic*?" Her question was loud enough to pick out over the music, but Far struggled to keep up.

Remember? Everything was a blur, thanks to that bottle of Belvedere. He could barely recall the past few minutes, much less the finer points of his last mission. "Um. Crates?"

"How did you get to those crates?" Eliot was cutting off his circulation. Far's fingertips buzzed; pins and needles pulse. *BOOM sting BOOM.* "Do you remember the exact route?"

Far frowned, thoughts spinning too fast to track. He remembered the plans: ship's schematics flashing across Imogen's screens and Bartleby standing by, looking dapper in a swallowtail coat. He remembered tossing said coat overboard before he descended into the cargo bay. But when it came to his actual jaunt through first class?

Nothing. The space was blank.

Shaking his head only made him dizzier. "Too much vodka..."

"Fex!" Far had never heard the word before, but he was pretty sure it was a curse for how hard Eliot spat it. "Fex! Fex! Fex!"

He stared at her, more dazed than not. How could he forget his entrance onto the *Titanic*? Far recalled his exit well enough—the polished staircase, the angry steward, chasing Eliot to kingdom come.

"It's happening too fast," she told him. "I forgot Charles."

Charles? Who was Charles? Everything she said was nonsense.... And yet it wasn't. The ground felt all tilty beneath him. Eliot's fingers turned tight as talons; she started tugging him through the dancers.

"We have to go back to Central. Right now." She said the same thing to Priya, to Imogen, to Gram as she led the group to the cabana. "Gather your things and let's go."

"Now, wait a second!" Imogen stood far closer to Gram than she would have four drinks ago. Her face was flushed from dancing, strands of glowing hair stuck to her neck. "No. We're on vacation. Farway, tell her!"

"We're on vacation," he said. "Like it or not, I'm still the captain of this—"

"If we don't leave right now," Eliot told them, "I will destroy the *Rubaiyat*."

The group went dead silent. Their expressions matched the savage beat of DJ Rory's song. Imogen looked as if someone had just shaved Saffron's tail clean down.

"You're bluffing." The stakes were too high for Far's poker face to hold. Dreams, freedom, life... "You—you can't do that to us."

Eliot's eyebrows rose. One of them was smudged, but instead of looking comical, it gave her an edge. "I can and I will. We deliver the book to Lux, right now. If we don't... it's gone."

Gone. The ground was tilting again, and Far had to fight

to stand straight. Why couldn't he remember walking through first class? That was a massive chunk of memory...minutes and minutes of his life. Now that Eliot had pointed it out, all he could focus on was the gap. The space in his mind where someone had come along and cut the film.

Had *she* erased things somehow? Disturbance. Result. Linked. Could she have doped him up with Nepenthe when he wasn't paying attention? Eliot was capable of anything. He saw all this and more in her eyes—the fire ready to light the pyre, send his entire world up in flames. Fear, anger, fear, fear, fear widening gyre all of it spiraling to places Far couldn't reach. Priya's hand on his shoulder was the calm during the storm. He would've keeled over without it.

Far puffed up his chest instead, tried to sound like the sober, in-control captain he wasn't. "It's decided, then. We go."

20.

NIGHT ARMOR

READINGS ARE 30% COMPLETE. REMEMBER CHARLES.

Vera's second sentence cut Eliot to the quick with every update. Each new percentage brought a fresh degree of panic: Were the measurements being processed fast enough? Charles was gone, reduced to a collection of pixels that Eliot played and replayed. His face blinked on her interface—a bit round, mostly innocent. There was something of a dreamer about him, as he talked about his recent European tour, his plans for school once he returned to Canada.

I hope I'm not boring you, Ms.—Forgive me, my memory has been wretched today. What did you say your name was?

Eliot, she whispered inside her head. *My name is Eliot.*

At least she remembered that.

The feed continued, into territory Eliot recalled with perfect clarity—producing the *Rubaiyat* and its oak case, appearing in the cargo bay, watching Subject Seven's face implode with recognition, the cat-and-mouse chase that followed. She even remembered passing Charles again before rushing up the Grand Staircase. He hadn't called out, just watched her yellow dress swish and vanish.

Had he ever made it to Canada? Eliot hoped so. Someone in this haze of a mess deserved a happy ending.

She switched off the feed and stared at her bunk's white walls. The DJ's spins rang through her ears, hours old, strong enough to dance to. It had been a fun evening—raking in cash from blackjack and blowing it on whatever she pleased. Gram and Imogen had made for excellent conversation—fashion and physics, history and the merits of twentieth-century gaming consoles. (Buttons, the Engineer had explained. It felt like more of an achievement if your hands were put to work.) She'd taught them both a Gaelic hex, as whimsical as it was wicked: *May the devil make a ladder of your backbones while picking apples in the garden of hell.* There was a beat, between the translation and the laughter, when everything around Eliot solidified, from her skin all the way to the flinted stars. She became a solid girl in a steady world, partying her arse off.

Life was for the living, and this one should have belonged to her. For an evening, for just a few hours, it did.

READINGS ARE 30.1% COMPLETE. REMEMBER CHARLES.

"Thanks, Vera," Eliot said, though thankfulness was the last thing she felt, this close to evanescing. "Keep updates to every one percent."

Racing against the unknown was enough to make anyone restless, and the bunk was no place for itchy legs. Eliot stepped into the common area. All was quiet, haloed in April 19's daylight. Through the vistaport she caught glimpses of a cloud-cluttered sky. If she leaned over far enough, she might even see the glittering carpet that was the Atlantic. The *Invictus* was flying itself over the ocean, on autopilot while the rest of the crew slept off their wild night. A few had been wilder than others.... They'd been forced to take a cab from Caesars Palace to the desert lot because Imogen and Seven were in no condition to walk that far without tangling themselves in their own legs, and there was no time to stumble.

Eliot walked a few laps around the couches, keeping time to the ringing in her ears. Notes that would've helped her dance the dawn into existence, had the past not fallen out from under her. The tear was growing, had grown while she partied, and who was she to take a break? Agent Ackerman would go full-on feral if he found out....

A flash of red and white, the beastie called Saffron, dropping from the pipes onto the couch. Its tail reminded Eliot of an old-fashioned duster—fur straight as static. A dozen curiosities dashed through the creature's gaze as it watched her. *Who? What? Yum?*

"You don't *look* like a panda," she muttered, walking to the other side of the couch. The more cushions between them, the better. "Stop staring! Return to the void from whence you came!"

"He doesn't bite. Usually." The voice over her shoulder sounded as if it'd been zapped by lightning. Its owner didn't look too different: *Himmeldonnerwetter* in human form. Imogen emerged from her bunk—palazzo pants crumpled, hair frazzled and glowing.

"A question…" she croaked. "Do I look as shazmy as I feel?"

"You look as one might expect after a night on the Strip and a more-than-healthy dose of Belvedere."

"*Ngh.*" Imogen held a hand up to block the vistaport's light, then frowned. "We're flying?"

"You don't remember?" Eliot wasn't worried. This was normal forgetting—alcohol-induced. "We're on our way back to Rome."

"Already? The *one time* we get started on a decent vacation! Why the Hades would Far yank us back to Central so soon?" Imogen stomped toward the washroom, pausing before she reached it. "Oh no."

"Hmm?"

"Bits are coming back." Fingers fluttered around her electric-storm hair—frantic. "I made Gram dance with me last night, didn't I?"

"Yes."

"Did I talk to him? Like, *talk* talk?"

"Dunno." Eliot shrugged.

"Of all the bluebox blunders…" The Historian massaged her temple with a groan. "Remind me never to drink vodka again."

"I don't think it's the vodka that's the problem."

"Right. Pining. Star eyes. I know. It's what I *don't* know that's killing me. What if I said something stupid? Like only he could make math sexy? Or that I already named our imaginary pet chinchilla?"

"You want *more* animals?"

"Its name is Dusty," Imogen offered. "This is some code-red stuff right here. I'm going to need you to do some reconnaissance. Toss Gram a few feeler questions. 'Hey, I heard you talked to Imogen last night. How was it?' That sort of thing. It'd help my pining immensely!"

Why are you so afraid of being vulnerable? Eliot should have asked the question aloud. She didn't. It was an answer she knew well enough. She knew other answers, too: Gram was a man of numbers, but he had heart, and some of it leaned in Imogen's favor. And Imogen? The girl was all tilt, all over, but with some direction she'd find her way. Both parties needed a shove....

Over the past year Eliot had become quite proficient at moving people around the chessboard. Arranging, rearranging, in order to reach *checkmate*. But Gramogen wasn't in her mission directives. Subject Seven was the one she was here for, and there was no time

no time

no time to stumble, dance, play matchmaker.

"Think on it. Oh, you've got—or rather, you don't have—" Imogen gave up on words, pointing to her own eyebrows instead.

"Ah. Happens sometimes. They need freshening up; it's been a while since I drew them."

With a wave, the other girl continued into the washroom. "There's a scathingly strong mirror in here, if you need it."

The area was roomier than expected, tucked along the ship's starboard side. It had all of the standard long-term time-travel fare—shower, toilet, vanity, closed-loop recycling water system. The mirror lived up to Imogen's descriptions: overachieving to a fault. Who knew skin had so many pores? Eliot's sunburn wasn't as bad as she'd feared, already pastel in shade. Most of her left eyebrow was nonexistent. She set to work washing her face clean, and—while Imogen's back was turned—pulled out her brow pen. It was a relic, label rubbed off from so many uses. Eliot sometimes composed new names as she drew: Black as the Souls of Mine Enemies, Widow Maker, A Humor So Dark, Night Armor.

Muscle memory took over her fingers. Swipe, swipe, fill in the blank. Eliot traced curves along her supraorbital ridges while Imogen watched. Fascinated. "Do you always draw the same arch?"

"More or less."

"Do you ever doodle secret messages into them? Something tiny and subliminal?"

"I've—never thought to do that," Eliot admitted. "What would you write?"

" 'Hello, there.' Or 'Cookies please.' It'd depend on the day, to be honest. Speaking of." Imogen hefted up a giant case of hair chalks stacked in rainbow rows—primaries, neons, metallics, white. Some had been used more than others: almost down to the nub. "What color do you think I should go with? Taylor Pink? Marigold? Silver Dream?"

Eliot couldn't help renaming the shades: Fairy-Tale Fury,

Earwax?, New Robot Overlords. "You change your hair color every day? Isn't that time-consuming?"

"I like colors and colors like me," the other girl said. "Anything's better than boring old blond."

"My hair was blond, before it fell out." One of the few memories Eliot actually wanted to dissolve. Standing barefoot in the tub, fingers around a fistful of golden strands. They'd looked so short apart from her head, so straggly when she dropped them and shrieked for her mother.

Her pen hand quivered, turning her left brow cartoonish.

"Shazm." There was gravel in Imogen's whisper. "I'm sorry, Eliot. I wasn't thinking. It didn't even occur to me—"

"Don't get me wrong. I like your colors, too." Eliot set down her pen, using a towel to scrub the deviant brow away. "The world gets gloomy. It helps having something bright around."

Imogen ran a finger down its color-blocked columns. Rainbow dust clung to her skin—as if she were a fairy gathering a spell. "It's all about perspective, isn't it? That's why Aunt Empra loved time travel so much. She always said the past helped her make sense of the present...sometimes even the future, too. I didn't understand what she meant until I started traveling. When you witness the breadth of history, you understand how small you are. And yet at the same time you realize how much your life matters...how much you shape the people around you. And vice versa."

There was still a tremor in Eliot's fingers. She stared at the pen nib, waiting for the shake to pass. Usually it wasn't this hard to put her face on.

"Anyway, I'm babbling," Imogen sighed. She plucked two chalks from the case. "If we're going back to our anchor date, I should default to aquamarine with a hint of bubble-gum pink, for continuity's sake."

"Nebula hair," Eliot offered.

"It does sort of look like a nebula, doesn't it? Celestial 'do, here I come." The Historian set the aquamarine and pink chalks on the vanity. "I'll let you finish your eyebrows before I monopolize the washroom. Take your time. I'm off to concoct something strong and caffeinated."

The washroom became ten times quieter with her exit, silence that felt more hollow than full. Eliot's hand had steadied, ready to trace what she'd show the world. She liked the secret message idea, wearing a war cry only she could see at a mirror's glance. She stared at her reflection—past the burn and the blackheads—and wondered what today's mantra should be. *Fex this? Brace yourself? Zut alors? Carpe diem?*

READINGS ARE 31% COMPLETE, Vera told her. REMEMBER CHARLES.

Eliot picked up her pen and started to write—spider-leg letters, backward to the casual observer. Once she was finished, she shaded over them, until even the most discerning eye couldn't pick out what was scripted beneath.

Make it count.

She fully intended to.

21.

WOBBLES

FAR'S FEAR HAD GONE VIRAL. It was the worst thing that could happen from a captain's perspective, watching your insecurities leak into the crew, nerves crawling all over the console room. Every one of the *Invictus*'s five passengers stared out the vistaport as Gram guided the time machine down the Tiber. Its water crept brown beneath the evening light. They drifted along with it, past the Castel Sant'Angelo, over bridge after bridge, to a section of river that the men of Central would choose to forget. What was now water would become earth, and what was earth would be hollowed out by Lux and used as a warehouse for his illegal TMs. During Central time, the place was buried in secrecy. Ships like the *Invictus* could only dock there by jumping through specific years, namely ones where drought had reduced the Tiber to a volume that wouldn't drown them on impact.

They'd made it to 2155—a year skies refused to cry and the earth thirsted—without incident, but the stakes were much higher with the docking jump. Lux's fleet left and landed on an airtight schedule to avoid collisions. One slipped landing became two TMs with volatile fuel rods in the same space became nuclear apocalypse.

So yeah, nerves.

Gram brought the *Invictus* to the exact landing coordinates, settling the ship into muddy shallows. He grabbed one of his Rubik's Cubes and began twisting.

Priya slipped on headphones, insulating herself in music.

Imogen chewed her thumbnail to a saw-toothed quick.

Eliot didn't have a tell, but this didn't stop her anxiety from being palpable. Far tasted it as well as his own. The only one without a care was Saffron, who'd planted himself in the captain's chair and would've melted into its abhorrent orange if not for his facial markings. Far was too hungover to *tsk* the animal off. It'd been a long sleep and a few waking hours since Caesars Palace, but the wooze of vodka clung to him. Nausea was inevitable for this jump.

"You sure we can land right this time?" Far asked.

"Nothing's sure now, Far," Gram reminded him.

Right. All conjecture at this point. Far turned to Eliot. "If you want all of us to get back to Central in one piece, you'd do well to dish anything you might know about wobbly landings. They only started happening when *you* showed up, and Gram here tells me you were asking about it. It's not much of a leap to assume that you can help us avoid blowing up."

"Which is preferable," Imogen added.

Eliot's eyebrows scrunched together. They looked different

today, more substantive. She'd put on another wig—a jet-black bob that added five years to her appearance. "These... wobbles, as you call them, are relatively random. As far as I know, this landing shouldn't be affected."

So she *was* connected to the wobble, which meant the wobble was linked to his memory loss. Again, Far felt his forgetting, the shock of it like a limb just amputated. Where had his entrance onto the *Titanic* gone, and why?

The question felt too big to ask. He couldn't imagine the size of the answer.

"How far do you know?" It was Gram who pressed for truth, because he couldn't not. "What caused the wobble? What made the numbers change? They *did* change, right?"

"Tick-tock, my friends." Eliot tapped her watchless wrist. "The *Rubaiyat*'s at stake."

Far turned to the nav system. Its center screen was crammed with digits, spattered with symbols, things the Engineer once swore by. Now as Gram sat by his instruments, he had the posturing of a gladiator: ready to attack, bracing for the wounding. His nostrils quivered. He set his cube down, unsolved. *Ready or not?*

"We jump," Far ordered.

Five breaths held. Five sets of eyes locked onto the vistaport as gloaming surrendered to absolute black. One red panda tucked his nose into his tail, for sounder sleep. Far looked back to the screen, where Gram was wrestling with equations. None of the numbers changed, though there were too many for Far to actually keep track. How the Engineer managed it was a few IQ points beyond him.

There was no length to how long this solving took, such was the nature of the Grid. Gram punched buttons, and light poured through the vistaport—the manufactured kind that belonged to the lamps of Lux's warehouse. Harsh under normal circumstances, stabby to the alcohol-soaked senses. Far fumbled his aviators back on, cursing the ingenious soul who had invented vodka.

"We're back to anchor time." He didn't need Gram's confirmation, not when he could see two of Lux's other TMs—the *Ad Infinitum* and the *Armstrong*—flanked by their latest shipments. The Engineer offered the time stamp anyway. "August twenty-second, 2371, 1:31 PM."

With one long sigh, the *Invictus*'s nerves unspooled. Its holo-shield dropped.

"Glad we're not dead." Imogen held two thumbs up, both nails ragged. "Good job, Gram."

"Er. Thanks." The Engineer's expression went soft. Crinkled brow, undecided smile. "Though I don't know if my skill had anything to do with it."

Is every jump going to be like this from now on? Far wondered as they pulled into their slip. The *Armstrong*'s crew was in the process of unloading. Their captain, Paolo, wheeled a dolly of crates down the dockside. The boxes were brimming with all sorts of goods: fresh oranges, specialty soaps, cages of extinct songbirds. Every one of these things would fetch a fat price from Central's elite, but they paled to the value of Far's one-of-a-kind cargo. The one he hoped they were actually carrying.

"The *Rubaiyat*?" He turned to Eliot. The way she stared

at Far's outstretched hand made him feel like a beggar. "Look, as soon as I leave this ship I'm going to have to meet with Lux—"

"*We're* going to meet with Lux," Eliot interrupted. "Together. I want to cement my position on your team."

What was she playing at, hanging on to the freelancer story when there was obviously so much more going on? Far's molars locked tight as the *Invictus* landed, settling into its own weight with a groan. He spied Wagner at the end of the dock, checking and double-checking the *Armstrong*'s crates. Lux's right-hand man was nothing if not thorough, which meant that the black market mogul already knew of Far's arrival. Commence catastrophe in three, two, one...

"Lux doesn't like unexpected guests," he said.

"I'm guessing he'd like your empty hands even less," Eliot challenged.

"Just give me the *Rubaiyat*. Please. You have my word that you can stay on as a part of this crew." Far tried not to think of everything that could go wrong if he took Eliot with him to Lux's villa. "What about mutual trust? Hmm?"

"What about it?" The girl cocked her head, most Antoinette-like. "Take me to Lux and the *Rubaiyat* will be delivered safely. I'm not here to haze you over, Far."

THEN WHY ARE YOU HERE? It was all he could do not to yell. Anger and alcohol banged against his skull, magnifying everything. Wagner glared alongside the lights, into the vista-port; his look let Far know he was already behind schedule. Lux hated to be kept waiting.

Imogen cleared her throat. "I think she's telling the truth, Farway."

He stared back at his cousin, sitting cross-legged in her twirly chair. Her hair reminded him of the cotton candy Burg once smuggled back from a mission—sweeter than anything Far had ever tasted. Only later had he realized how much was risked to bring it to him.

"You sure? Are you willing to bet your entire future on Eliot? Because if she doesn't deliver, it's not just my tail Lux will skin. Every one of us signed our names to his contract. Every one of us just used five jumps' worth of fuel to bring him *nil*. That kind of loss won't blow over."

Wagner was walking dockside, only twelve paces away. Terror was a physical thing in Far's chest—clawing him short of breath. Could he do it? Could he face Lux with his life in Eliot's palm? His crew's lives? Could he trust this blackmailing, timeline-meddling thief *not* to turn all turncoat on them?

Thud thud. "Captain McCarthy? Everything all right in there?"

"Everything's peachy keen, Wagner!" he shouted at the hatch.

The hatch shouted back. "Peachy what?"

"It's all hashing brilliant! I'll be out in a moment."

There was no choice—only knives at his back and a cliff at his feet. Far looked around at his crew. They'd picked up his fear once more, and the emotion carved grim lines in their faces: scaffolding light eyes and dark. Gram Wright, Imogen McCarthy, Priya Parekh…all of these names were on Lux's contract.

Every one of them signed at Far's request, letters spreading red as open veins.

The fall should be his to take, and his alone.

"Get a new fuel rod in and keep your comms on, just in case." Far looked to Priya. Her headphones were only half off, the notes bursting through them as rampant as his heart. "If stuff goes south, I'll send a distress signal and you guys get the hash out of here. Got it?"

"We're not ditching you," she said.

"Knowing Lux, there might not be anything *to* ditch." Far nodded at Gram and Imogen. "Fly at my say-so. That's an order."

Thud thud thud. Time to go. His kiss with Priya held every promise he wanted to keep, including the one she herself had planted in him: *We'll figure this out.* The BeatBix slid down her neck, its song beating between their throats—golden and ferocious—and he wanted to keep listening through to the end, wanted his fate to be *this*. Eyes on her, lips too, closest joy this side of eternity.

But Eliot was waiting at the hatch, the devil he'd dealt with waiting beyond. The longer he lingered, the more apt Lux would be to increase the forfeit. No doubt there *would* be a forfeit. The white jumpsuit Eliot wore was flowy in places, but nowhere near baggy enough to hide a book the size of the *Rubaiyat*.

He was so, so hashed. "This is the first time I want you to have something up your sleeve, and you've got no sleeves."

Eliot laughed—she would be the type of person who reveled in gallows humor—and waved her very bare arm at the door. "Shall we?"

22.

THROUGH LIGHTS
AND TIME

Replacing the fuel rod was a task for hazard suits with steady hands. Priya managed it well enough, even though her insides matched the cyber-metal songs she was listening to. Clanging chaos *CRASH*. The playlist—dubbed "Unintelligible Screaming" by Imogen—was usually reserved for workouts, so it was fitting that she felt both the adrenaline and the drain of two dozen crunches.

This stress was beyond the power of tea, and music only agitated it. Loss breathed down her neck. Was *this* why Far was moving, always moving? Priya knew his mother's disappearance haunted him, but only now did she connect his forward motion with grief. Stay a step ahead, always, lest it catch up. Waiting for a distress signal to punch across her interface was the last thing Priya wanted to do. (As if she'd ditch anyway: Love was *all* and home was *here*.) She paced from one end of the infirmary to the other, trying to outrace the tightness in her throat.

"Hiya!" A wave—Imogen trying to steal Priya's attention through her headphones. "Need some company?"

Priya pulled back her BeatBix and put on a smile that made her lips feel wobbly. "Sure."

The other girl flopped onto the workstation stool: fresh flower hair, a sigh that reckoned with savannah rains. "He's going to be okay, you know. Sure, Lux is scary enough to make a shark shazm itself, but Farway's wiggled out of worse scrapes. I mean, just take a look at the wall o' chalky wonders out there. As much as I tease him, he's got plenty to brag about."

"This is different." Far's talent was never in question. "This is...Eliot."

"Eliot's not all bad," Imogen offered. "In fact, I'm not sure she's *any* bad. She's just really lonely. Can't you hear it, beneath her words? Every time we talk, it aches...how sad she is."

There was something, now that Imogen mentioned it, now that Priya thought to listen. Some fragile desperation she couldn't quite cling to, lengthening, thin, thin as the echoes of the *Titanic*'s phantom orchestra, threatening to make wraiths of them all. Who was this census-ghost of a girl? Why was she trying to take everything from them?

If anyone had pulled answers out of Eliot, it was Imogen. The Historian could talk a fish into walking. "What kinds of things did you two chat about?"

"Normal people stuff. Eyebrows. Clothes. Cursing. Boys.

She thinks I should talk to *you-know-who*, too. I'm afraid I might have taken the advice to heart."

"Wait, what? I've only been telling you to do that for..." Priya counted up their time as a crew in her head. "Eleven and a half months. What happened?"

"I'm not exactly sure." Here Imogen launched into a familiar monologue. One Priya had heard dozens, if not scores, of times: all the feels. This was a bonus edition, complete with angst, amnesia, and alcohol. *I drank, we danced, what then???* Told at a whisper so "you-know-who" wouldn't hear. Not that he would— Gram was entirely in his *Tetris* game, tongue edging his lips as he mashed buttons. Why was it so easy for guys to get lost in screens?

"I take it that's why you're in here and not the console room?" Priya asked, once the story reached its inconclusive conclusion.

"No comment."

"Oh, Im. You have nothing to be scared of—"

"Easy for you to say. You and Far just *happened*."

"Not exactly."

Just happening had happened over months. It was song recommendations and history lessons and late-night interface messages that felt around feelings: HOW'D YOUR EXAM SIM GO? WHAT WAS THE NAME OF THAT TROPICAL HOUSE BAND? TOP TEN FAVOR-ITE DATASTREAMS, AND GO! It was Priya's heart sparking each time she saw that tell-the-world-I'm-here smile across the examination room. It was that very same grin glowing a thousand watts brighter when she crossed the threshold. It was Far on the night of his failure, tugging the edges of his flowered waistcoat, hope on his face where there should have been heartbreak, saying, *I think we both know that we... Well, what I'm trying to say is, I've been offered a job, one I can't do alone, and I can't think of anyone else I'd rather have with me.*

Of course, Imogen had met Priya in this very docking bay on the eve of the *Invictus*'s debut heist, so she hadn't seen any of that. Her perspective began when Far took the entire crew to twenty-first-century India on Priya's behalf—a first vacation that turned into a not-so-thinly-veiled first date.

They'd landed in the city of Varanasi amid Dev Deepawali, a festival of lights of the gods, when the night dripped with thousands of candles and the lush, golden promise of things to come. Fireworks splashed across the sky, birthed again in the reflection of the Ganges River, where the gods were believed to bathe. A brush of the hand led to interlocked fingers as Priya and Far walked through the festivities—marveling at the ghats lined with tiny earthen lamps, steps of flames descending to the water's edge. She knew then she could keep wandering with him: through lights and time and whatever else came their way.

"Everything looks easier from the outside in. I liked Far for a long time, but when he asked me to join the *Invictus*, I almost told him no." It was hard to imagine now: a single-time existence, soundtrack provided by fake BeatBix. "Doing what we do, it puts a lot in peril."

Imogen nodded. She had her own parents, her own cover job at the boutique. She, too, faced jail time if they were caught by the Corps. "So why'd you say yes?"

Cyber-metal shook Priya's headphones. She gripped each

earpiece; the voice through them was more scream than song, licking her fingertips. "The *no* would've haunted me. Far and I had talked so much about wanderlust, places I wanted to go, times he wanted to see, and there he was, offering all of it. Remaining in Central suddenly felt like half of a life.

"Risk nothing and you'll stay where you are," she told Imogen and reminded herself. Her eyes landed on the dead-screen diagnostics machine, Ganesh's likeness beside it: There were answers out there. Priya just had to trust it wasn't too late to find them.

She exchanged her real BeatBix for the poseur pair and grabbed her purse.

"What, what are you doing?" Imogen blinked. "Far said—"

"Let's both make a deal to be brave. Far's coming back." And Eliot with him, presumably. If Priya was going to purchase the equipment they needed to scan the Ancestral Archives without raising suspicion, she had to do it now. "He's coming back, and I have an errand to run before he does."

❖ ❖ ❖

The bazaar of Zone 4 was an organizer's nightmare, a bargain hunter's dream. It was the size of a small town, made up of corridors so winding they required interface GPS to navigate, though many window-shoppers chose to get lost in the market's charm. There was more than a whiff of the Old World about it. Estate salvagers sold whatever they could: pages torn from magazines (back when magazines *had* pages to tear), keys to doors long rotted, thumbdrives no modern machine could read.

Priya's mother came here every week to sift through these offerings. Her eye for value and relentless bargaining kept her own Zone 2 store well stocked. Priya had spent many afternoons listening to her haggle over stained glass windows and teak furniture. Whether through DNA or osmosis, she, too, had acquired the skill; it would serve her well today.

She walked with throngs of shoppers into the digital district. There were several shops with the tech she needed, touting their wares with loud lights and louder hawkers. Priya perused ten of them before she ventured to make her first bid.

"Five thousand," she told the shopkeeper. Even the low number was high; operating systems with enough bulk to run something as comprehensive as the Ancestral Archives were stupid expensive. Add the price of software on top of that and it could easily cost every credit on Priya's palmdrive.

The vendor wrinkled his nose, replied with a line he'd probably recited twenty times that day: "Bah! Are you trying to rob me? This is a top-of-the-line diagnostics machine. Twenty thousand. No budging."

"Eh." Priya shrugged, trying to keep her heart off her grease-spotted sleeve. This part—feigning disinterest—was always hardest for her. "Six thousand, maybe. I'm sure I can get a better price next door."

Again the shopkeeper balked. "Eighteen."

So the numbers went—high, low, to and fro—accompanied by stubborn grunts and shaking heads. Priya walked off at one point, only to have the vendor wave her down and cut his quote another twenty percent. From there she wiggled him down to eight thousand, Ancestral Archives software included. A decent enough price, though she still winced when the credits were transferred.

The package fit in her purse, but only if her knockoff Beat-Bix took their rightful place over her ears. Priya wore them through the crowd as she wove back toward the hoverbus stop. Tight hips, bags jostling, adverts splashing her interface, dash, dash, hundreds of strange faces, and then—

A familiar one.

Roshani Parekh stood with her back to the street, examining a vase. Priya stopped, her thoughts spinning through the calendar—of course, it was Sunday. Shopping day. Her mother had been discussing it at dinner last night, several days ago, before the *Titanic* and Vegas and Eliot. She'd even invited Priya along....

Priya stood, watching her mother watch the vase, hating this distance. She wanted to tap her mom on the shoulder. She wanted to brew her a batch of chai with sunshine-fed spices and sit at the kitchen table, chatting the way they once did. She wanted to describe the treasures she'd seen, the places she'd walked, the boy she loved. Far, especially. She'd wanted to bring him to Saturday dinners too many times to count, but it was unwise. Though he also had a cover job—same as Gram's, employed by one of Lux's many non-illegal companies as independent contractors—how could they cover a one-year relationship?

She wanted, she wanted, yet she had to keep moving. Priya's mother thought she was working a Medic shift today, and if she turned to find her daughter with an eight-thousand-credit diagnostics machine in her bag, there would be questions.

Priya rallied her tangled-garden heart and kept walking.

23.

MAGIC *E VINO*

As the crow flew, Lux's villa was a good ten kilometers away from the TM warehouse. This distance was best conquered by underground magcart, which could make the journey in under two minutes and often did, zipping past the catacombs of Old Rome and the skyscraper pilings of Zone 2. Safety lights flickered every half kilometer, the sole sign of speed. Far counted them through his sunglasses to keep insanity at bay. The tactic only half worked.

The magcart exited into Lux's wine cellar, where bottles of the mogul's favorite port were stacked by the score. Far ran a finger along their necks as he passed, the way he did every visit, carving a line through velvet dust. The walks he'd made before were still there, in varying states of waning. Dustfall come again.

He left his mark—bold and unbroken—all the way to the stairs, wiped off the grime on his shirt, and headed up. Eliot followed, a specter he couldn't shake.

Lux's villa was the kind of place only reckless money could afford. It had the skeleton of a grand house, though many of its original amenities had been altered to accommodate state-of-the-art everything: auto-dimming windows, hologram platforms, a hovercraft landing pad. Even though there were pollution filters around the windows, the smell of city emissions was unmistakable: *home, hazy home*. Today Far's lungs refused it, as if his organs knew the end was nigh and decided to get a head start. Respiratory shutdown. His heart threatened to do the same when they entered the mansion's main room. Lux sat where he always did—in a high-backed leather chair facing the vista wall. His was an opportunistic view of the skyline, the New Forum's gold gleaming through his eyes like some strange pupil.

"Run into trouble, Captain McCarthy?"

That's one *name for her.* "Not trouble, exactly..."

"Lux." Nothing about the figure in the chair seemed to intimidate Eliot. Far wasn't sure if it was sheer bravery or a not-so-blissful ignorance. "Can I call you Lux?"

Hades's clangers in a hashing bluebox. Far's too-short life flashed before his eyes, best-of reel bouncing off his sunglasses. Piggyback rides with Burg. A sweltering summer day visit to the Colosseum with his mother. His first kiss with Priya, after their second heist, his back to the old Forum stones; testosterone swam through his veins, and her lips tasted like moon rays made human: silver light secrets.

"Take those things off." Lux waved the aviators away. "I like to see eye-to-eye."

Daylight was murder on the retinas, but Far did as instructed.

"Who is this? I do not like surprises, Captain McCarthy." The words held poison, the slow kind that killed you as soon as you thought you might be fine. "Nor do I like the noticeable *lack* of a package in your hands."

"Let's not get ahead of ourselves." Eliot stepped forward, so that Lux had no choice but to see her. "My name's Eliot. I'm the newest member of the *Invictus*'s crew."

"You're nothing until you sign my contract," Lux said, though his voice wasn't nearly as strychnic as before. "Have we met? You look familiar...."

"I have one of those faces," Eliot told him. "It makes me very effective at what I do."

"What *do* you do?" the black marketer asked.

"I'm a Renaissance woman. Dabbling here, meddling there. Recording, observing, snatching." She held her palms aloft, wiggled her fingers. "Captain McCarthy is good at what he does, but I'll make the team even better. You get one shot at each disaster because of timeline crossings, right? With twice the hands, you get twice the loot."

"A compelling argument. Or it would be, if you had any loot to deliver." Lux stood. "Where's the *Rubaiyat*?"

Far's tongue stuck to the roof of his mouth. He looked at Eliot, who was so hashing bright—white suit in sunlight—he had to shut his eyes.

More fragments: Imogen's smile when she first held the fluffball that would become Saffron. That time he played a game of chess with Gram and won—though there was a 99.9 percent possibility the Engineer had conceded the game to make

207

Far feel better. Silver letters—*I-N-V-I-C-T-U-S*—engraved onto the hullplate, shimmering along with the realization that the ship was *his*, ready to go to anytime. Crux, what a moment. He could live in it forever. He could die in it now.

Might as well get the unpleasant parts over with. "I—"

Eliot cut in. "*We* have delivered it as promised."

Far's eyes opened, unable to believe what they were seeing. An oak case. *The* oak case. Same size, same lock, perfectly polished. Eliot held the item in both hands, offering it to Lux.

When Far was younger, he used to beg his mother to stop and watch the street performers in Zone 1's piazzas. If you deposited a few credits into a living statue's outstretched palm-drive, it moved: a sweeping bow, a wink. Do the same for a musician and they'd strum any song you wanted. There was an old man with an even older word processor who sat by the *Fontana dei Quattro Fiumi* and wrote custom poems for wooing lovers-to-be. Far's favorite performers were the magicians. They could make almost anything vanish—flowers, scarves, doves, playing cards—and reappear in the strangest places. As a child he'd been awed, filled with the wondrous sense that the world really was a place of magic.

All of this washed over Far once more as he stared at the oak case. How was this possible? Lux accepted the item without comment. The book's cover sprayed shine across the room when he opened it, glitter glancing off the villa walls. Imogen might've *ooooooh*ed and called them fairy lights; there was still enough magic in Far's thoughts to agree with her.

Three peacocks. Gold-lined pages. Jewels. All of it seemed

to be there. Lux wasn't a fan of *seems*, though. His inspection was thorough—involving tweezers and gloves and a magnifying glass that made his nose look comically large from the other side. Far kept waiting for him to cry foul, but the book was undeniably *the book*.

Eliot had been telling the truth. She hovered by Lux's shoulder, sending Far a smirk and wink in turn. He was too verklempt to gesture back. It occurred to him that he should be angry, nay, raging, but relief was the emotion of the hour. How couldn't it be? Priya, Gram, and Imogen were safe. The *Invictus* remained his. Nothing was ending today.

Lux set down the magnifying glass; his scrutiny refocused on Eliot. "Where did this come from?"

"The *Titanic*'s cargo hold. London's Sangorski and Sutcliffe bookbinders before that."

"Not historically," he snapped at her answer. "Presently. There was nothing on your person when you walked in this room. How is it you pulled something out of thin air?"

"I'm a smuggler," Eliot said. "I smuggle things. The *how* would take all the fun out of it. My secrets make me the best in the trade, and if that doesn't suit your operation, I'll take my services elsewhere."

"Elsewhere?" Lux was caught off guard. His pause teetered. "I *am* the trade."

"If that's what helps you sleep at night," Eliot said, dismissive. "The world is a large place and time is even larger. The question is, do you want my skills working in your favor? Or beyond it?"

It made Far feel slightly justified, that he wasn't the only one Eliot threw for a loop. That she could make Lux Julio—a man whose very presence invoked a baseline of terror in his subordinates—go splotchy at the neck.

"What might such a favorable alliance look like? I'm assuming you have a proposal."

"I do, in fact." Eliot nodded. "I have a buyer interested in several artifacts from the Library of Alexandria that were destroyed in the siege of 48 BC. I'd take the job as a freelancer, but they want more scrolls than I can recover during the burn window solo. With Captain McCarthy's assistance, I can get everything I need and more besides."

"The cut?"

"Fifty-fifty. You. Me."

"Those aren't my usual terms."

"It's that or nothing," Eliot told him. "The *Invictus*'s crew might be the best, but they certainly aren't the only Academy graduates chomping at the bit for a spin through history. Consider my portion a finder's fee."

The silence that followed made the room feel very fragile. Floor tiles, vases, the glass of half-drunk wine by Lux's armchair—all of it quivered in anticipation of an answer. Far found himself shaking, too, a shiver that couldn't be seen, only felt, taking root beneath his toenails.

"Sixty-forty. Me. You. As long as you sign my contract."

"Fifty-five–forty-five," she shot back. "I sign nothing. My clients remain anonymous. This is the best you're going to get."

The mogul's stare could break glass. Eliot's could crack

worlds. Far stood off to the side, watching what passed between them. All the fear and frustration this girl had stoked inside him had transformed into something else entirely. Admiration? Awe?

"Captain McCarthy," Lux addressed him without looking. "What say you?"

"Two pairs of hands *would* snatch up more than one." This conversation was a minefield—pocked with Lux's anger and Eliot's endgame. Far navigated his response with tiptoe words. "Eliot seems to know her way around history, and the *Invictus* is always game for a good disaster. From what I've heard about Alexandria—the salvage we get there could be invaluable."

"Invaluable. Yes..." Greed dripped down Lux's lips. "Though I don't like entering into agreements without a form of insurance."

"You have my image on your security feeds. That's enough collateral to make anyone amenable, wouldn't you say?" More magic: Eliot's hand emerged from behind her, clutching a bottle of port. Its scripted label looked old but unaged. 1906. Fresh as yesterday. "Also, I picked this up from the *Titanic*'s first-class dining saloon, as a gesture of my goodwill."

Lux accepted the bottle, examining it like a second relic: blood-dark contents, cork made of actual cork wood, glass the color of deep-sea sorrow wherever daylight struck. "From the *Titanic*'s menu? Truly?"

"Vintage *and* morose," Eliot assured him.

"Extraordinary." The mogul turned back to the vista wall, where the city hummed through the afternoon's golden haze.

"Your goodwill has been noted. We have ourselves an agreement: fifty-five percent to me. The *Invictus*'s cut will come out of that."

Far glanced behind Eliot to get a glimpse of the port's origins, but there was nothing to see. Strap-backed jumpsuit, crossed hands. Once more she'd put Far to shame—he'd thought himself a master negotiator and here she was a sorceress, her sleight of hand so distracting that Lux hadn't even done a background check. *Shazm*. If Far had known a vintage bottle was all it took to transform the black marketer from a *kill you in your sleep* control freak to a *pat you on the back* boss, he would've become a hashing sommelier ages ago.

"We'll get started with mission prep," Far said, fighting back the urge to upchuck his hangover nerves into the nearby potted bougainvillea. Lux's goodwill probably wouldn't extend to vomit on his houseplants.

The mogul ignored him. His stare slid from the wine label to Eliot. "Excellent haul. I'll inform Wagner about the updates to our business agreement and have the payments processed accordingly."

There it was, said and done. Eliot had become a part of the crew. Far was still alive, thank Crux, but now he'd have to walk back through the cellar and draw his line into a life he had no agency over. One that spun at *her* whim, leaving him fearful, always fearful.

What kind of future was that?

24.

AN AGREEMENT

ELIOT'S STEPS FELT KILOS LIGHTER WHEN she climbed back in
the magcart. The meeting had gone as well as possible. Subject
Seven hadn't thrown any tantrums—a good thing, too, since it
would have ended badly for him. He'd just stood there glower-
ing as the drama unfolded. Oh, and what drama! Men like Lux
were easy to bait; she'd given him everything he wanted—the
Rubaiyat, some wine, the promise of more—all while upend-
ing his authority through technological trickery. Eliot acted on
every cue, tossing breadcrumbs to get the scene to end the way
she wanted.

READINGS ARE 57% COMPLETE. REMEMBER CHARLES.

So far she was on course.

Seven reclaimed his magcart seat. His aviators were back
on, making him look far more suave than he likely felt after
so many vodka shots and a face-off with Lux. "Some warning wouldn't have gone amiss, you know. Maybe a 'Hey, Far, I

actually *do* have the *Rubaiyat* and I'm not going to let Lux rip out your entrails and roast them for breakfast.'"

"Lux is too refined for that." Eliot clipped her safety belts into place. "I imagine he only eats eggs Benedict with a silver spoon."

The boy smiled. Eliot could tell he was trying not to—the fight of it all wrinkled his cheek. "Fine. My guts would be hors d'oeuvres, then, right before he'd drink my blood as an aperitif. Why didn't you just tell me you could magic things into existence? It would've saved me a hundred gruesomely imagined deaths."

"Would you have believed me if I had?" Eliot traced the bracelet-that-was-not-a-bracelet on her wrist—holding everything, the least of her secrets.

"I don't know!" Seven's expression snapped with his voice. "Maybe if you'd slice the shazm with all this cloak-and-dagger business and talk to me, we'd get somewhere. Hades, I'm not asking for a bottle of wine, just some goodwill explanations!"

Subjects like Seven were harder to wrangle once they caught the scent of the truth. Eliot would need to feed him some, if they were to keep moving forward. "I don't travel as light as I look. I have a—well, it's kind of like an invisible, bottomless bag."

Far's brows twitched over his glasses. "Got any mints in there?"

"No." Though there were plenty of other items: wigs, eyebrow pen, outfits for a vast array of times and occasions, extra storage for the memories she kept losing, a first aid kit, her laser knife, her gun. Thinking about the last item always made her stomach clench. "I keep it to the essentials."

Seven exhaled, and Eliot realized that mints actually *were* essentials. His was a special kind of halitosis. Hangover, stress, and morning breath all in one. "Anything else you feel like sharing? Like why we're really going to Alexandria? Or why I keep forgetting what happened on the *Titanic*?"

"You remember that?" Eliot figured he'd had enough Belvedere in his bloodstream to forget what he'd forgotten. She hadn't touched a drop of alcohol and even she needed Vera's prodding to gather what was being lost.

"Hard not to. Usually you're so composed, and the look on your face..." Far paused. A frown slashed his lips. "Ever seen your life flash in front of your eyes?"

Eliot stared at the boy on the other side of the magcart. Her reflection stared back through the silver of his glasses, smaller than life, hardly recognizable with a fresh wig and What Abyss Waits shaded eyebrows. What could she say that was true? What could she tell him that he would believe? Nothing Agent Ackerman would clear, that's for sure.

Far went on. "I used to think it was a line poets pulled out of their tails when they couldn't come up with something better. But this job gets dangerous: bullets, flames, the works. Once I started getting shot at on the regular, I realized there was truth in the saying. When you start facing death, all you can see is life. That was the feeling I just had in Lux's villa. That"—he pointed at her—"was the feeling on your face last night. When you appeared on the *Invictus*, I thought maybe you were running some sort of con. But that wobbly landing, the memory gaps, your fear...those things add up to something bigger."

Their magcart sped along. Earth's darkness cut through its windows again and again as they passed the tunnel's lights. Bright, shadow, bright, shadow, life, death. The Eliot trapped inside the aviators flickered and squirmed.

"When you showed up on the *Invictus*, you claimed you wanted a fresh start, which makes me think you're running from something," Far said. "You want to work with a crew? Well, here's your chance. Take your thumb off my operation, come clean about what's going on. Gram, Priya, Imogen, and I...we can help you."

Help? Had any of the other subjects been so generous? This olive branch was a stretch for him, Eliot knew. What a shame she had to spit on it.

"What's happening—you're right. It's big and very, very complicated. I can't fill you in on the details." There were too many holes and forgettings—all following her—and talented though this crew might be, they couldn't stop what was coming. "I didn't tell you about my storage situation because I wanted to demonstrate that I'm good on my word. I told you I'd deliver the *Rubaiyat* to Lux and I did. Trust is falling. Now you know I'll catch you."

"Trust isn't a plunge off a cliff," Seven countered. "It's something you build."

"Then consider this the first brick."

"No." His voice edged to a shout. "Trust is a two-way street, Eliot Antoinette. Give and take. All you've done, from Versailles to Vegas, is the latter."

Eliot couldn't stand her own stare anymore. Her gaze cut to

the window. "When's the soonest the crew can get prepped to depart for Alexandria?"

"So that's how it is? You're gonna keep dragging me and mine through the dark? Use Lux to make us your compliant puppet ship?"

"I need a timetable, *Captain*."

She watched the boy's window face—just as transparent as hers. Bright, shadow, still, motion, bright, shadow, spite, surrender. "Depends on the mission. Imogen likes to get the lay of the land before we go tumbling into a new era. That means wardrobe, proper translation equipment, building schematics, a timeline down to the second, a backup wardrobe. All that can take from twenty-four hours to a week."

"She's a good Historian. Thorough." Perhaps too thorough. They didn't have a week to spare. Even twenty-four hours was a stretch, though it was impossible to establish parameters within the Fade's whim. "Could she get it done in twelve?"

"Assuming this is *just* a snatch-and-grab?" Seven prefaced. "Yeah. Imogen might not think she can do it, but she can. It wasn't just nepotism that got her a spot on the *Invictus*."

No, Eliot thought. *It was trust.* Thicker than blood, made of years and tears and toil. Seven was right. The feeling—though *was* it a feeling? It seemed to her more of a mandate—had to be built. But no matter how firm your bricks, no matter how high your wall, there was always a part of the act that became a plunge, because though your trust might be steady, the world never was.

Trust is built. Trust is falling.

Give and take, take, take.

Who would catch her?

Ache curled over Eliot's left lung as the magcart slowed into the light. They were back dockside, where the *Invictus*'s hull shimmered like a waterfall's fringe. Gram waved through the vistaport, calling behind his shoulder to Imogen. Home filled Far's sunglasses as he lifted a hand and waved back.

No matter how long Eliot stared, all she saw was a ship.

25.

CLICKS AND SWIRLS

INVICTUS SHIP'S LOG—ENTRY 4

CURRENT DATE: AUGUST 22, 2371

CURRENT LOCATION: CENTRAL. HEART OF THE WORLD, BOTH ANCIENT AND NEW.

OBJECT TO ACQUIRE: CLOTHES. LOTS OF THEM.

IMOGEN'S HAIR COLOR: CELESTIAL NEBULA 'DO

GRAM'S *TETRIS* SCORE: 380,000

CURRENT SONG ON PRIYA'S SHIPWIDE PLAYLIST: "JAI HO" BY A. R. RAHMAN

```
FARWAY'S EGO: ADRIFT. NOT UNLIKE A TOY ROBO-BOAT
ABANDONED IN THE FONTANA DI TREVI.


ELIOT: ISN'T HALF BAD. MAGICIAN STATUS VERIFIED
BY FARWAY. DRAWS KILLER EYEBROWS. POSSESSES
INVISIBLE BAG? OTHER DETAILS TBD.
```

IMOGEN HAD TWELVE HOURS TO INGEST an entire civilization's worth of knowledge. No biggie.

[Insert maniacal laughter/endless weeping here.]

The feat would've been easier if it had involved a more recent century, where documentation abounded. The 1990s with its addictive sitcoms and newspapers. The 2170s with its virtual reality chambers and pictogram feeds. But 48 BC had little to offer when it came to primary source material. Sure, Julius Caesar wrote a firsthand account of the fires he set to his enemy's ships in Alexandria's harbor, but even that was vague, stopping at the very flammable docks before the library's destruction could be pinned on him. It was a frustrating endeavor—depending on the fallible accounts of victors to create a portrait of past events. Imogen couldn't imagine how historians such as her great-great-grandfather Bertram managed it.

Datastreams held more answers. There were none from their target landing year, but a Recorder had taken a long wander through the library in 52 BC. Imogen watched the footage in 8^x to get a sense of the layout. The place was large, with three stories of rooms for every activity: reading, greeting, lecturing, even eating. There were windows galore, wide open to views of gardens and the harbor, complete with its iconic lighthouse. For the library's scholars, this meant ample daylight to read by. For Farway and Eliot, this meant escape routes. Imogen took note of each one, just in case. With its walls and walls of diamond-shaped shelves stuffed with papyrus scrolls, the place looked awfully combustible.

It was fire they were facing; she was certain. Though there were no expeditions present at the event, later Recorders had managed to glean enough oral history to fill in the gaps. December 16, 48 BC. Alexandria, Egypt: a city under siege. Caesar. A battle with boats. Lots o' flames. The Roman ruler hadn't destroyed *all* of the library, just made an ash pile out of hundreds of thousands of its irreplaceable books.

Oops.

If she were Caesar, she'd probably omit that not-so-tiny detail, too.

It never ceased to amaze Imogen how much she could get done alongside a ticking clock. In the span of hours she had a date. She had a (very loose) time frame. She'd set the translation tech to a combination of Greek, Coptic, and Latin.

Now all she needed were clothes.

This particular errand was tight. Imogen had gotten so caught up in datastreams and note-taking that she'd almost forgotten the wardrobe component. Most of the boutiques, including her not-really-former place of employment, locked their doors at sunset, and Imogen had no desire to break into the store, so she found herself jogging along Zone 2's ground level, racing the Flaming Hour. Walkways buzzed with the onset of dusk. Even on Sunday it was a time for rushing, when government officials broke from their work stupor to put sustenance in their bodies. Vendor tents popped up at the base of each skyscraper, numerous as spring weeds, selling everything from meal blocks to stimulant patches to obscenely priced pizza with garlic and greenhouse tomatoes—and CHEESE. Imogen's stomach growled at her to stop, but her watch vetoed the motion.

"Make way!" She mucked through the masses. Elbows, bags of roasted nuts, shoulders, holo-paper zines, toes she could not avoid stomping on. "Apologies. Condolences. Make way! Make way!"

Gram moved in a silent path behind her. He was much better at navigating a crowd—those with Recorder training always were—probably imagining it as one big *Tetris* game. Imogen would've let him lead, but she had a better idea of where they were going. It was a path she'd walked most mornings through periwinkle haze, past the Department of Agriculture, with its fifty-story-high wall gardens, through the financial district—Imogen had often bought her morning stimulant patches from the vendors here, since they were twice as strong to keep the bankers goinggoinggoing—along a man-made canal and into the Palisades, a residential district where new houses put on their best old-money faces. Many of the senators had "cityhouses" here, and Imogen often wondered how many of the globe's laws were decided behind their lion-knocker doors.

The boutique—Before & Beyond—sat at the edge of this

neighborhood. Its ground-level walls were made of holo-glass: programmable to a variety of vistas. Right now they mimicked a jazz club from the 1930s, which meant it was Bel's shift. The shopkeeper's expression flickered when the door opened—veiled annoyance, Imogen knew. She felt it, too, when customers sauntered in five till close. Once he spotted *the hair*, his face went just as bright. He set down the poodle skirt he was clipping to a hanger.

"Imogen! Dearest! Come to check your schedule? You could've just comm-ed."

Schedule? Oh right. Technically she still worked here, though it'd been ages since her last shift: a few days in Central time, weeks for Imogen. As much as she wanted to hand in her notice, having access to the store's closet was worth staying on its payroll.

"Hi, Bel! I—we were hoping to get into the closet before you left."

"We?" The man's face lit even more as he looked over Imogen's shoulder, where Gram stood, studying an early-twenty-third-century mirror gown. "Oh! Who is this?"

"My..." *Oh Crux*—she couldn't say coworker. *Bel* was her coworker.

"Your...?" Bel prodded.

Bluebox blunders on a blathering whale's tail! She couldn't even say his *name* now because then the pairing would be *My Gram* and her pause had gone on a beat too long. Welcome to the pinkest skin that had ever graced her cheeks.

"Friend," Imogen finished, flustered. "Gram's my friend."

223

At least she couldn't see Gram's fallout face, mercifully behind her. She'd already spent most of the day analyzing his expressions, trying to scrape whole memories from Vegas. They'd danced together. His smile had made Imogen feel floaty. After that the night went splintery. Lights. Blur. Bodies. Booze.

Curse Belvedere and its ability to make her talk!

Something important had happened during those lost moments...Imogen was sure of it. A raw, fundamental thing had shifted; there'd been such a *tension* between them all day. Stumbly words, caught glances, cleared throats, all while her heart pitter-patter wilted. It was every awkwardness she'd feared, plus some.

Gram was far from awkward now. His levitating grin returned as he introduced himself to the shopkeeper. "Gram Wright."

"A pleasure. Bel Fisher." Bel shook the Engineer's outstretched hand; his eyebrows waggled at Imogen in a terribly unsubtle fashion.

"Can we get in the closet?" she croaked. "Please?"

"Sure, sure. As long as you make it snappy. I'm meeting Jansen for dinner. Well, dinner for me, breakfast for him, seeing as he works nights and all. I've told you about Jansen, right? Redhead. Dreamy. Does security for the Corps. It was Mrs. Chun who introduced us—"

"We're on a bit of a time crunch as well," Gram prodded.

"Indeed?" Bel's gaze bounced between the pair. "What's the occasion? Dinner? Dancing? Dalliances?"

Imogen wanted to crawl under the mink coats and hibernate

for the rest of her life, but the shopkeeper was already heading off to the back room to unlock the closet entrance. "We're going to a toga party," she said.

"How retro! There are plenty to choose from down there. Virilis, candida, trabea, praetexta. We might even have a few picta, too." Bel waved at the wrought-iron stairs. "You know your way around. Just bring up what you need and I'll run it through the system."

Imogen muttered her thanks before rushing down the staircase. Gram's steps echoed behind her, accented by the fact that they were alone.

What had she said in Vegas?

What should she say now? *Talk, talk, tell him* was the only thing on her mind, thanks to Eliot, who hadn't been as helpful at salvaging the dark hours as Imogen hoped. Instead of doing reconnaissance, the girl had suggested that Gram make the wardrobe run in Farway's place.

Now they were here and Imogen had no words.

Gram didn't, either, but his speechlessness was caused by the view. What the employees of Before & Beyond called a closet was more along the lines of a warehouse—millennia's worth of styles on hundreds of racks. Some eras were better represented than others. The 1920s had an entire row dedicated to beaded gowns, while the 1120s consisted of a few flared-sleeved tunics, probably on order for a Recorder expedition.

"Some closet." Gram whistled. "Got any string we could tie to the bottom of the stairs to find our way back?"

He was making jokes. That had to be good, right? Should

she joke back? Should she smile? Would that scare him off? Why was her brain rushing along at a thousand kilometers an hour while she stood there paralyzed?

Pull it together, McCarthy.

"No need." Imogen knew this place backward and forward. "The BC section is this way."

"So this is where you come to get outfits. I always wondered."

"The Corps uses it, too. All of this stuff is accurate, sometimes painfully so." Imogen paused to take a whalebone corset from the eighteenth-century rack. "These reshaped women's rib cages, you know."

"That's"—Gram's eyes went wide, and Imogen realized exactly just *what* she was holding—"awful."

"Right?" NOTE TO SELF: AVOID SHOWING OFF LADIES' UNDER-WEAR TO CRUSH. INCITES DEER-IN-HEADLIGHTS LOOK. She returned the corset to its rack and kept walking toward the BC section. It was smaller than the closet's AD portion, if only because the citizens of the ancient world had less to work with. Plant dyes, flax fiber, and sheep's wool. Hades, some of the Greeks preferred no clothes at all!

Even still, there was plenty to choose from. Alexandria was a port city founded by the Greeks in Egypt, which meant that Farway and Eliot could get away with numerous styles. Imogen's magpie nature gravitated toward traditional Egyptian garb—jewels, kohl, gold—but such shininess would draw too much attention. Best to go with something simple.

"A toga virilis or a chiton?" She took one of each from the racks. "That's the question."

Gram squinted at both linen garments. "Is there a difference?"

"Roman or Greek. There'll be some Romans about, especially since they'll be in Caesar's section of the city. Farway is fluent in Latin, so it'd be safer to go Roman if anything happened to his translation tech."

"You did tell Bel we were getting togas," Gram pointed out.

Imogen chose a toga virilis for Farway and an unadorned stola for Eliot. Below the rack was a row of leather shoes. They weren't as finely crafted as hers—straight from the source—but one would be hard-pressed to tell the difference between the reproduction and the original.

CLOTHES: CHECK

SHOES: CHECK

DIGNITY: MOSTLY INTACT, NO THANKS TO BEL. AS LONG AS YOU GET OUT OF HERE WITHOUT SAYING SOMETHING IRRETRIEVABLY STUPID.

Gram, however, seemed in no rush to leave. He'd taken a bright purple toga picta off the rack. "These must have been comfortable."

"Hashing comfortable. Like walking around in a cloud all day." Imogen nodded to the golden embroidery on the outfit's edges. "Showy, too. It's what generals used for their victory parades."

"You know so much." Gram looked out over the warehouse:

Regency gowns and neon jumpsuits, armor and tuxedos. "There's so much *to* know."

"Says the boy with two Academy tracks to his name."

"Never did make it to Historian." His smile went past wry into crescent-moon territory. "It's amazing, everything you do."

Imogen's insides were starting to go zero G again. She grabbed the rack next to her to keep from floating off, an impossibility that seemed very likely, because dimples! "Well, I mean, guiding a ship full of miscreants through time is pretty snazzy, too."

"That's just numbers." Gram shrugged.

"Just numbers! Ha! There's a reason I make you sort out multicentury exchange rates. 'Twere I an Engineer, we'd probably get stuck halfway between the Grid and the late Cretaceous Period, watching T. rexes tromp about through the vistaport."

The Engineer's grin grew, lifting Imogen another few centimeters. "Getting stuck like that isn't possible."

"Exactly." She smiled back. "I'm that bad at math. Being a Historian is just teaching yourself to learn. It's about knowing the landscape to a T, but also being flexible for whatever curveballs the past tosses your way."

"I wish I could live in the tangled places so confidently."

Really? One of the things she loved about Gram was his neatness. There was always an order to the way he did things, a predictability that was more comfortable than boring. He was steady, stoic, smart. He was always there, in the chair across from hers—taking them beyond, bringing them home. He was perfectly him.

"Your brain works in clicks and mine in swirls," Imogen said. "The *Invictus* needs both."

"Clicks and swirls." The words had felt like mist from her lips; they solidified against Gram's when he repeated them. "I like that."

This exchange was going well. She hadn't said anything stupid. The awkwardness she'd feared between them all day was nowhere to be felt. There *was* a tension, but it was a good kind—less like scraping teeth, more of a whisper down her skin, shivering to the end of every capillary.

Priya and Eliot popped up on her shoulders, cartoon consciences. Instead of the normal angel-devil routine, both said the same thing: *Tell him.*

Imogen squeezed the Roman garments to her chest and wondered if she could. Was there enough courage clinging to her? Enough to say *I like you*, maybe, but could she survive the break if he didn't feel the same way? Could she walk back to the *Invictus* with him in one piece? Could she sit in the chair across from him every day after, feeling the jaggedness between them, a fresh wound every time?

She had to say something. This silence was getting ridiculous.

Her breath hitched. Her mouth opened.

Gram's did, too. "Look, Imogen. Last night—"

The darkness cut him short. Above them the warehouse lights died, then hummed slowly back to life. Bel's way of saying *Closing time! There are places to be and people to see!*

"We'll be up in a second!" she yelled at the stairwell, mind tumbling. *Look, Imogen* was a phrase ripe for disappointment; nothing good could follow it. She could still get out of here with her dignity intact, but she'd have to act fast. "It was great, wasn't it? Look, we need to jet. If I'm the reason Bel's late for a date, I'll never live it down. Do you want to pick up some pizza for the crew on the way back?"

Swirling, swirly, swirls. The lights hadn't recovered from the switch, the closet dim around them. Imogen's vision was broken down to outlines—linen rumpled in her arms, the sharp edges of racks. Though Gram stood close to her, most of his expression was lost. The only thing she could see for sure was that his smile was gone.

"Yeah, sure. Pizza sounds great."

He turned to leave. Imogen followed, wondering if she'd said something irretrievably stupid after all.

26.

TUMBLING INTO A
PAPYRUS TINDERBOX

THE *INVICTUS* WAS ALREADY IN FLIGHT, gliding over the Mediterranean with all the grace and shape of a moon-stung cloud. June 11, 2155 was a beautiful night—stars blanketing the black like a chorus—but none of the crew paused to savor it. Far and the others were eating pizza instead, nibbling through two large hot-boxes of Margherita pie, plus a pan of tiramisu. The dinner and adjacent planning session were a shipwide affair—even Bartleby was there, dressed in a toga. The stola meant for Eliot hung by Saffron's tail with the rest of the wardrobe, linen hem just long enough to graze Far's head every time he moved.

He fought the urge to swat at it.

Imogen stood by the mannequin's side, walking the crew through the finer points of their heist. It wasn't like his cousin to get stage fright—but her briefing came across shaky. Throat clearing, hair tucking, sentences riddled with *um*s.

"The Library of Alexandria was, um, the most significant collection of knowledge in the ancient world. Poetry, physics, philosophy, astronomy…This place had it all, until Caesar's conflagration situation. Eliot's, um, buyers have their credits set aside for two works in particular: the manuscripts of the Greek lyric poet Sappho and the history of the ancient world as recorded by Berossus. The exact locations of these scrolls are unknown, but, um, the librarians had an elaborate cataloging system. Sappho's writings are thought to be kept somewhere in the, um, northwest corner. The *Babylonaica* is on the other side of the building. We think."

"We think?" Grease leaked down Far's fingers with his first flashing bite. *Ow!* The hot-box had done its job too well. He felt mozzarella scald its way down his throat, sticking to the side of his chest. Some of the burn regurgitated with his words. "I'd like more than *thinking* before I go tumbling into a papyrus tinderbox."

"I'm doing the best I can," Imogen protested. "Considering."

"Of course you are." Priya nudged Far's rib cage as she said this.

It was hard not to be irritable—the relief of *not being dead* negated by the magcart ride. Eliot's caginess stung extra hard after his offer to help. He was a hero spurned. No, it felt worse than that. He'd become a bystander in someone else's story.

There was one bright spot to cling to: Priya's new diagnostics machine, currently cross-referencing Eliot's DNA with a world's worth of people. The process was—understandably—ponderous. Priya had spent most of her afternoon in the infirmary, installing the Ancestral Archives software out of Eliot's sight. In a few more hours they'd have a lead on the girl's identity. An ancestor, an origin year, something seizable.

"There's evidence to support the locations," his cousin went on. "Previous expeditions...and, um, Eliot's intelligence."

Far tried not to choke on the water he was sipping.

"My intel's solid," Eliot assured him. "I've been to the library before."

Imogen cleared her throat, schoolteacher style. "Things get rather, um, fuzzy when it comes to the timeline...."

Far chewed the rest of his slice and listened to the long list of everything they didn't know. The mission felt more slipshod than anything they'd ever tackled. Lux had never before sent them into such a vaguely documented event, nor had they ever had such a short prep time. Twelve scrambling hours. And for what? They were time travelers. Time was one thing they possessed in abundance.

Eliot remained zip-lipped on the reason for her rush order and, to tell the truth, Far wasn't sure more time would help. December 16, 48 BC, was one of history's grayer, unmapped areas. Imogen's homework would only take them so far. The rest was down to vigilance and improvisation. To get through this heist unscathed, they'd need all hands on deck.

"Gram, how do you feel about putting your Recorder skills to use?" Far glanced at the Engineer, who looked even more unsettled than Imogen: too tall for the couch, kneecaps tilted at awkward angles. "I'd like all eyes I can get on the ground."

"Sure thing, Far—"

Eliot broke in. "I don't think that's the best idea."

"Oh?" Far asked. "What happened to more hands, more loot? I thought you wanted as many scrolls as we could manage?"

"We'll need an Engineer on the *Invictus* in case..."

All eyes in the common area settled on Eliot, waiting for the rest of her sentence even as it slipped away. Her expression added to the room's uneasy air. It was not unlike the look he'd seen in Vegas: big and very, very complicated.

"In case?" Far prodded.

"There's a possibility that we'll need to make a quick exit," she admitted.

"What do you mean by that?" Gram sat up straighter, frowning. "Corps interference? Birthing a paradox? Timeline crossings?"

All good guesses, especially the last, considering that Eliot had been to the Library of Alexandria before, but Far had a suspicion he couldn't shake. "This has to do with the forgetting, doesn't it?"

The girl's eyes shivved him—filled with every sharpness and the *yes* her lips trapped.

"Forgetting?" Priya echoed. "What forgetting?"

"The *Titanic*—" Far stopped to feel the hole in his memory. It was larger now—swallowing not only first class but the whole hashing ship. He *knew* he'd been aboard the steam liner; the fact hung above him with a workman's shirt. "I can't remember being there."

The room grew quiet enough to hear red panda chirps— tackling shins in his dreams, most likely—as the crew sifted through their own memories. Gram's spine turned into a ramrod. Priya held her breath, while Imogen's shock was all exhale.

"Me neither." His cousin's voice became tiny. "I remember the prep, but the mission itself is gone."

"The numbers changed," Gram murmured, "then it goes blank."

Far looked at Priya. She shook her head: mustn't lose it, already lost.

His mind wasn't the only one crumbling.

"Mass memory loss? How's that possible?" Imogen asked Far. "How could we all forget the same moment?"

"You're asking the wrong person," he told her.

All eyes fell to Eliot—girl who'd sprung out of the forgetting. When during those black hours had she joined their crew? Had she taken the *Rubaiyat* and wiped their memories of it? Why did she look as if she'd been bled to a husk?

"Nepenthe," she answered, when it was clear she had to. "I dosed all of you to protect some sensitive personal information that slipped out during our first encounter. But that has nothing to do with the mission at hand. This city is under siege, which means things could go sour at any moment. We may need a quick evacuation, so it's best if Gram stays at his post. Far and I will take care of things on the ground."

Heads shifted back to Far. He knew them all so well—Imogen's green gaze. Gram's brown eyes. Priya's smoke-soft stare. He could feel the doubts squirming behind each, waiting for him to step up to Eliot's explanation with a challenging *what where when why exactly?* Useless queries. If this girl had ripped away their memories, she wouldn't hand them back on a silver platter. Besides, the details of the heist wouldn't sort themselves. The *Rubaiyat* might be safe in Lux's hands, but Far's remained tied. They had to retrieve these scrolls to keep the *Invictus* flying.

"Gram, you'll stay at your station," Far said. "No games this time. Sounds like we might need a swoop in. I want you to be extra vigilant."

The Engineer nodded.

Priya stood, walked to the infirmary, and shut the door. Were there answers behind it yet? Far needed them more than ever, so he waited an unsuspecting amount of time and followed. His girlfriend started when he entered, tossing a lab coat over the Ancestral Archives screen.

"Anything?"

Again, she shook her head. "Eliot's lying."

"That baseline's been established."

"No, you don't understand. Nepenthe is an incredibly potent drug. The human body can only handle enough to forget forty minutes. An hour *max*. According to the *Invictus*'s systems, your *Titanic* feed was live for over an hour and a half."

Priya paused, let her words sink in. "If Eliot dosed all of us with Nepenthe, as she claims, we should all be dead."

❖ ❖ ❖

December 16, 48 BC, was an excellent day, weather-wise. Cloudless skies, emboldened sun, low humidity. A breeze swayed through the palms, threading scents of sea brine and cinders through the *Invictus*'s open hatch. Far had known worse smells. Between a lack of consistent bathing and suboptimal sewage systems, history often wreaked havoc on the olfactory nerves.

"The fires have already started." Imogen stared in the direction of the harbor, where smoke twisted in mangled black pillars, wind stretching it thin. Haze crept across the horizon, clung to the silhouette of the ancient world's seventh wonder: the Lighthouse of Alexandria. Far could see Poseidon's likeness on top from half a city away. The god's trident stabbed the sky, trying to bleed it blue again.

"Are we too late?" The least of Far's worries, and a mammoth one.

"The flames haven't reached the docks yet," Eliot said, adjusting the drape of her stola. "We have time."

For once.

Far fluffed his toga. "How do I look?"

His cousin's arms were full of fur—securing Saffron so he wouldn't bolt into BC Egypt. She hugged the red panda close as she studied Far's outfit. "Appropriately ancient."

Priya drew near. Her shoulder to his, cheek against cheek. "Be careful. Your life isn't worth a few papers."

She kissed him in the doorway to a city in flames, their bodies melting together in two-sided surrender. Far forgot the sting of smoke, the taste of ashes. For a moment the world was her— all her. Priya lingered even when her lips left, their eyelashes close to tangling.

"You might want to start hauling tail." Imogen was gazing out of the hatch again, sunlight playing iridescent off her hair. "That smoke's getting wickeder by the minute."

Far turned to Gram. "Vigilance!"

"Vigilance." They nodded at each other as most boys do: quick and curt. "Good luck, Far."

Normally Far laughed such tokenisms off—*Luck-schmuck! He made his own fate!*—but he kept his lips pressed tight as he faced the warring city. Imogen was right; the smoke was already worse, thunderstorm thick. Flecks of ash had begun falling onto clay-tile rooftops. Desert snow.

They had to get moving.

Three, two, one. *Mission: Rescue Scrolls from Inferno* is a go.

The team dispersed: Imogen and Gram to their console stations, Priya waiting by the hatch to close it. Eliot's wig fluttered against acrid wind as she stepped into the street. Far followed her into Alexandria's royal quarter. North and west, where the smoke was thickest. The way the girl moved reminded Far of a rat in a maze—one that ran the course from memory. She turned corners with automatic precision, sought out side alleys that he never would've spotted at first glance. Scurry, scurry, hurry!

The city's syncretic beauty—statues of Egyptian deities nestled alongside classic Greek structures—passed in a blur. The *Invictus* was already well in the pair's wake by the time Imogen was settled enough to provide directions.

"Hades, Eliot's hauling tail! Where are you guys?"

"You're the one who's supposed to tell me!" Thank Crux the Romans believed in underwear, for while Far hated tight pants, he wasn't a fan of going commando, either. Especially in an airy toga. Especially, especially when running was involved.

Dust licked their heels as they dashed past old gods still new. Horse-drawn chariots. Columns wrapped in hieroglyphs. Roman centurions in full regalia. *This* was the feeling Far traveled for. The exhilaration of running through an age not his own, battle-shout harsh on the air, a stranger among the strange. He wondered if Eliot felt it, too—the thrill of being where they shouldn't, the bending of time beneath every step.

She halted. Far followed suit, though everything inside him kept lurching.

They'd reached the library.

Like many of Alexandria's buildings, the library was built in a style that honored both its Greek patrons and the Egyptian soil beneath it. Stately columns were guarded by statelier sphinxes. Stairs led to a courtyard flanked on either side by extensions of the symmetrical main building. Three stories made doubly magnificent by the courtyard's reflecting pool.

This is the last time anyone will see this sight. The library's edifice, and some of its collection, would survive the fire, but it would never be the same. This was the dusk of its old glory, moment before ruin.

Imogen saw the same view, shared the same sentiment. "Crux, that's beautiful...."

Smoke billowed heavier than devil's breath over Far's shoulder. Ruin had risen; it was well on its way. Eliot didn't even glance toward the approaching flames. Ashes that should've caught on eyelashes tumbled down her cheeks instead. Her eyes pierced across the waters, past the columns, through doors, almost as if she was searching for something....

They were searching, Far reminded himself. "Let's be quick about this. You collect Berossus's *Babylonaica*. I'll go for Sappho. We'll meet back here in five—"

"Sappho's mine!" Eliot was already running up the staircase, past a crowd of gaunt, scholarly-looking men at the courtyard's edge. All were too focused on the building wall of smoke to notice her.

"Go, team!" Imogen muttered. "Guess we got *Babylonaica*, which means you'll be going to the right. Southeast corner. Try not to trip over any librarians. Notice most of them are wearing chitons. I'm starting to second-guess the toga choice."

Eliot had reached the main entrance, its hungry doorway swallowing her. Far wished invisibility on himself as he clattered up the steps, past the onlookers. Again, flames won out. Why were they just standing there? Why weren't they *doing* something? Maybe they didn't know *what* to do, in the face of something so massive. It was a feeling Far could relate to, with so many fires of his own: amnesia and Eliot and keeping his ship and completing this half-baked mission.

One step at a time. He moved across the courtyard, through the doorway, into the library.

Doomed sterling light fell through glassless windows, magnifying the building's magnitude. The sight was foot-stopping, breath-seizing. There were gods here, too—Greek, Egyptian, painted, carved—standing between the pillars, guarding books they could not actually protect. Imogen had told them there were nearly half a million scrolls in the library's collection. The count sounded make-believe, zeros on a screen. Only now, with his chin tilted high as he took in row after row of shelves, did Far understand the breadth of it. The smell of papyrus was overwhelming. So much of it had been etched with ink, rolled tight, and placed onto diamond-shaped shelves. Histories, poetry, philosophical revelations, epics, so many thousands of years of progress...

All about to burn.

"To the right," Imogen reminded him.

Far's footsteps didn't even echo against the floor stones, such was the library's size. He passed a likeness of Anubis—pointy ears, fangs of a dog, torso of a man—and started down the row. He wasn't alone. There were people who'd taken the smoke for the warning it was, desperate to save what they could, gathering as many scrolls as their arms could carry. Far found himself hoping that the *Babylonaica* was on one of the higher shelves, less likely to get pilfered by random passersby.

"Imogen, talk to me. What am I looking for?"

His cousin sounded just as lost. "Hold on...."

Far narrowly missed a collision at the end of a row. The other patron swerved, dropped a scroll, but did not stop. Probably wise. Smoke was slithering through the windows, steadier and steadier. Soon it would get hard to breathe....

"Am I hot? Cold?" he asked once the man was out of earshot. "Should I ask for directions?"

"No!—Sorry, I misplaced my notes. You're heading for the southeast corner. Last row. Fourth shelf up. Fourth cubby from the left."

Far twisted through these instructions, all the way to the final row. Its fourth shelf was well above head height. He'd have to use the ladder to reach the manuscripts. This sat at the end of the row, and despite its rudimentary set of wheels, Far was panting by the time it was in place. The air was too thick—he couldn't fit it in his throat without choking.

"You okay, Farway? Try not to breathe too much."

Yeah, I'll just switch that basic function off now. Far didn't say this aloud, if only to conserve oxygen. He held his breath as he climbed the ladder to the predetermined cubby. It held dozens of scrolls, far more than he was capable of carrying.

"Which ones?" he asked Imogen.

"Eliot says the top six."

"Six?" These scrolls weren't small; they held the history of the world, after all. Far wasn't sure how he was supposed to get them down the ladder, much less haul the bunch back to the *Invictus.*

242

He'd figure it out. He had to. Far plucked the scrolls out one by one and dropped them to the floor below. Battered loot was better than none.

"Ow! Eek! Ah! Oof!" His cousin winced with each manuscript's impact. "Careful!"

Far leaped off the ladder with the sixth scroll under his arm and set to collecting the others. He was even *more* thankful for the Romans' love of undergarments as he scrambled on his hands and knees, trying to roll the books back into place.

"Hic tu non sis."

You shouldn't be here.

Far froze. It wasn't the words—spoken in Latin, no translation tech needed—that caught him, but the voice that gave them form. Everywhere the air was filmy and the library had turned opaque as a dream. The woman at the end of the shelves seemed the only solid thing. Her Greek chiton shone white, and Far knew he wasn't sleeping, but maybe the smoke had seeped into his head, because he'd imagined this moment for so many years, sought it, and this was the wrong time, the wrong place, but here she was in front of him.

His mother.

27.

AN EXPLOSION OF RUBIK'S CUBES

Turns out *VIGILANCE* was code word for "boring."

Gram sat at his station, reading through the numbers of their landing for the umpteenth time. All was well with math and universal order. He wasn't sure why he kept checking them or what he feared to find. Nothing had changed since the landing he'd had trouble solving. Or so he thought... Fallible memory was something Gram's brain was struggling to calibrate.

He was regretting his promise to keep *Tetris* on pause. No games meant just sitting. Just sitting meant his mind started wandering, analyzing things that were better off left alone.

1.2191 meters: the space between his chair and Imogen's. He'd never measured it before. He'd had no reason to. Imogen was his friend. She'd always been his friend, from the very first day Far had introduced them. Four Central time months ago—one biological year past—Gram had been invited to the McCarthys' flat to celebrate Far's seventeenth unbirthday. Her hair had been highlighter yellow that evening, but it was her laugh that really struck him. The ease and flow of it, how often she let it out...Everything about Imogen felt bright.

It was impossible not to like her.

But did he *like* her?

It'd be a lie to say that Gram hadn't thought of her in an amorous way with increasing frequency. In such close quarters, it was hard not to form attachments. 1.2191 meters was comfortable. They shared so much: jokes, near-Far-death experiences, celebratory high-score gelato. Even though Imogen's hair color changed every twenty-four hours, the change itself was a constant clockwork rainbow. A cycle he could count on.

For all his love of patterns and predictable steps, Gram was rubbish at dancing. He could manage a formulaic waltz. He might even be able to eke out a fox-trot if the situation were dire. Not that there were many emergencies involving ballroom dancing. Club dancing was a special brand of torture—no rules, go with the flow. He'd only ventured into the fray at Caesars Palace because Imogen had called him out. Five flailing songs and two stiletto-smashed toes later, Gram had slipped back toward the cabana, certain that Imogen wouldn't notice. She had, though. A tug on his vest and he'd turned to find her much closer than 1.2191 meters. Shiny eyes made shinier by a combination of alcohol and nuclear-green hair.

Don't go, she'd told him. *You're the only one I want to dance with.*

He'd stayed. Not for the dance, but for her.

Gram tried not to read too much into the statement. People said all sorts of shazm when they were inebriated: unfiltered truth, brazen lies, things to be regretted in the morning. Imogen certainly seemed to regret it. She'd avoided him all day, sliding out of whatever room he entered, averting her gaze. Had his dancing been that heinous?

Things had started to feel comfortable again in the wardrobe. Too comfortable...

He'd almost said something to regret of his own.

He didn't want to upset their balance, but it was off anyway. All the weight was on Imogen's side of the room, her presence gravitational. Gram had to fight to keep from staring at her. He studied his Rubik's Cubes instead. Again, there were no answers there, just a mug of tea beside the green one. The drink was cold when Gram picked it up; milk had formed a skin over the top. It'd been there awhile.

"I'm starting to second-guess the toga choice." Even Imogen's frown was vibrant as she guided her cousin through the library. Her screen's glow was all-encompassing, making the blues in her hair bluer. Saffron curled tight in her lap.

Gram took a sip of the tea. It was still good. Maybe even better for age. He scanned his own screens again. The numbers were steady. All systems sound.

This was fine. This was normal. This was working.

Everything was where it needed to be.

Best to let sleeping feelings lie.

"To the right." Imogen looked up from the screen during

her instructions, eyes drifting toward Gram's chair. The glance didn't feel intentional—it had the automatic slowness of a habit. This time, when their gazes locked, hers didn't skitter away. She didn't seem to realize she was looking. He hadn't, either.

See? Gravity.

"Hold on...." The moment caught up with them. Imogen tore her stare from his, back to the screen. A chasm opened up between their chairs. "No! Sorry, I misplaced my notes...."

1.2191 meters. Exactly what it was before.

Completely different now.

Gram's palms tightened around the mug. He looked back at his frozen *Tetris* game, his color-coded cubes. Not too long ago everything had fit. If Eliot hadn't brought up how pretty Imogen was by the blackjack tables, he might not even be dwelling on this...this...imbalance. Then again, maybe he would. Gram still wasn't sure if the newcomer was the cause or the effect. The problem or the solution.

"HOLY SHAZM!" Imogen shrieked.

Chaos ensued. Gram dropped the mug—chai went projectile when the ceramic shattered, hitting the chalk wall. *1922: Hunted down Hen With Sapphire Pendant* washed down to *1946: Recovered Yamashita's Gold from the Philippines* until all thirty missions became a polychromatic soup. Saffron scattered from his owner's lap, leaping to the closest high point he could find: Gram's console. Paws mashed the *Tetris* score back to zero before landing in an explosion of Rubik's Cubes. Green side became orange flipping over to white, which was sure to become brown after landing in the pool of tea. Gram's stare fixed back on Imogen, and hers to her screen. Both hands were on her face, framing trembling lips.

"Oh Crux, oh Crux, oh..."

"What's wrong?" Priya appeared in the doorway. Fear enough for all of them circled her eyes: three times pale. "What's happening?"

Imogen seemed incapable of answering. Gram looked at the screen that swallowed her so, view via Far. He picked out shapes through the haze: shelves, the face of a woman who was not Eliot. She was staring at Far and Far stared back, meeting her eyes in a way no Recorder should.

"Who is that?" he asked.

"It's Aunt Empra," she gasped. "Aunt Empra is in the library."

Empra McCarthy. Gram had never met Far's mother but he'd heard plenty about her. She was one of the most respected Recorders of her time—fluent in Latin without translation tech, Recorder of several staple datastreams. Her career was matched by few, but most of Empra's fame sprang from a different source: her disappearance.

If Empra McCarthy was here, the *Ab Aeterno* was, too. But...that didn't make sense. No official Corps expeditions had ever been sent to this date. Gram and Imogen had checked and double-checked the Corps' logs. They would have noticed any crossover, especially if the CTM was the *Ab Aeterno*.

Unless...

Unless this was the *Ab Aeterno*'s final mission. The one Empra and her crew had never returned from.

Click, click, click. These thoughts snapped into place, building up to a terrible realization. No one had been able to deduce where or when the *Ab Aeterno* had vanished—several rescue expeditions to the CTM's last logged destination (the Giza Plateau, before it possessed such a name, some two centuries *earlier* than this date) had come up empty, including several ventures by the *Invictus* itself. Nor had anyone been able to determine what prevented Empra and her crew from jumping back to Central time eleven years ago. Something unprecedented, something catastrophic enough to keep a mother from her son... Gram had no idea how the *Ab Aeterno* came to be here now, but if his theory was right, something drastic was about to happen.

His gaze swung back to the *Invictus*'s nav systems: *Vigilance!* What he saw struck him to the core.

The numbers weren't just changing this time.

They were disappearing.

28.

CONFLAGRATION
SITUATION

FAR WAS SEVEN YEARS OLD AGAIN. Chocolate gelato danced over his tongue, sweet with a seep of bitter. He'd taken too many bites too fast, and the cold of it climbed through his molars into his brain. Morning sunlight stole into their flat, transforming the most ordinary objects into gold: the rim of his bowl, a vase full of forget-me-nots, the boxes Burg had turned into a make-believe CTM. His mother—beneath these rays—was royalty. Her hair was bound in several braids, but the flyaways caught the light, betraying amber beneath the brown. When she frowned, these Celtic roots became a crown of fire.

"What's wrong?"

"You just went on an expedition!" Far tapped his frozen temple, wincing. "Why do you have to go again so soon?"

"It's my job, Farway. I'll be back before you know it," she

promised. "Besides, what's a week for me will only be a day for you. Time travel is funny like that...."

It was. Motherhood had shortened Empra's expeditions—no more yearlong surveys—but even the shorter missions added up after a month or two. Every time the *Ab Aeterno* returned, Far's mother was changed. New freckles pollocked her arms. Her eyes had seen more and were heavier for it. The sadness that swamped their brown never left, even with sunlight's Midas touch.

Far stared across the table. She'd be back this evening, but she wouldn't be the same mother sitting across from him now. So fiery, so ready to leave... He decided to take a picture with his interface. *Click!* Sun and gold and flowers blue. When his mother came back, he'd show her the image. Maybe then she'd realize how much she changed.

Empra McCarthy was the unchanged one now. Eleven years and she hadn't aged a day, torn straight from Far's childhood. Her hair was even bound up in the same braids, as if someone had crafted a hologram from the footage of that last-sight photograph.

No hologram could stare like this, though, eyes brighter than any memory could burnish. Smoke clung to Empra McCarthy's silhouette, proving her to be flesh and blood and here. "Gaius?"

Strange. She'd never called Far by his middle name before.

He scrambled to his feet, plane of existence tilting. His mother had gotten shorter—no, he was the one who'd grown. The years had slid sixty centimeters into Far's bones, and now he could see the fine white part of his mother's hair.

"Mom?" he croaked.

"Farway?" His mother had the look of a dreamer waking, settling slowly into the realization that she stood in Alexandria's ill-fated library, face-to-face with her grown son. "But—what? What are you doing here? Crux, how old are you?"

Imogen was yelling something in Far's ear, and the surrounding smoke had gone from filmy to fuzz—fires closing in. Neither of these things moved Far, for he was a waker falling back into dreams. Eleven years he'd fought for this moment. Academy Sims and orphan nights, jewel heists and laughing his lungs sore with the crew. Everything had been done with this at the back of his mind: son to mother reunited in the heart of history. The scene had been imagined a thousand different ways—in just as many ages and locations. Now that it was manifesting, Far found it difficult to believe that this was *the* version. All true.

It was too good to be....

But then Empra clasped Far's face in her hands. It was a mother's touch—instantly familiar, twisting his emotions upright.

"I'm eighteen now," he managed.

"Eighteen," she whispered. "Burg, are you seeing this?"

Burg was here? Of course. He was the *Ab Aeterno*'s Historian, missing alongside the rest of the crew. Technically, Far had only lost one parent to the disaster, but in his heart, the number doubled. Burg's bedtime stories, his cardboard time machine missions, his crush-your-shoulders hugs—Far missed those comforts something fierce. Then and still.

"Burg?" His mother was frowning. "Do you read me?"

"You never came back." The words hurt more than Far expected, as if eleven years of sobbing into pillows and surrounding adults' conversations wilting into *a shame, such a shame, we'll never truly know* could be crammed into a sentence. "None of you came back. Eleven years I waited, Mom...."

"Eleven years?" Empra McCarthy stiffened; her heart-shaped face broke a little. Far knew he might be ruining things—telling his past her future—but what was lost was lost, etched in stone on the granite memorial walls at the Corps' headquarters. "But it was just yesterday. Oh, Farway...Farway, I'm so sorry. I thought we could make it right...."

There was a tremble in her fingers, against his cheek.

"Make *what* right?" Far asked.

"Our nav system fritzed, and we landed hundreds of years off course, and as luck would have it, our fuel rods were never restocked. We don't have enough juice for a second jump. The *Ab Aeterno*'s been running on fumes, and we used a lot of those getting here from the Giza Plateau. Burg knew the library burned today, and we thought if I came on-site I might find a Recorder to pass along our SOS. Here you are...."

"You've been stranded?" No wonder the Corps' rescue unit never found the *Ab Aeterno*, stuck in a date two hundred and some years from when they were supposed to be. "But—"

"FARWAYFarwayFarwayFarwayFarwayareyoulistening?" Imogen's words melted into an indistinguishable shout. "Getbacktothe*Invictus*now!"

The smoke beyond the shelves parted, giving way to a wild

Eliot—arms thrashing, wig as skewed as her eyes. Her sandals skidded through scrolls as she grabbed Empra and Far and started dragging them through Berossus's spilled words. She screamed while she did: "Tell Gram to fly the *Invictus* over the courtyard! We've got to get out of here!"

Far dug his heels against her pull. "The scrolls—"

"Leave them!" Eliot snapped. "They'll only weigh us down."

Her fingernails formed five fierce moons—close to blood— in Far's biceps. Still he fought to stay. "I'm *not* getting my tail skinned alive by Lux—"

"Lux doesn't matter!" Eliot kept yanking; papyrus shred beneath her feet. "Lux never mattered!"

"Quickexitisagowe'recomingrightawaygotit?" What the Hades was Imogen saying? It was too much, pouring into Far's senses alongside the smoke, twisting everything dizzy.

"Farwaywe'rethirtysecondsoutlistensomething'shappening- somethingbigGramsaysweneedtojumpnow!"

His mother seemed overwhelmed as well, staring at Eliot with a misty-strange expression. "Have we met before?"

Eliot's grip tightened. Far hissed. If she hadn't drawn blood before, she certainly had now. "We have to get out of here before it reaches us!"

"We're well away from the flames still," said his mother.

"Not the fire!" Eliot pulled and tugged and tore. Her wig slipped off, black hair tangling with ink just as dark. "The Fade!"

"The *what* now?" Far asked.

254

"This moment is—it's decaying. It's unbecoming. So will we, if we stick around much longer. We have to get back to the *Invictus* and haul arse into the Grid before the Fade erases us!" Fear yawned beneath Eliot's explanation: the death-facing, life-flashing kind. "Time is collapsing."

Collapsing? Decaying? Unbecoming? What?

"She'snotlyingFarwayGramsaysthenavsystemnumbersare-vanishingwhatevertheHadesthatmeans!"

"Hashing blueboxes!" Far hissed and started running. "Let's get to the *Invictus*!"

"I'm not leaving my crew!" It was Empra who stood her ground this time. Eliot clung to her wrist, but the connection was taut, arms stretching. "Burg...Burg? Do you read me? Doc? Nicholas?"

"Mom! Come on! We have to—" Far's voice shriveled in his throat when he stared back at his mother. Shorter than him, so much the same; eleven years clashing with a day. These shocks paled in comparison to what poured through the window behind her.

The smoke billowing at the end of the row was not really smoke. It wasn't made of dark cinders or white ash. It was...*nothingness.* The world had become a Sim and was shutting down panel by panel, only there was no mother-of-pearl hologram tech shining beneath. Alexandria's lighthouse: gone. The harbor's warships: vanished. Lush palms, glimmering water: erased, unmade.

Every disaster Far had ever witnessed had one thing in common—noise. *Do not go gentle* events were punctuated with shrill bullets, screams, fire hissier than dragon's breath, war drums, orchestras—take your pick. Destruction was a loud, roaring thing.

Unmaking wasn't.

The Fade's silence was absolute, made for hearing your heartbeat in your ears. As the absence reached for them, dissolving the library's windows, devouring stones and shelves and scrolls, Far's blood became sludge inside his body. He was a dreamer back in the dream-turned-nightmare; everything around him tinged a red, colorless shade. His mother yelled into her comm, oblivious to the void over her shoulder, even though it was beginning to swallow her voice's sound waves—"Burg! Burg! Burg! Burg!"

Eliot's reaction to the vacuum was instantaneous. She dropped their arms and ran.

"FOLLOWHERYOUHASHINGFOOL!" Imogen's yell crashed through the comm, loud enough to move him.

Far lunged for his mother. The Fade was so close that the words coming from her mouth took no shape at all—they fell out of existence with the floor just a step away. His hand to her wrist, Far ran and Empra followed. Together they crashed through the stacks, clipping the shoulders of librarians rescuing manuscripts, trying to keep up with Eliot. The girl was several lunges ahead, her stola winging past Anubis.

What are we running from?

Far looked over his shoulder and found, to his terror, that the library's southeast corner no longer existed. Nothingness pushed toward them, claiming shelves and statues, refusing to be processed by logical senses. No mind could link vocabulary to what Far was seeing.

"GETTHEHASHOUTOFTHERE!" Imogen screamed. "GRAM'SBOOTINGUPTHESYSTEMWE'REGOIN GTOTRYTOJUMPEVENTHOUGHTHENAVNUMBERSA REDISAPPEARINGANDIWANTYOUTOBEINHEREW HENWEDO!"

There was little air left in his lungs, and everything burned for it. Calves, thighs, eyeballs, veins. Empra's strides had equaled out with Far's, so he let his mother go as they dashed toward the library entrance and the courtyard beyond. The *Invictus* was already there, hovering a few centimeters off the ground with the holo-shield dropped. A massive iridescence, impossible not to see. Several scholars were pointing from the steps—by far the worst breach of the Corps of Central Time Travelers' Code of Conduct that Far and his crew had ever managed.

It didn't matter now. The Corps wasn't coming here. No one was coming here. If the nav numbers were disappearing, no time machine could land in this moment.

Far only hoped they could leave.

Priya stood in the *Invictus*'s open hatch, waving them forward. Eliot was already on board.

"HURRYHURRYHURRYKEEPRUNNINGTHE-FADE'SCOMING!"

His cousin's screams were all the louder for the dead quiet rolling in behind them. The Fade? It must be. The sky was disappearing, the vast expanse above them peeling back into something vaster. Blue and smoke and ashes gave way, their dimensions draining as destruction without a shadow curled over the *Invictus*, one beat from crashing down.

Far ran from his own fading footsteps, toward Priya's outstretched hand. His blood, his veins, his everything had gone kinetic. He was existence in motion. He wanted to stay that way. As soon as his sandals hit the hatch, his heart exploded, bits smearing the time-machine floor. He gasped past them, into Priya's arms, unable to gather anything as he turned to see what was—and wasn't—behind him.

Empra was only a few strides from the hatch, braids flaring as she lunged. Everything else was nothing. The vacuum licked for his mother's heels, snatching courtyard stones out from under her. Her face was afire once more, ready to leave *with* him this time. Far could see his name on her lips—

"Mom!" he screamed, reaching for her. Priya clutched his toga tighter than life. "Hurry!"

"ELIOTWHATAREYOUDOINGTHEHATCHISN'T—"

His mother was staring straight at him when the nothingness latched on. Foot gone, calf gone, thigh now, she was falling…tumbling to a ground that was not there. The sadness in her eyes turned infinite.

Far kept screaming. Silence honed in on the sound, hungry for it. "Noooooooooooooooooo!"

Everything vanished.

29.

DEVOURER OF ALL THINGS

Far had always thought of the Grid as the definition of nothing. Central's scientists often used words like *void* and *vacuum* when trying to describe such an indescribable place. Now he knew that couldn't be further from the truth. There was some allowance for matter, some level of existence here. Theirs was proof of that.

The *Invictus* was an island in the endless dark. Priya and Far sat on the edge of eternity: her gasping, him screaming. The noise was back to full volume, no echo, no fade, just agony rolling on and on and on and on. The Grid gaped in front of Far, inside him. The sight of his mother—falling down and apart—was easy to conjure against the lightless space, a horror just starting to hit.

Priya's arms were the one thing keeping him from the black. She dragged Far farther into the ship, while Imogen shut the hatch. His cousin had his mother's nose—narrow down to a delicate, pointed end. Almost whittled. Far had never noticed the similarity before, never would've noticed if Empra had stayed lost.

He never would've known what happened to her....

What had happened?

Far had no idea. His scream was gone and he was trembling. Priya draped the couch throw over his shoulders and told him to sit, but how could he? The blanket clung to him, lopsided, dragging over sticky Rubik's Cubes and mug fragments as he entered the console room. Gram sat in his chair, hands up, as if to say *I didn't touch anything; the jump was all her.*

Eliot braced herself by the nav system with thunder-white knuckles, eyes closed. The glow of the *Invictus*'s lights would not stick to her skin; instead it beat back, harsher than the numbers on the nearby screen.

"Turn this hashing ship around!" Were those his words? Leaving his mouth? "We have to go back!"

"There's nothing to return to." Eliot's knuckles bulged at the seams, but she didn't yell. "When the Fade destroys a moment, it's lost. Forever."

"One more second and my mother would have made it on the ship!" he screamed, if only to get his insides' ragged edges out, where the hurt could stretch its legs. "If you hadn't jumped this ship, she'd still be alive!"

"We didn't *have* one more second. Don't you understand?" Eliot opened her eyes; their darkness went deep. "The Fade is the devourer of all things: matter, moments, memories, even time itself. Your mother was unraveling. She was already gone."

260

"WHY DID YOU BRING ME HERE? WHY DID YOU MAKE ME SEE THAT?" He'd always thought that knowing what happened to the *Ab Aeterno* would make things hurt less. *Closure*, his childhood counselor once said, was the emotional equivalent of a scab. Instead, Far's grief felt more open than ever, gaping with the knowledge that his mother was gone now, really gone, and he hadn't been able to save her. "Why do you care about my mother? Why do you care about any of this? All you've done is destroy my life!"

"All I've done?" Eliot barked. "I gave you a chance to fexing rescue her! That's what I did! That's what I always do!"

She was speaking in riddles again. Holding something—everything—back. Far was sick of secrets. "Cut the shazm, Eliot! You knew this Fade thing was coming!"

"I didn't know." Eliot let go of the console. "I feared...and that fear came to pass. I've told you before, the Fade is relatively random. It can happen at any moment in our timeline. It *is* happening in lots of moments—"

"LIAR!" Yelling just to yell, just to have something loud outside of him. "You never told us about the Fade. I would've remembered being told about a void bigger than the hashing SKY!"

"Do you remember landing four hours late on the *Titanic* mission?" The girl cocked her head. "Of course you don't, because the Fade doesn't just cause wobbly jumps but amnesia, too."

There was no Nepenthe. They should all be dead. Far's mother *was* dead, uncreated before his very eyes, and how had they gone from a breathless reunion in the shelves to this...another hole. Had he had this conversation before? There was no telling with his temporal lobes going Swiss cheese on him. Far couldn't trust himself, couldn't stop fighting. "There has to be something we can do! Go back to Alexandria earlier in the timeline, find Mom before the Fade!"

"We can't! It's too dangerous! Your mother's gone and you have to move on! You have to keep going!" Eliot slammed her fist into the console, knuckles catching the corner. Real tears ribboned her cheeks. "Fex, that hurt!"

"Why does everyone keep punching my stuff?" Gram muttered. "Bartleby's a lot softer."

Eliot's hand bloomed with blood and nerve endings—skin sliced off. Far knew exactly what it felt like: the punch, the hit, the raw. Shock was catching up with him, overriding every other emotion. *Keep going?* He couldn't even move. He stood there staring as red wreathed down Eliot's fingers.

"Playing punching bag with Gram's instruments won't help anything. We don't want to get stranded here." Priya was on the scene, hand full of gauze, lips pressed as she took in the damage. "This laceration is deep. You're going to need stitches."

When the bandage pressed to Eliot's wound, she flinched. White grew heavy with scarlet and her tears fell thicker. *Why is she crying?* She had no right to sadness or pain when she'd brought all this on herself. On them.

Far was about to say as much when Priya cut in with a steady, take-no-shazm tone. The deck was hers now. "Imogen, try to make Far sit down. Gram, find us a time to land when we won't crash into the library—"

"No!" Eliot gasped. "Stay in the Grid. We're safe from the Fade here."

"Fine." Priya's jaw locked. "We stay in the Grid. But after I sew you up, you're going to tell us everything. Who you are, where and when you came from, why you're here, what the Fade is. Understood?"

To everyone's surprise, Eliot nodded. Something inside the girl had wilted: Her shoulders slouched, and her steps dragged as she followed Priya into the infirmary. The door slid shut.

Suspension gripped the console room. The Grid's timelessness mixed with held breaths. For a second, for an eon, no one spoke. It would've felt silent, but now that Far knew what *true* silence sounded like, all he could hear was noise. The *thud, thud* of a heart begging for oxygen. Red panda claws tapping the common area floor. The *Invictus*'s stealth engines made more commotion than he'd realized—their background hum more feeling than decibel.

"The universe is falling apart." Gram glared at his equipment; his voice boomed.

"Farway." Even Imogen's presence was muted—neon gone gray. Far hadn't noticed her in the doorway until she said his name. "Come sit. I—I can try to make tea. Maybe."

Far didn't want tea. He didn't want to sit. He didn't want the universe to fall apart. But every ounce of fight-or-flight had abandoned his body, so he let his cousin guide him to the couch. It wasn't just Imogen's nose that matched his mother's. It was the clean part through aqua hair. It was the great sorrow molding her face as she sat on the cushion beside Far's. He kept expecting her to say something sunshine-y, but each of Imogen's exhales was as empty as the next. There was no buoying grin. No honeycomb gelato. She'd seen everything that had happened through his eyes. He'd lost a mother and she'd lost an aunt, and this time words wouldn't help either of them.

30.

FAR FROM THE TREE

THE GIRL BLED LIKE EVERYONE ELSE: red. It was a nasty gash, but Priya had seen nastier. Eliot stiffened when the curved suture needle was retrieved from its drawer, snake's-tooth sharp. In Medic school Priya had learned that bedside manner made all the difference in situations like this. Keep the patient chatting. Talk about the weather, family members, their favorite datastream, anything to keep them from focusing on the pain at hand.

But it was all Priya could do to keep her own focus. The Ancestral Archives program glowed from the other side of the infirmary, details of its search-in-progress hidden beneath a lab coat. *Does that truth even matter, now that the questions have changed?* Gloves on. Heal-All spray applied. Suture thread strung. Eye on the needle. *Don't think about what you just saw. Don't think about how Far might have reached his mother, if you'd let go. Don't think about how close he came to being erased, too....*

"You're shaking," Eliot said.

"Can you blame me?"

"Is there a less old-fashioned way to do this? I don't want crooked stitches." Eliot attempted enough of a smile to show she was trying to lighten the mood.

As if that were possible, after watching the sky disappear. Colors, light, matter all peeling back...It was the surety of an end, coming for them with the wrath of a merciless god. The sight reminded Priya of a line from the Bhagavad-Gita, oft quoted by men who knew they held desolation in their hands: *I am become Death, the destroyer of worlds.*

Translation was a funny thing. Some scholars thought it was time, not death, that destroyed worlds. Both versions were chilling, made her ache for warmth and masala chai, still points and perfect moments.

"We don't have skin glue on board," Priya told the girl. "Scar will look the same no matter what."

At this, Eliot held out her hand. The bleeding had slowed after the Heal-All, but she remained quite pale, insides a blue-veined story against her skin, pulse an ode to terror. Whatever it was they'd seen in Alexandria, it upended this girl. She'd become as much a shadow-person as the rest of them.

It only took four interrupted sutures to close the cut. Priya sliced the thread and applied the bandage as steadily as she could. "All better now," she said, even though nothing was. "Now, go out into the common area and start talking."

"It's—a long story." Eliot stood. "I'm going to need to use the washroom first."

Because they were suspended in the Grid, Priya nodded. The *Invictus* was all there was out here. Eliot would be hard-pressed to find a place to run, though she certainly did her best on her way to the washroom, tripping over Saffron before she shut herself away. The red panda bristled thrice his size, his misery made well known as he yowled and leaped up to the safety of the pipes.

Priya checked on her crew. All of them were in the common area. Gram sat on the couch, cleaning off one of his Rubik's Cubes. A steam cloud surrounded Imogen in the kitchenette, which explained both smells—karha spice and burning. Far sat with his back to the infirmary, unmoving. Priya couldn't see his eyes, but she suspected they were glazed, reliving the same moment she was. Death or time—whatever windless force it was—bearing down, snatching Far's mother out from under him, his toga linen feeling like a thousand threads ready to snap beneath Priya's fingers.

She'd been right to hold on, hadn't she?

Priya tossed the garnet gauze and the needle in the trash; her gloves followed. So much sorrow, so much fear—Eliot's ache had spread to the entire ship. The Ancestral Archives results might be slight, but they mattered, because everything stemmed from this girl somehow, and all she'd done was lie. Nepenthe. Ha! If only...

Whatever story Eliot chose to spin next could be held to the tale her genetics told. This diagnostics machine also featured an hourglass cursor. Its eternal sands had been pouring most of the day, were still pouring when Priya lifted the lab coat. Results wouldn't take much longer, *shouldn't* for how many credits she'd dropped on processing power. Though who knew what *soon* meant in a timeless place...

"I think I murdered the chai." A glum announcement on Imogen's part. "There aren't supposed to be floaty things in it, right?"

"I usually strain the spices out," Priya said, and made her way toward the kitchenette. The pot in Imogen's hands was a piece of work: too much milk, burnt at the bottom, bubbling over the sides. Not enough spice, despite the bits that flecked the top. Poor, precious karha mix. Murdered, indeed. "What is this?"

"I don't know...." The Historian's chin wobbled. "I'm sorry, Priya. I tried."

They'd all tried. They were all on the edge of tears. They all felt as if maybe the nothingness actually *had* managed to graze them, stealing something essential. Priya looked back at the pot and decided to save what she could. Something hot in their hands would be better than emptiness.

She poured out five cups this time, substituting two bowls. One for Eliot and one for the mug that was now in pieces on the floor. The washroom door stayed closed. Priya found herself dreading its opening. She wanted answers, yes, needed them, but whatever came out to face them couldn't be good.

The whole world was unsettled now, not just theirs.

Her eyes kept traveling the same path: washroom door, Far, hourglass. Closed, unmoving, ever-pouring. Closed, unmoving, ever-pouring. Closed, unmoving...results! The hourglass vanished with a chime, and it was everything Priya could do not to spill the rest of the pot as she set it down, rushing for the infirmary.

The screen greeted her with the program's motto—ANCESTRAL ARCHIVES: ROOTS AT YOUR FINGERTIPS—and the picture of a tree. (Some marketing person sure fancied themselves clever.) Priya had no patience for it as she clicked to the next screen. This layout of results was easier to read than the initial DNA profile—ancestral lineage branching out from the strongest percentage, following census records and haplogroups down the generations.

NO NO MATCH FOUND this time. Eliot's closest relative shared a whopping 50 percent of her DNA, which meant she wasn't from as distant a future as they thought. One of the girl's parents or siblings existed in Central time, and as soon as Priya selected that profile, she'd know who it was.

Time to pull back the curtain...

A glance at Ganesh. A prayer. A click.

The profile filled the screen, picture first. Priya didn't read the name or birth date beneath it because the face, painted in pixels before her, needed no ID. She'd seen it in person not a moment ago. The sight was more than familiar; it was hashing impossible....

It was Empra McCarthy.

31.

100 PERCENT

READINGS ARE 99% COMPLETE. REMEMBER EMPRA MCCARTHY.

Eliot sat on the covered toilet seat, head in her hands. The right one screamed through the Heal-All's numbing agents, palm shaking because her world's end had come too close. This was the second time she'd faced the Fade in the flesh, and Eliot's edges felt less solid for it—warped fingernails, caving chest. No clever foreign curse word or dance party could pull her back together after such a sight.

"One more percent." Even her whisper felt cobwebby, syllables ready to snap. "All you have to do is make it to one hundred. Then you'll be certain."

But what if this boy *wasn't* the one? Could she move on to Subject Eight? Nine? Ten? Twenty? Could she keep drawing on eyebrows with her All My Friends Are Dead Again pen while the lifetimes piled over her groaning bones?

Blank slate? Ha. If anything she was overwritten. There shouldn't be *room* for any more of these traumas, but Eliot's interface accepted the upload of the Alexandria mission none-theless. SUBJECT SEVEN, DECEMBER 16, 48 BC. The label's letters looked too neat for such a nasty business.

WOULD YOU LIKE TO PLAY THE FILE? Vera asked.

Eliot didn't want to watch the footage again, but it was necessary. She'd already forgotten most of her flight from the Fade, as Far certainly had, as the others certainly would. Only the Grid was preserving those final, fatal seconds, and once the *Invictus* landed back in time—any time—the Fade would feast on that memory, too. If Eliot didn't relive Empra McCarthy's unmaking again, she'd forget it. Though, in truth, forgetting would be easier. It was tempting to highlight the lifetimes of footage in her drive and hit Delete—Agent Ackerman's orders be fexed. She'd remember the ones she'd already watched, sure, but once the Fade caught up to her, none of it would matter.

Nothing would.

Eliot started to sob: water, water everywhere. Vera kept repeating the question in her most polite text-speak, the act of crying beyond the interface program's comprehension. Eliot had tried to operate like that—bionic, aloof, apart—but she was too hazing human for her own good.

The mirror caught Eliot when she looked up. Through the tears, at this distance, everything was warped, the washroom engulfing her blotchy face. How could Agent Ackerman expect her to shape the fates of billions when she couldn't even fill in her own reflection? Eliot's eyebrows anchored her in the smallness, their message untouched by weeping. She couldn't not hear her mother's voice when she read it. *Make a wish.* **Make it count.**

"I'm trying," Eliot croaked.

READINGS ARE 100% COMPLETE. REMEMBER EMPRA MCCARTHY.
Vera's question changed. WOULD YOU LIKE THE RESULTS OF THE
SCAN FOR COUNTERSIGNATURE EMISSIONS?

Up, up her hope soared, and Eliot hated how high it felt
because it meant the crash would be that much worse, and she
was only human, after all, only a girl trying her best to save the
world, and her mission rode on whatever came next.

"Hit me, Vera."

I AM A COMPUTER. I DO NOT POSSESS PHYSICAL ARMS TO
PERFORM SUCH A TASK.

"It's a blackja—never mind. Show me the results. Please."

THE FADE'S CATALYST IS CONFIRMED. SUBJECT SEVEN IS A
COMPLETE COUNTERSIGNATURE MATCH.

Subject Seven. Out of all the candidates in all the universes
this boy was the one. Solara—and the other cousins—would've
called it lucky, for the number, but Eliot didn't believe in luck.
The best way to wrangle fate was to seize it by the fexing throat.

She knew what was coming next. She'd spent seven lives
bracing for it.

NEUTRALIZATION ORDER CONFIRMED.

Eliot reached into the pocket universe wrapped around her
wrist, feeling through gowns and wigs and tools for the item she
needed. There! A steel so cold her fingers solidified around it.
She hated to do this, especially in front of Imogen.

She had to.

Eliot turned toward the washroom door and pulled out
her gun.

32.

WEIRDEST WORST DAY
EVER

No time whirled around Far, mixing with the scent of scalded tea. His crew was talking, but he couldn't pick their words apart from the roar in his brain. All of his senses were on overload, blasted into static. He barely felt the blanket's wool fringe scratching his throat. He didn't see the washroom door open. Priya's scream—that made it through, if only because the sound was so out of place.

"FAR! LOOK OUT!"

His daze twisted into tight focus. Eliot was emerging from the washroom—pink-faced, blaster in hand. Far had seen more than a few gun barrels in his day, but this one was unique: shaped like an X instead of an O, ready to punch a cross through his chest. There was no flourishing pause, no dramatic monologue, no time for Far's Recorder reflexes to throw him out of the weapon's range. Eliot pulled the trigger and he was a dead man.

Or would've been, if not for Saffron. The red panda launched from the pipes with a *step on me and I'll fall on you* vengeance—landing on Eliot's head, every claw flailing. She yelped. The blaster swung, its laser reducing the cushion by Far's shoulder to a blackened smolder. Gram launched himself over the second couch, wresting the weapon from Eliot and tossing it back to Far, who caught the blaster midair—*Way to finally make an appearance, Academy training!*

When he turned the weapon's sights back at its owner, Eliot froze. The whole hashing room did. Gram had managed to secure the girl's arms behind her back. Priya paused by the charred couch and Imogen was brandishing the chai pot, though Far doubted she'd use it. There wasn't a violent bone in his cousin's body. There weren't many in his, either, but almost getting blasted through the heart was enough to whip up aggression in anyone.

"You can't shoot her, Far." Priya was the first to move, bringing the moment back into itself with a touch on his arm. "She's family."

"Not on *this* crew, she's not."

"It's not a metaphor," Priya insisted. "The Ancestral Archives results came through. Eliot shares half of your mother's DNA, which means she's either your sister or your aunt."

"What?" The worst day of Far's life was also now jockeying for the weirdest. "No. No! I don't have a *sister*. And Uncle Bert is Mom's only sibling. There must be a mistake. We were both eating blood orange gelato when you gathered the sample; you must've snatched my spoon instead."

That was it. The only thing that made sense...

"The DNA is Eliot's," Priya pressed. "It has all of her markers. Female. *Alopecia universalis*. She's a McCarthy."

Far stared down the blaster sights. Eliot stared back, no more smirks left to give. Those eyes *did* look an awful lot like his: same color, same stark stubbornness. "Is this true?"

"In a sense." Hers was one of the most earnest sighs ever exhaled. "My name is Eliot Gaia McCarthy. I'm not your sister, or your aunt. I'm the daughter of Empra McCarthy, born on April 18, 2354 AD, in a parallel universe."

Parallel universe.

As in...

Another world.

Weirdest worst day ever. "So you're my doppelgänger?"

"Doppelgängers look the same," Gram corrected him. "What Eliot posits, what the evidence substantiates, is that there's a different universe in which Empra McCarthy had a daughter instead of a son. That would mean Eliot is an alternate version of you."

"Far's the alternate version," Eliot muttered.

"I think we all know who's the original here," Far shot back, blaster steady.

"Really?" Imogen lowered the chai pot. "We just found out there are *whole other worlds* and you're arguing for an *ego boost*?"

Fair. Far looked back at the Engineer. "Is this even possible? Parallel worlds and shazm?"

"Hypothetically? Yes." Gram's eyes brightened: Geek-out

mode greenlit. "String theory has maintained the existence of a multiverse for centuries, but we haven't figured out how to communicate with these theoretical universes, much less attempt interdimensional travel."

"A lot of the universes haven't," Eliot said. "Mine only joined the fun about twenty-seven years ago."

"That's remarkable!" Gram glanced down at her. "How'd your scientists manage it?"

Far broke in before things spiraled into quarky atomic talk. "If you've been able to jump worlds for so long, how come we haven't heard of this multiverse before?"

"For the same reason your world's history hasn't caught on to the fact that the future walks among them. Much like the past, the multiverse is delicate. The Multiverse Bureau doesn't like disturbing worlds that haven't discovered parallel universes. It's their policy to remain observers in such spheres."

"You call trying to shoot someone observing?" Tiny tongues of smoke licked off ruined satin, dispersing when Far waved toward them. "I, for one, am very disturbed. If not for the deus ex machina à la bear-cat, that would've been my chest! Why would you want to kill yourself? I mean, your alternate self. Crux, we need a term for this."

"I don't *want* to kill you." There was a crack in Eliot's voice, threatening to spill out all sorts of emotion. "I have to."

Far wasn't sure he wanted her to go on.

"Why?" Priya asked for him.

"You just saw why." Eliot's eyes slid toward the hatch, meaning clear.

The door was the same as it'd always been, yet the crew's hearts quickened when they stared at its metal and bolts. As if the *why*—the Fade—remained on the other side, apocalyptic storm front rolling, ever rolling, toward them, edges heavy with a skeleton army. Far could almost hear the clip-clop of ghost hooves, galloping in infinite silence....

"You mean that fady cloud-thing?" Imogen murmured. "What's that got to do with Farway?"

"Everything," Eliot said. "It's—well, it's hard to explain. It'd be easier to show you. There's a memory chip of datastreams inside my pocket universe."

"Your bag o' secrets is a *pocket universe*?" Far snorted. "No way am I going to let you rummage through that. You probably have another weapon tucked away in there somewhere."

Eliot looked to Priya. "The pocket universe is on my left wrist. It's easier to open if you stretch it horizontal."

So the bag o' secrets was a pocket universe was a... bracelet? The chain was, for the most part, invisible. All the naked eye could see was a distortion—a ripple of wrong air strung between Priya's hands, paper-cut thin. She stretched it out, eyes widening as they registered what she held: porthole to a different world. Slender fingertips vanished, first knuckle, second, third, wrist, as she reached into a space the rest of them couldn't see. For a terrible moment, Far feared the disappearing would swallow her, too.

But her hand resurfaced, clutching the edge of a daffodil dress. Lace frothed out of thin air, until an entire gown stretched before them. The whole thing looked as magical as ever. *Whoa* was a common theme the room over, except for Imogen, who was making grabby hands for the dress itself.

"If you set the pocket universe on the floor, it's easier to see what you're grabbing," Eliot offered. "You can stretch it wider, too. Just take care that you don't fall in."

Priya did as instructed. The dimension's edge was malleable, warping to her touch until Far could see where space itself had split open, allowing for a cavity that was both there and not. One of the *Invictus*'s floor panels now went a level deeper than ship schematics dictated.

"What I wouldn't give for a purse like this." Priya pulled out another gown. "It's ... well, I mean, it's phenomenal."

Gram craned his neck for a better view. "This tech's from your world?"

"Standard issue from the Multiverse Bureau." Eliot nodded. "Light packing makes interdimensional travel worlds easier."

"Ha!" Imogen grinned as she hung the dress in the wardrobe. "Punny!"

"What's the Multiverse Bureau?" the Engineer asked. "How do you travel between worlds? Is there an interdimensional equivalent to a TM?"

"Like I stated, it's easier to show you," Eliot said. "The answers are inside the chip, which is in a blue velvet box."

Annoyance worked Far's jaw back and forth. Had everyone already forgotten Eliot's transgression, still sizzling a hole in the couch? Perhaps *forgiven* was the better word, because the Fade sure as Hades hadn't snatched that moment yet: Eliot nearly knocking him out of this life, not even lifting a scribbly eyebrow about it.

"Blue box, blue box…"

Priya's hand kept dipping through the floor, producing a new item each time. There were powdered wigs, fishnet stockings, muddy trousers—more clothes than the wardrobe above them. A case stamped with a blue serpent twining around an orange cross contained curiously labeled silver packets. *Medicine*, Priya declared, though she looked uncertain when she read the names. There were gadgets, too—near as silver, just as strange.

"Careful," Eliot warned when a metallic cylinder was drawn out. "That's—"

A scarlet bright light leaped from the instrument, stopping short of Priya's jaw. The burning smell of the room went three-fold; a generous swoop of raven hair fell to the floor.

"A laser knife."

The beam retracted when Priya let go of the hilt. Hair that had flowed past her shoulders was chopped in a ruthless line far too close to her neck. She brushed the loss with fluttering fingers, unable to reconcile where hair ended and air began. "Well. Guess there's no need to worry about split ends for a while."

Imogen was considerably more distraught. She tugged her own locks back, making a noise that could only be attributed to a robot-roadrunner: "*Meeeeeeep.*"

"Any more lethal surprises hidden in there?" Far remembered he was holding a gun, remembered it was aimed in Eliot's general direction. He nudged it at her. "Speak now."

"No. Just the laser knife." Light bounced off Eliot's head as she shook it. The welts from Saffron's claws were a bloody tiara, finely scrawled. "Trust me. I don't want to hurt any of you."

"This from the mouth of the girl who claims she has to kill me." His hand ached against the blaster. Did he even *know* how to shoot this alternate-universe tech, if it came down to it? "I'm sure you understand why I'm not terribly trusting at the moment."

"Aha!" Priya had recovered the box. It was blue—the shade's truest version, found on primary color wheels—and small enough to fit in her palm. The chip inside was translucent, with the dimensions of a pinkie nail. When held up to the light, it resembled a snowflake on the verge of melting, patterned with a delicate labyrinth of circuits. Dropped, it would take hours to find, minutes to step on.

Gram squinted from across the room. "Is it compatible with our tech?"

"Not without modifications," Eliot told him. "There's a shortcut hologram function that responds to voice command, though."

"This is a hologram platform?" Priya asked. "But—it's so tiny."

"They get smaller every year. If you put it on the table, we can get started."

The box was set down first, the chip placed back inside, where it was least likely to vanish into the common area's knick-knack landscape. One word from Eliot lit the air above it; files appeared in the form of several more boxes, each a different color, most bearing a Roman numeral. 0 through VII. White through black.

"Zero." The lid to the white box opened at Eliot's command. "Start at the beginning."

A scene unfurled from the container, blooming before the group. It looked as solid as the Sims, but everything had a miniature quality—doll-sized people sat at aluminum tables the length of Far's arm. Some held forks. Others chopsticks. Both utensils looked elementary in the hands of the fresh cadets, who'd grown up on meal blocks. Far did a double take at the uniforms. These kids were being groomed for the Corps. They were eating lunch inside *the Academy*.

The mess hall looked the same as the one from Far's schooling, but also different. Its checkered floor was a red-white pattern instead of navy-gray. The security camera this footage had been lifted from was in the wrong bird's-eye corner—facing the grub line instead of the stage where Instructor Marin rattled off his list of *don't*s at the beginning of every term. Some of the people were the same. Mrs. Benucci was running the kitchen— harried curls sticking out of her hairnet, dishing out the pasta she claimed was an ancient family recipe. Ekstone Elba sat where he always did, picking tomatoes out of his sauce. Instructor Lee—who taught the wildly popular Pop Culture Through the Centuries class—sported his acerbic lime hair.

Far's eyes skipped to his usual seat: second table, far end. Logic told him what—who—he should expect there, but the sight jarred him anyway. Eliot didn't look like Eliot. Cap off, hair gone, she sat in a ring of friends, laughing so much she couldn't get a bite in edgewise. Her smile was...real.

Everything was familiar. All of it strange.

could've been could've been could've been

This was his life.

This was another's.

An announcement poked through the mess hall speakers: "Cadet McCarthy, please report to Headmaster Marin's office."

"Marin's *headmaster* in this universe?" Far spluttered. "What is this? The darkest timeline?"

"It gets darker. Marin's the least of our worries from here on out." Eliot's hologram grin quivered; by the time she replaced her cap and stood, it had vanished. Something about the way now-Eliot regarded the scene made Far doubt the expression would return anytime soon. "You guys might want to get comfortable. Grab a seat, make a snack. This will take a while."

33.

WHAT THE HASH/HAZE IS GOING ON

THEY ENDED UP CUFFING ELIOT TO one of the wardrobe pipes—though there was no need. Her exhaustion had scraped through to her soul, her resolve as fleeting as the blaster's laser. The Multiverse Bureau's directive haunted her interface, reminding Eliot she *could* take back the gun, quite easily, but her limbs refused to move. She just didn't have this killing in her.

Not anymore.

Not yet.

Eliot almost didn't recognize her hologram self; the girl in the datastream had a bounce to her steps as she walked to Headmaster Marin's office—unaware that life as she knew it would soon be over, in five steps, four, three, two, one....

❖ ❖ ❖

Security footage switches from the Academy's hallway to Headmaster Marin's office. The door opens and Eliot McCarthy enters. At the sight of her mother seated by the desk, she halts. A shadow settles on her face.

Eliot: Mom? What are you doing here?

Headmaster Marin: At the Academy you're to refer to her as Instructor McCarthy. [gestures toward an empty chair] Have a seat, Cadet McCarthy.

Eliot starts for the chair, pausing when she notices the second man, dressed not in a Corps uniform but in plain clothes, seated across the room. His is a face crowded with life's little annoyances. The porkpie hat on his head is either his prized possession or his clumsiest afterthought.

Eliot: Who's this?

The man's only way of introduction is a lift of his jacket, a flash of something gold. The security camera can't capture the details, but Eliot's nostrils flare at the sight. Something's wrong, and she knows it.

Headmaster Marin: [more forcefully] Have a seat, Cadet McCarthy.

Empra: It's all right, Eliot.

Headmaster Marin coughs in a nonrespiratory manner. Empra's smile frays.

Empra: It's all right, Cadet McCarthy.

Eliot: [takes a seat] What's going on? Did something happen with my final exam Sim?

Headmaster Marin: Your final exam Sim results are beyond reproach. The licensing board was overwhelmingly pleased. There was even talk of sending you on a mission to the real Versailles—

Eliot: That's all I've ever wanted.

Headmaster Marin: Do not interrupt me while I'm speaking, Cadet. I'd take marks for it, but there'd be no point in my doing so. While the results of your final exam were extraordinary, different results have brought you into this office today. Your physical examination threw up some flags with the Multiverse Bureau. Their very own Agent August Ackerman is here to escort you to their facilities for further tests.

Eliot: Tests? What kind of tests?

Headmaster Marin: They wouldn't deign to say. Typical cloak-and-dagger red-tape nonsense.

Agent Ackerman: The Multiverse Bureau, unlike the Corps of Central Time Travelers, actually adheres to the guidelines it sets. We keep our classified information classified.

Headmaster Marin: I'll have you know that this universe's Corps hasn't created a single pivot point—

Agent Ackerman: Yet. It's only a matter of time with you lot.

Eliot: But what about graduation? What about my Corps assignment?

Empra: The Corps has agreed to keep a position open for you.

Eliot: But, Mom—

Headmaster Marin: [coughs] *Instructor McCarthy.*

Both women ignore him.

Eliot: I can't just drop everything and leave. Solara's been planning my graduation party for months.

Empra: Wait, you *know* about that? It's supposed to be a surprise.

Eliot: Your niece is dash at keeping secrets.

Headmaster Marin: Cadet McCarthy, I have to insist that you keep your language civil in this office.

Agent Ackerman: This isn't a request. This is an order from the Bureau's highest levels, a matter of multiversal security.

Eliot: How can I be a security threat to multiple universes? I've never even stepped outside this one!

Headmaster Marin: No one's saying you're a threat, Cadet McCarthy. Once the Bureau is finished with this little power game, you'll be back under our jurisdiction and out on assignment before you know it. For now, please hand over your practice Sim pass and campus credentials.

Eliot looks at her mother. Empra tries to tamp down her frown. There's nothing either of them can do.

Empra: Everything's going to be fine, Eliot. Solara will understand. We'll celebrate once all of this is over. I promise.

❖ ❖ ❖

SUBJECT ZERO

MAY 10, 2371 AD

More security footage. Different building.

The lab is white—most of its surfaces flat. As seen through the hologram, it resembles a paper pop-up greeting card, something to be tucked away in a junk box after reading. Eliot looks fragile, too, elbows one degree from crumpling as she props herself up on the examination table. Her pale medical gown blends into pale skin, pale walls. When the scientist makes his entrance, he has to use Eliot's eyebrows as a reference point. August Ackerman steps in after him—the charcoal fabric of the Bureau agent's hat becomes the darkest thing in the room.

"Do you know what we do here, Cadet McCarthy?" the scientist asks.

"Aside from giving people frostbite on their arses?" Eliot's lips quirk, a premonition of many smirks to come.

"That kind of talk might fly in the Corps, sweetheart, but you're dealing with the Bureau now." The feathers in Agent Ackerman's hat quiver when he speaks: red, partridge, pissed. "Show some respect!"

"*Ik laat een scheet in jouw richting,*" Eliot mutters loud enough for everyone's translation tech to register—here and then. The phrase is Dutch for "I fart in your direction."

"Listen here—"

"Agent Ackerman," the scientist intervenes. "I think it best if I handle this exchange. Why don't you wait outside?"

"I'm this girl's official handler." Agent Ackerman crosses his arms. "I should be present for the briefing."

"Yes, but this conversation requires some bedside manner. You can watch over the security feeds if you want. I assure you none of your superiors in MB+251418881HTP8 will take issue with it."

The Bureau agent considers this—protocol tick-tocking through his thoughts, behind his flushing face. "Fine. I'll be in the security office if you need me."

Breathing becomes easier, the air ten times lighter, when he leaves. Both Eliot and the scientist take advantage of this levity—filling their lungs, sighing. Hers sounds relieved. His pushes back at something.

"Bedside manner?" Eliot asks. "Am I dying?"

"Answer my question and I'll answer yours."

"What do you do here?" Eliot sighs again. "Let's see. The Multiverse Bureau is a cross-universal organization that dedicates itself to maintaining balance in the multiverse through interdimensional communication, observation, and travel. The branch in our own universe—MB+178587977FLT6—opened up after Dr. Marcelo Ramírez discovered the key to communicating with alternate realities over a quarter century ago."

"Quite the textbook answer."

"Still counts." Eliot looks around the room, blank as fresh snow, made of few dimensions. There are eyesight charts on the wall—letters from the Roman alphabet alongside characters that did not originate on this earth. Her shoulders peak at the sight. "Level with me, Doc. I've been scanned left and right, up and down. What's wrong with me?"

"With you? Nothing." The scientist scratches at days-old stubble. All he needs is a cup of black coffee and the *emergency deadline* look will be complete. "The name's Dr. Ramírez, by the way."

"Ramírez?" Eliot straightens. "As in Marcelo Ramírez, the head of this Bureau branch and brainiac of the centuries?"

"The one and only—" Dr. Ramírez catches himself. "In this universe, at least. I've met a few of my alternates and they're all very smart, though I suppose that's conceited to acknowledge."

"Alternates? You mean other yous? Other Dr. Marcelo Ramírezes out in the multiverse?"

"Not all of them are named Marcelo. There's Maricella—she's in universe MB+318291745FLT6, as well as MB+318291747FLT6. In several universes, I go by Mache. The bloke in MB+143927121FLT6 struck the jackpot in our DNA pool and got all the looks."

"How many alternates are there?" Eliot's head tilts, dizzy with numbers. "How many universes are there?"

"Unknowable alternates and infinite universes," the scientist says. "The Multiverse Bureau does its best to catalog the worlds, but the task is, by its very nature, endless. They cannot be counted, and yet we keep counting."

"Tell me, in some of these endless universes, are there other Eliot McCarthys currently attending their Academy graduation, not sprouting icicles from their arsecheeks?"

"No one's forcing you to sit on that table, Cadet McCarthy. If your posterior is so cold, feel free to remove it from the offending surface."

"Can I remove myself from this building? My cousin's throwing a party, you see—big bash. She already put a deposit down on enough gelato to sculpt a snowman. Solara's freezer isn't big enough to store it all and it'd be a travesty to let it melt."

Dr. Ramírez vises his head in his fingers. His sigh is a puzzle box—irritable edge, sleepless fears, something bleak inside waiting to be unlocked. "You do have other alternates in other universes. Everyone does. Some of them are probably attending their Academy graduation, and one of them is the reason you're here."

Painted eyebrows clash with each other. Eliot says nothing.

"To the best of our knowledge, the multiverse is infinite. As I said before, the Bureau tries its best to categorize all the universes we've been able to map. The worlds in our universe's grouping—FLT6—are the ones that most closely mirror our own. We share basic biology, geography, and languages. There's an entire gradient of common histories and alternate selves through this series. Naturally, it's the universes that most closely parallel the timeline of our own that hold our alternates. Family trees have to match down to the parents' DNA."

The breadth of Dr. Ramírez's explanation—universes upon universes through universes—adds a new layer to the lab, something palpable. This depth reaches through the hologram, so that even the listeners aboard the *Invictus* shudder.

"The Bureau has been studying the multiverse for an untold number of collective years. So much of it's beyond our comprehension, but the discoveries we have made..." Dr. Ramírez trails off. "You learned about ecosystems in school, yes?"

Eliot nods. "It's all they teach after the bee fiasco. Symbiosis. The web of life. Everything on Earth is connected, and a single change can wreak massive consequences, et cetera."

"Exactly. The same holds true in the multiverse. We're linked to other universes in ways we never could've predicted, connections that transcend dimension. As a Corps cadet, I'm sure you're familiar with the immutability threshold. If a time traveler eats an apple in the past, the world goes on undisturbed. But time can only self-correct to a certain point. If the interference is large enough, a pivot point is created; a new universe with an alternate future is born."

"Our mistakes screw up your filing system?" Eliot concludes. "No wonder the Bureau hates the Corps."

"That's one reason for our organizational animosity, yes. But my point is that the multiverse is interconnected. It's the web of life on a massive scale, all of us tied to other lives through common strings. Do you understand?"

"Um..." Eliot's shoulders jut even higher. "Sure?"

"You're here because there's an aberration in your string."

"A what in my what?"

"One of your alternates has triggered a cataclysmic event." Dr. Ramírez's hands fall to his side. "We've been receiving reports from other FLT6 Bureau branches of a force that annihilates everything in its path, including time and space."

"Like antimatter?"

"Antimatter annihilates, yes, but it releases energy when the matter disappears. This is different. It's...nothing. Creation reversed. We call it the Fade. This decay has been attacking universes, eating their timelines until there's no future to move forward to."

"How long has this been going on?"

"It's impossible to know. The first documentation of this decay was a decade ago, a few spots in universe MB+110249100FLT6. But the Fade is amnesiatic in nature—it not only destroys moments, but people's memories of those moments—so it's possibly existed for far longer without anyone remembering they encountered it. We've been studying it, carefully, for several years: tracking its growth, taking readings, recording the Fade's varying effects on people in its path. Three days ago, something caused the decay to metastasize. Universe MB+110249100FLT6 has unraveled from existence and would've been forgotten if we hadn't kept such diligent digital records of it. Universe MB+110249101FLT6 has an entire decade missing, and MB+110249102FLT6 is also showing signs of erasure. Worlds are meeting their end. The Multiverse Bureau has declared a state of emergency."

It's hard to tell how much of the explanation Eliot has taken in—she's alabaster still, made motionless by the weight of it all. "You said my alternate triggered it. How? How would you know something like that?"

"There's a pattern to the Fade's decay. Only certain universes in the FLT6 category are being eroded, and the deterioration has a cutoff date. Everything that takes place after April eighteenth, 2354, falls apart."

"My birthday..."

The scientist nods. "We're dealing with a reactive force. Are you familiar with how antibodies function?"

"Yes." Eliot taps her hairless head. "And how they mal-function."

Dr. Ramírez goes on to explain anyway. "There are over a trillion antibodies in the human body, each one designed to deal with a specific threat. Whenever a foreign antigen enters our systems, the corresponding antibody responds by attacking what doesn't belong. It's a lock-and-key system, built as a safe-guard to protect our bodies. We believe the decay is acting in a similar manner. Through our studies this past decade we've noticed that the Fade emits a very specific charge, or signature if you will, before it unravels matter. Something—or someone—is calling it.

"We've reverse-engineered the lock to the decay's key and developed a way to scan for it. Since the state of emergency was declared, the FLT6 Bureau branches have been combing their worlds for signs of the Fade's countersignature. Children born on April eighteenth, 2354, were a logical point of interest. Your alternate in MB+136613209FLT6 was flagged first. McCarthys throughout the multiverse have been brought to their branches for testing."

"So you've been scanning me for this countersignature?" Eliot asks.

"Yes," Dr. Ramírez tells her. "You have it. Partially. All of your alternates are emitting the countersignature in varying concentrations. Every universe the Fade has eroded thus far holds one of your alternates, each with a consecutively stronger countersignature. The distribution pattern suggests an echo, a

293

bread crumb trail for the decay to follow until it reaches the source. The way a spider follows the vibrations of its web to secure its prey."

"Spiders. Webs. Locks. Key. Antibodies. Ecosystems. For a scientist, you sure enjoy your metaphors...." Eliot sits up straight: shoulders flat, elbows locked. "Are you going to kill me?"

"Kill you?" The scientist scratches his jaw again. "Why would I do that?"

"If the web is shuddering, why not just cut the string?" Eliot makes a snipping motion with her fingers. "*Not* that I'm endorsing my demise, but if I'm a walking beacon for some cosmic antibody..."

"That's where the metaphor falls apart," Dr. Ramírez admits. "You aren't the *source* of the countersignature. Your death won't stop the Fade—only the neutralization of the catalyst might do that."

"Might?"

"Nothing like this has ever happened before. Everything from here on out is theoretical.... But if we can find the catalyst and neutralize her—or him—first, then it's possible we'll be able to halt the Fade's progress and protect the universes between. Including ours. None of the branches' scans have come back with a complete countersignature, which leads us to believe the subject we're searching for—the epicenter of all this—dwells in an MB-negative universe. One where the Bureau doesn't yet exist. As you might imagine, this presents complications. There's a portable scanning process, but the readings take longer than those with the lab instruments. Plus, the subject has to be within a hundred meters for the scan to work."

"Why are you telling me all this?" The table shimmers as Eliot shifts her weight. "Don't you have schools of interdimensional travelers who can skip universes on command?"

"Universes, yes. Time is a different beast. Seeing as many of your alternates are time travelers, it's best for us to cover our bases with an operative who can navigate both. The scan won't work if we can't keep up."

"You—you want me to conduct the scans." The realization sinks in, carving deeper marks into every corner of Eliot's face. "But I don't know the first thing about world-hopping."

"It's easier for time travelers to pick up interdimensional travel than vice versa. Similar mechanics, different contexts. Traveling through time requires historical finesse, and thus years of training, which you've already had. The world-hopping tech is similar to the Corps' solo-jump equipment—only you're traveling sideways instead of backward. We've no doubt that you'll be able to adapt to the terrains of this mission. They are other versions of your life, after all," Dr. Ramírez tells her.

"How *many* versions? You just told me that the number of universes is infinite. That's more than a Hail Maria or haystack-needle odds...."

"We've narrowed the epicenter's search window by projecting a path using various strengths of the countersignature in each alternate. There are 3,526 worlds most likely to host the catalyst."

Eliot considers this number. "Better than infinite, I guess."

"You won't be the only you searching. We've divided the window into manageable sectors, a few dozen universes each. You're to scour your assigned worlds, scan your alternates as discreetly as possible, and—in the event that you find the catalyst—neutralize them."

"Neutralize. As in...?" Eliot blanches, making scissors of her fingers again.

Dr. Ramírez hesitates. "If there's a string that needs to be cut, it is the catalyst."

Murder is as cold as the room. Eliot shivers—white—into it. Her hand drops.

"And if I fail?"

"Annihilation," the scientist says simply. "Your cousin's gelato will have to melt, Cadet McCarthy. You have worlds to save."

❖ ❖ ❖

SUBJECT ZERO

MAY 15, 2371 AD

Eliot stares down the camera, no trace of smile left. She looks tougher than she did in the lab—less likely to tear, more ready to do the ripping. "My name is Eliot Gaia McCarthy. I'm recording this message for myself in the event that the Fade reaches my universe—MB+178587977FLT6—before the mission is completed."

Her flinch is understandable. She's talking about the destruction of everything she's ever known.

"If you see the decay, jump through time immediately. The

Fade is running along a timeline parallel to your own, but as long as your present doesn't collide with the decay's present, you will continue to exist. Your memories won't be so fortunate. The Multiverse Bureau has equipped you with recording tech that preserves moments even after they've been erased by the Fade. It's imperative to your mission that you record everything you see so no essential knowledge is lost. Knowing what you've forgotten will also help you track the Fade's growth and—hopefully—stay ahead of it. Your interface, Vera, will remind you to file these feeds every twenty-four hours. You have three types of jump equipment: interdimensional, time, and teleportation. All three of them are linked into Vera's systems and can be controlled via voice. Your handler for this mission is Agent August Ackerman. He'll be monitoring your progress from universe MB+251418881HTP8 and dropping in from time to time. Beware: He's a complete arse. His sexism is pointedly ancient, despite his disdain for time travel. Protocol is his Achilles' heel, so if he starts giving you grief about something, just mention his superiors in HTP8. Your mission directives are stored in Vera's systems, so I'm not going to waste time going over all of them here...."

There's a pause.

"This mission won't be easy. It's long and solitary, with terrifying consequences and possibly no reward. Mom, Strom, Solara, entire universes of people are depending on you, Eliot." She stares at herself, at all of her selves—future and alternate, despairing and dumbfounded—through the lens. It's a warpath gaze, blazing across time, beyond dimensions. "Make it count."

❖ ❖ ❖

Files played on, compact lives lived again in the *Invictus*'s common area, all meticulously labeled with subject numbers and time stamps—a system made even more essential with hindsight. Eliot had organic memories left, but after seven alternates with seven lives alongside seven sets of friends in seven sets of universes, they began blending together. Was it Subject Three or Subject Five who named their time machine *Icarus*? Which one had tilted teeth? The cousin named Maribel? It was such a snarl of details—shared histories, subtle differences—made all the more indistinguishable by Fade-induced amnesia. The early lives were moth-eaten blankets—frayed at the edges, gone where it counted. Holes, gaps, holes. No matter how hard Eliot tried, she couldn't place herself back in Dr. Ramírez's lab. Had the examination table really been that cold? What had it felt like, before all those metaphors of his sank in, took root? Before she realized she had to scour dozens of universes to kill her other self?

It was a learning curve—diagonal travel, across universes, along timelines, all over the map. Subject One was already on a CTM crew when Eliot landed in her world. Tailing her—through the streets of 2152 New York, medieval castle corridors, the redwood forests of pre-colonized North America—while staying inside the countersignature scanner's operating radius had taken far too long. By the time Eliot realized Subject One wasn't a match, she'd lost months—months the Fade had used to creep from world to world.

Eliot wasn't just racing against time, but the ruination of it.

Every moment spent searching for the catalyst meant the destruction of another. She had to pick up the pace of her observation, which meant that she had to get close to her subject, far closer than the Corps' MO would ever allow. As long as her alternates were traveling through history in an official capacity, she wouldn't be able to obtain speedy reads on them without getting arrested by the institution she'd trained her entire life to serve.

And so Eliot was forced to do what every instructor had warned her against: Change the course of history. She suspected the Bureau wouldn't be too pleased with the idea, either—sowing pivot points, growing fresh universes as casually as garden tomatoes—but this *was* the apocalypse they were talking about. Best-case scenario: She'd find the catalyst quickly, neutralize the original and any spin-offs. At worst, she was creating more fodder for the Fade.

Altering her alternates' timelines was a process of trial and error. The natural starting point? Corrupting their final exam Sim. It was Versailles—it was always Versailles: pastel gowns, mercury mirrors, evening gardens in bloom—and with a bit of quick-coding and alt-tech, Eliot was able to project herself into the Sim's programming. One blown kiss from a Tier Three mark queen and her alternates' time-traveling futures would be ruined.

But time pushed back, where Subject Two was concerned, self-correcting in the form of Empra, who intervened on her child's behalf. Her rank in the Corps caused them to overlook the final exam Sim. Back to square one, version two. More months were spent chasing Subject Two through history, trying to avoid Corps detection. An unsustainable pace.

No match found. On to the next life.

Subject Three. Eliot started even further back. Dr. Ramírez had warned her against scanning alternates outside of a present parallel to her own, since doing so might skew the results, leading to unnecessary neutralization or a skipped catalyst. She lingered in Subject Three's past just long enough to ruin it, sabotaging what would become the *Ab Aeterno*'s final mission. Altering the nav system and stealing the extra fuel rods meant that Empra's ship landed a few centuries off course, with no way back to Central and no chance of rescue. Making her own mother a castaway in history was a heartless move: palatable only through necessity. Eliot promised herself she'd rescue the *Ab Aeterno* once everything got sorted.

The immutability threshold was breached, and this time, when the final exam Sim went awry, the Academy did its part, tossing a protesting Subject Three out on his arse. But he wasn't as grounded as Eliot had hoped, for wherever time travel existed, so did the black market. Every universe had its own version of Lux, whose sights were always set on Cadet McCarthy. Subject Three was skipping centuries inside an illegal TM within days. It was all Eliot could do to keep up, aligning his present with hers through burning buildings and pirate battles, scavenging scanner percentages whenever Subject Three brushed shoulders with her mid-disaster. The process was even slower this time around. Something had to change....

She had to get closer to the subject. She had to join his crew. The task was harder than it sounded; theirs was a tight-knit group and approaching them led to more suspicion than open arms. Subject Three—their captain—was wary. He remembered Eliot's face from the Sim, which led to questions she couldn't really answer. They elected *not* to take her on board, and so more weeks were lost chasing them through history for the final few percentages. Subject Three was not a match.

Agent Ackerman checked in. As predicted, he wasn't thrilled with the new universes in Eliot's wake, but he was even less pleased with her pace. "Hurry it up, history hopper! My superiors in MB+251418881HTP8 are breathing down my neck to get this situation contained and resolved." Not the best pep talk.

Round four. Eliot did everything over again, but this time, when the present points in their timelines intersected in the den of the Caponian Collective, she resorted to blackmail. They faced off in the vault: Subject Four in a rainbow-bright suit, Eliot palming the Cat's Eye Emerald. There was a chase—there was always a chase—and after a begrudging agreement, she was part of Subject Four's crew: bunk, nickname, and all. It seemed she'd worked out a system. The scanner finished its read inside two days: not a match.

Eliot didn't skip worlds immediately; it didn't feel right, leaving the *Ab Aeterno* stranded, making Subject Four's loss of mother permanent. She stayed just long enough to guide the crew in Empra's direction. Their universe might be doomed, but they found each other—embracing in the flaming city, hearts made light by the fact that for now, the *Ab Aeterno* was saved.

The fifth world. A pattern had emerged: strand the *Ab Aeterno*, sabotage the final exam Sim, intersect the subject's timeline at present point, blackmail, join crew, take scans, rescue mother. It wasn't easy, but it felt rhythmic, something Eliot could keep up with. Something that might even outrun the Fade...

Then the forgetting started.

They weren't small losses: no five-second delay recalling the name of Solara's childhood pet. What Eliot could not remember were large swathes of past: sophomore year at the Academy, her first kiss....Logic told her these things had happened. Freshman year, junior year. Never-been-kissed, second base. Memories fit in the middle, but—much like a secondhand jigsaw puzzle—whole picture pieces were missing.

Universe MB+178587977FLT6, the world Eliot came from, was fading.

If there was a fate worse than death, it was a life unremembered. Mom, Solara, Strom, her Academy friends...moment by moment they melted away from Eliot's recollection, herself with them. She found no solace in her interface footage, for photographs were meant to preserve memories, not resurrect them, and so her family pixelated—three strangers on a Venetian boat, adrift in ruins.

Eliot watched the datastream of Dr. Ramírez again so she wouldn't forget what she was doing, why she was here. Why *was* she here? Who was she trying to save, really? How could she *make it count* when the life she'd lived was falling into oblivion?

It wasn't a question she could contemplate for long. Decay

was hot on Eliot's heels. The forgetting stretched on, over, out, spilling into the universes of Subject OneTwoThreeFour, hounding their countersignature through history with gathering strength. Subject Five was not a match, and Eliot left him in the arms of his mother in Alexandria. Once more saved, once more on the edge of burning.

Subject Six. Same routine, new haste. Eliot had no way of knowing when the Fade would find her, but she knew the force was close, its fingers of forgetfulness scratching at every universe she'd ever traveled through. Her days were spent on high alert—watching every moment for signs of the Fade's arrival. Dr. Ramírez had shown her footage of the decay, but even watching herself watch it, Eliot knew there'd be no comparison between screens and life. The hologram's projection looked fake, something stripped from a Sim programmer's nightmares.

Her first encounter with the Fade was in Far's universe. The sight was as horrible as it was magnificent—view of all views. Eliot stood on the *Titanic*'s first-class promenade, hip bones pressed against the railing, awaiting the arrival of the *Invictus*. Atlantic wind whispered salty nothings into her ears; water sped below, folding froth into the ocean liner's hull. There was a peace to the scene Eliot only felt in hindsight: the calm before.

It started at the horizon, where the blue of the sea struck the blue of the sky. A pinpoint of not-blue appeared between the two elements. The spot mushroomed up and out: drinking the ocean, gnashing the heavens, devouring two of the vastest expanses known to twentieth-century man in seconds. Eliot stood on deck, transfixed by the magnitude of the force. It was too *big*, too massive for holograms or descriptions or human feeling. Even her fear was dwarfed in its presence....

Presence. Present! As soon as the Fade reached the promenade and clashed with Eliot's present, she'd be unmade.

Jump immediately!

She did. The leap was through time, not dimensions, and even then only into later that evening. Eliot spent much of the night in the first-class dining saloon, waiting for the *Invictus* and the Fade in turn. The decay *did* follow at a delay, creeping into a not-distant-enough past, savoring the minutes she'd also spent eating, stripping the taste of poached salmon from Eliot's tongue even as it sat in her belly.

She would have abandoned the day altogether, if her present wasn't scheduled to intersect with Subject Seven's present here. Roughly. The hours she was forced to skip worried her, but they mattered little in the end. The *Invictus* bounced off six o'clock—a time that no longer existed—and the resulting ten o'clock crash landing meant Eliot only had to jump another thirty minutes to realign their timetables, giving Far an extra half hour to fumble through the cargo room.

From there it was a familiar story, mostly remembered. Flashing the *Rubaiyat*. Teleporting onto the *Invictus*. Blackmail. The party in Vegas. *Cucurbita* conversations with Imogen. The meeting with Lux. Mission prep for Alexandria. Eliot had recorded every moment—even the ones that seemed too simple to store. The crew of the *Invictus* watched themselves through her eyes, their own transfixed. Only Imogen had moved, sliding from couch to floor, drowning her face in aquamarine hair while starry-eyed confessions played. Eliot was surprised at how much she felt for her, for all of them. In a matter of days, her loved ones had become strangers, while the strangers themselves became people she wanted to save....

The chip held almost a year's worth of footage—but the Grid's timelessness allowed them to watch it in a single sitting. A year. A minute. A month. A life. Seven infinite lives until only one memory remained in the systems. It opened with Imogen gazing into ash-strung skies. "The fires have already started."

"Are we too late?" Then-Far asked.

"That's enough." Now-Far stood. "Pause."

But the chip was programmed to respond to Eliot's voice alone, and as much as she wanted to spare them the horror of Empra's unmaking, she couldn't. The *Invictus*'s crew knew what happened next, but soon they wouldn't. They had to watch the footage to understand what the Fade took and remember the stakes....

"Stop!" Far tried again, louder. The stitches in Eliot's hand throbbed alongside his shout—a fresh and oozing grief. "Make it *stop*!"

She wanted to. She didn't.

The hologram dashed through Alexandrian streets, up the library steps. Eliot hadn't rushed to Sappho's scrolls but kept to the central stacks instead, watching to make sure Far got to the right place. Empra was always in the library's southeast corner on this date, at this time. Her children always turned at the sound of her voice—their reunion always curdled inside Eliot's heart. Empra McCarthy looked identical in every world, and even though Eliot knew these were other mothers, it was easier to imagine her own as a transient soul than to accept the Fade's sentence.

That erasure wasn't so abstract anymore. On the *Titanic*, it had been the decay's size that struck Eliot; from the ground, it was the hunger. No element was safe. Water, air, earth, fire, stone, paper. The Fade destroyed *everything*.

Skin. Bone. Soul.

Empra was gone the instant the Fade touched her: presents intersecting. The *Invictus* would have unraveled, too, if Eliot hadn't initiated the TM's jump into the Grid. And so they were here, watching until the moment in the hologram overlapped with the moment they were sitting in. It could've gone on—ouroboros endlessness: serpent's tail to serpent's mouth to serpent's tail to serpent's mouth—but Eliot finally spoke.

"End sequence."

The world within a world folded in on itself, becoming a clear chip in a velvet box once more. The crew stared at the space the hologram had filled—its emptiness played back in their expressions. Imogen hid beneath waves of hair. Gram, too, had turned inward, making calculations of everything he'd heard. Priya sat more still than steady, parted mouth vacant of words. There was no need to observe anymore, but Eliot watched them anyway, all too aware that they could look back and *see* her. The veil of secrets had been ripped away and here Eliot stood. World-hopper, alternate cousin, other self, executioner, girl forgotten by her universe—

she was who she was, but only because he was who he was

—boy unmoored from time, snag in the fabric of the multiverse, eye of the storm, system error, catalyst. Farway Gaius McCarthy didn't look like any of these things, seated on the scorched couch, blaster drooping at his side. Often he carried himself with the surety of someone convinced they were destined for greatness, but after realizing what he actually *was* destined for, the boy sat with his shoulders hunched.

When Eliot spoke again, he flinched. "Don't you see, Far? You're the epicenter. My countersignature emission scans confirm it. You're the reason the Fade has torn apart these universes, and there's only one theoretical way to stop it...."

No one said a word.

They understood now, all of them did.

"You have to die."

PART III

Things fall apart; the centre cannot hold;
Mere anarchy is loosed upon the world.

—W. B. YEATS
"THE SECOND COMING"

34.

PAST THE END

IT WAS A BAD MED-PATCH NIGHTMARE, Far told himself. Reality couldn't possibly morph like this, until it had more in common with a Salvador Dalí painting than the world he'd wandered for eighteen years. Everything was swimming, as if he'd fallen back-first into a river and was seeing the rest of the *Invictus* through its flow. Bright hair, bloodstained scrubs, rainbow cubes on the floor. The ship full of colors seemed to be moving and swirling, yet nothing was.

"I'm the catalyst? Why? How?" Far knew the answer. It was something he'd carried his entire life—a badge of honor. Being born outside of time had always felt like a mark of something greater, culling him out for an extraordinary existence.

But this existence was becoming a bit *too* extraordinary.

"It's your unbirthday," Gram said. "Think about it. Every one of your alternates is your genetic match, which means you all share the same father. Nothing aberrant there. It's the birthday, or in your case, a lack of one, where you diverge. The rest of them were born on April eighteenth, 2354."

And Far was born in the *Ab Aeterno*. Eternity. Surely there was a scientific reason for the collapse of the multiverse, but all Far could think about were the Linear protesters who sometimes gathered on the Academy steps—their digital ONE LIFE, ONE TIME banners blazing. Their leader's magnified words rapped at the school windows: *When humanity steps into the shoes of gods, things will go awry.*

You don't belong here. Eliot wasn't just a premonition. She was course correction, God's will, karma, fate—call it what you will. This was the universe's way of righting itself, handing Far an eviction notice....

The dreaming feeling ebbed enough for Far to recognize Priya's breath beside his—thick with emotion, too thin to hold back her sob. Their hands turned into a tangle of each other's fingers. *Hold on for life, dear.*

He didn't want to go.

"But if it really was my birth that set all this off, why'd it take the Bureau so long to find me?" Far asked. "Everyone in Central knows about my unbirthday. Surely that would've set off some red flags."

"The Multiverse Bureau isn't omniscient or omnipresent. Your universe is just a number to them—MB-178587984FLT6— though I suppose that number's changed since I broke the immutability threshold twice...." Eliot trailed off. "Regardless, I think Gram's correct. You're the only alternate who was born outside of time. It's not a stretch to believe that your birth broke something."

"So why's the Fade attacking the other universes first?" Far knew it wasn't important in the end, but maybe, if he could wrap his head around his doom, it'd be easier to accept. "Shouldn't it go the other way, if I'm the epicenter? Inward out?"

"The Fade isn't springing from you," Gram said. "If I understood Dr. Ramírez correctly, it's hunting you down. Does anyone have a pen? Imogen?"

"What? Pen." The Historian started at the sound of her name. "Yes, pen. I have. Somewhere. Definitely."

"Could I borrow it?" Gram prodded.

Imogen brushed her hair from her face, set to scouring the table. She found the felt-tipped pen and handed it to the Engineer over her shoulder. "Yeppers."

"Thanks, Im."

She nodded, still not looking at him, and sank back into her hair.

Gram grabbed the sole paper they had on board—the Corps of Central Time Travelers' Code of Conduct—and traced a circle on one of the cover's un-doodled spaces. "Inside this circle are all of the FLT6 universes where your genetic alternates exist. Here you are"—stick figure jotted in the middle—"the epicenter. Now here's your birth, causing the countersignature." Tiny lightning lines, splintering out of the toothpick man. Were they signals, or cracks? To Far, they looked like both. "Crux knows where the Fade actually comes from, but for this illustration we'll just say outside the circle. It's honing in on you, following the trail through the other universes, and obliterating them in the process."

His friend etched arrows, until Far's entire likeness was ringed with points, every one of them aimed inward. A dozen sharpnesses. *You don't belong, you're wrong, wrong, wrong!*

Far looked to Eliot. The gleam of her handcuffs was mirrored in her eyes. "You said the Grid keeps us safe from the Fade. If I was born here, maybe I should stay. That way the decay wouldn't have anything to follow."

"No can do, Far." Gram placed the pen back on the table. "All time or no time, our resources are finite. We'd run out of fuel and food if we didn't land."

"Food." Imogen perked up again, rising off the floor, drifting toward the kitchenette. "Good idea."

Far's stomach was hollowed past the point of appetite. Saturated fat wouldn't repair the universe—*universes*—his existence had broken. Sugar couldn't resurrect his mother. "The *Ab Aeterno* didn't wreck because of the Fade. You—you stranded it." Eliot wasn't the villain. Far knew this, but the knowledge didn't translate into feeling. "You took my mom away."

"She's my mother, too," the girl whispered.

The blaster in his hand had grown heavier. Far wanted to lift it but found that he couldn't. Who was he going to aim it at anyway? Himself? His different self? No shot would make anything that had happened untrue....

"You had eleven more years with her than I did—"

"And I can't remember any of them. You want to toss around

blame, Far? Those years are gone because you exist. I stranded your mother because I was trying to save her. I tried to save all of them...." Eliot sagged, marionette past motion. Wardrobe clothes shuddered from the extra weight on the pipe. "If I'd known the Fade was going to appear in Alexandria, I never would've taken you there and let your present align with Empra's."

"So why bother with target practice?" Far looked past the brown-white weave of his and Priya's fingers, at the burnt satin below. "You should've just left me in Alexandria, let the Fade do what it set out to."

"The countersignature scan wasn't complete. The Multiverse Bureau wants hard evidence that you're the catalyst, proof that the Fade might halt with your death."

"It won't." Gram's grave words buried every one of them. "Dr. Ramírez said the Fade has been active for over a decade, though I suspect it's been closer to eighteen years. Far's carried this countersignature his entire life; shooting him now might cut the signal and stop the Fade's reach into the future, but it won't keep the decay from chasing down his past self."

Eliot squeezed her eyes shut. Far stared at the illustration: boy radiating brokenness. His future, their fate prophesied in one small scribble. He wasn't the blood threading through history's veins, but a poison, polluting every time he'd ever touched. All the seconds he'd lived—the sights he'd seen, the pasts he'd walked—were damned, and his friends' lifetimes with them.

There was a rattling of pots in the kitchenette and Imogen emerged with a half-eaten pan of tiramisu. The scene was heartbreaking for its normalcy. His cousin set the leftovers on the table like she always did. She'd brought enough forks for everyone.

"The world's ending," she explained as she sat down and started digging into ladyfingers and cocoa-flecked cream. "Might as well have dessert."

"You're going to give up on Far that easily?" Priya bristled, too distraught to hide the fact that she was. It was so unlike her to fall apart in the open, for all to see. "Stuff yourself with sweets while everything goes to *shazm*?"

"What else *can* I do?" Imogen's voice hit a pitch that made Saffron scramble into her lap, ears perked. "Dress him up in his finest flash-leather suit? Teach him the proper etiquette for meeting a universe-gobbling evanescence? 'Smile, Farway, take a bow as you go to your doom. Always remember that gentlemen never run. Oh wait, we can't remember anything, because the Fade has an insatiable appetite for our past.' Eating some fexing tiramisu is currently the only thing between me and drowning in a puddle of my own tears. I'd be happy for anyone to join me!"

Priya grabbed the Code of Conduct and waved the book about. "We've broken these rules for trinkets and thrills so many times...but when things get hard, when lives are on the line, we tuck tail. We make ourselves feel better by saying they've already died and we don't have a choice and we can't change history and I swallow it every time, because what else is there to do?"

"P..." Far couldn't feel his fingertips, couldn't let go of her. "There's nothing to fight here. Imagined heroics—"

"You're *not* already dead!" Priya broke in. "And I refuse to act like you are."

"Far shouldn't be alive in the first place," Eliot said. "Gram's right. I don't know why Dr. Ramírez didn't see it. The Fade won't stop until every trace of Far's existence is erased. Our lives were doomed from the start."

"That's it!" Gram leaped to his feet, snapping both sets of fingers, embodiment of an exclamation point. "The start!"

"What?" Imogen paused between bites.

"Dr. Ramírez ordered Eliot to neutralize the catalyst. Far isn't the catalyst." All the Engineer got were blank stares. He kept snapping, as if the sound might jog their IQs up to speed with his own. "I mean, yes, he's carrying the countersignature, but he himself isn't the aberration. His birth is."

"What difference does that make?" Eliot asked.

"There might be nothing to fight, but there is something to save," Gram told them. "If we go back and alter the circumstances that led to Far being born on the *Ab Aeterno*, we could pivot point into a future where the catalyst has been neutralized. We can give our universe, our own lives, a second chance."

The common area was quiet as their minds ran the track. It felt a bit like an infinity loop—internal histories and external forces and what about all the other universes? What about themselves? What was the cost of this hope?

"That's dash..." Eliot blinked. "It just might work. I mean, it's making a lot of assumptions. That Far's birth is the aberration. That the time we have to travel back to doesn't fall to the Fade. Plus, how do we know the countersignature won't echo into this new world?"

"We don't." Gram crossed his arms. Excitement was writ beneath his skin, pulsing with the veins there. "But if we fail, everything goes to shazm anyway. Succeed and we get a new lease on life."

"My vote goes for saving stuff," Imogen offered. "What's there to lose?"

"Ourselves." Priya looked to each of them in turn, her stare ending with Far. The whole room wavered. "We might be alive in this new world, but we won't be who we are now. This life on the *Invictus*, everything we've been through together..."

More silence, another track. This one more finite: May 7, 2371, dawn—hazy, like all others—when the four of them stood at the helm of an unnamed ship, admiring the flawless holo-shield invisibility plates and their reflection in them—a fine, shiny crew. Their very first mission to eighteenth-century Portugal that same day to retrieve a bottle of port for Lux's stores. From there it was a life of historical snatch-and-grabs: the Cat's Eye Emerald, Klimt paintings, Fabergé eggs....For each treasure, an adventure; for each adventure, a mess of tears and laughter, kisses and scrapes. For all of this?

A family.

"Who we are now can't stay." It was Imogen who pointed to the chalk wall, where Far's cursive cried into itself, running ruins of color. "How many of those mission descriptions could you rewrite? How many would we never know we lost? How soon until we don't even know each other? I'd take a total system reboot over rotting through the brain stem any day. No offense, Eliot."

"I'd take that, too," Eliot told them. "If it's any consolation, there was no *Invictus* before I arrived on the scene."

This was a strange thing to consider. Far walked over to the creator of his world, still a head shorter. She had no parted hair for him to ponder, just the cuffs, which made her wrists look far thinner than they were. "Tell me, why haven't you teleported out of those yet?"

"A rather pissed-off boy once told me trust is something that's built." *Ah!* There was her smirk, making a comeback. "I figure I'm a few bricks down after trying to murder you."

"Yeah, well...if I were you, I would've shot me, too."

"If you were me? Ha. Good one." Eliot's laugh was made of brass, as hard as it was deflective. "At least our humor is equally morbid."

Far didn't echo the sound, because he meant every word. So much fury, so much fear spent on this girl's behalf and for what? Hers was the ruined life, his was the fault. "I'm sorry, Eliot. About your mom, your cousin, your childhood...I'm sorry it's gone."

Dimples mussed Eliot's chin.

He went on. "There's a place for you on this crew, if you want it. I know it won't last long. We're all about to take a fall, and I'll need every hand on deck to create this pivot point—"

The air before him flickered, and again Far was reminded of Central's street magicians. Top to bottom, stola and all, Eliot had vanished. Her cuffs dangled from the pipe, chaining nothing. Displaced air wove through the wardrobe's garments—the yellow dress among them.

"Did—" Gram blinked. "Did she just haul tail on us?"

Far stared at the daffodil gown, swaying its phantom waltz.

Everything was disappearing on him. Everyone...

He looked back to the couch, where Priya was staring at the crumpled guidebook, tracing the cat ears over each C. Her haircut looked extra drastic from this angle: short, long, two versions of herself pasted together.

"Look!" Imogen pointed toward the console room, where Eliot was stepping from behind Bartleby's cloth-and-wire frame.

"Let's start over, fresh." The girl reentered the common room, rubbing her wrists back to white. "New mission, new world. We're going to have to be quick about this if we want to beat the Fade."

"How quick?" Far felt better shifting back into mission mode. Fighting for a future, albeit an alternate one, was preferable to waiting for oblivion. "What kind of timeline are we talking? Days? Weeks?"

"My best guess is the former." Eliot grabbed a fork, gouged a V-shaped hole into the top half of the dessert. "Imagine the multiverse as a piece of tiramisu. Each layer's a world. My universe is the top layer, the one below that is Subject One's world, and so on. This universe is at the bottom, with Far's moments mostly intact. But the Fade's growth"—she scooped out a fuller bite, scraping the pan—"is exponential. The longer we take, the faster it spreads."

"Vera isn't equipped with any sort of mapping system?" Gram asked.

Eliot shook her head.

"We can use the wardrobe to make our own." Imogen planted her own utensil in the tiramisu and started pulling down clothes. Yellow dress, workman's shirt, tricorne hat, a camouflage field jacket... "Put anything we don't remember into a pile, figure out the dates that are being erased. That'd at least give us a sense of scale...."

"Ingenious, Imogen!" Gram turned to Far. "What mission was the *Ab Aeterno* on before you popped out?"

"December 31, 95 AD," Priya offered, voice raspy. "It's what he always tried on the med-droid."

"Never worked," Far muttered.

Priya smiled at the memory, tucking her longer hairs behind her ear. Far was thunderously struck by the sight—there was only one Priya, *his* P, who hummed songs long after they ended, who told the most gruesome medical stories with a stone face, who *felt* on a level most of them couldn't comprehend. Far had never imagined love could be such a solid thing, yet here it was. He wished he could go back in time and tell himself to drop everything, to go to Woodstock for no reason at all but to be with her....

"We got the when. What about the where?" Gram prompted.

There was a good deal Far didn't know about his origins—i.e., most of it. His father's identity had always been a question mark, a dead halt in conversations. He only knew the circumstances of his birth because Burg had turned the story mythic with so many retellings. Certain details were cemented in canon: Empra's indigo stola, Far's wild curls. Others—such as the ship's pre-Grid location—had been meticulously cut out.

"Um, Rome." It was a guess, one he'd pieced together over the years. Where else would a Latin-speaking time traveler be wearing a stola in 95 AD? "I think. Mom never talked about it."

"You think?" Gram frowned. "No offense, Far, but we can't run this op on hunches. We need a clear picture of what we're trying to change, a timeline down to the minute."

"What about the datastreams?" Imogen kept sorting through clothes. A dinner jacket here, a pair of trousers there. So much forgetting, above them all along... "Every Corps-sanctioned mission has them."

"The 95 AD streams were never released to the public." Every year on Far's unbirthday, he tried to look up the mission's footage. Every year he got the same answer: *Please refer to archive 12-A11B.* A restricted section his cadet badge couldn't come close to accessing. "Someone locked them up nice and tight at the platinum-black level."

The original crew groaned.

Eliot placed her hands on her hips. "We'll have to hack it out, then."

"You don't *hack* a platinum-black-restricted Corps archive." The mere thought was sacrilegious to their Engineer, schooled in the Academy's computery ways. "Their restricted servers are isolated, so you have to be on-site at the Corps Headquarters server room to access them. Teleporting might get you in, but the place is bristling with cameras, all running facial-recognition scans. Anyone who doesn't belong there would be spotted before they could touch the server, much less hack it."

"Enter Corps, stage left." Far shuddered thinking about it.

"Are you black market thieves or are you *black market thieves*?" Eliot hissed.

He shrugged. "We're realists."

"Which is something only pessimists say." Imogen brushed her hands together. The pile of fabric at her feet was substantial enough for Saffron to nest in. The creature looked downright blissful.

"I made alterations to Far's final exam Sim via remote hack. We can do the same with the Corps' facial-recognition system," Eliot suggested. "My face isn't in their files. If we create a profile with platinum-black clearance, that'd prevent the alarms from tripping when I tap the restricted servers."

Gram's brow furrowed, considering. "We could. . . . It won't last long, though. Once the Corps realizes their firewalls are breached, they'll spot the forgery."

"What if I told you I had a traceless way of hacking the systems?" Eliot asked.

"It's true." Marin's nasally sneer stuck to Far's memories. *Diagnostics showed all systems are untampered with. You failed.* "Corps had no idea she screwed up my Sim."

"Then I'd say our odds just improved incrementally," the Engineer conceded.

"All right, then." Far regarded his crew. Only the chalk puddles knew everything they'd carried him through; not even the future knew what they might face. Nothing was certain except this: They were up to the task. "Let's make ourselves a world."

35.

THROUGH AND THROUGH

THE PLANNING OF THE CORPS HACK went on for hours or seconds or years, until the crew's bodies realized that they were, in fact, mortal and very, very sleep-deprived. No one had caught z's since the flight from Vegas, and the chance to enter REM cycle would be nonexistent once they landed back in Central.

Priya had never struggled with insomnia before, but the thought that this was the last sleep she'd ever have as herself kept the ceiling in sight. Ocean noises hushed through her headphones and dreams licked her peripheral vision—*come to us sink in deep sleep sleep*—but memories kept getting in the way, washing her back into wakefulness. Many of them were firsts: the sight of a cadaver's waxy lips, the Acidic Sisters concert her father took her to for her thirteenth birthday. That fateful day when, on the angrier edges of a caffeine headache, ERROR: MANUAL MED NEEDED flashed across her interface and she'd marched into the examination room to find a cadet whose grin punched through all defenses.

These memories…who would she be without them? Identity was never something Priya had taken for granted. *You are a Parekh*, her mother reminded her every time she stressed over study notes. These were double-sided words. Encouraging: *You come from a long line of medical professionals.* Daunting: *You must live up to their accomplishments.* It was something she remembered every single time she put on her ID card at the Academy infirmary: PRIYA PAREKH, MED, mirrored in Hindi.

The thought of being rewritten kept her turning on the bunk. Reincarnation—sloughing off old bodies for new—had always been such a distant promise, seventy, eighty, ninety years off, and yet here she was, on the eve of it. How much would change in this next life? Would she still be a Parekh? Yes. She was a few months older than Far. If she was a Parekh, she'd probably end up being a Medic.

The ocean rolled through Priya's ears, out of her eyes, on, on…

Tap, tap. The knock was soft, and might've been lost to the nautical noises, if Priya wasn't so familiar with it. Many of the *Invictus*'s lights had been dimmed, and gloom pressed through the door when she opened it, settling in the corners of her bunk, dripping from the ends of Far's curls.

She pulled back her headphones and wiped her eyes. "Did I wake you?"

Far shook his head.

The space between them reeked of lasts. Priya wanted to be brave, wanted to say what she meant—*I love you. Good-bye.*—but the words withered inside her vocal cords, trapped by the deadened tangle of what never was jealousy, but fear. Fear of a loss now realized. "I wanted to let you sleep. We've got a big day ahead."

"You've been crying."

Her lips trembled, attempted a smile. "This haircut looks abysmal."

I love you. Good-bye.

Good-bye.

It was almost as if Far heard. He tilted his head. "You don't have to hide from me, P."

Open the floodgates. This was more than ugly crying. It was the grief that came with truth: They were past saving. Their love was all, but soon it would be nothing, and the certainty of it clutched Priya's spine, shook and shook and shook, until her sobs became wretched, waterless things. Far sat on the bunk, his arm around her shoulder. There were tears on his face, too, aqueducting down his nose. One for his mother, two for the worlds, more for this life.

"I know it's not everything we'd hoped, but we're giving ourselves a chance," he whispered. "We'll live."

"But the *Invictus*, Saffron, Gram and Imogen, us..."

"We'll find each other."

"You'll have a birthday, so there will be no need for me to come in and reset the med-droids every time you have a medical exam." Priya's breath shook. She was a drought inside. "We'll never meet."

"Maybe we'll bump into each other on a street corner. I'll flash my impish grin. There's a vendor a few meters away selling real coffee, but since I'm still a cadet and too broke to pay, I'll invite you to sit on the curb and share a stimulant patch while we smell the roasting beans instead."

"Maybe…" She'd never been one to accept random invitations from boys on the street, and the chances of two souls colliding in a city of millions was slim. Even if both of these things happened, as soon as Priya discovered Far's future profession, she'd stick to her no-time-travelers policy. But these doubts were nails in a coffin, no point in voicing them. "Make it a tea stand and I'm there."

"Of course, tea!" Far laughed—a light, ragged sound. "We'll smell smoggy chai and I'll ask you your name and you'll ask me mine first because you like to know the lay of the land before you commit to anything and I'll say Farway Gaius McCarthy, just a normal guy with a birthday who likes your smile and your cutting-edge hairstyle."

"It really is awful."

"It really isn't."

They sat, wordless. Waves crashed through Priya's headphones, became the pulse in her neck, the beat of her heart, the *want want want* to not just stay here with Far but to go back to when they had a future. She thought back on all the other times they'd sat like this, where she'd wasted the silences between them wondering about their trajectory: Rings? Vows? A villa in Zone 6? Children?

None of that now.

This was it. The moment they'd rushed to.

There was a shudder, Far clearing his throat. "Back in Vegas, when we were at Café Gelato, I was on edge because I knew Eliot was playing us for something. The sparkler was burning down, and you and Gram and Imogen were singing, and as I looked around that table, all I wanted... all I wished for was a happy ending."

Priya shut her eyes. According to the rules of ancient birthday lore, Far was only telling her because he didn't believe it would come true. If only the Fade were a force that could be bargained with...

"Lux grilled me pretty good before he offered me this job. He asked me what my biggest fear was. Dying without living, I told him. I had no idea the living part could be stripped away, too." Far's arm shifted, so he was no longer holding Priya together, but gathering her in. "For all of its faults, I want to remember this life. I want to remember you."

When they kissed, the water on their cheeks mingled, salt into salt. Priya thought she'd been wrung dry, that there was nothing deeper to feel, but Far's lips were proving otherwise. This couldn't be what *good-bye* felt like: his hands on her hips while her breath grazed his ear and more than tears began to meet. Neither of them held anything back.

This was all.

This was *I love you*, through and through and through.

❖ ❖ ❖

It was dark when Priya woke. She lay in her bunk, memorizing every point where Far's body met hers: kneecap to thigh, hand to waist, nose to neck. Sounds of the sea poured through her BeatBix, and for one sweet moment, Priya forgot that she was going to forget. But dehydration buzzed against her skull, a reminder that she'd cried herself out.

There was no point in checking the time to see how long she'd slept, but she felt rested, and it'd be wise to check the *Invictus*'s fuel rods to make sure they had enough juice to jump back. The air cooled a few degrees as she pulled away from Far, into a clean pair of scrubs. She stumbled over her purse on the way to the door. The thing was so pedestrian compared to Eliot's pocket universe—overlarge and yet far too small. How much easier would life as a thief-patcher be with an entire hospital's worth of medicine stored around her wrist?

Have been, Priya corrected herself. Not *be*. Existence had changed tenses.

The common area was empty, not to mention in shambles. The pan of tiramisu was scraped clean, thanks to the ladyfinger-laced paw prints that skipped up the couch. Floor panels were sharp with Rubik's Cube corners and mug shards, sticky with tea. Normally, Priya would've cleared a path before anyone else needed stitches. Now she just stared at the clutter. Her eyes landed on the Code of Conduct, pages splayed so the stick figure was out of sight. Their paper crinkled and torn and not made to last.

Everything was still. Everything was urgent.

Far's snores drifted from the bunk alongside ocean sounds.

Priya grit her teeth and thought of the Fade, not as she'd seen it from the hatch of the *Invictus*, but through Eliot's eyes. She could almost feel it rolling over the waves, obliterating an entire seascape, DESTROYER OF WORLDS so hungry, tugging every one of her hairs to itself as her hands locked around the railing, but what was the point of holding on? It was strange to think that she herself had never stood on the *Titanic*'s deck. The chip made everything feel so real, as if she herself had lived it. . . .

Priya regarded the room again—five full cups of subpar tea, red panda tail poking through bare pipes, Empra's profile shining from the infirmary. The gape in her chest grew a thousand-fold as her fingers furled into fists. *This* was the life she'd chosen. There had to be a way to save it.

She wanted, she wanted, and this time, when she rallied, it wasn't to walk away, but forward, to the table where the velvet box sat. It felt lighter than when she'd first plucked it from the pocket universe, silver hinges soundless when she opened it. The chip within—with its see-through circuits, its nano-dimensions—was a marvel.

Seven worlds should weigh more.

Is there room for another one?

Priya snapped the box shut and knocked on Eliot's door.

36.

FINALLY

INVICTUS SHIP'S LOG—ENTRY 5

CURRENT DATE: AUGUST 23, 2371. WHICH STILL
EXISTS! YAY!

CURRENT LOCATION: OVER THE MEDITERRANEAN. EN
ROUTE BACK TO WHERE WE CAME FROM.

OBJECT TO ACQUIRE: A PIECE OF AUNT EMPRA'S PAST,
WHICH IS OH-SO-INCONVENIENTLY STORED IN THE
CORPS OF CENTRAL TIME TRAVELERS' MOST SECURE
SERVERS.

IMOGEN'S HAIR COLOR: HIGHLIGHTER YELLOW. EVEN IF
THE FUTURE ISN'T BRIGHT DOESN'T MEAN ONE'S HAIR
CAN'T BE.

GRAM'S *TETRIS* SCORE: 0

CURRENT SONG ON PRIYA'S SHIPWIDE PLAYLIST: OCEAN SOUNDS? METHINKS?

FARWAY'S EGO: SURPRISINGLY CENTERED, AND NOT IN A SELFISH WAY, DESPITE BEING THE LITERAL CENTER OF SEVERAL UNIVERSES. CHARACTER GROWTH? PERHAPS SO.

ELIOT'S SECRET EYEBROW MESSA—

"What are you typing?"

The tap on Imogen's shoulder made her jolt—skin-out, fresh yellow hair whipping back. It wasn't like her to be so jumpy, but she figured her nerves had the right to be high-strung, with assured destruction threatening to pop up any second and all. There was no cloud with the munchies behind her, however, just her cousin. Clarification: cousin several universes removed.

This was all so incredibly *weird*.

"Hiya, Eliot. I've tried to make a habit of writing ship's logs. To keep track of dates and quirks and stuff. I haven't really decided what your quirk should be. Eyebrow messages?"

Said eyebrows went all wiggly. There was definitely a message hidden in them—Imogen spied an Ǝ and a ⅃Ƨ beneath the Saffron-induced welts. "That's actually what I wanted to talk to you about...."

"Eyebrows?"

"No." Eliot shook her head. "The ship's logs. Do you keep datastreams of the *Invictus*'s missions?"

"Sure do. Every one of them's saved under the label 'You Rat You Burn.' It's our insurance policy against Lux." As if any of that mattered now. "Why do you ask?"

"No reason."

"You're lying." Imogen's eyes narrowed. Like Farway, Eliot had a penchant for swallowing too much when she fibbed. Their similarities were easy to spot, now that the truth was out. Maybe this was why she and Eliot got along so well, before. Eliot's Farway traits cross-wiring and connecting with Imogen's Solara-isms—she must've had them, if her MB+178587977FLT6 alternate threw gelato-centric surprise parties.

"You're right," Eliot said. "I just—I don't want to get anyone's hopes up."

"I don't think there's anywhere else for our hope to go, considering."

The other girl offered a smile, wry as the day's flavor. "If it happens, you'll know."

"Hmm." Imogen spied an etched ꟼ, a scripted M. There was an exclamation point, too. "So what *do* your eyebrows say today?"

"Eliot, would you take a look at this coding? Whenever you get a sec?" Gram sat at his console, where he'd been typing for the past half hour. Imogen had spent that entire time avoiding eye contact, trying to ignore the fact that he'd heard every one of her confessions to Eliot: a chinchilla named Dusty, sexy math.

Crux, where did she think of this stuff? Was it too much to hope that those heartfelt rants had gotten lost in all the doom and destruction bits?

When it came to Gram? Yes. The Engineer caught everything.

She'd told him without telling him and nothing had changed, except her blood sugar.

"Sorry, Im. I didn't mean to interrupt—"

"Your thing's more urgent," she told him. "Code away, my friends."

Gram grinned. Imogen swore not to analyze the expression as she clutched her twirly chair and failed immediately.

Back to the ship's log. There wasn't much more to say, so she just watched the cursor blink. Into existence, out again. Her heart flickered at the same pace: *Tell him, tell him before your world ends, what do you have to lose?*

"My composure," she mumbled.

You're talking to yourself in a room full of people who watched you single-handedly inhale a quarter pan of tiramisu to cope with doomsday, her heart pointed out.

"Touché."

"Battling something?" Her original cousin this time, sidling next to Bartleby, squinting through his fray of curls at her screen. "You're working on the ship's logs?"

The *why* of Farway's question was missing, and there all the same. Imogen looked back at the letters she'd typed and the emptiness beyond the cursor—so much unwritten. She became a speck where she sat. Itty-bitty, infinitesimal. Yellow-haired pollen dot drifting through galaxies. There were too many battles to fight: Aunt Empra's unmaking, the Fade, world in the balance. Little wonder she opted for an angst that made her feel life-sized, focusing on boy problems when existence as they knew it was about to croak.

"I'm about to go through the wardrobe again and map out more decaying dates. Everything else on the Historian end is sorted. Eliot's going to wear one of her old Corps uniforms." A disguise that wouldn't hold up under scrutiny. The sleeve's badge had the same infinity hourglass symbol, but an alternate universe meant an alternate motto. *Spes in Posterum in Praeteritis Latet* was replaced by *Temporem Ullum Homo Non Manet.*

Translation: "Man Waits for No Time." New twist on an old phrase, far cleverer than their Corps' "Future's Hope Is in the Past" maxim.

"We're set up on the comm front." Eliot's datastream was already linked to the *Invictus*, and when Imogen pulled up the feed, she could see herself seeing herself: lemon-bright hair, killer denim jumpsuit. Dressed to go out with a bang. "Gram's connection is all we're waiting for."

"Oh?" Farway's head cocked, a reminder that he, too, had seen *Blubbering Heart à la Imogen.*

"Don't you have some jitters to exercise out or something?"

Her cousin's eyebrow waggled. "Depends on how long that connection will take."

Oh really.

"It's going to be a few more minutes—" Gram was immersed

335

in his work, fingers glued to keys. It was hard to tell if the light honing his face was from the screen or within. "I want to make sure we do this right."

❖ ❖ ❖

This was the puzzle of a lifetime, everything Gram never knew he'd been looking for. Life had gone so far outside his imagined possibilities: multiple universes, teleportation, the entropy of universal constants...Eliot had disassembled his Rubik's Cube knowledge, shown him he didn't just have to twist along the axis.

Brain = unleashed.

Slipping through the Corps' security system's firewalls was a hack of epic proportions, even with Eliot's coded shortcuts. Corps techheads were among this world's best, and their digital fortress was chock-full of defenses. Such stakes should've coiled around Gram's throat, but the fact that everything was going to Hades in a bluebox regardless took the pressure off. Things he used to fret about—complications, probability, everything in its place—were inconsequential.

He understood now why Eliot had gambled so manically at the Fortuna Pool's blackjack tables. Shuffled cards and some dollars couldn't crack the immutability threshold, but what did it matter when everything was breaking anyway? Chaos was inevitable.

Might as well roll with it.

He was knee-deep in code, covering his tracks with Eliot's

program, grafting her forged credentials into the system as seamlessly as possible. Door badge scans, facial ID, mission records. The profile wouldn't fool a full-on manual read, but it was enough to keep the alarms at bay while Eliot accessed the server. Speaking of—

"Did we keep that networking cable Far used during the 2318 heist?"

"I think so. Let me check." The question was directed at anyone, but Imogen caught it. She flounced off to the common area, too colorful *not* to look at. Her hair was the same yellow as on the evening they'd met. Gram wondered if she chose the pigment on purpose, if she knew it reminded him of dissolved sunlight, laughter, and birthday sparklers, and all the shine his life had taken on with her in it.

1.2191 meters was too far.

Especially when she felt the same way.

Especially when the world was ending. That made things much less complicated.

It was so unlike Gram, to jump from his seat and into the moment, go with the flow, climb onto the ash-strewn couch where Imogen was reaching above the pipes for the cable he'd asked for, close enough to note that her hair smelled of lemons.

"Imogen, there's something I want to—"

"Ilikeyou." She blurted this out as one word. Gram didn't have time to dissect the syllables before she went on. "There. I said it. I like you, Gram Wright, and I meant everything I said about math and chinchillas and—"

"I know," Gram broke in.

"Well, then." Her face fell. "Don't mind me."

"No, I mean, I like you, too."

Imogen stared at Gram. Gram stared at Imogen.

Her eyes *were* galactic—green swirling with stars. Her laugh soared. "Really?"

"Really."

"FINALLY," Far called through the open door of his bunk.

They had an audience, Gram realized. Priya's hands clasped together over her heart as she peered from the infirmary. Eliot sat by Gram's console, grin strung ear to ear. Even Saffron stirred from sugar-induced dreams: pink yawn, paws stretching over wardrobe hangers.

Their captain set down the kettlebell weights he'd been lifting. The look on his face could only be described as impish. "This is the part where you kiss."

Kissing? Gram hadn't thought that far ahead. Kissing Imogen *would* be the next logical step in this series of events, but there were so many things to consider. Eyes open or—closed, definitely closed. Was he the one who was supposed to lean in? What if they bumped noses or, worse, teeth?

It turned out kisses didn't have to be planned. Imogen's citrus hair tickled his face as their lips found each other. He was surprised by how well she fit. Steps A, B, C melted away, and Gram found himself on a Mediterranean beach, bottle of sparkling water in hand, watching the sun drip orange against evening clouds. Pebbles—still hot from summer's languorous day—kneaded the arches of his bare feet. Wind whispered secrets down the shoreline. Horizon turned to neon dream. It felt like one of his favorite memories, but he wasn't even sure it was a memory at all. Just a summation of feelings—glow, fizz, fresh, warmth, rest.

Just Imogen.

"Crux," she swore when the kiss ended. "I mean, definitely the good kind of Crux. But *Crux*!"

Gram couldn't agree more. His dopamine levels surged as if he'd hit the highest possible *Tetris* score. How had it taken this long to find her?

"A chinchilla, huh? I'm more partial to sugar gliders. Or a quokka."

Imogen smiled. "Then we'll get one of each."

"I refuse to let any more fuzzies onto this ship!" Far hopped from his bunk, glaring into the pipes where the red panda was crouched. "That ginger devil is enough of a handful."

"Saffron *saved your life*, thank you very much!" Imogen reminded her cousin. "He's the unsung hero of an unborn world!"

"Imagine those ballads! *What creature of flaming fur is this, which hath scratched back the apocalypse*—" Far's laugh was slain where he stood. He kept staring upward, his expression fogged. "Then again I suppose we'll all be unsung after this."

"What is it?" Priya stepped in close, following his gaze. "What's wrong?"

Far pointed to one of the hangers, where a jacket hung. Its black leather was roughed up at the elbows, as if it'd had a run-in with some road. "What mission did I wear that jacket for?"

The *Invictus*'s long-term crew stared at the item of clothing.

Had it always been hanging there? Gram couldn't recall a time when it wasn't. Then again he'd never paid much attention to clothes.

"I picked it up from Before and Beyond. We were planning for a trip to 1950s America," Imogen recalled. "You said it made Bartleby look like a gang member from a musical when I was briefing you. We flew to Kansas City and then…"

Then what? Based on the state of the jacket they must have jumped, and Gram did have some memory of the equation. Numbers, numbers all blending together, now bled from this world's gaping wound.

"Another time bites the dust!" Imogen plucked the garment from its hanger, tossed it into the growing pile. "Let's see…that's one mission in the twenty-third century, two in the twenty-first, three in the twentieth, one in the nineteenth, two in the eighteenth, two in the seventeenth, a BC blip."

There'd be more, Gram knew, and soon. To have this many lost hours in their log, this many clothes crumpled on the floor…Eliot was right. The Fade's decay was accelerating, which meant their window for a reboot was closing. Imaginary chinchilla children and second kisses would have to wait.

"I'm going to need that networking cable," he said.

"Yeah, yeah." Imogen nodded, breathless. "It's up here somewhere. Maybe you can reach it."

After fumbling through fur tufts and something…*sticky?*… Gram found the hardware, a cord connected to a wireless transmitter. It would work for Eliot's on-site hack, assuming the Corps hadn't rehauled their servers in the past few months.

"Once you plug this into archive 12-A11B you should be able to access the server's data through your interface," he explained, handing it off to her. "I'm expecting there will be other security protocols, but those should be a cakewalk after what you showed me."

Eliot tucked the cable inside her pocket universe. Though Gram knew a rational explanation lay in interdimensional mechanics, the sight of hardware sliding straight into the girl's pale wrist twisted his insides. So much was weird and wondrous and bent.

"Good job on the profile planting." She nodded back at the hack on his screen. "I'll be a wraith as far as Corps alarms are concerned. I think it's best we find a parking spot, so I have solid coordinates to teleport back to."

"All of time at our feet and we're running out of it." Far marched toward his orange chair, back to mission mode: "Let's get a move on! Gram, find us a place to land. Priya, get ready to switch out the fuel rods for our next jump when we do. Imogen, give that wardrobe another comb-through. Eliot—"

The cut in Far's silence was clean. In it Gram heard how much this bothered his friend, handing this heist to another. He'd never not been on the ground, and the stress of it winched his neck tendons tight—muscled mountains, valley skin.

"Yes, Far?"

"What else do you need?"

"I'm all set."

Gram returned to his console and guided the *Invictus* to a safe landing spot, one of the many islands dotting the flight path from ancient Alexandria to Central. At this hour, both nearby towns would be asleep. Their outcrop was occupied solely by spotted goats, which didn't even twitch a tail at the invisible TM's arrival. Once the ship hit earth, the crew rushed against the clock—fuel rods were switched, teleportation coordinates pinned, comm connections confirmed for the third time—until no more details could be finessed and all five of them gathered in the console room.

Priya was in the doorway, peeling the gloves from her hazard suit. Imogen and Gram sat at their stations, and Far on the edge of his chair. Eliot stood in the center, making adjustments to her wig. The *Invictus*'s mood was somber and spectacular, everyone a laugh away from tears.

"Hey, Eliot?" Imogen's fingers were crossed, as Gram knew they would be. He hoped he'd get a chance to kiss her again.

"Yes?"

"What do your eyebrows say? For the record."

There *were* new letters on Eliot's face, Gram realized. Fresh ink, fully scrawled, a mystery until she said them: "*Carpe* the hazing *mundi*!"

The air swallowed her.

37.

A HAT AS FINE AS THAT

JUMPING THROUGH SPACE WAS MUCH WORSE than leaping through time, in Eliot's opinion. The latter took the world and rearranged it beneath her feet, but teleportation rearranged *Eliot*. The breakdown of her cells into travel-sized pieces was a painless process, but every time she disappeared from one place and materialized in another she felt the dissonance. A quiver in her bones, intestines knotted, blood thick as mud.

It was no different when she appeared in the Corps Headquarters restricted server room. The coordinates Gram had given her, the same numbers she'd fed to Vera, placed Eliot in one of the room's blind spots, so the cameras wouldn't catch her stepping out of nowhere. Her boots found purchase against the concrete, but it took a moment to settle into herself—elbows and knees rehinging, stomach sloshing with smaller and smaller waves.

"This teleportation thing is so hashing cool!" *I've just been kissed* GLEE oozed from Imogen's every word.

"Sure." From Eliot: a grunt. She was as thrilled with the pair's *carpe* kiss as everyone else, but it was hard to maintain a cheery demeanor with liquefied insides. "Where to?"

"Start heading south," Imogen instructed. "You'll have to walk a ways to get to the twelfth row. Keep an eye out for foot patrols."

To call the server room a room was a disservice to its size. The place stretched for blocks, disappearing into its own largeness. Servers glowed through glass-faced racks, a crimson light that cramped the air around it. Everything felt ominous, one slip away from sirens and stunrods. But Eliot's digital mask held when she began walking down the aisle. No alarms were triggered. She was alone with her footsteps, gliding past rows of hive-hum data. *Bzzzzzzzzzzzzz.* So many Recorders' memories—her teeth rattled with them. It was strange to think of how many datastreams were inside these machines. *They cannot be counted, and yet we keep counting.* Dr. Ramírez had acknowledged the impossibility of the Multiverse Bureau's task of numbering infinite universes, but the Corps' mission fell under the same *schlep your boulder up a hill only to watch it tumble down again* category. Thousands of Recorders and years of footage could be spent trying to capture a single day and still something would be lost.

History could not be collected, and yet they kept collecting.

Worlds could not be saved, and yet...

TRANSFER OF "YOU RAT YOU BURN" FILE IS 35% COMPLETE.

The *Invictus*'s memories were much closer, loading through Vera's interface onto the chip Eliot carried in/on/outside her wrist, joining her own observations of her crew. Could she say that? *Her* crew? Eliot had brought them together, through chess piece disasters and Gramogen nudges, but the phrase felt true for a different reason.

There's a place for you. Maybe it wouldn't last long, but Far's offer, spoken through the smoke of a laser she'd aimed to end him with, was enough. Gram, Priya, Imogen—they all knew Eliot as much as she could be known—nothing bigger to add up to, the sum of her shrinking, blank slate, too full. They'd welcomed her. They...trusted her.

We're all about to take a fall.

Could Eliot catch them? She hadn't even considered the possibility, until Priya knocked on her door. The Medic was determined to move mountains, jaw set and hand steady as she'd held out the chip. "Can you save us in it?"

"Yes," Eliot had answered. That part was easy.

The chip, like Vera's and most of Eliot's tools, was standard-issue Bureau equipment. All of them had been manufactured in Agent Ackerman's universe MB+251418881HTP8, outside of the affected string. The Fade wouldn't touch the tech, as long as it passed through the pivot point, into a countersignature-free universe. This last detail made Eliot an imperfect messenger: echoes of Far's wrong existence continued to cling to her, *would* as long as he lived. How could they transport the chip into the new future?

"If we could find a way to get this on the *Ab Aeterno*. Maybe pass it to Empra. Please, Eliot. I want to find Far, in this next life...." Priya's words had ended with a limp. The silence that followed had made Eliot flex her bandaged fingers and take the chip. Debt without interest; promise without words. Here was a girl who made a way, bloodshot eyes lined with silver sunshine, *thank you* melting into a smile. Eliot understood why Far loved her, why the chip meant more than memories.

But, just as she'd told Imogen, she didn't want to get hopes up. Even if the chip could be transferred, there was no guarantee Far would watch the memories inside, or feel compelled to act on them if he did....Love was kin to time and infinity, too vast to be contained by men's machines.

"Twelve! Gotcha!" Imogen's shout broke into real time, catching the number etched into the end of the row before Eliot did. "Rack A should be right in front of you."

It was. Eliot opened the frosted-glass door, scarlet glow dimming enough to see server 11B. Next she fished the networking cable from her pocket universe. In accordance with the Law of Strings, the cable had tangled itself into three giant knots since being packed. Red light crowded the edges of Eliot's vision as she wrestled the cord into a functional line.

"The pointy end goes in the hole," Imogen said, simply to say something.

Tempted as she was to point out the phrase's double entendre, seconds were too precious to spend on banter. Eliot bit her lip and stuck the pointy end into the hole. The not-pointy end connected to a wireless transmitter, which in turn, linked to Vera.

TRANSFER RECORDINGS FROM THE CTM *AB AETERNO*'S 95 AD MISSION, DEPOSITED BY BURGSTROM HAMMOND ON APRIL EIGHTEENTH, 2354 AD? Y/N?

Eliot's throat swelled when she saw the name. Burg in this universe, Strom in hers, both burly men with silver crew cuts. How alike had they been? She knew more about Far's Burg: father figure, smuggler of sweets. He'd be the same in the pivot-point world, if Eliot could make it.

"Y," she answered. Definitely Y.

THIS TRANSFER REQUIRES PLATINUM–BLACK CLEARANCE. PLEASE SUBMIT CENTRAL ID NUMBER AND PASSCODE FOR VERIFICATION.

Eliot sighed. Security protocols. Predicted, but no less annoying. Hacking this would take minutes they might not afford. While she typed, the Fade fed.

CLEARANCE ACCEPTED. DATASTREAM IS NOW TRANSFERRING.

Juggling downloads from two different systems only slowed Vera's transfer times, so Eliot opted to pause "You Rat You Burn." The sooner she teleported back to the *Invictus*, the faster they jumped back into the Grid, the better. Eliot shifted from one foot to the other, watching the *Ab Aeterno*'s recording percentages climb. Imogen hummed an off-key tune into the comm. The server room's air-conditioning kicked on with an icy *wumph*. Though Eliot was wearing long sleeves, the draft made her shiver.

"Cadet McCarthy."

The shiver became a bristle—no hairs needed.

Eliot turned.

"Whyyyy are these missions always getting interrupted?" Imogen's song became a wail. "Whyyyy him?"

Him being a porkpie-hat-wearing arse, and a very good reason to curse. Eliot chose a Norwegian one: "*Dra meg baklengs inn i fuglekassa!*"

347

Agent Ackerman was different outside the hologram footage—he wore his third dimension heavily. Jutting shoulders, knuckles clenched. He'd materialized not a meter from Eliot, yet the only alarms going off were the ones in her head. Rack A's open glass door was interfering with the security camera. Nothing was ruined.

Yet.

A lift of the coat, a flash of badge. "I'm Agent August Ackerman. From branch MB+251418881HTP8 of the Multiverse Bureau."

"I know who you are," Eliot said, stiff. This wasn't their first meeting, or even their fourth, though the Fade had left neither party with in-person memories of the other. For the best, judging by what she'd watched. "You're my handler for this mission."

"So you *have* been reviewing your footage, which leaves you no excuse whatsoever for creating unauthorized pivot points! I'd have responded to your beacon hours ago if I didn't have to wade through two half-eaten bastard universes—"

"What beacon?" Eliot asked.

"What beacon?" Imogen repeated.

"*What beacon?*" It was a wonder Agent Ackerman's eyes didn't roll right on out of his head and under the servers. "This is what the Bureau gets for sending a history hopper to do an interdimensional's job. Though it seems, by some farce of fortune, that you've done it. Sloppily. Your interface alerted the Bureau branches that you found the catalyst."

"Vera?"

YES, ELIOT?

The Bureau agent's face twisted. "Are you one of those girls who names everything?"

"One of those girls?" Imogen seethed. "Crux, this guy really *is* a total jacktail."

Eliot was in agreement. "Are you one of those perpetually bitter men who uses his anger as an excuse to shazm on everyone else?"

"Listen, sweetheart, I'm just here for the cleanup. I already neutralized the catalysts in your pivot-point worlds." He said this so casually Eliot almost didn't catch the spatter of blood on his sleeve. Red as the feather in his hat, bright as the light around them. "Take me to Farway McCarthy's body and we can be done with each other."

"Oh Crux..." Imogen noticed the color, too. "He killed them. He killed the other two Farways!"

And now he was here for the third.

"You need to get out of there," Imogen whispered.

She did, but she couldn't. Too many things tied Eliot here, the cable among them. Its download wasn't finished yet, and it was the datastream's ending they needed most. As per Vera's updates: TRANSFER OF CTM *AB AETERNO* 95 AD MISSION RECORDINGS IS 87% COMPLETE.

Even if she was able to stall 13 percent more, there was the matter of the beacon. Ackerman had tracked her here, would continue to hound her as long as Vera ran. Eliot couldn't teleport back to the *Invictus* without bringing a load of trouble with her, and warning Imogen would only tip off this *cucurbita*...

89%

"Shazm," Imogen breathed. "He can teleport-track you. Time to storm the brain.... Got any ideas, Gram?"

Eliot couldn't hear what the Engineer suggested. She was too lost in her own whirlwind thoughts: *Stall, just stall. Tangle him up in by-the-book rules, the way Dr. Ramírez did.* "If you're asking me for a report, I'd prefer to give it in person to your authorities in MB+251418881HTP8."

"I'm under strict orders not to let you leave this universe until you scan free of countersignature emissions. The Fade must be contained at all costs." The man's voice went a shade deeper, his shoulders a notch larger. "I asked you a question, Cadet McCarthy, and as my subordinate you're required to answer. Where is the catalyst?"

91%

"I'm working on the neutralization."

"The boy's still alive?" Agent Ackerman reached past the ellipses of blood on his sleeve, hand vanishing through his wrist. It returned from his pocket universe holding a blaster. "Figures you'd be too softhearted to pull the trigger. Take me to the catalyst and I'll get the job done."

92%

Eliot didn't have another eight percent of stalling in her. She held up her palms. "I'm not so sure point-and-shoot is the solution here. The Fade was kicked off by an event, not a person. If we go back in time and alter—"

"More pivot points are the *last* thing this mess needs!" the Bureau agent snarled. "Besides, do I look like a history hopper to you?"

"A porkpie hat as fine as that would throw anyone."

93%.

Imogen returned, her suggestion soft: "Get him to step a smidge to your left."

Eliot shifted to the side. Agent Ackerman mirrored her, fingers tight around his gun as he moved away from the glass door, into the security camera's line of sight. The room began to wail from the ground up—throaty sirens, strobe lights slashing every which way. *Alert. Intruder. Face not recognized.*

How did adding the Corps to their list of complications help anything? The situation only escalated: blaster barrel rose to meet Eliot's chest, and Agent Ackerman's forehead veins filled with squiggly-worm rage, rooting from the brim of his hat. A scream warped his mouth, but Eliot couldn't hear it for the alarms. 96%. Seconds crawled. Agent Ackerman was turning into a tomato of a man, trigger finger too twitchy for her liking.

97%. Noise from every source—alarm, comm, the Bureau agent's mouth—crashed into an incoherent blur.

98%.

She could jump soon, but where? Ackerman would only follow her, unless—

Another brightness joined the strobe lights. Corps security had arrived, along with their highly charged weapons: stunrods. Agent Ackerman's eyes went white with the voltage, one hit to the neck and another to the side. Eliot—hands lifted high, wearing what passed for a Corps uniform—was spared the onslaught. The closest guard of the four, a man with copper hair whose name tag read J. DYKEMA, held out a hand to steady her.

"Are you okay?" he mouthed.

99%.

Eliot nodded, looking down at Agent Ackerman. His fetal position was halfhearted, porkpie hat flopped feather-side to the floor. No chance he'd be tailing her anytime soon. Both his body and his interface had absorbed too much electricity to function properly. A genius solution. No doubt she had Gram to thank....

But solving this problem only made way for a dozen more. J. Dykema was doing a double take of her Corps badge—reading *Temporem Ullum Homo Non Manet*, realizing the Latin didn't add up with the motto on his own sleeve. His freckled fist tightened around his stunrod.

"Hey..."

TRANSFER COMPLETE.

Eliot vanished, in full view of everyone, leaving the cable, an unconscious Bureau agent, and four shocked security guards in her wake.

38.

THE LAST DAY

FAR WATCHED THE OUTCROP GOATS FROM his captain's chair, taking in their shadows against the growing pulse of Central time's dawn. The animals were a poor distraction: The few that weren't asleep grazed on dew-coated grass, boring and bored. He wanted to move, but with clothes strewn across the floor there was no room for pacing. Instead Far began picking a hole in his armrest's leather—worrying the orange wider and wider, while the rest of the crew troubleshot behind him. Having never been on this side of a mission, Far had nothing to offer.

He sat it out in the chair, picking it to pieces, watching goats take shape against the sunrise. Eliot's landing—and consequent scrambling—made enough noise for the animals to perk up their ears and stare at the empty patch of field. Had their eyes and minds been sharper, they might've noticed the seam where the TM's holo-shield met true air. Being livestock, they just went back to eating.

The *Invictus* tore out of Central time, goats giving way to the Grid. Absolute dark stared into Far, and the truth hit him: They weren't going back. Whether they succeeded or failed, he would never see Central as himself again. It was a smaller good-bye, but even the tiny *lasts* felt huge stacked up like this.

"You were right." He swung his chair toward Eliot. Her comm was still connected to the *Invictus*'s systems, every breath magnified. It sounded as if she'd just run a marathon. "Agent Ackerman is a total arse."

"I forgot"—*gulp, gasp*—"about Vera's beacon. It wasn't in my self-briefing. The zapping was brilliant, though. Even if Ackerman gets his teleportation system back online he won't find us. Multiverse Bureau agents aren't equipped to travel through time."

"Great clicking, Gram!"

"Good swirling, Imogen!"

The two grinned at each other, bridging the space between their consoles with a high five. Far couldn't shake the feeling that these celebrations were preemptive. They'd only escaped the Multiverse Bureau by poking the dragon that was the Corps, who *did* possess time-traveling capabilities.

"When the alarms sounded, I wiped the security footage," Gram explained when he caught Far's expression. "The Corps will have no idea what went down."

"That's something, at least." Far turned to Eliot. "Did you download the file?"

She pulled off her wig, nodding. "One hundred percent."

"Shall we watch the last day?" Far gestured to the common area.

They gathered in the usual clusters—Far and Priya on one couch, Gram and Imogen taking the other. There was hand-holding on his cousin's side, pheromones finally focused into smiles. Though Far had seen Imogen with this hair color before, he couldn't remember it being so incandescent. She was all lit, all yellow. Happy as it was, the sight stung.

A *first* and a *last*, they never even had a chance....

Eliot settled on the floor, cross-legged, freezing when Saffron hopped into her lap. Fear braced her shoulders, but all the red panda did was curl into a ball.

"Ooooh!" Imogen's expression went up in wattage. "Saffron doesn't nap with just anyone, you know. He *likes* you."

Eliot patted the beastie's head, her palm flat and awkward. "I guess it's not that bad."

The sting settled deeper in Far's chest. He hadn't thought he'd miss the *Ailurus fulgens*, but it seemed the creature had sunk its claws into more than just his shins....

"Before we get started, I think I'll make us some tea." There were no arguments to Priya's proposal. How could there be when *one final time* hung unsaid at the end of her sentence?

Eliot pulled the chip from her pocket universe, drew up the file. Imogen rested her head on Gram's shoulder while the Engineer stared at their hands, marveling at the pattern of interlocking fingers. Far watched Priya in the kitchenette with the same wonder. He'd seen her make tea on countless occasions, but every detail felt new. The way she smelled each spice before adding it into the boiling water. How she counted each stir beneath her breath. Her care in lining up the mugs' handles before divvying out the chai. So many *lasts* adding up, not even a scalding swallow could wash this grief away.

Losing her might just kill Far before the Fade did.

They sat with mugs of steaming chai, outside of time, watching Far's beginning. He didn't know what to expect when the *Ab Aeterno*'s final 95 AD footage flickered to life. What the hologram showed was both familiar and surprising.

Far's mother had walked the Colosseum's crumbling circumference with him many times. She was full of facts during those visits, pointing out the thumbprint masonry of the hypogeum, describing how lions used to be stored beneath the arena floor. Not once had she mentioned that she'd seen men bleed there.

Far had watched datastreams of gladiators before; they were impossible to avoid in Central, where the clash of their blades still echoed round and round the ancient ruins. But this one felt different. It was unedited—raw footage that didn't skip over ugly things. The violence of the first fight was enough to make Imogen—a seasoned Historian—squint through her fingers.

How strange to think that his mother had taken this in without blinking. Stranger still to realize that Far had been there in fetus form. He'd heard this crowd with his own ears, racing alongside his mother's heart: *Blood! Blood! Blood!* A noise urgent enough to call him out into this ruthless world...Burg's voice—which Far associated with bedtime stories—sounded surreal as he urged Empra off her bench, down the stairs.

"Why would Aunt Empra ever want to watch this?" Imogen wondered aloud. "Why does she keep looking back?"

"*Pause.*" At Eliot's command, the hologram froze on the pair of gladiators. "Look at who she's looking to."

"Ugh." Imogen peeked between her hands. "All I see is blood."

"Far..." Priya, her own steel stomach unfazed by the insides of men turned out, leaned toward the projection. "That gladiator looks just like you."

Now that the footage was paused, Far had time to study the fighters. Priya was right. The gladiator with his back to the wall wore no helmet. Though what helmet could contain such dead-ringer curls? And the nose... Far had always wondered where his most dramatic feature had come from.

Now he knew. He knew so many things: why his mother insisted on teaching him Latin, why she'd called him by his middle name in the Library of Alexandria, why she'd stayed to watch this brutal match, why his skin was always tan while every other McCarthy's burned at the first glimpse of sun, why he forever needed to move-move-strive-fight. It wasn't just time-lessness in his blood, but battle, too.

Eliot was the first to state the obvious. "That's our father."

"Oooooh, Aunt Empra!" Imogen gasped. "Courting a gladiator! No wonder Burg classified this datastream! She would've been in such deep shazm had anyone found out."

"That's why your DNA is fudged in Central's systems," Priya said. "It wasn't just a common discretion clause. It was so no one could prove your father wasn't one of the *Ab Aeterno*'s crew members."

Far should have felt surprised, but facing his father's image—back to wall, blade to throat—struck a much deeper chord. The sadness that was always beneath his mother's eyes, dictating her smile, made sense now. This wasn't just a one-night sperm donation.

This was love.

"Why does anyone look back?" It wasn't hard to imagine the emotions behind the datastream when Far's own chest was a pulpy mess. When he turned to see Priya—still here, still next to him, but for how long? "She didn't want to leave him."

Her lips went tight. He wanted to cry again.

Instead, Far braced himself for the worst as the datastream played on, but that view of his father was the *last*. Empra ran from the stadium's roar, pausing every few minutes to lean on columns, huffing through her pain while Burg recited encouragements: "C'mon, McCarthy! Keep going. You're almost here!" The datastream's visual had gone misty when Empra finally did reach the *Ab Aeterno*, her tears turning Burg into a giant blob. The time stamp, at least, was clear: 9:10 AM when she boarded the *Ab Aeterno*, 9:14 when the clock froze and froze and froze and Far's very first breath of ageless air expelled with a scream.

The boy who should not have been was born, and something disastrous with him.

The datastream ended. Far stared through the vistaport, wondering if that very birth was happening out there in the black.

"Poor Aunt Empra," Imogen whispered. "Poor gladiator. This is so hashing sad."

"It doesn't have to be." Priya's eyes went from smoky to steel: a hard shine. "Far's father doesn't have to die."

"I'm pretty sure his name is Gaius," Far offered.

Priya went on, "We want to get Empra back to the *Ab Aeterno* well before nine ten. If she was lingering to watch Gaius's fight, then it makes sense to free him. Yes?"

"You can't just *free* a gladiator," Imogen told them. "There's a whole system in place. Most of them are slaves or prisoners of war, and even the men who volunteered are bound to their lanista overseers to the point of death. If Gaius goes missing, his lanista will rip apart the city searching for him. And it's not as if he can hitch a ride to Central...."

"So what do you propose?" Priya asked. "Letting Gaius die while one of us drags Empra back to the ship by force?"

"Maybe not that." Far's cousin made a face. "Farway and his father look so much alike that Aunt Empra called him Gaius in the Library of Alexandria. Perhaps there's a way to fool her back onto the *Ab Aeterno*."

The footage of his father was gone, but Far kept seeing him: curls splayed against the stones, ready to fight until the end. The image reframed his entire childhood. Seven years with his mother and her mourning, she didn't want to leave Gaius, she'd always regretted it....

The Code of Conduct lay open before him, title down. Far could see where ink from Gram's illustration had bled through—arrows and cracks, a picture in pieces. The stick man didn't appear on this side of the page.

He knew what he had to do.

"I'll take my father's place. If I claim Gaius's spot in the arena, the lanista won't think my father escaped when one of you takes him to meet my mom. Empra can say good-bye to Gaius, and she'll leave in time to create a pivot point."

"You? A gladiator? Are you *out of your hashing mind*?" Imogen's shout supernovaed through the common area. "Far-way, these guys live and breathe slaughter. A few fencing lessons at the Academy won't mean squat when you step into that ring."

Yeah, he'd figured. Far had never been *that* great at sword-play anyway, as the scar on his biceps reminded him. "I don't have to win the match. I can't. The Fade's present is linked with mine, right? My death won't stop my past from being erased, but it's the best chance this new universe has at living. It's the only thing that might prevent the countersignature from passing through the pivot point. Cut the string, end the signal before the *Ab Aeterno* takes off, stop the echoes of my wrong birth before I'm born *right* again."

Priya became a statue, leg rigid against his. Far wasn't sure he could bear her expression, so he stared at the ceiling instead. The ship's skeleton pipes were too easy to see through the thinning wardrobe. Why the Hades would he wear such an eye-gougingly bright flash-leather suit?

His next question was a footnote: "What's a little extra blood in the scheme of things?"

"It's awful!" Imogen cried. "It's awful and you're being too hashing heroic to see straight! If you die before the Fade finds our present, where does that leave us? With a pile of clothes and no minds to call our own? Playing pincushion will only make a mess! Tell him, Gram!"

"I can't." The Engineer cleared his throat, and again, harder, as if to dislodge some hidden feeling there. "I mean, I don't like it, but Far's theory about the countersignature has merit. For all of Ackerman's horribleness, the man was right. The Fade must be contained, and this is the cost."

"It doesn't have to be sad." There wasn't much left to Far—his memories shedding like autumn leaves, time sliding in the wrong direction—but his fate was yet in his hands. More fates, still. He looked around at his crew: Imogen, Eliot, Saffron, Gram, Priya. Priya... "If we succeed, the pain won't even be a distant dream."

Stone, all stone, stayed her lips. No words left them, nor did they tremble.

"I'm with Far," Eliot said. "We'll find a way to free Gaius—"

"How?" asked Imogen. "He'll be locked up in his cell at the *ludus*."

Eliot held up her wrist; a seam between dimensions shimmered against hairless skin. "This pocket universe doesn't just hold clothing and sundries. I can carry Far into the cell and take Gaius out. If I intercept Empra on her way to the Colosseum and redirect her to the *Ab Aeterno*, they'll have a chance to say good-bye."

"I can be on the ground," Gram volunteered. "Something as important as this requires a second set of hands."

Far's cousin walked over to the clothing pile and dug the toga from the bottom. "If this is really what we're doing, we'll need another toga. As for three live datastreams... Gram might be able to keep up with that many screens, but I'll be overloaded."

"It's okay, Imogen. I can get to the arena without comm support. You shouldn't have to watch..." *My death*, the silence said, and Far faltered. How could he give himself over to the sword when he couldn't even form the words? Talking talk, thinking thoughts was easy. But to stand where his father had stood, to feel the years wasting behind, the ones ahead sliced short...

"I'll manage your comm." Priya reached for his hand. "Through lights and time and whatever else comes our way. Even this."

Her palm filled his with warmth, the kind that seeped through pores and lit a path to the heart. Fortitude? No. Bravery? No. Hope? In any other circumstance, Far might have said so. But as the saying went: *Dum spiro spero*. Hope could not outlast the breather. Love, however... Love was something not even death could conquer, because at the end of everything, even life, he was hers. If Far could wield his father's trident, wear his father's wounds, claim his father's quietus, this *last* might give way to *next*.

Maybe not for him—blade and Fade, dead and done.

Maybe not for her—past lost forever at best.

But for them.

Blood or none, it was a chance worth seizing.

39.

DENTAL HYGIENE IS THE MAIN CONCERN

INVICTUS SHIP'S LOG—ENTRY 6

OUR UNIVERSE IS COLLAPSING. WHAT ELSE IS THERE
TO DO BUT MAKE A NEW ONE? RAGE, RAGE, AND ALL
THAT. AT LEAST I GOT KISSED BEFORE MY UNTIMELY
SPIRAL INTO SENILITY. YOU HEARD IT HERE FIRST,
FOLKS. IMOGEN MCCARTHY AND GRAM WRIGHT KISSED.
A HAPPILY EVER MOMENT, WORTH DECLARING BEFORE
THE AFTER PART JOINS THE PARTY.

HERE ARE SOME BRAIN YOGA EXERCISES: ARE YOU
YOU WITHOUT YOUR MEMORIES? IF NOT, WHO DO YOU
BECOME? IF SO, ARE YOU ALSO *YOU* IN A PARALLEL
UNIVERSE?

I HAVE TO STOP WRITING IN THIS LOG AND MAKE
A TOGA. STAY TUNED FOR MY TAKE. TO BE HONEST,
YOU'LL BE WAITING AWHILE. TO BE HONEST, HONEST,
YOU DON'T EXIST, BECAUSE NO ONE IS READING THIS.
RIP SPIRIT OF THE *INVICTUS*.

THE SHEETS WERE A THOUSAND THREAD count, so soft that kings might weep to sleep on them. Imogen herself had spent many a slumbering hour in the bedding—as evidenced by the neon streaks on her pillowcase. She tossed this aside. Nuclear Green + Taylor Pink + Aquamarine were *not* shades common to Ancient Roman fashion. Neither was cotton woven with a high-speed automatic air-jet loom, but options for craft-your-own-toga fabric were slim at the moment. Using bedsheets wouldn't be the end of the world—*HA*.

(Sardonic humor must be genetic, huh? Dominant McCarthy trait.)

Even Imogen's seamstress tools were makeshift. From the infirmary: curved needles and surgical thread. There was dental floss, too, in case she ran out. Floss upon unused floss. Some of the *Invictus* crew members must've been lying to their dentist-droids.

"Need any help?"

Blushing when she heard Gram's voice—sonorous song of a sound—was reflex at this point. Imogen's cheeks fuzzed pink, but she didn't curse herself this time. Instead, she looked toward the door, where the Engineer stood, elbow propped to frame. The air between them was Grid-dizzy. Her smile swam in it.

Gram's dimples grew as he stepped closer. "What?"

"I like you."

"Haven't those parameters been established?"

Kiss number two was even better than its predecessor. For as many day—and night—dreams Imogen had spent on the subject, kissing Gram, really *kissing* him, was something fantasies couldn't hold a candle to. It was give and receive, find him, show him, warmth exchanged. It was a sparkle in her spine, thrilling to her fingertips.

"Just making sure the words still worked," she murmured, forehead resting beneath his chin. "Do you floss?"

Sealed lips stunted his laugh. "Not a question a guy wants to hear post-kiss. Are you insinuating that I should?"

"Oh, no. You have very nice breath. The best." Alas, Imogen's foot-in-mouth curse had no fairy-tale cure! "I was only wondering because I have too much floss to sew this toga with. After the gelato and tiramisu we've been eating, I fear we may have some cavities on board. Naturally, our dental hygiene is my main concern at the moment...."

"Naturally." Gram's embrace tensed, biceps going sharp through his sleeves. "I floss every twenty-four hours. You?"

"Not enough." Imogen couldn't remember her last plaque-be-gone session, probably because the Fade had stolen it, the way it was stealing everything else. *STUPID LIFE-GUZZLING FOR-GETTING.* Standing here in Gram's arms should've had the chance to become a memory, recounted to their many fur-babies. Chinchillas and quokkas and sugar gliders and other pint-sized cutenesses. "I'm not sure I did enough of anything...."

"We're not over yet," he whispered above her.

Chalk dusted his chin—bumblebee yellow—when Imogen pulled away. She brushed it off with her thumb, thinking of the many colors this could've been, had she *just told him* earlier: every pillowcase shade, a rainbow's entire reach. Maybe their 2.0 versions could span that spectrum in the next life... whatever *next life* meant. Limber though Imogen's thoughts might be, they couldn't wrap around the pivot point's existential implications.

"You're right." There was a toga to be sewn. "Were you serious about wanting to help?"

"There's nothing else I'd rather be doing."

"I need a pen to mark out the panels. Do you still have the one I lent you?"

"It's in the common area." Gram looked through the door, where the others were reviewing Empra's datastream on repeat for planning purposes. "I'll go get it."

One more kiss left her insides swirling like a glitter snow globe.

SUCCESSES IN IMOGEN'S LOVE LIFE: **TEN THOUSAND SPARKLE-HEART EMOJIS**

Saffron skipped in from the common area. Imogen intercepted the animal, scooping him up before he could turn the clean sheet into his personal art project. The garment would be avant-garde enough without a red panda paw-print pattern.

Her fluffy ward gave a series of chirps. The noises often had a conversational quality—*Insert food here!* or *Why so sad?* or *You humans are interrupting my daily twelve hours of slumber.*

Imogen didn't translate so much as choose the subject matter. This *cheep cheep chirrup* turned into *I always liked Gram. I'm glad you two found each other. Not like this was a game of hide-and-seek or anything. I love hide-and-seek. Especially with your favorite hair chalk colors. No one will ever find Mint Medley now....*

"I know." She smiled down at the creature. "I got lucky."

40.

A NEW LOW FOR ACKERMAN

Agent August Ackerman's vision was beginning to pull itself back together. Instead of three steel tables, twelve men, and an infinity mirror, his surroundings were thirded. He found himself restrained to a chair with handcuffs. There was a coppery residue coating his tongue, but a swallow determined it to be the aftermath of the stunrod's current. Not blood.

"He's awake!" one of the guards announced.

This was August's first good look at his assailants. His eyes focused on their sleeves' loopy hourglass symbol. *Corps.* August came from a long line of career Bureau men and consequently had a patent dislike for anything to do with the Corps. They were forever stealing things—funding, recruits, public interest—and leaving messes in their wake. *Pivot point* had become akin to a curse word in Ackerman families across the HTP8 string. Unauthorized worlds popping up like fungi, all because *this lot* was so obsessed with looking backward. August couldn't understand why. What sort of person would want to make a career wallowing around in history's diseases and odious smells?

These sorts. Amateurs who thought a few links of metal could tie him down....

...

...

When August did not vanish, he sat straighter in his chair. His interface—and the teleportation equipment linked to it—had been scrambled by the surge of electricity. Much like August's body, it needed a reboot. He wouldn't be going anywhere for some time, unless these guards decided otherwise.

The flame-haired one leaned in, elbows locked as if he was bracing for something. "What were you doing in the Corps' restricted archives?"

That explained the servers, as well as the alarm. Both had been unexpected. This entire assignment was, really. He'd spent most of his twenty years with the Bureau mopping up time-traveling messes—observing *oopsy-daisy* universes, numbering them in the ever-changing system—but the Fade was a first for his career. Whatever Farway McCarthy had done to cause it was a muck-up of catastrophic proportions. Despite the many Dr. Ramírezes' valiant efforts, it could not be cleaned up, only contained. The quarantine should've been simple: Follow the beacon, X out this final catalyst, confiscate Cadet McCarthy's jump equipment before she could create more spin-off worlds. Of course, history hoppers never made *anything* simple.

Lightning bolts streaked down the side of August Ackerman's throat as he swallowed a second time.

"Who was that girl?" the guard tried again. "How is it she vanished into thin air? Why was the motto on her badge different? Why was she tapping into the *Ab Aeterno*'s 95 AD archives?"

Because Cadet McCarthy was foolish enough to think time might change things, and she would keep creating pivot points, spreading the Fade into world after twisted world, until she gave up and jumped to an innocent string, dragging the countersignature's infection with her.

That couldn't happen. Metal bit into August's skin as he tried to lift his wrists. Chained to this chair, stranded in this rotting universe...He wasn't going anywhere if he kept silent.

"Some very unfortunate events are about to occur," he informed his questioner. "I was in the process of preventing them when you intervened."

Eyes widened. The guards glanced at one another.

"You're from the future, aren't you?" the red-haired guard offered. "Explains why we didn't recognize your credentials."

The thought of the respected emblem of the Multiverse Bureau—the infinity symbol linked over and over again into a circular chain-mail pattern—being mistaken for a time traveler's badge ticked August's blood pressure up a few notches. Somewhere in universe MB+251418881HTP8, the Ackerman forefathers were rolling in their cryonic suspension chambers.

"Sharp young man you are." Agent Ackerman's gaze flicked past the guards, to the mirror. Whoever was calling the shots of this interrogation stood behind the glass, listening. August stared past his reflection as austerely as he could. "Your present is in peril. Cadet McCarthy is traveling back into the past to alter events, but she is playing with forces vastly beyond her qualifications—"

CRACK! The door to the interrogation room opened so hard August expected the sound to spread to the mirror and spill into a thousand silver shards. The glass held. Agent Ackerman recognized the newcomer from the datastream of his trip to MB+178587977FLT6. Headmaster Marin's alternate was identical in this world—right down to the mustache. It was an admirable lip wig, waxed into knifepoint ends that quivered when their owner spoke.

"Did you say *McCarthy*?"

"Yes," Agent Ackerman answered with care. The name was obviously an explosive one.

"First day of a new promotion and that hashing family shows up. Never could stand Farway, always preening about being born outside of time. As if having a mother irresponsible enough to watch gladiator matches during labor is a bragging point!"

Ah. The history hoppers had a history, something painfully personal, gathering from the mustachioed man's tone. It was the born-outside-of-time bit that piqued August's interest. Could the circumstances of Farway McCarthy's birth be the event to which Cadet McCarthy had been referring? Was 95 AD the time she was so determined to alter?

"Who is this girl? Farway's daughter?"

"What she is, is a danger to you and your timeline." Cadet McCarthy was probably in 95 AD already, catalyst alive at her side, attempting to spread this decay even farther....Even if August could get his teleportation capabilities back online, they wouldn't do him much good. "It was a disaster I was in the process of preventing, but your stunrods have interfered with my equipment. Headmaster Marin—"

"Headmaster?" It wasn't until Marin frowned that Agent Ackerman realized his slip. Different world, different title. "No, no. It's *Commander* Marin."

"Commander Marin." Frozen Ackerman corpses kept rolling round and round, but family honor could wait. The Fade had to be contained. If Agent Ackerman had to time travel to kill the final catalyst, so be it. "I'm going to need a ride."

41.

THAT TIME GODS POPPED OUT OF THE FLOOR

THE DREADED DAWN HAD COME. GAIUS fought it off, clinging to dreams as long as he could, for Empra was in most of them. Empra—woman who'd come from the clouds, or so she'd always claimed. It was the glib answer to his serious question: *Where are you from?* He'd wondered this ever since his first sight of her in the stands in the *ludus*'s training arena, bright spot in the bleakest winter of Gaius's life. His debts had hounded him to the foot of a lanista, forcing him to make an oath—to train, to fight, to slay, to die in the man's name. Sunrises became numbered, nothing more than a reason to wake and begin the litany of blood and blade anew.

Whenever Empra watched Gaius's practice spars, he felt life's gray slip away. Food stuck to his stomach, jokes became laugh-worthy. On the evenings she visited him, to break bread and ask Gaius about the gladiator's lot, he remembered that spring smelled of warmth and star-edged flowers, and love felt much the same.

During the day, Gaius fought. During the night, he lived.

Their conversations wound through many things. Questions, answers, fears, the dreams of youth. Nothing about Empra added up to a single city or province, nor did she ever commit to one when he asked.

Where are you from? The stars.

Where are you from? Heaven.

Where are you from? Not here. Elsewhere.

The thing was, it was believable. Empra *was* sky—vivid and vast with possibilities. But Gaius? Gaius, as his name so literally claimed, was a man of earth. He felt this gap between them even after their love became a spoken thing, even when she lay in his arms: shoulder blades sprouting like wings into his chest, a beat or two away from taking flight. Not even a child, *his* child, growing inside her womb, could keep Empra from leaving, going back to wherever it was that she'd come from.

Why? There was no fanciful answer this time.

Nor was there sky above Gaius when he opened his eyes, just the dull stone of ceiling, made for tamping down dreams. A rooster's cry announced that morning was nigh. Soon he'd be fighting his first official match.

"Gaius? Is that you?"

The accent was Empra's, and the woman standing on the other side of his cell door had a complexion just as alabaster. But the torchlight called up several differences: Her eyes were darker, her hair, too. Empra was *gone* and this woman was here when she was not supposed to be—even wealthy matrons didn't frequent the gladiator school at this hour.

"How do you know my name?" There was crust in Gaius's eyes. He made to wipe it out, yet the motion was in vain. He was still dreaming. He must be, for the woman was now inside his cell, while the bars themselves had not moved.

Gaius blinked. The sight only grew stranger. The woman—girl? She looked to be that in-between age where both words applied—removed the thinnest bracelet he'd ever seen, stretched it out in front of her, and *pulled the air apart.* She stared into this hole, speaking tooth-jarring words that belonged to no tongue Gaius had ever heard.

Hair appeared, black curls spilling out of nothingness. A head followed.

It was his own.

Gaius forgot to breathe.

The head frowned and spoke in the tumbling language. The woman—Girl? Goddess?—knelt down, placing the torn air before her. Two arms sprouted from the floor; an entire second Gaius pulled himself into the cell.

Somewhere the rooster kept crowing, reminding Gaius that he was *awake.* Awake and sober, unlike his cellmate, Castor, who'd tried to drown his fears in a goblet at last evening's banquet, and was now a pile of limp limbs in the corner. Gaius drank only a single glass of wine at the festivities, even after Empra had melted off into the darkness and the night caved in on him. Yet if he was neither drunk nor dreaming, what explanation could there be for the scene before him? Had he already died in the arena? Was *this* Elysium? He'd expected more grass and fewer bars in the afterlife....

"Wh-who are you?" he managed.

The two newcomers exchanged a glance and more spear-head syllables.

"We are..." the woman began in Latin, "...friends of Empra. Though she must return to the realm she came from, it is not her wish that you perish here."

This was not Elysium; these were gods come to earth. *Clouds. The stars. Heaven.* None of Empra's answers had been false. Like most Romans, Gaius had grown up with the stories—where deities such as Venus and Aurora lit their eyes on mortal men. Tempestuous, whirlwind tales of love that ended in sorrowful partings and children who shook the world.

He'd never expected to be a part of one.

"We've come to free you," said the second Gaius. "So that you can say good-bye before she departs."

The longer Gaius studied this divine version of himself, the more he realized the imitation was inexact. The god—Man? Boy? He was also of the age where both words applied—had nicer teeth, and a scar on his arm. Something about him, about *both* of the beings in his cell, reminded Gaius of Empra.

"But my oath—"

"I will fight in your stead. Your oath to your lanista will be fulfilled. You'd do best to start your life anew elsewhere." The god pointed to his toga. The textile's weave was too small to see, an impossible feat for mortal hands. "We should exchange garments."

The rooster's call was fading, soon to be replaced by armor clatter and lashing whips as the *ludus* prepared for the day's bloodshed. Gaius tried to understand what was being said, that he might be spared all this.... Would it be cowardice, to accept another's offer to fight and possibly perish for him?

No, Gaius realized. For immortals did not die.

Who was he to deny the gods?

He began pulling off his garment.

❖ ❖ ❖

For eighteen years, the word *father* had been a fill-in-the-blank where Far was concerned. What was the fudged half of his DNA hiding? Who had he come from? A CTM captain? A Medic? A senator? Math made the last option impossible, but that hadn't stopped young Far from adding it to his rotation of imagined father-son reunions. His captain dad taking him for a whirl over pirate-riddled seas. A Medic father letting him wear his lab coat, even though it was years too big. The upstanding senator, guiding Far on a tour of the New Forum, telling everyone he met *This is my son!* in a voice as proud as it was booming.

None of the scenarios had come close to this. Far, standing half naked in a prison cell, December air grazing his chest as he swapped Imogen's floss-strung bedsheets for a ragged tunic. Gaius wrapped his new toga with care, running his fingers over and over the cotton. It must've felt otherworldly compared to the fabric Far was yanking over his own head. Scratchy as Hades!

"Eliot—er, this is Eliot—is going to take you to Empra now. But you will need to step into her..." *Shazm*, what was he supposed to call it? "Invisible chariot now."

"Chariot?" Eliot repeated in Central dialect, her *Mundi* eyebrow raised. "Does that make me a horse?"

"*Pocket universe* was too tricky to translate."

"How do I ride this unseen chariot?" Gaius's question brought them back to Latin.

"Step in." Eliot pointed at where the floor gave way to dresses. "Carefully."

Quaking brow, disbelieving lips—both children made cameos in their father's expression as he peered into the dimensional rift. "I can fit in there?"

"Yes." Far knew because he'd asked the same question on the same edge, before leaving the *Invictus*. Once he'd climbed into the space, it felt more universe than pocket. "It's bigger when you get inside."

Gaius took the words of his unknown son on faith. There was a lump in Far's throat as he watched his father slip into the floor. His entire life had been lived as a McCarthy and only a McCarthy, but there was 50 percent *more* to him, landing among hemlines and lace. How had Gaius become a gladiator? What were the names of Far's grandparents? Where did his blood call home?

Far wished he could ask his father these things, but the

sun was rising, and any answers would soon be forgotten. He watched Gaius settle into a pile of petticoats instead, marveling at their tulle netting. His windpipe kept clogging, too much to manage a farewell. Then again, he'd hardly even said hello.

Black curls became earth when Eliot sealed the pocket universe, wrapping it back around her wrist. Far looked around the cell's flickering lamplight walls, interrupted by the graffiti of past inhabitants—*Antiochus was a stallion among women* and *Today I made bread*. These marks made the place less bleak. He wondered if his father had carved any of them.

"Your link with the *Invictus* should go live around eight o'clock," Eliot told him. "Priya will be there to walk you through…"

"My death?" The words were utterable now, both cathartic and piss-in-your-Roman-underwear terrifying. How could the guy in the corner sleep so hashing soundly when the same fate loomed?

"Fingers crossed, the Fade won't show up between now and then."

"You sound like Imogen." Far tried to crack a smirk; the expression was too breakable for his face. "Do we believe in luck now?"

"I think we have to." Eliot clasped his shoulder. "Far, I know we've had our differences—"

"Differences?" Far snorted. "That's a delicate term for a blackmailing, blaster-wielding, mother-snatching Marie Antoinette impostor."

"You were the best version of myself." It was enough to

knock the laugh out of him, enough to see glimmer by her lash-less lids. "Die well, Farway Gaius McCarthy. I'm going to try my fexing hardest to make sure you live again."

Gaius's cellmate began to stir, mumbling Latin too foul for a mother to teach. Far caught the gist without his translation tech: The gladiator was waking up with a horrible hangover, a mass of muscles and rags assembling into wakefulness.

"You were the best version of myself," Eliot repeated. "Of course, that could be the amnesia talking."

She winked.

And then she vanished.

Far stood on the solid cell floor, comm dead in his ear, his shoulder indented from Eliot's fingers. His stare went straight to the window, not for the violet sunrise, but for the bars in front of it. He was trapped. The thought itched inside his legs and made him want to pace, back and forth, tiger-in-the-cage style, but he'd seen what his opponent's blade could do. His energy was best saved for the battle. Far would die, because he had to, but he wasn't going to leave this life without a Hades of a fight.

He owed himself that much.

42.

AN EMPRA IN A HAYSTACK

GRAM HAD SEEN THE COLOSSEUM'S CARCASS too many times to count. Most of these views had been from an eagle-eye height, through skyscraper vista walls and hoverbus windows. The circle of scarred stones, host to a never-ending stream of tourists, had never particularly captivated him. Even the ground-level sight, amplified by a datastream tour, had ill-prepared Gram for the *Amphitheatrum Flavium*'s towering prime.

According to Imogen, this land had been a valley once, complete with a lake. The Romans raised the earth with ruins from Nero's fire, so necks would have to crane *up* to take in this marvel of engineering. Every one of the amphitheater's outer wall stones had been set without mortar—*Tetris* before its time—coming together into unmatched dimensions: 48 meters tall, 189 meters long, 156 meters high, 80 ground-level entrances to accept the ebb and flow of fifty thousand people.

This was Rome's glory, her heart, throbbing with the footsteps of a blood-callused mob.

Gram walked among them, searching. At nine months pregnant, Empra should have been easy to spot, but the flood of game-goers drowned out all shapes. Colors blurred his peripheral—yellow togas, rust togas, white togas, every tone of skin—made even more chaotic by the constant crush of body odor. It was tempting to bury his nose in his own dated toga, which smelled of an inferno nearly 150 years dead. The attire, equally out of date, had garnered Gram some sideways glances, but it was best he not blend in. Empra McCarthy was in Recorder mode, which meant she'd try her absolute best to ignore him. An old costume was a way to catch her attention. Or so the plan went. He had to *find* Far's mom first.

Indigo, indigo...Gram searched for this shade in a thrash of ochre oranges and goldenrod fabrics. He waded through the crowd, bumping elbows and jostling shoulders, turning every few seconds to get a view from all angles.

"You sure know how to make a lass dizzy!" Imogen told him.

"It can't be just me." The *Invictus*'s Historian console had three feeds going at once: his own, Eliot's, and the recording of Empra synchronized with their time stamp. "Did you try minimizing some windows?"

"Imogen is flirting, Gram." The grumble through the comm belonged to Eliot. She'd returned from her jump into the predawn *ludus* and was searching the same crowd. "As adorable as you two are, now isn't the best time for that."

"It's the *only* time to flirt!" Imogen protested. "Oh, hey—Aunt Empra just passed arch LVII. Turn around!"

"Are you talking to me or Gram?" Eliot asked.

"Gram."

He spun on his heels and scanned the closest arch—*LVIII* were the numerals carved into its stone. A single digit off. Empra had to be nearby, but none of the women in the passing throng wore indigo. Nor were any of them pregnant to the point of waddling.

"I'm not seeing her, Im."

"I *see* that you're not seeing her." Nervous energy frayed Imogen's voice. "She should be right on top of you, but you don't show up on her feed since you weren't there the first time. Okay...she's passing gate LVIII right now."

Except she wasn't.

"Are you sure the feeds are synchronized?" Gram asked.

"Surer than sure," Imogen answered. "Atomic clock sure. I don't understand. Aunt Empra was supposed to be there. She *was there*."

The one constant in their plan had shifted, leaving Gram stuck in place. The crowd kept moving around him—colors of fire and earth, swarming into the amphitheater's many entrances. Dirt, halitosis, shouts that cluttered up his translation feed...What did Empra's absence mean? Gram hardly had time to work out a theory when the Recorder appeared.

Empra McCarthy's belly caused a break in the pedestrian traffic—everyone slowed to give the pregnant woman a wide berth. Her own walk was ponderous but persistent. It wouldn't take much for Gram to catch up and recite the Latin lines Imogen had taught him: *Cruenti sunt ludi. Oculo intimo spectare non sapiat.* The words would—hopefully—signal Empra to cut off her datastream feed without alarming the *Ab Aeterno.* They needed the CTM to stay where they could find it.

A hand landed on Gram's arm. Eliot appeared at his side, soundless as ever, shaking her head as Empra McCarthy shuffled past.

"Guys, Aunt Empra is *right there*! Go get her! We've got a world to jump-start!"

"That delay was ten seconds long." Eliot's whisper doubled—next to Gram, in his comm. "Something's changed and I don't think it's on our end."

Hers was a logical conclusion and, unfortunately, correct. Not fifteen steps behind Empra was a face caricatured in countless Academy restroom stalls. The mustache that made these illustrations so comical was gone, but there was no mistaking the militant frown beneath.

"Blistering bluebox barnacles!" Imogen recognized the man, too. "What's Instructor Marin doing here?"

It wasn't just their disgruntled instructor. An entire Corps unit trailed Empra at a distance. Gram recognized three other men from Central's hallways, canvassing the crowd in togas loose enough to hide their stunrod holsters. Familiarity went both ways. Instinct urged Gram to run, but his Recorder training held strong. Hauling tail would only jerk eyes in their direction.

"Duck," he advised Eliot.

Size worked to Eliot's advantage—where she slipped, her Corps pursuers smashed. Latin curses mixing with harsh Central yells.

Her veins were all pulse, high on the fact that this plan was working. Marin and his men had abandoned Empra, so intent on pursuit that they blazed past Gram in the second-tier corridor without registering his out-of-time outfit.

"Good job!" Imogen sang in Eliot's ear. "All you have to do is keep them running like the wind!"

All. Ha! Were Eliot able to spare the oxygen, she would've laughed aloud. She was fast, yes, but speed came at a higher cost out in the open. There were no corners to turn here on the ground level, and the crowds around the amphitheater had thinned. Eliot was much too easy to see in these streets. Time to haul arse.

"McCarthy!" Marin and his unit spilled out of an arch. Their togas flapped as they ran, ready to take flight.

Eliot's premeditated path had ended, but the chase had to keep going. She turned north, away from the *Ab Aeterno* and any route Gram and Empra might take to it, and began running. Hades licked her heels, hounding her until the Colosseum's roar began to recede, deflected by a maze of red-tiled roofs. Other, more urgent sounds took over: heartbeat in her ears, Marin's stunrod unsheathed, the air around the weapon crackling. It smelled of pennies and clean fire, too close for comfort. The man's silver-hair-to-speed ratio was admirable, and Eliot figured she had only another minute or two before the *ZAP*.

TRANSFER OF "YOU RAT YOU BURN" FILE IS 90% COMPLETE.

"Not now, Vera!" The word *Rat* disappeared, but Eliot couldn't help feeling like one, scrambling past palatial columns, up a road she saw no end to. She was tired of running. So hazing tired. The fact that this was her final dash only compounded her weariness. Without memories holding her up, her skeleton felt one step away from splintering. It would be such a relief to collapse, let the dust take her....

"The distraction's working, Eliot! Keep going!" That voice became the only thing keeping her up. Imogen—pumpkin-swearing, cocktail-umbrella-wearing, aurora borealis girl who felt like family because she was—counted on her. All of Eliot's friends did, and if she fell now, she wouldn't be able to catch them. "You've got this!"

Ten meters ahead the air shuddered and Eliot's insides with it. She knew that shimmer: atoms arranging into molecules, stacking into the shape of a man wearing a porkpie hat. He stood in the middle of the road, live stunrod in his fist.

His was a broken-record question: "Where's the catalyst?"

"Ackerman? *Take off that hat!*" Marin bellowed. Never mind that the rest of the man's wardrobe was just as ill-suited to 95 AD. The hat was the heart of the offense. *"You call yourself a Corps man?"*

The Bureau agent hadn't just tipped off the Corps. He'd hitched a fexing ride with them! His teleportation systems must have rebooted, for when Eliot veered to avoid getting trapped, Ackerman bloomed out of the ground in front of her like a hazing beanstalk. She could still see the blood on his sleeve, a streak he seemed determined to lengthen.

"Warning!" Imogen screamed. "Evil man ahead!"

"Take me to the boy, and this ends!" the Bureau agent snarled.

Eliot had the perfect Yiddish curse—*A zisn toyt zolstu hobn a trok mit tsuker zoldid iberforn.* "I wish you a sweet death: a truck full of sugar should run over you."—and no time to say it. Stunrods barricaded her back and chest, each just a few steps from scrambling her systems. She couldn't stop. She couldn't run.

Teleporting was her only option.

Random coordinate numbers wiped away Marin's shout when she jumped, arranging a whole new scene. Well-groomed paths, hedges wrapped in the cool of the morning, sunlit quiet punctuated by birdsong. The garden Eliot had landed in seemed a peaceful place, somewhere to get acquainted with deep philosophical thoughts. Any other hour she would have taken a seat beside the marble peacock fountain, let herself get lulled by the water streaming from beak to basin.

But her bones could not be stilled, for five seconds later a new set of feet crunched the gravel. Electricity tugged at the air and sparks flirted with Eliot's shoulder as Ackerman swiped his stunrod. She threw herself into some bushes, collecting a leg full of thorns. Nothing was singed. Not much was saved, either. The Bureau agent materialized in front of Eliot, causing her to double back.

This wasn't a chase. She was already cornered.

"Can you turn off your beacon thingy?" Imogen asked.

Eliot dodged Agent Ackerman's second jab by teleporting to the other side of the garden. "Dunno. Vera, shut off the beacon."

I AM UNABLE TO COMPLY, the computer told her. TRANSFER OF "YOU RAT YOU BURN" FILE IS 93% COMPLETE.

Et tu, Vera? The interface *wanted* the Multiverse Bureau to track her down. As long as Vera stayed online, Eliot was a moving target. Jump, jump, always in the crosshairs. Shutting off her interface wasn't an option, either—it would cut Eliot's link with the *Invictus*, stranding her with no way to flee from Ackerman.

The agent appeared on Eliot's side of the garden, stunrod in full swing.

She scrambled her coordinates.

Sparks showered across the frescoed wall, not a girl to be found.

The garden vanished, Eliot had landed...underground? She couldn't see much in the swampy darkness, except for open-flame lamps lining tunnel walls. These offered more heat than light, temperatures that ripened the smells of urine, feces, and blood. Noise raged above, at a volume matching her nausea, which had already been stirred by the previous two jumps. Eliot's insides boiled with bile as she stumbled down the passage. This place couldn't get any more hellish—

She saw Ackerman's stunrod before she saw him. The scepter's crackling light cut farther than any flame, revealing cages filled with lions. A sure sign they were underneath the Colosseum. The beasts rippled behind the bars, muscles and honeyed fur; yawns peeled back into fangs. One of the big cats roared.

The Bureau agent froze at the sound. Eliot teleported behind him, managing a kick to the back of his knee. Ackerman yelled

392

and a whole line of lions snarled, ready for this fight, any fight, fangs at the ready, *take him down!* Her second strike found nothing but air. The target had evaporated, realigning on her. She lunged two steps ahead, missing Ackerman's reappearance by centimeters.

Run, jump, a bathhouse. Run, jump, a field. Run, jump, a temple. Wherever Eliot went, Agent Ackerman appeared five seconds later, automatically locked onto her coordinates. There was no way to shake him.

"I can't keep this up," Eliot croaked on the seventh jump. Her body wasn't used to so much rearranging. She was an over-loved ragdoll, limp and coming apart at the joints. "If he hits me with that stunrod I'm done."

"Can you jump to a different time?" Imogen asked.

"That won't help." Not in the long run. Eliot might get a breather, but the consequences would be the same as shutting off Vera—Gaius wouldn't get to say good-bye to Empra, the *Invictus*'s memories would not pass through the pivot point. Even worse, the Bureau agent might find his way into the next universe and kill the new Far. Countersignature or no. Who would've thought a man with fexing feathers in his hat could be so dangerous?

"This only stops if he does."

44.

INTERVENTION, MAYBE
NOT DIVINE

RECORDER EMPRA MCCARTHY SAT IN THE bleachers of the *Amphitheatrum Flavium*, her pregnant belly round as a globe under her indigo stola. The Colosseum was a frenzy of life around her. Everything had the sheen of a fever from the moment Empra had awoken in her bunk; the entire day felt warped. She'd been in such a daze walking here from the *Ab Aeterno* she thought she saw Edwin Marin, her tailhat of an ex-fiancé, studying the games' red-letter *edicta munerum* announcement on the side of a building. She'd even paused, Marin's name on the tip of her tongue, before realizing it was the wrong year, and this man was the wrong age. Silver temples, some twenty years Empra's senior.

So much seemed off. Her thoughts were fuzzy, spinning her head into itself. Empra wasn't sure if it was a side effect of pregnancy or heartbreak or the crowd's chanting. The three were a trifecta for misery as she stared at the sands below.

Empra didn't register the newcomer on the bench beside her until he spoke. *"Cruenti sunt ludi. Oculo intimo spectare non sapiat."*

Translation: *Bloody are the games. With the inmost eye to watch would not be wise.* It was a strange thing to say, in even stranger-sounding Latin. Empra frowned, but didn't break her gaze into the arena. Conversations with ancient Romans went against her Recorder training, and even though she'd already shattered these rules—off-record interview with a gladiator x 320—none of her felt like talking. She was here for one reason alone.

"I'm placing my bet on Gaius. What about you?"

Empra's heart rate spiked. She wondered if Doc would notice—connect the reaction with the name. More pressingly, she wondered how this young man knew to say it. One look and Empra knew she was sitting beside a fellow time traveler. Plenty of others in the amphitheater had skin as dark as his, but her neighbor's toga virilis was dated by over a century. Besides, how else would he know about Gaius? Or want her to know that he knew.... A whole new meaning slid into his greeting: *With the inmost eye to watch would not be wise.*

She cut off her feed. "Who are you?"

The teenager frowned, his silence carrying until Empra began to second-guess herself. Maybe he was from this time, unable to understand her Central dialect. Maybe this was all some fever-haze coincidence.

"I'm not recording," she tried again. "You can speak freely."

"I'm a friend. Call me Gram." These words fit the newcomer's tongue much better than his Latin. A learned language, not one cobbled together by translation tech. "I'm here to take you back to the *Ab Aeterno*."

Again, her heart seized. "You don't understand. I can't leave—"

"Gaius isn't fighting today." Gram gazed down at the imperial box, where the emperor was arriving to a lash of cheers.

Empra wanted this to be true, which made the lie even worse. Gaius's match was among the day's first—he'd told her at the banquet last evening, unable to veil the fear in his voice.

"He is. And I—I have to watch." The sob surprised Empra. Usually she was better at hiding things. She'd kept her pregnancy a secret from the *Ab Aeterno*'s crew for six months thanks to loose stolas. "I need to know how his fight ends."

"We came to an arrangement with Gaius's lanista. He's free, and he's waiting to say good-bye near the *Ab Aeterno*. I'm here to take you to him."

"Free?" Empra's dizziness was growing worse. Her hands fell from belly to bench, clutching through its splinters. "The Corps would never allow that."

"We're not with the Corps," Gram explained. "How do you think I'm sitting here talking with you?"

"If you're not with the Corps, then who *are* you with?"

"That answer would take far more time than we have. Your water's going to break soon, and if you don't get back to Central before your son arrives, things are going to get very hashed up. Er, pardon my language."

It wasn't the profanity that had startled Empra. *Son.* Her palm flew back to her stomach. Despite Doc's offer to reveal the child's gender, she'd refused, because that was a secret she could not keep from Gaius, and it would expose far more than she could afford.

"Hashed up how?"

"Come with me." Gram stood, extending his arm. "I'll explain as much as I can on the way."

The *Porta Sanavivaria* was going to open soon. Empra studied its latticework. Standard Roman design—composed of triangles or Xs, depending on how one stared. The rest of the crowd watched the door, too, shouts growing hot with restlessness. Her baby—her *son*—began kicking to their beat.

"Gaius?"

"He'll be there," the other time traveler promised. "The sooner we leave, the longer you have to say good-bye."

That was the farewell Empra wanted—unmarred by blades and bars.

She took Gram's hand. The steps were steeper on the way down. Empra's shifted center of gravity didn't help things, but Gram was as strong as he looked, and held her steady all the way to the exiting arch. She did not miss how often he glanced at her belly. Nor did she miss his pause in the passageway, his last over-the-shoulder look at the sands.

Gaius's son kept kicking inside her.

This is a miracle. Intervention, maybe not divine, but just as effective.

She couldn't help but wonder what it cost.

45.

MEMENTO MORI

Farway Gaius McCarthy only ever wanted to see the world, not save one.

His view had shrunk down to a door. The *Porta Sanavivaria*. Gate of Life. Sunlight shone through the grand exit in triangle shards, too sharp after an hour in the amphitheater's underworld. Tigers and lions roared in the tunnels behind Far, but the beast on the other side of the door was louder. The crowd screaming at morning's first fight wasn't driven by primal survival instinct, and that made them all the more terrifying. They *wanted* to watch men bleed. For fun.

Far's opponent seemed indifferent, though it was hard to tell. The man's helmet covered most of his face, two eyeholes hinting at the human beneath. His right arm looked just as robotic, covered in metal armor. The scars on his bare chest spoke of a brutal life; the muscles beneath put Far's kettlebell/ pull-up routine to shame.

It was the sword Far eyed with the most envy. He felt like a fountain statue with his trident and net—armed for display, nearly as naked. No helmet. No legionnaire shield. Not even hashing shin guards. His rival's blade wouldn't have much trouble finding flesh, no matter how fiercely Far fought. He was *going* to fight. That much was decided. It'd take Gram a while to guide his mother back to the CTM *Ab Aeterno*, more minutes still for her good-bye to Gaius. Far wanted to cling to every second of life left to him. Maybe that made him selfish or stubborn.

Most likely it made him human.

Far stared at the Gate of Life and wondered if he was always meant to end up here, at his beginning, full circle, stop. Priya's breath joined his own through the comm, reminding him why he stood at this threshold. Love. A love that was bigger than just them. Their heartbreak now had been his mother's then, and this was the only way to end it. This was the only way to make things new.

He could hear the first fight's end through the door, stabbing alongside the sunlight. Not long now. Once the first defeated gladiator knelt for his quietus, once the victor's sword landed in his neck, once the blood clumped garnet on the earth, once the body was dragged by its heels to the *Spoliarium*, once the arena was cleared . . .

The door opened. No number of datastreams could prepare Far for the sheer force of fifty thousand throats rattling the sky, showering back to earth. Sand shuddered beneath his feet—grain by unsteady grain—as he strode to the center of the Colosseum. Ahead, the *Porta Libitinaria* loomed: second passage, Gate of Death.

His grip on his trident tightened.

Not yet.

"Walk to the imperial box," Priya reminded him. She wasn't a Historian, but she didn't need to be when Empra's datastream played a few seconds ahead on an adjoining screen. "You're going to bow to the emperor."

Bright fabrics framed the imperial box, eagle statues' golden wing tips stabbing the sun. Emperor Domitian could have been a prop in his chair, for all he moved at the gladiators' tribute. More men about to die…another day in the life. Officials examined Far's trident and tested Sir Robot Head's blade. Both weapons were deemed kill-worthy and returned to their bearers.

"Now you walk back to the center of the arena." Priya spoke quickly to hide the shake in her voice. "At the sound of the horn, you fight. He's going to come at your right side first—"

"I love you." Far could say it, now that there were no ears close enough to hear his non-Latin. He hadn't said it enough, so he tried to make up for lost words as he took his place. "I love you, Priya Parekh. I *will* find you in the next life."

"Far—"

The horn sounded. His enemy charged.

"Jump left!"

Far blocked the blow with his trident, tossing his net. It slid off the gladiator's helmet, became a good-for-nothing pile of ropes in the dirt. Better for catching fish than feet…

"He's going to strike," Priya warned. "Feign right!"

Again, Far was spared. He twisted right, thrusting his weapon as he did. Three shining prongs found a gap in the other fighter's defenses, metal to flesh. Red, red, red down the gladiator's scarred side, roar pouring out of his eyeholes. The crowd's cries turned to thunder as he scrambled back.

"The net! Grab your net before he recovers!"

It was too late. Far's opponent had steel-coated nerves to match his robot head. Though bleeding bad enough to make bettors wince and clutch their coin purses, the gladiator didn't even wobble. He held his shield close to his side, raised his blade, and attacked.

Left or right or block?

Priya had no directions this time. History was changed and Empra's datastream could no longer give Far his much-needed edge. His mind went for the parry, but his reflexes chose to dodge. The result was a half-tail combination of both. His enemy's blade glanced off the trident, path diverted from Far's neck to his arm. The hurt was too shocking to feel, at first. Far only knew he was wounded because the storm screams were back, raising every hair on his neck. Lightning soon followed, nerve endings opening up all at once.

His trident arm. Oh Hades, his *trident* arm. The sword had found his scar and split it right open again. Had there been this much blood the first time? Far couldn't remember. The Fade had whittled memories of the injury down to Priya's needle and swift stitches. She'd hummed then, to distract him, a song called "Fix You," written by one of her favorite bands of yore. *Cold—something? Cold, cold.* That, too, was slipping. . . . Far's red-rain blood dribbled into the sands as he stumbled away.

This was the beginning of his end.

"Far!" When Priya saw the wound through his eyes, she cried, "Don't you dare stop, Far! Keep fighting!"

"P…" He was never supposed to win. Both of them knew that.

There was a rustling sound. Far spun around, bracing for a blade, but the other fighter had dropped back, side trauma and heavy armor taking their toll. The noise must have come from Priya's end.

"I love you. I—I have to go."

What? No…

"Keep fighting," she said again.

"Priya?"

Dead air ached in his ear. Far felt as if something far more vital than his arm had been cut. How was he supposed to keep fighting now? How was he supposed to die alone? Like this: The other gladiator began circling, slow, stalking steps. His sword was edged with Far's blood, poised for more. Not that it was hard to find. Half of Far was red as he switched his trident to his good arm, struggling to secure the slick handle.

Not yet.

But soon.

He couldn't blame Priya for leaving. No amount of love in the world could make a person strong enough to watch this.

46.

THE MOTH WHO KNEW HER WINGS WOULD BURN

PRIYA HAD NEVER BEEN SQUEAMISH AROUND wounds, even her own. Playtime scrapes were a source of fascination, something to be studied through the glittery fray of Madam Wink's mane while her father sprayed on Heal-All. He often recited facts as he did—things to distract her from the sting, truths to tuck away for later.

"One minute is all it takes for a drop of blood to run through your body. Heart back to heart. The hemoglobin in your red blood cells threads oxygen through your veins to keep you alive. It's pretty phenomenal stuff."

"Why are some people so scared of it?" Priya had asked, thinking of Tommy, who'd abandoned his own hoverbike to help her off the ground, only to freeze when he saw her torn-up knees.

Her father went quiet. This silence went past tired, the kind of pause that meant something important would be said.

So Priya had waited, squeezing her stuffed unicorn so tight its stuffing pushed back against the practice sutures.

"It's not the blood people fear," Dev Parekh said finally. "It's the pain."

Now, at eighteen, watching Far's wound ooze through the screen, Priya understood. Here was a sight that turned her stomach. The pain was *not* a distant dream, but red and roaring, all of Far's blood spilling out too fast to replace. His medical readings scrambled across the infirmary screens—fight-or-flight wild, a beat no song could match. Even if there were such a tune, playlists were a thing of the past. Both sets of Priya's headphones, BeatBix and rip-offs, sat quiet on her desk, mirroring their surroundings in their gold plating: the see-through surface of a dead holo-paper zine, useless needles, Ganesh's curled trunk. All appeared four times and shining, reminding her that this was the only way to make a way. Everything would be better when the string was cut.

But it hurt watching Far bleed out of life. It hurt watching life bleed out of him. Neither force crackled.

"Far! Don't you dare stop, Far!" Priya's own heart bled through the comm.

She was afraid.

"Keep fighting!"

"Priya! Priyapriyapriya!" Imogen appeared, a lemon-colored blob in the headphones—too frantic to register her cousin's injuries. "We've got an *emergency* emergency. The Bureau jacktail showed up with the Corps, and he's trying to fritz out Eliot's equipment with a stunrod. His teleport equipment is working again and he's chasing her all over the city and she's still got Gaius in her pocket universe and I don't know what to do. Do you have something *zappy*?"

If Gaius was in the pocket universe, then the chip was as well. They were supposed to be passed on to Empra together. Priya had even written a letter to Far's mother, filling the inside cover of the Code of Conduct with instructions to give the chip to Far on his seventeenth birthday. The guidebook's paper tore as easily as it folded and was now a tiny square in a small box in a pocket universe on Eliot's wrist, hopping all across Rome. The *Invictus*'s whole past and possible future hinged on this: Stay with Far at the hour of his death, or save their lives for later.

All or nothing.

It wasn't even a choice.

"I love you." Priya's finger trembled over the Mute button. "I—I have to go. Keep fighting."

She cut the audio link before Far could answer and tossed a lab coat over the feed. Grief settled gray below her eyes, dry, yet dark enough to tarnish the BeatBix. "Why do you need zap? What about Eliot's blaster?"

"Are you an ace shot?" the Historian asked. "I'm not. Anything short of a kill means squat when teleportation is involved. I figure it's better if we can fritz Agent Ackerman's jump systems before he fritzes Eliot's. Less death, less hopping, everybody wins."

"We don't have any stunrods on board." But they *were* in a ship full of live wires. Priya turned her back to the lab coat's shine and pushed into the common area. A few floor panels remained crooked from Far's *Rubaiyat* ransack. Sharp corners, tilting plane, covered in costumes from a blank-page past. Neon fires flared as Priya shoved aside the flash-leather suit, prying up the panel beneath. More rainbows appeared in the form of wires, bundled together by the dozen.

"Welcome to the *Invictus*'s nervous system," she announced. "Very colorful, very electric."

Imogen knelt next to her, gaping at the Medusa mess. "You're gonna gut the ship?"

"This is all the zap we've got." The correct combination of wires—high voltage, low current—could substitute as a stun-rod, stopping a man, but not his heart. It was the ship itself Priya was worried about. Disconnecting the wrong line could bring down the holo-shield, the comms, the mainframe…any number of systems essential to their mission. "We can do without overhead lights or speakers, right?"

"Affirmative."

Which wires were which wires were which wires were which? So many colors streamed together, and Priya found it hard to keep her head on when her heart was in the arena. Green? Light blue? Orange? Red? Red? Red?

"Hurry," Imogen urged. "Eliot's been through enough jumps to scramble an egg inside a hen."

Purple and green. Priya wasn't certain about the wires she chose, but this didn't stop her from yanking them free. The *Invictus*'s overhead lights cut out, sparks scattering through new-found darkness. She'd gotten at least one of the wires right. The comm system had stayed online, too. Far's datastream glowed through the infirmary screen, ghastly in new shadows. Priya couldn't look at it. Her concentration was best served focusing on the wires in each hand, frayed ends far from touching.

Keep fighting, Far.

One more minute. That was all she needed: heart back to heart.

I'm going to save us.

"These wires don't stretch much," she told Imogen. "The Bureau agent has to land on this side of the common area."

The other girl nodded. "Copy that, Eliot? Your order of save-the-day is ready. Come on home."

The final word wasn't even cold when Eliot appeared. Sweat streaked her eyebrows. Her eyes had gone from haunted to hunted. She slouched against the couch, ash in her warning: "Five seconds. He'll be here."

Priya's fists tightened around the wires. A flickering in the infirmary called to her, but she could not look. She *could not look*. Priya wondered if she'd feel it—the moment Far died—or if that was a sentiment created by ancient poets. Souls twined so closely together one could feel when the other was severed....

Agent Ackerman's materialization made Eliot's teleports look mystical. Where she slipped, this man slammed, crushing the tricorne hat beneath his feet. His stunrod was pointed at Eliot, and it might've landed, had he not been so blindsided by the brightness of Imogen's hair.

"I have *had* it with you history-hopping betch—"

Poke. Poke. *ZZZZZZAP.*

Thud.

One touch and the Bureau agent was grounded. Priya stared

at the wires she held, shocked in a different sense. She'd never harmed another person before, had never thought she could, under the unspoken pressure of the Hippocratic oath. Everything was upside down, inside out. At the end of the couch, Eliot doubled over, charred fabric crumbling beneath her nails while she heaved. There was a wet splash of something on the floor panels.

Priya took an extra breath to keep her own sickness down. "Are you okay?"

"Too much—dashing—rearranging!" Eliot explained between gasps. "My—molecules—can handle it. Stomach—not so much."

"Is *he* okay?" Imogen nudged Agent Ackerman with her toe. The man was face to floor, pinned by a force heavier than gravity. His hat had tumbled into the rest of the clothes, blending in with forgotten times.

"He seems to be breathing." Eliot gathered herself enough to pick up the Bureau agent's stunrod. She flicked it on, then off, white charge leaving a jagged imprint in the air. "Good call on the wires, Priya. You just saved the whole hashing day, and more besides."

"The files? They're intact?"

"Locked and loaded." The eyes that were so like Far's—and altogether different—blinked. "I'm feeding all of the ship's current datastream into the chip as we speak, including mine. Anything you want to say?"

Priya's fists buzzed and shook, no volts involved. What could she voice that hadn't already been shown? How could she put love into letters, life into words?

"Far, you're in the arena right now, fighting a really terrifying guy with a sword, because you believed this life is worth dying for.

Please, give it a chance. Give *us* a chance. When we met in this life, I was working shifts in the Corps infirmary. Priya Parekh. Find me. Bring a mug of chai from the tea stand on Via Novus."

"The files..." If Imogen were an animation, a lightbulb would've appeared. "You mean the *Invictus*'s logs! Clever, clever. Oooh, breaking news! Gram and Aunt Empra have made it to the rendezvous. Her second contraction just started—ah! It's loud!"

"I should go. I'll do my best to make sure the chip gets transferred." Eliot pulled off her wig as she said this, elaborate Roman updo tossed into the pile. "Don't let him out of your sight, okay?"

"You'll warn me before the *Ab Aeterno* leaves?" Far couldn't live past the time machine's takeoff, no matter how much Priya wanted him to. "So I can tell Far when it's time...."

Eliot vanished midnod, her exit just as sudden as her entrance all those days ago, prelude to doomed violins. No songs rose to meet Priya now as she looked toward the infirmary. Somewhere on the other side of this city, Far's eyes were open, datastream transmitting a sight bright enough to sear through her lab coat. What a fearsome light, calling her, the moth who knew her wings would burn.

Let the flames come.

Let the watch end.

Clear sight or tears, she'd be there to see it.

"Im?"

"Yeah, Priya?"

"Will you hold these wires away from the metal floor?" Priya passed them to her friend one at a time. "I need to say good-bye."

47.

AMONG THE TOMBS

ONE MORE JUMP.

These coordinates—not random—brought Eliot to Rome's southern outskirts, where buildings yielded to tombs. All along the Appian Way, the dead made themselves known with epitaphs; patricians' stone likenesses guarding whatever was left of their mortal husks. Trees stretched alongside the stillness, their branches scratching blue, making the sky that much larger. Eliot felt like the only soul beneath it. She wasn't, of course. The *Ab Aeterno* lurked behind these tombs; Burg and Doc and Nicholas going frantic within its unseen walls at Empra's blackout. Empra, who was nearer than they knew, seized by a new contraction Eliot could hear through Gram's side of the comm.

"You're doing fine, Ms. McCarthy," the Engineer coached.

"Ms. McCarthy? Way to make a woman feel old. Where's Gaius—*ah!*" A stab of pain, heard not just through electronics, but from the other side of the road.

"He's coming," Gram assured her. "He'll be here."

Sun glared off Eliot's bare scalp as she slipped the pocket universe from her wrist. Her exhaustion bordered on sinister: two palms to earth, a few dry heaves, *collapse now, rest your bones.* The background voices twining through her comm wouldn't let her: Empra huffing, Priya calling Far's name, Gram's encouragements, Imogen apologizing for not being at her station. All of them were connected, close to a turning point, and it was up to Eliot to push them through.

Once the worst of the nausea rolled past, she opened her pocket universe. Her father's curls were the first thing she saw through the interdimensional slip, followed by brawny arms. He'd been...napping. On a pile of dresses nonetheless. Gaius blinked at the sudden daylight, starting when he saw Eliot haloed in it.

"It's okay," she reassured him in Latin. "Could you pass me that box?"

Gaius frowned at the velvet as he grabbed it. "What creature did such fur belong to?"

"A velveteen rabbit."

"Truly? I've never seen a rabbit so blue." The sincerity in Gaius's voice only sharpened her guilt. This was no time to go planting stories of cerulean wildlife into ancient Roman mythos. Though a velvet blue rabbit paled against everything else her father had seen today. Eliot wondered what he made of all this....

Gaius passed her the box. Eliot opened it, lifting Priya's letter to see the chip beneath, items as fragile as they were forever. Paper covered with permanent ink. See-through circuits filled with everything Eliot was, everything the crew members of the *Invictus* wanted to be. Was it enough, to place these in Empra's hands? With so much on the chip, would future Far bother watching a file called "You Rat You Burn"? Certainly, the name was in their humor set, but the label needed to be more than just funny. It needed to be life—drink of water, breath of air, undeniable.

But what? "Watch Me Now" or "Yield to New Life Course"?

Both were throat-snatchy. Neither felt right.

Her father pulled himself out of the earth, staring at the collection of pale tombs around them. He walked like a man unused to freedom—hesitant at first, then overswift—toward the nearest stone, and placed his palm over its chiseled letters: TU FUI, EGO ERIS.

"Not a dream," he declared once he found the world solid enough to push back. "Where is Empra?"

The final cry of a contraction answered him. Gaius's face went sharp at the scream, and when he took off running, Eliot did not stop him. It was good that he hurry....

"Vera?"

YES, ELIOT?

"Program the memory chip's hologram function to respond exclusively to Farway Gaius McCarthy's voice. Also, I'd like to relabel 'You Rat You Burn.'"

VOICE RECOGNITION HAS BEEN REASSIGNED. WHAT WOULD YOU LIKE TO RELABEL THE FILE?

Eliot stared at the words her father had touched. The poetry of them tugged, their undertow meaning stretching through her.

Not déjà vu but a similar feeling: cat paws splayed in sunlight, fireflies clinging to dusk's edge, a wave's foam getting caught between your toes, bursting one bubble at a time. *Life*. As it was, as it would be.

Her skin prickled when she read the phrase again, aloud.

Once the naming was done, Eliot sealed her pocket universe and went to join the others. She found Gram standing behind one of the nearby tombs, trying his best to ignore the fact that Far's parents were kissing. Kissing being the G-rated term. Their level of PDA was impressive, turning Eliot into the embarrassed teenage daughter she was.

"Good job convincing Empra to leave with you." Gram nearly leaped from his skin when she sidled next to him. "Sorry! Not much I can do in the way of sloshing here."

"Suppose not." The Engineer looked around the tombs, laced with grass that had seen better seasons. The *Ab Aeterno*'s field was a few corners away, out of sight, within sprinting distance. "I return the felicitations. Heard some trouble through the comm."

"Nothing Priya and Imogen couldn't manage." Speaking of... "I can take this from here. You should get back to the *Invictus*. Far's fight is almost over, and you'll be needed."

"Five minutes." Gram paused one step in, half torn. "That's all you've got. Any longer and Far might make his debut on the *Ab Aeterno* again. We shouldn't risk the window with this pivot point."

"I won't," she assured him. "I've come this far. Go back to Imogen."

With a nod, Gram left. Eliot pressed the velvet box to her

heart and waited while Empra and Gaius exchanged hungry gazes, quiet Latin. Her fingers wove through his curls and his hands stroked her face, thumbs wiping tears that sounded different from the ones on the datastream—sad, yes, but not broken. There was room for a laugh when Empra caught sight of Gaius's garments.

"Is he wearing *bedsheets*?" The question, meant for Gram, stalled when Empra found Eliot in his place. "Who are you?"

The velvet box was stronger than it looked, for how Eliot gripped the corners. It was her own flesh that dented, her own thoughts that winced: *I'm your daughter from another life.* "No one important. I have to take you back to the *Ab Aeterno* soon, so say your piece."

" 'From eternity.' " Gaius caught on to the ship's Latin name. "That's where you must return, yes?"

"Yes. I—I don't want to leave you, Gaius."

"You were never meant to stay, Empra of the Elsewhere Skies. That our lives intersected and created something new—" Gaius looked to her swollen belly. "That has blessed me more than I can say."

Fresh tears spread daylight across Empra's face. Were they for birth or good-bye, Eliot wondered. Agony made itself known in each, and both were drawing near.

"Tempus venit." Eliot spoke Latin as she stepped away from the grave, so both her parents could understand. Imogen, too. There was background mumbling as the words were passed along to Priya, and to Far through her.

It's time.

Empra nodded, her arms twined around Gaius. She leaned forward, kissed him, whispered something only he could hear, listened as he whispered something back. She kissed him again. She let go.

"The world you return to..." Eliot switched to Central's tongue. "It won't be the same as the one you left, but you shouldn't fear. It means the universe didn't end."

"End?" Empra flinched. "I hashed things up that much?"

"You won't, if you jump back to Central as soon as possible." Eliot pressed the box into her mother's hands. "This is for your son. Give it to him on his seventeenth birthday—no sooner, no later. His future depends on it."

Empra didn't seem to know what to make of the gift or its giver. "My son, you know him?"

"I did." The tense slipped out, caught both women in the gut. Eliot didn't try to recover. "Let's get you back to your ship. The longer you stay, the more you risk."

At this, her mother accepted the box and walked to the end of the tombs, into the field beyond. Its emptiness shimmered with morning. Strings of dew caught the edge of Empra's stola as she crossed the grass, turning indigo into darkest night.

Gaius didn't fight when Eliot grabbed his arm to keep him from following. "Where is she going?"

"You'll see."

The center of the field—that was where the *Ab Aeterno* hid in the open, holo-shield heavens matching the true thing. If Eliot hadn't watched the datastream, she might've jumped when the hatch opened, time machine's inner workings punching out sky. Burg emerged, beside himself, scooping Empra off her feet with windmill arms and rushing her back to the ship. There was a second of panic—white lab coat, blinking console lights—and then the door shut.

The field was just a field again.

"Eternity." Gaius knelt to touch the dry grass. His curls wrote haywire lines around him as he looked back at Eliot. "But why did you not join them?"

"Mine is a different route." Once the *Ab Aeterno* peeled out of this time, a new world would branch out, and if Eliot crossed the pivot point, she risked dragging the decay with her. If she jumped to the past, she could scan herself to make sure Far's death had eradicated the countersignature.

Best move fast. Empra's CTM was due to jump any moment.

"What about me?" Gaius asked. "Where should I go?"

"You're a free man—" Eliot's explanation dried up as she stared at the equations on her interface, where digits had gone from steady to soluble. Numbers vanished, and when Eliot looked past them, she found the rest of the world disappearing, too.

Air above and earth below, unbecoming as one. Trees bent from the roots up. Sunlight shuddered. Tombs forgot their own names, and the soil no longer understood its purpose. Eliot's own shout was stripped from her throat, but at least her hands still worked. The bedsheet-and-floss toga held when she pulled her father close.

It was too early. It was too late.

It was no time at all.

48.

EVERY GOOD-BYE

IMOGEN STARED AT THE WIRES IN her hands. Green, purple, emerald, violet, jungle leaves, deep dusk, green...What was another word for *green*? She couldn't think of one, which freed her mind to wander to any number of awful things.

Lost memories above and around her—jackets and suits, days evanesced.

Aunt Empra's love story ending.

Another love story coming to a close: Priya in the next room, watching as Farway died.

As Farway died.

As Farway died.

As Farway die—

Swirling thoughts became a spiral. Imogen cut them short. She looked to the least of the current evils, flat on the floor, frazzled to the eyebrows. "What's another word for *green*?"

Agent Ackerman didn't seem to be in a thesaurus mood.

He tried spitting, but the saliva made a sad trail down his lips. His groans had evolved into obscenities, albeit, not very creative ones. "Betch!"

"I am a girl," Imogen corrected him, wagging the wires. "A girl who likes to name things. This is Electro and this is Cute. They're both very eager to get reacquainted with you, so I'd lay off the insults if I were you."

The Bureau agent's answer consisted mostly of drool. Imogen wondered if she should layer a red attack panda to her threat—Saffron was more apt to do damage anyway. The creature was already stalking the porkpie hat, eyes fastened to its feathers.

Daylight scorched through the common area as the *Invictus*'s hatch opened. Saffron scattered. Imogen brightened. Gram was here. He'd run with lung-popping speed down the Appian Way to make it so.

"Quick! Tell me a synonym for *green*."

Gram shut the hatch, but his smile wasn't dimmed so easily. "*Viridescent*."

"And *purple*?"

"*Violaceous*."

The words sounded too preposterous to belong to a language, much less colors, but Imogen wasn't one to judge. She loved how Gram had these at the ready, even as he sat down next to her.

"So you got stuck with guard duty?" he asked.

"More of a *don't let the wires touch the floor or we'll see everyone's skeleton through their skin* duty. Plus, I volunteered."

Imogen's eyes darted to the infirmary door. Closed by Priya, with mercy. "I don't see how she can be in there ... watching."

"Far needs someone with him." Gram reached for the viridescent wire, held it so they could sit closer. Knees touching— Electro in his hand, Cute in hers. "We all do."

❖ ❖ ❖

Far's fight dragged on. The battle was harder without Priya, but easier, too, for the next time the gladiator's sword found Far's flesh, the hurt of his wounds belonged to him alone.

Alone.

It wasn't the way Far wanted to die, but death did not care what its victims wanted. The force clung shadow-close, a fell breath against his neck, waiting, waiting for the final strike. Blood trailed Far's footsteps as he tried to outrun it, frantic scarlet signature. Despite his injuries, he'd managed to stay a trident's length away from his opponent, but the crowd was growing bored of the chase. Hisses prickled the air—*Get on with it. We've a schedule of slaughter to keep. Your death isn't entertaining anymore.* Imaginary voices, real thoughts, growing, swelling, louder, until Far didn't know why he was still blocking the other gladiator's blows, still trying to land some of his own.

Death caught every man alone.

"Far! I'm here!" Priya's voice: solid as ever. "Eliot and Imogen needed help."

"You're here?" Far asked, dazed.

"I'm here. I promised I would be." She'd come back to him,

his courage. His heart. "Eliot just left. Your mother and father are saying good-bye to each other."

Clash, block. Thrust, bleed. Sand in the eyes. Cuts full of grit. Steps began to falter. It went this way for a few more minutes, until Priya passed along the words *It's time* and a blow from the other gladiator sent Far's trident flying. Far's hands flew up, too—though there was no surrender, just a pause for the crowd's will to make itself known. Thumbs up, thumbs down. *Let him go!* or *Kill him!*

Shouts tangled together. Thumbs turned.

These men were hungry. These men were bored.

Emperor Domitian rose from his chair, twisted his wrist to please the masses.

"I'm here. I'm here. I'm here. I'm here," Priya kept saying, until he felt her hand in his, holding tight as he knelt in the sand. "I'm here. I'm here. I love you."

His opponent placed his sword's point on the back of Far's neck. He stared past the crowd, into the sky, and wondered if the *Ab Aeterno* had left yet.

The clouds quivered. The blue around them began ripping, dripping...

The Fade had found his moment at last.

Hurry up, please.

Tempus venit.

"Far?"

"I love you, too, P," he whispered. "Meet you at the tea stand."

The sword fell.

❖ ❖ ❖

Far's vitals slowed. This dying dirge pressed against the infirmary walls, ran through Priya in place of her blood. Sixty seconds and there'd be no heart to return to, no death to mourn, for silence was already blooming. Nothingness grew around her, a whole garden of decay fed by med-patch cabinets and fuel rods. When the gold of her BeatBix began to fade, taking every reflection with it, Priya Parekh shut her eyes and waited for the distant dream.

❖ ❖ ❖

The *Amphitheatrum Flavium* was caught up in the death of the moment. The defeated gladiator had faced his end with honor. He was a name struck off a lanista's roster; a life bleeding out on the sand. Most were too mesmerized to see that they, too, were being scratched out of history's ledger, the clouds above crippling their firmament. The few who caught the sight were reminded of the tales from Pompeii, after the great eruption. But those stories had been filled with ashes and darkness. This sky wasn't filled with anything.

The Fade fell on Rome's past and Far's present, bringing interruptions and ends. It moved as a fog, creeping through windows, winding down roads, consuming all it could. Four stunrods blinked out, their bearers with them. The *Invictus* dissolved along with every soul inside. A girl on the edge of a field held her father tight.

There was one CTM the decay did not reach, for though Nicholas wasn't a knee-jerk kind of guy, he found that—between Empra's order to *Get us the Hades out of here* and the glitches on his screen and one year of cabin fever—he was all too happy to jump. The *Ab Aeterno* vanished from a vanishing sky, just as that vanishing vanished. At last, the Fade had reached what it had ravaged so many worlds for, sliding through stilled lips, seeking that final shudder of a heartbeat.

Lock and key.

Severance.

The boy who should not have been became the boy who never was. No one blinked when the gladiator's body disappeared. His fight, too, slipped from fifty thousand memories second by second as the unraveling stretched back. Not a soul noticed, for they were already placing their bets for the next battle.

The games rolled on.

Two thousand two hundred fifty-eight years later, a child was born.

49.

TAMÁM SHUD

———

THERE WAS AN END.

There is a beginning.

They're one and the same.

PART IV

In my end is my beginning.

—T. S. Eliot
"East Coker"

50.

THE BOY WHO NEVER WAS

PASSING OVER ZONE 1 WAS FAR'S favorite part of his Academy–home commute—the hoverbus always took the same preprogrammed path, slicing straight over Old Rome. Every morning and evening he stared through the window, picking out the monuments below. The Pantheon. St. Peter's Basilica. The *Fontana di Trevi*. His chest twinged, as always, when they passed the Colosseum. Far never knew *why* he felt the way he did whenever he saw it—nostalgia and homesickness and wanderlust and none of the above. Something about the stones made it hard to look away.

Gram seemed just as enthralled with the rainbow box he was twisting around in his hands. After arranging the colors into solid sides, he offered the puzzle to Far. "Wanna try?"

"That way lies humiliation," Far told him. "I don't like humiliation."

His friend passed the cube over anyway. "Then hash it up, will you? If I do it myself, I'll solve it too easily."

This, Far was happy to do. He twisted the little box at random, until it resembled Imogen on an oil-spill hair day. The hoverbus crossed into Zone 2—skyscraper forest—until Old Rome became a sliver in the rear window. Passengers drifted on and off at each stop, too consumed in their spheres of pop-up adverts and datastreams and *Central News Tonight* snippets to do anything more than swipe their palmdrives to pay the fare. Far knew almost all of them by sight, none by name. It made him eager to go to an era where strangers actually talked to each other.

Today a true stranger boarded the hoverbus. The girl's features were striking, not for any particular beauty, but for their starkness. She was as pale as a mist on the moors. Her hair was nearly as light, with the exception of her eyebrows, which had an almost scripted quality. It wasn't until the newcomer winked that Far realized he'd been staring.

He averted his gaze back to the puzzle—jumbled enough—and tossed the cube to Gram. "Hey, want to make a bet on what color my cousin's hair will be tonight?"

"That's an unfair proposition."

"Not so! I haven't seen it today."

"The odds favor you nonetheless, seeing as I've never met your cousin and only know of her behavioral patterns through your anecdotes." Gram wasn't even looking at the puzzle as he twisted it. *Show-off.* "It's basic statistics."

Far snorted. "There's nothing statistical about my family."

This was true. Though Imogen was unpredictable, it was his mother who was the real outlier. She and the rest of the *Ab Aeterno*'s crew not only made history when their time machine landed on April 18, 2354 AD, at 12:01 PM, but a scientific discovery as well. Empra McCarthy, Burgstrom Hammond, Nicholas Nylle, and Matthew "Doc" Hiott stepped off the *Ab Aeterno* to find themselves already waiting on the dock. Mirror doubles pulled from the glass, identical but for Empra's bursting belly. Both crews were stunned. The Corps went into frantic lockdown mode, cross-examining the eight time travelers who should be four. Questions only led to more questions; neither set seemed to be a past or future version of the other. Each *Ab Aeterno* had just returned from 95 AD, but the nonpregnant crew only spent a few minutes in the year before abandoning the assignment. The reason? They'd been spooked to discover themselves already there. Far's mother's crew, ostensibly, who couldn't seem to remember the final hours of their own mission. The mystery thickened when an investigative team tried traveling to the morning of December 31, 95 AD, only to find that their landing equations wouldn't add up. Their time machine kept bouncing off the hours, as if that time did not exist. . . .

After countless interviews to rule out timeline crossings, datastream reviews, and blood tests, the Corps could only conclude that Far's mother's crew had changed history enough to create a parallel universe, which meant that when they traveled back to the future they arrived in a world where they already existed. Voilà! Two Empras! Two Burgs! Two Docs!

Two Nicholases! A whole new branch of science! Bright minds flocked to the theory of a multiverse, both *Ab Aeterno* crews elevated to celebrity status in intellectual circles. Gram, who'd read every single one of Dr. Marcelo Ramírez's papers on the subject, knew more about Far's possible origins than he himself did.

"I look forward to meeting them," his friend said. "You sure they don't mind me crashing your birthday dinner?"

"It's not crashing if you're invited."

"A valid point."

"I make those sometimes."

The cube's colors were back to their sides in thirty seconds. Gram returned it to Far: Mess up, solve, repeat. They spent the next few stops laughing over Instructor Marin's latest assembly rant about *not* placing the Historians' wardrobe mannequins in compromising positions. An advert for the Acidic Sisters' June concert (FEATURING THEIR NEWEST HIT SINGLE "EVERYDAY PAST"! DON'T MISS IT, FARWAY!) popped up on Far's interface. He X-ed it out before the tune turned into an earworm.

"Our stop's next," he warned Gram. "Via Appia. Zone Three."

Far and his mother lived in a flat two buildings away. Burg's name might as well have been on the address, too, for how often the Historian was there. He'd taken pains to make sure the living space had *character*, filling shelves with books, stocking the kitchen with appliances that would never be used. Far was pretty sure over half of the flat's contents were contraband, though some of the old things were genuinely old—such as the stained glass window his mother had discovered in a Zone 2 antique shop. She'd used it to replace the vista in their dining room, where its colors glowed no matter the hour, thanks to a blazing advert on the opposite building.

It was their own little McCarthy time capsule.

Far opened the door—also antique, carved from cypress wood—to smells that must have cost a fortune. Meat, tomatoes, something bready. A banner had been strung over the window; rainbow light dappled its letters: HAPPY 17TH BIRTHDAY, FAR-WAY! The table beneath was set for eight. Mom, his mother's double (affectionately known as Aunt E), Burg, Imogen, Aunt Isolde, Uncle Bert, Gram, himself. Every guest had a plate, but Far couldn't shake the feeling that the number was off.

"Nice place." Gram surveyed the front room the way any Recorder-in-training might. "The vintage touch reminds me of a Sim."

"It's what happens when you're beset on all sides by Historians," Far told him.

"Surprise!" Imogen appeared in the kitchen doorway. Her hair was *yellow* today, scraped into a bun. Burg's kitchen appliances were being put to use after all, as evidenced by the flour that avalanched down her apron. It created a faint cloud around Far when she hugged him.

"This isn't supposed to be a surprise party," he protested.

"The surprise is that you've made it to seventeen without any significant mishaps!" Imogen turned to Gram and held out her hand. "Also, you. You're a surprise."

"The name's—"

A shattering sound cut their introduction short. One of Burg's carefully curated platters was on the floor, in pieces. Even more tragic were the cheeses that had fallen with it—manchego, gouda, cheddar—all over the place. Far's mother stood above the mess. There was no flour on her face, but she looked as pale.

"You...you're Gram?" Her voice crackled. Intense. "Do you remember what happened that day?"

His friend frowned. "I beg your pardon? What day?"

Oooookay. Far had never seen his mother fritz out like this. He tried his best to make the encounter less awkward. "What'd I say, Gram? Your genius reputation precedes you. Gram, this is my mother."

"It's a pleasure to meet you, Ms. McCarthy." Gram's response was straight out of an Old World etiquette lesson. "You have a lovely home."

"Please, call me Empra. 'Ms. McCarthy' makes me feel so old—" His mother frowned. "Are you certain we haven't met before?"

Gram shook his head. "Maybe you've seen me around the Academy?"

"Maybe."

"Or *Central News Tonight*," Far suggested, though he knew his mother rarely tuned into the show. "They did a profile on Gram a few months ago. He's about to finish his second Academy track."

Imogen looked up from the floor, where she was saving as many cheese slices as she could in her makeshift apron pouch. "Your second? What's the first?"

"Engineer. I'll be a Recorder next month, too, if all goes well in the final exam Sim. Historian is the only track that's eluded me." Gram bent down to help collect manchego slices.

"You don't want to be a Historian," Imogen warned. "There are no jobs. Graduating with honors leaves you at the beck and call of Senate spouses who are in denial about their tag size. Okay pay, eternal boredom. The best thing I get out of it is this floor cheese."

Gram examined one of the pieces. "This stuff smells genuine."

"It is. A Senate wife who shall remain unnamed bribed me with her mysterious black market connection to get a peek at the CTM *Churchill*'s next expedition wardrobe. Er...pretend you didn't hear any of that, Aunt Empra."

His mother's eyes were dazed, misted. "Any of what?"

"Exactly." Imogen winked.

Far didn't think his mother was in on the joke. She should've called for the housekeeping droid by now. When he sidestepped the broken pieces and touched her on the arm, she jumped, mind a whole other world away. "Mom, what's the matter?"

"Nothing." For as long as Far could remember, his mother was a force to be reckoned with: independent, certain, *never back down, laugh while you live*. This answer was the opposite of that. It brought out her years—skip-forward silver hairs, solemn lines around her mouth.

"Mom," he prodded.

She shook her head, stepped over the cheese, went into her bedroom, and shut the door. Imogen shot Far a *what the hash just happened?* look. He passed back a *Hades if I know!* shrug. Brusque exits and smashed plates were not a part of Empra McCarthy's MO. Something had glitched, and Far wasn't quite sure what to do about it. Maybe Burg could help, when he got here. Burg always helped.

Ding! Imogen leaped to her feet at the timer, not accounting for her apron full of cheese. Every piece she'd rescued went flying again, double-floored. "Rat barf!"

"Rats don't barf," Gram volunteered. "Their esophageal muscle isn't strong enough to induce vomiting."

Far could have gone his entire life without knowing this. Imogen laughed at Gram's fact, raised him one. "Did you know it wasn't rats that spread the bubonic plague through Europe in the fourteenth century but gerbils?"

Gram was fascinated. "Gerbils? Really?"

"Fuzzy creatures," Far muttered. "Can't trust 'em."

"Guess I'll have to cut rat barf from my rotation," Imogen sighed. "A shame. I liked that one."

"Rat farts would work if you wanted your expletive to be more biologically accurate," Gram told her.

It struck Far that this conversation had happened before, but that was impossible. Imogen and Gram had never met. So why were they hitting it off so well talking about rodent flatulence?

Ah, the universe's mysteries...

51.

THE ROOTS WE DID
NOT CHOOSE...

EMPRA MCCARTHY SAT ON THE EDGE of her bed, attempting to fit her heart back inside her chest. One breath in, two beats out. Her pulse kept escaping, fluttering toward the kitchen. She'd heard plenty about Gram Wright over the past semester—stories Farway told during dinner about his new Sim study partner. The kid was not unlike her son: capable and restless, the kind of cadet who'd make his mark.

Except, Gram already had.

Empra was sure of it.

She couldn't *remember* meeting him, seventeen years and over two millennia ago, but there was footage in archive 12-A11B that proved otherwise. Farway's friend had sat next to her on the fourth-tier benches of the *Amphitheatrum Flavium*, had spoken Gaius's name, had...what? Her feed went dark soon after; next thing she remembered was holding a blue box the same way Burg held her: tight to the chest. Empra had no idea where the object was from, but she refused to let it go, for reasons her mind hadn't been sharp enough to cut. She'd gripped the corners through labor, cradled its velvet alongside her newborn son. When the Corps officers arrived at the maternity ward to question Empra, she'd hidden the item inside her fist, continued hiding it—in word and deed—during every following interrogation to avoid confiscation. Empra had even kept it from herself—the double who shared her shock, along with her family, her fingerprints, her job, her ex-fiancé horror stories.

Here she was, seventeen years later, holding the box again, fingers fitting into the grooves they'd created during childbirth. Had it really hurt so bad, to leave such deep marks? Memory was a fickle thing—erasing pain, branding the box's contents into her brain. When Empra cracked the soundless hinges, she knew what she'd find, down to the letter's letters.

She unfolded the paper gently to spare its ever-tattering creases. Some plucky soul had taken a pen to the former cover of a Corps of Central Time Travelers' Code of Conduct guidebook, lending the Cs a faint feline quality. The doodles went on—hearts and stars and widening gyres. A crescent moon. A flaming sun with a stick man inside, arms outstretched. None of these meant much to Empra, though she'd spent many hours studying them.

The note on the other side was marginally less mysterious. Its handwriting wasn't practiced enough to belong to a

Recorder, building words too blocky and big. Sentences took up twice the space they needed: *Empra—if you're reading this, it means we've succeeded. Mostly. There's not enough room on this page to explain, but all the answers are inside the chip. It holds your son's past, and possibly his future, too. Give it to him on his seventeenth birthday.*

Here the author had run out of room, no end in sight: period, signature, or otherwise. The *y* simply leaped off the page, leaving Empra with the sensation that she'd been interrupted. Her train of thought picked up at the same place every read: Who'd written this? How could there be answers inside the chip, when it was incompatible with Central's technology? Empra had approached dozens of programmers over the years, but none had been able to extract data from its circuits. How could her son have a past before his birth? Was it connected to the *Ab Aeterno*'s crew splitting the universe in two?

If so...this box could be akin to Pandora's. Better left shut.

She wanted the best for Farway: the one thing in this world that kept her *her*, made in his father's image, filled with her own wanderheart. As a child he'd watched her past expeditions with wide eyes, soaking in ancient cities, dinosaurs, volcanic eruptions, worlds unwired. He'd enrolled in the Academy because he wanted to make these adventures his own, and had worked his tail off to become class valedictorian. Rumor had it the Corps had already set aside his sergeant's uniform, final exam Sim pending. The future ahead of him was bright enough.

Why complicate it?

It was an oft-thought cycle, one Empra had pondered this very morning. She'd stared at the bed she sat on now, looking over Farway's birthday gifts, blue box in her hands, unable to let go. Maybe when Farway was eighteen or nineteen or never...

But Gram's reappearance, today of all days, had rattled her resolve.

There were deeper things than fear at work.

"What the Hades is going on, McCarthy?" Burg filled her doorway like he filled every doorway. He didn't take pains to distinguish himself from his duplicate, the way the rest of the *Ab Aeterno*'s crew did through hairstyles and jewelry, but Empra always knew which Historian was hers. There was something about the way he softened around her, surly-old-man performance crumbling in the second act. "Your son's worried, says you went white as a meal block in the kitchen. Feeling all right?"

She felt on edge, sweat from her fingertips mussing the box's velvet. "Burg, if you could choose to remember what happened to us the day we left ancient Rome, would you?"

"I suppose so. Yeah." The Historian was too burly for her bedroom, but he'd maneuvered it often enough to learn smallness. When he reached the bed, he picked up the letter to keep from crushing it. "A person's got the right to know their history, don't they?"

The chip looked one sneeze away from disappearing, so Empra held her breath when she stared at it. Her heart slowed to real time. Farway's past...If someone had gone to the trouble of putting it on a chip, it must have been worth saving. Handing this to her son would be no different from letting him watch her old datastreams. That was all futures were really—stories passed down, lived forward.

History: *The roots we did not choose.*

Who was she to stop it?

52.

. . . BUT CHOSE US

THE DINING ROOM TABLE HAD BEEN reduced to plates of pizza crust. None of the black market cheese had been harmed by its two-time tumble to the floor. In fact, the entire incident seemed never to have happened. Far's mother had reemerged from her bedroom with color in her cheeks, placing a new gift on the table before going around and taking everyone's drink orders. The evening proceeded like most birthday celebrations in a McCarthy household: eating, laughter, the pause between dinner and dessert for embarrassing stories. Imogen shared the one about their childhood petting-zoo visit from Hades—Far had begun that day with a white shirt and went home in a half-eaten yellow rag thanks to a nervous rabbit and a goat kid, forever cementing his dislike for pint-sized mammals. Gram countered with Far's more recent Sim triumphs. The tale of Far's birth was told by Burg and both Empras in a rotation that was practically memorized.

The dessert was gelato, chocolate with chocolate chips—Far's favorite. Aunt Isolde brought out a whole tub of the stuff, but only made it two steps before her daughter cried "Wait! The sparklers!" and disappeared into the kitchen. Light frothed from Imogen's hands, creating a trail of spilled sparks as she cometed back. Uncle Bert started off the first notes of "Happy Birthday," and everyone sang.

At the end his mother smiled. "Make a wish. Make it count."

Far wished he *would* count. He'd lived his entire life with the feeling it was a size too large. He looked around the table—Aunt Isolde scooping gelato into bowls as Uncle Bert and Aunt E passed them out, Burg holding his mother's hand, Imogen testing Gram's Rubik's Cube, the plates that weren't there—and felt the possibilities.

could be could be could be

This was his life.

How would Far fill it?

He wished he knew.

Gifts came next. Uncle Bert, Aunt Isolde, Burg, and his mother had all pitched in to buy him a hoverbike—no more public transportation to school! Imogen bought him a pair of goggles to reduce windburn while he drove. Gram gave him credits toward a new datastream. Aunt E's gift was a family heirloom, judging by his mother's reaction. She reached for the tweed jacket as soon as he opened it.

"This belonged to your great-great-grandfather, Farway," she said. "He was a history professor at Oxford, back when

Historians had to rely on books. Crux, it's been ages since I've seen this."

Years, Far knew. Seventeen plus one, to be exact. Crashing into one's own life was exactly that—a crash. As much as his mother and Aunt E had adjusted to themselves, casualties such as this jacket sprang up every once in a while. Identical child-hoods, not enough inheritance to go around. He let his mother hold on to her memory, returning to the final gift. It had been wrapped with haste—no bow, no tag, small enough to fit into his palm twice-over.

"Who's this from?"

"Open it." More strange behavior from his mother...The only time she ever skirted subjects like that was when Far tried to bring up his father.

He tore the paper, fast. Silver hinges, plush blue—the box looked like something from a jeweler. The kind of thing that would hold cuff links or a ring or a corneal implant upgrade. It *was* tech, Far discovered, but none he'd ever seen before. Clear and nearly invisible, the chip had the feel of a futuristic prototype.

"What is th—"

Far spoke. Light bloomed. Everyone at the table gasped.

Gram moved to get a better look at the item. "This is a holo-gram platform? How?"

Far didn't know the answer to the second question, but the first was obvious. It was a hologram in front of him, displaying some kind of menu. Eight boxes sat in a neat gradient of colors, tagged 0 through VII. Above them sat a box with an altogether different label: TU FUI, EGO ERIS.

What you are, I was. What I am, you will be.

"Strange." Imogen leaned forward in her seat. "That's a gravestone phrase. The Romans used it to warn the living about death."

Death. Far didn't think that was what it was referencing this time. He had no proof, nothing beyond a gut feeling—the very same longing he got every time he flew over the Colosseum, magnified. It was a twinge turned roar: *WILL BE WILL BE WILL BE.*

"*Tu fui, ego eris,*" he repeated the words to let some of their feeling out.

WILL BE WILL BE WILL BE

The box opened. Out spilled ship's logs for a vessel called the *Invictus.* Far read his name in the documents, along with Imogen's and Gram's and two others that felt on the brink of familiarity, as if his tongue had recited them many times before. Priya, Eliot, Priya, Eliot, Priya, Priya, Priya. He used to be the captain of a time machine, four months from now, and there were over thirty datastreams to prove it, time-stamped all over history: AD, BC, take your pick.

Far cleared his throat. There seemed to be only one thing to do. "Start from the beginning."

EPILOGUE

M<small>AY</small> 5, 2371 <small>AD</small>

T<small>HE</small> <small>GROUND</small> <small>LEVEL</small> <small>OF</small> Z<small>ONE</small> 2's financial district proved a perilous place to walk. Its walkways swarmed with brokers, all of them edgy with stimulants and distracted by the stock numbers on their interfaces. *Toes beware! Coffee cups, too!* Eliot's reflexes were being put to good use as she tracked Far through the fray. The cadet's Recorder training brought out the chameleon in him, causing him to step at the same tempo as the surrounding suits. He was too easy to lose: no curls to draw in the eye, uniform melding into the gray of the walkway.

Eliot—with her flash-leather moto jacket, her ice-blond wig—was the one who stood out in this swarm of corporate monochromes. Her eyebrows felt a few font sizes too large, though she *had* written them with a freer hand today. The color? Darkest Before Dawn. The message? *Forget me not.* She'd scripted the phrase rightside forward, for Far's sake.

All he had to do was pause, see her, read it. But Far kept forging along Via Novus. It was a roundabout route to the

Academy. Especially strange, considering his final exam Sim was scheduled to start in a few hours. Eliot hadn't planned on hacking this test, at least in the digital sense. Her scheduled interruption was of the manual variety. Or *would be*, if the boy would just stop moving. She could run to catch up, but so many lattes sloshing about made her nervous, especially with the invitation tucked in her non-universe pocket. Real ink bled, and though flash leather was expensive as Hades, a stain wouldn't be the worst of it. Lux Julio wasn't the sort of man who deigned to write things twice.

Eliot slid her hands into her jacket pockets, thumb pressed against the envelope's corner. It was quite sharp, for paper. Heavy, too: worth its weight in steals. She'd had to produce more than a bottle of port to gain the black market mogul's trust this go-round.

It seemed unlikely that Far had business in the Central World Bank, where gold letters swirled around a globe just as bright, assuring customers that their credits belonged nowhere else. Rotating glass doors swept in person after person, the odd droid. Far broke away from this flow before the grandiose steps, to the plaza lined with pollution scrub bushes and vendors.

Curiosity, more than caution, was the reason Eliot hung back, pausing beside a crouched marble lion. She leaned against the statue and pondered this break in pattern. Of all the times she'd followed Far during the fortnight since his seventeenth birthday, he'd never stopped at a tea stand. The boy was energetic enough as it was; caffeine was apt to make his heart explode.

"I'll have a chai," he told the vendor. "Extra hot, if you could."

Twenty-five credits. Far flinched when the price came up. Eliot knew this was because he couldn't cover it, not even by half. She, on the other hand, had plenty of money to spend. After two snatch-and-grabs for Lux, she was sitting pretty, but what use were so many credits without friends to enjoy them with?

Eliot stepped in, swiped her own palm over the scanner as payment. "It's on me, this time."

The vendor began preparing the order—using spices that smelled of heaven and home, and made Eliot long for something she couldn't quite remember. Story of her life—lives. But that forgetting was over, thanks to the boy beside her. Far was already reading Eliot's eyebrows when she turned, his own high enough to get lost in would-be curls. It was the strangest thing: meeting someone for the first time once more. Even though there were a thousand places to begin, Eliot had no idea what to say.

Hello. Again?

"You! You saved us. Me and Gram and Imogen and—" Far's voice cracked. His eyes darted to the tea stand, where chai was being poured. "This whole world. All of history."

None of these statements were true in their entirety. Early history had its holes: The morning of Far's death was gone, along with the hours he'd visited pre-dating it. When Eliot tried to retrieve Berossus's *Babylonaica* from Alexandria's burning library for Lux-baiting purposes, the Fade's tear forced her to land too late. She found the smoke impassable. The past steadied out, post–pivot point, for this was a different world. Every time after 95 AD remained as it was, unfaded. The *Titanic* sank; Las Vegas sparkled. CTMs landed without a hitch, collecting bees and seeds and history to revitalize Central time. All was as it should be.

Except for Eliot. She'd been wiped blank again, with only streaks of Grid-protected memories to cling to: shooting at Far, watching seven subjects' worth of footage, brainstorming ways to build a world. Beyond that? Her earliest recollection was from a month ago, standing in an empty field, pulse thrashing with terror her mind couldn't register. The Fade. Why else would Eliot forget? Why else would she flee? According to Vera's logs, she'd jumped from December 31, 95 AD, to a morning in 90 AD. A glance into her pocket universe confirmed she hadn't done it alone. Gaius, too, had survived.

She wasn't sure the same could be claimed for Far, Gram, Priya, and Imogen. They were alive, yes, but they'd also been lost. Eliot's comm link with the *Invictus* kept SEARCHING FOR CONNECTION... and *saved* was a word she didn't quite know how to define. If you never were, were you ever? Could people be dead if their existence was erased?

"I was there," Eliot said, partly to reassure herself. "From what I can remember, it was a team effort. The chip was Priya's idea. Imogen kept ship's logs. Gram figured out how to end the countersignature, and you..."

"Died?" Far didn't seem to mind that the vendor was within earshot, placing the steaming hotmug into the pickup window. "Yeah, I figured. Pretty hashing noble of me, don't you think?"

So she did. The sentiment became a lump in Eliot's throat, swallowed back. Grief didn't feel right with Far standing here. The sadness didn't feel wrong, either. Just...misplaced.

A few extra credits swiped as tip and Eliot passed the hotmug to Far. "At least your humility came through unscathed."

"As did your humor. Your fashion sense, though..." He squinted at her jacket, which translated the morning light into something psychedelic, colors stretching to the edge of expected. "Methinks you took some cues from Imogen."

"Girl's a bright influence." *Is, was. Same, different. Flesh, ghost...*

Far's laugh brought Eliot to the land of the living, where the plaza stones became unshakeable beneath her feet. *This* was a memory she would not forget: bantering beside a tea stand, breathing in factory spice and sky smog. She slipped her hand back into her pocket, where the envelope was.

"Priya wanted the chip to reach you on your seventeenth birthday, before your final exam Sim. I've been keeping tabs on you for a few weeks now, waiting for the right moment—"

"You winked at me on the hoverbus!" Far interrupted. "Why didn't you say anything?"

"Explaining was the chip's job. I'm here for the fallout." With all jump systems functioning, she had everywhere else to go. A multiverse awaited: Choose a number, lotto random, and that universe was within reach. But this world—with its solid ground, its booming black market trade, its many McCarthys— was Eliot's now. She'd put down roots here, or vice versa. They were already a few weeks old, growing as deep as she could ever remember.

"The chip didn't explain everything. My"—the boy paused—"our father. What happened to him?"

"Gaius lived his life." Again, it was hard to choose a tense, but for happier reasons. Eliot still checked in on her—their—father from time to time, visits that eased her guilt for leaving him in 96 AD with nothing but some coins and a toga sewn from sheets. She'd worried for nothing, though. Said garment had fetched him a small fortune. "Long and free."

"What about the Multiverse Bureau?" Far's face tightened, until she could see every muscle in it. "Will their agent check in on us again?"

Again? Agent Ackerman must've turned up during the lost moments. What a hazing *cucurbita*…"Anything's possible, though I wouldn't fret over it. Your countersignature emissions scan comes up same as mine. Clear. Nothing particularly special or apocalypse-inducing about either of us."

"I can live with that." Far only became self-aware of his pun until after the fact—evidenced by his wince. "So what's this fallout you referenced?"

Eliot realized she'd used the wrong word. Fallout? No, it was more of a catching.…It was convincing Lux to allow the use of the fourth, unnamed TM in his fleet. It was the red panda cub, the *Tetris* cartridge, and the satchel of karha spice—welcome-home gifts Eliot collected and placed in their respective bunks. It was the envelope she pulled from her pocket.

Far stared at the stationery. "Is that..."

"This is your life, Farway Gaius McCarthy. I'm not going to bust into your final exam Sim as Marie Antoinette—"

"Wait, what?" He must not have watched that part.

"I got you thrown out of the Academy, which caught Lux Julio's eye, which landed you on the *Invictus*. All that to say, fate's in your court this time. You can soup up on chai and go crush that exam, or you can accept this invitation."

"The tea isn't for me," Far said, as if that explained everything. Maybe it did. He considered the envelope another second before reaching for it. "A life worth dying for has got to be a life worth living, right?"

"It won't be the exact same setup," Eliot warned. "I've already signed a contract with Lux. Think you can handle being co-captain?"

"Only time will tell." The boy's expression bordered on wicked; he tucked the paper into his uniform pocket. "I assume the invitation extends to the rest of the crew? Can't fly a TM without an Engineer, and Gram and Imogen are a package deal as of a week ago. Who knew talk of rodents' digestive anatomy and past-life kissing would lead to...well...kissing?"

"Assemble the dream team." Eliot's smile felt much like her sadness. It amazed her, that joy and sorrow could be so intertwined. Sweet to the bitter. This start wasn't fresh, but perhaps she was better for it. "Eleven o'clock tonight. The Forum. Zone One."

A winking light. The chai in Far's hands took on a whole new meaning when Eliot spotted the gold headphones bobbing through the crowd. Of course Priya was headed toward the tea stand. Ships of Theseus in the night, moments from colliding.

Eliot wasn't about to get between them.

"Tonight," she said again, before stepping back into the current of financiers. There was no need for a farewell, not when she and Far would meet again in a matter of hours. "The *Invictus* is waiting."

❖ ❖ ❖

The boy waiting beside Priya's tea stand was not a regular. A grin as bold as his would be memorable any morning of the week, pre-caffeine or post-. So why, oh why, did it feel so familiar? Why did her heart do a tiny cartwheel inside her chest when their gazes locked? She'd never been one to swoon, especially when it came to Corps cadets. The uniform alone should have been grounds for dismissal: *Strike one, he's out.*

Strike two. He was... waiting for her? It seemed this way, when he held out the hotmug. Priya regarded it, skeptical. His grin didn't waver. It held more than just straight teeth and confidence—something she couldn't name, but echoed inside her anyway, a song apart from the one she was listening to. She removed her rip-off BeatBix and met his eyes, dark enough to see constellations in.

"Do I know you?"

"In a manner of speaking? No. I'm Farway McCarthy. Far for short."

Priya had seen the name around—inscribed on a 24-karat

plaque, popping up on med-droid reports, referenced in Edwin Marin's faculty memos. By nature of the Academy's size and the lack of Medic-to-cadet contact, this was the first time she'd met the boy himself.

Wasn't it?

She gestured at the tea in Far's hand. "What's this?"

"Chai. For you."

"I don't date cadets." There wasn't much heart in the rejection, since her own kept flip-flopping. "Even ones who wait at my favorite tea stand with my favorite drink. Whoever tipped you off was ill-informed."

"Is that so?"

"It is *so* so."

Far's smile grew past his lips, until it charged the air about him. Priya could think of at least a dozen songs with a similar feel, half of them about L-O-V-E. This made her grip her headphones by their backward BB logos, intent on placing them back over her ears. Her Medic shift was starting soon, and she didn't have time for a time traveler—

"It was you, Priya."

Pause. One headphone on: half song, half stun. She hadn't told Far her name, yet she must have, because it sounded so right when he said it, earnest enough to believe.

"You told me to find you," Far went on. "I know it sounds like some time traveler's pickup line, but it's the honest-to-Crux truth. I've got the datastream footage to prove it. You said to bring you a mug of chai from the tea stand on Via Novus. You told me to give us a chance, so that's what I'm doing. If the cadet part's a deal breaker, it shouldn't be. I'm about to quit the Academy."

"When?"

"I was just about to go over there—"

"No." Priya's headphones slid down. She did nothing to stop them. "When did I say these things?"

"Short answer? December 31, 95 AD." Star-stories aligned behind the boy's stare. "Complicated answer? In a different life."

A different life. It sounded crazy, but so many things did these days. Time travel had made a mess of nature's order. Pasts might not fall before futures on the calendar, people lived side by side with themselves, and the promise of parallel worlds lingered behind every *Central News Tonight* headline. The impossible was all possible.

Priya might have turned her back anyway, had this first sight not felt so much like a second. Or a tenth, times infinity. "What about the long answer? The one with the corroborating datastreams."

"I was hoping to fill you in over tea." Far nodded at the hotmug.

"I'm already running late for work." Twelve hours of reading through charts, tuning up med-droids, and trying not to spill blood samples on her scrubs. Followed by a long hoverbus ride home, reheated leftovers from Sunday dinner, an Acidic Sisters behind-the-scenes datastream, creating tomorrow's get-through-the-day playlist, and falling asleep to it. She'd gone through these motions before, but only now did they truly feel like motions. Priya wasn't sure what *a different life* looked like, or if she even wanted what this boy was offering. All she knew was that she couldn't stay where she was, without knowing.

She reached for the chai. Her fingers brushed Far's—warmth, all warmth, and a shiver, too. "But it seems we're headed in the same direction. Why don't you walk with me?"

ACKNOWLEDGMENTS

Although this story is more of an ouroboros than not, the novel itself had a definite beginning. In 2012, Jonathan Sanchez—owner of the renowned Blue Bicycle Books—asked me to take part in Piccolo Spoleto's Fiction Open. The resulting short story followed a time-traveling thief on a chase through the streets of Charleston. "You have to turn this into a book!" was the general consensus of my friends. My to-write queue was long—sequels, a thriller, an alternate-history series—but the Hunters and the Hiotts kept hounding me about time-traveling thieves. Turns out, after three years of creating a grim, Axis-ruled world, *Invictus* was the escape I needed.

Though fun, the switch from history with a tinge of sci-fi to sci-fi with a tinge of history was intimidating. Time travel requires brains, and mine would have broken several times if it weren't for Jacob Graudin. The way my brother untangles paradoxes would make Gram proud! Amie Kaufman instilled in me a confidence that sci-fi *was*, indeed, a genre I could tackle. Kate Armstrong has been another constant cheerleader of mine, continually asking me for more pages of SparkleBook (as this story was known in the early stages). The Ladies of Tall Trees Lane gave me life through revisions—seriously, those dock sunsets and kraken invocations did wonders. Roshani Chokshi, my fellow meeper, thank you for your notes, your joy, your chai. Speaking of joy, thank you, Rachel Strolle, for your constant supply of red panda GIFs. Saffron would be pleased. Megan and Jesse: Shepherd's Cottage was a lifesaver; thank you for offering shelter in the storm. My poorly remembered middle school Latin wasn't going to cut it for this project, so I'm indebted to Hannah VanSyckle and Soraya Een Hajji for their translations. I also owe much to my sensitivity readers: Kheryn Callender and Aneeka Kalia.

Writing careers are built with sweat and tears and stellar agents. I'm still in denial that this is my sixth novel, and I have Tracey Adams to thank for reaching this milestone. Alvina Ling, Nikki Garcia, Pam Gruber, and Hannah Milton were the editorial superteam this book needed. (So. Many. Paradox. Phone. Conversations.)

To the rest of the Little, Brown gang—Saraciea Fennell, Victoria Stapleton, Jenny Choy, Jane Lee, Svetlana Keselman, Megan Tingley—I am forever grateful for your support.

David, thank you for proving what a solid thing love can be. Mom, I am so proud of your strength in the face of entropy. Family, you mean the multiverse to me. Friends, I include you in that, because if there's one thing I've learned in this life, it's that kinship goes far beyond DNA. God, thank you for glimpses of eternity. *Soli Deo Gloria.*